WOLFSANGEL

WOLFSANGEL

M.D. LACHLAN

GOLLANCZ

LONDON

Copyright © M.D. Lachlan 2010

The right of M.D. Lachlan to be identified as the author
of this work has been asserted by him in accordance
with the Copyright, Designs and Patents Act 1988.

First published in Great Britain in 2010 by Gollancz
An imprint of the Orion Publishing Group
Orion House, 5 Upper St Martin's Lane,
London WC2H 9EA
An Hachette UK Company

A CIP catalogue record for this book is
available from the British Library

ISBN 978 0 575 08957 0 (Cased)
ISBN 978 0 575 08959 4 (Trade Paperback)

1 3 5 7 9 10 8 6 4 2

Typeset by Deltatype Ltd, Birkenhead, Merseyside

Printed in Great Britain by Clays Ltd, St Ives plc

The Orion Publishing Group's policy is to use papers that
are natural, renewable and recyclable products and made
from wood grown in sustainable forests. The logging and
manufacturing processes are expected to conform to the
environmental regulations of the country of origin.

www.orionbooks.co.uk

To my son James

Prince you cannot
talk about me
like that,
scolding a
noble man.
For you ate
a wolf's treat,
shedding your brother's
blood, often
you sucked on wounds
with a cold snout,
creeping to
dead bodies,
being hated by all.

FIRST POEM OF HELGI HUNDINGSBANI
THE POETIC EDDA

If only there were evil people somewhere insidiously committing evil deeds, and it were necessary only to separate them from the rest of us and destroy them. But the line dividing good and evil cuts through the heart of every human being – and who is willing to destroy a piece of his own heart?

ALEKSANDR SOLZHENITSYN

1 White Wolf

Varrin gripped the shaft of his spear and scanned the dark horizon, fighting for balance as the waves rocked the little longship. There, he was sure, was the river his lord had described, a broad mouth between two headlands, one like a dragon's back, the other like a stretching dog. It fitted well enough, he thought, if you looked at it with half an eye.

'Lord Authun, king, I think this is it.'

The man sitting in his cloak with his back to the prow awoke. His long white hair seemed almost to shine under the bright lantern of the half moon. He stood slowly, his limbs stiff with inaction and the cold. He turned his attention to the shore.

'Yes,' he said, 'this is as was revealed.'

Varrin, a giant of a man a head and a half taller than the king, touched an amulet he wore at his neck at the mention of prophecy. 'We wait until dawn and then try the river, lord?'

Authun shook his head.

'Now,' he said. 'Odin is with us.'

Varrin nodded. Normally he would have regarded it as very unwise to negotiate an unknown river in the dark. With his king at his side, anything felt possible. Authun was a Volsung, a direct descendant of the gods and was a vessel for their powers.

The tide was slow but with the boat, and the crew were well rested from the favourable wind that had carried them for a couple of days and eager to get to the oars. Everything was going well, and no wonder with the king on board. His magic, Varrin felt sure, had blessed their journey.

The men bent their backs pulling through the waves, propelling themselves at speed towards the river. The ship was more stable under oar than under sail and its sudden steadiness seemed to reflect the purpose Varrin felt as he heaved the boat through the surf. They were going into a fight, no question, and Varrin was ready.

Ten warriors crewed the ship, only ten including the king, but Varrin felt no uncertainty, nor scarcely any nervousness. He was with his lord, King Authun, victor of innumerable battles, slayer of the giant Geat, Gyrd the Mighty. If Authun thought ten men were enough for their task then ten men were enough. It was a trick of the gods that such a man had not produced an heir. The rumour was that Authun was descended from Odin, the chief of the gods. That battle-fond poet felt threatened by his fierce descendant and had cursed Authun to sire only female children. He could not risk him producing an even mightier son.

Varrin shivered when he thought of the consequences if Authun did not father a boy. He would have to name an heir, with all the trouble and bloodshed that would cause. Only Authun's name held the factions of his kingdom together. Without it, there would be slaughter and then their enemies would pounce. He glanced at the king and smiled to himself. He wouldn't put it past him to live for ever.

Varrin looked into the black hills and wondered why they had come to that land. It was more than just plunder, it seemed, because their ship had slipped away from a quiet beach a day up the coast from their hall, no kinsmen to bid them farewell, no feasting before they left. Only the war gear, the bright heads of the axes, a shield decorated with a painted wolf's head, another with a raven, spoke of their mission. The images bore a clear message to their enemies: 'We will make a feast for these creatures.'

They rushed upon the river's mouth but slowed as the water became more shallow. They did not stop for soundings; Authun just made his way to the prow of the ship and leaned out over the water, directing the rudderman. Varrin smirked to the man at the oar opposite as the ship slid into the river like a knife into a sheath. The other oarsman, a young man of seventeen or so who had never travelled with Authun before, grinned back. 'You were right – he is incredible,' his expression said. They were proud of their king.

The flood tide took them up the river. The channel became perilous and narrow, split into the land between sharp cliffs and hard boulders, but the king found the course. An hour inland with the dark tight about them, their only light a pale slice of moon high in the sky, the push of the current began to fade and the rowing got harder. In front of them a sandbank loomed midstream and Authun signalled for the boat to beach upon it. The small ship was designed for just such a landing and grounded with a slight judder.

Authun turned to his men and spoke their names in turn.

'Vigi, Eyvind, Egil, Hella, Kol, Vott, Grani, Arngeir. We are kinsmen and sworn brothers. There can be no lies between us. None of you shall return from this journey. Only Varrin will come back with me to the coast to steer the ship. By the time the sun rises you will all be feasting with your forefathers in the halls of Odin or Freya.'

The men largely received the news of their impending deaths without expression. They were warriors, raised with the certainty of death in battle. A couple smiled, pleased that they would die at their king's side.

'I would die with my kinsmen,' said Varrin.

'Your time will come soon enough,' said Authun.

He looked at Varrin, the nearest he had to a friend. The giant would be needed to get the boat back into the river and to help him with whatever perils they faced back down the whale road to their home. After that he would let him die.

'I have no responsibility to tell you why you must die, other than it is my will that you should. But know that they will sing tales of your deeds until the world ends. We are here to take a magic child, one who will secure the future of our people for ever and one who will be my heir.'

'What of the child your wife carries?' said Varrin.

'There is no child,' said Authun. 'It is a deception of the mountain witches.'

The men drew in breath. Authun was a good king, fair and generous, a giver of rings. He had never even killed a slave in drunkenness, as kings were wont to do. This was shocking news, though. The men despised liars and this was very near to a lie. Also, it bore the mark of magic, and women's magic at that.

The warriors shifted in their seats. Death did not scare them; they found it as companionable as a dog. But the mountain witches terrified them. Only the king, half a god himself, could speak to the witches and even he had to be wary. Their advice had proved true in the past but the sacrifices they demanded were terrible and always the same – children: boys for servants, girls to continue their strange traditions.

'The child is a captive in the village here, taken from the sorcerers of the far west,' said Authun. 'He is a son of the gods and will lead us to greatness. These farmers do not yet realise what they have. We will part them from it before they do. The village is defended only by farmers but there are warriors not two hours' ride away.'

He looked out into the dark. Somewhere in the distance the sky was taking on a soft pink glow.

'Their beacons are lit,' he said. 'We can expect opposition. We will find the child with a priest of their god. The building is marked like this, as their holy places are.' He made a cross with his fingers. 'Follow me as we fight to their temple, then we cut our way back to the boat. By that time the tide will have turned and I will leave you to your glory. You will be heroes and your fame will be everlasting. The village is five bends of the river away. Prepare.'

The men nodded and went quietly to their work. Spears were unstrapped from the rear of the ship, helmets and thick tunics taken from barrels, war axes unpacked and tied to their backs. Varrin and Egil had the honour of dressing the king, helping him into his precious mail hauberk – a byrnie, as the men called it – and placing the golden wolf helm, symbol of his family, onto his head. The helmet was the best that could be made, open at the face save for shining cheek guards that made it look as if a giant wolf was swallowing Authun's head from the rear. From a distance, in the splendid helmet, his eyes blackened with soot, the king would appear as a terrifying wolf-headed man. The warriors placed rings on the king's arms, tied a golden belt at his waist, took off his sea cloak and put on one of golden thread.

Varrin passed the king his shield with its snarling wolf's head. Then it was time to take out the sword, the only one on the boat, in its white-jewelled scabbard. As Varrin took it from its storage barrel, it caught the moonlight. It was a sword unlike any other. The Norse blades were short and straight, useful for hacking close up in conjunction with a shield. This sword though was long and thin with a pronounced curve to it. It was stronger than any straight sword and, though lighter, had cut through enemy weapons many times. Authun had bought it for a fortune from a southern merchant who said it came from 'beyond the dawn' – by which Authun had supposed he meant the east. Wherever it came from, Authun knew it was enchanted, forged – as the merchant said – by magical smiths in the legendary kingdoms of the sands. The merchant had named it Shamsir, and Authun had kept the name as it seemed to contain the stir of the desert winds, or at least how he imagined they would sound. His men called it the Moonsword.

The king was ready. In his war gear he looked terrible and splendid, a god. In fact, compared to his kinsmen, Authun had little taste for ornamentation. The display was for a reason – to inspire awe in his foes. Varrin looked at the king. The West Men would need their courage, he thought. Before long the others were ready too. Authun filled their drinking horns himself.

'To the endless feasts in the halls of the slain,' said Hella.

'To the endless feasts in the halls of the slain,' replied the rest of the men, under their breath in case the enemy should be nearby. They all drank a deep draught, and then another. The horns were refilled and refilled as the boat was prodded by oar from the sandbank and got under way again, rounding the bends towards their prey. As Authun had noted, they had been seen. The West Men were no fools and kept watch on the mouths of the rivers. Already, even before the village came into view they could see the flickering lights of its warning beacons filling the sky. They would have to be quick, to strike before a body of men could be mustered to face them. No matter, they were used to that.

The final bend was taken and Varrin had the impression of a village already being sacked. The beacons were blazing all along the beach and up a hill. The fires revealed what Varrin considered a very large settlement of twenty houses leading up to a building with a cross on its roof. Well, at least they knew where it was.

The West Men had been clever. The beach was backed by cut staves on top of a cliff the height of a man. There was only one entrance to the settlement from the river, a gap you would struggle to fit a cart through. It would have been easy to defend had the defenders been proper warriors. Even from the boat in the flickering firelight Varrin could see by the way the men held their spears and shields that they were more used to tilling fields than fighting. There were gaps in their shield wall and a couple of spears pointed at the moon. They would have been better advised to direct their tips to the invaders, because the moon wasn't going to cut off their heads.

The king was the first off the boat, splashing into the knee-deep water and walking up the beach at the pace of a man carrying a basket of mussels rather than a warrior facing his enemy. The troop followed him, three behind, then four in a shield wedge. Two remained on the boat to guard it.

Twenty yards from the enemy, Authun stopped and his men began to rattle their weapons on their shields, to bay and howl like beasts. Those who still had drink finished it and cast the horns aside. Four horns a man, enough to be courageous, not enough to be clumsy. Authun stepped forward, unsheathing the Moonsword, the torchlight turning its metal to fire. His helm too seemed to burn, the jewels of the wolf's eyes sparkling out a bloodlust.

The king lifted his sword high and screamed, 'I am Authun the Wolf, king of the sword-Horda, sacker of the five towns, son of Odin, lord of battle! No man has ever faced me and lived. See the plunder I have taken!'

He waved the sword again, its blade bright in the light of the moon and the fire. The torches caught the jewels on the wolf's eyes, turned the rings on the king's arms to burning snakes, made the scabbard of his sword dance like fire itself. His cloak seemed alive with sparks and even his mouth, the teeth inlaid with tiny red sapphires, seemed to burn. Only the space where his eyes should have been seemed dead, dead and pitiless.

To the West Men, Authun seemed a strange, glittering eyeless alien, and they knew there was only one place you obtained wealth like that. In battles, and plenty of them.

The enemy understood only a word or two of what the king said but were cowed by the force of his delivery. It could have been a spell and, even if it wasn't, the meaning of his message was clear: prepare to die. Imagination blended with fear and, to some of the West Men, it seemed that the king really did have the head of a wolf, that his wolf banner, held high by Vott, did snarl and snap in the breeze. A couple of boys fell away and ran. Three men at the rear melted off to go back to their wives and children and get them away. From somewhere a bowman, his aim made unreliable by fear, landed arrows into the sand ten paces away from Authun's feet. The king didn't move. The arrows had dropped quite softly, meaning the bow was at the limit of its range and, even if the archer improved his shooting, Authun thought himself well covered on that side by his helmet and shield. His impassive posture terrified the West Men. A spearman in the front rank ran, dropping his shield, and the others, paralysed by the sight of the sparkling, fearful king, did not move to close the gap. The raiders charged.

The farmers were not quick enough to flee, but their instinct, to step back and lift their spears under the onslaught, was fatal. The king, transformed from the cold old man who had sat in the boat, knocked two men down with his shield charge. A third, who had dropped his spear in fright, had his leg taken off at the knee by a flash of the Moonsword. Varrin and Egil, in the raiders' second rank, struck at two more with their spears. The men deflected the blows but the fight had left them and they fled. Fear is catching. Two heartbeats after the king had felled his first opponent, the West Men ran for it. Only one man had been cut down but panic had set in.

'To the temple, before the warriors arrive,' shouted Authun. Varrin quickly killed the fallen man with his knife and then swiped off his head with a couple of blows from his axe. He put the head on his spear and held it up as a warning to any others that might try their luck.

The Norsemen drove on up the hill in their wedge formation. As they went they cut down two beacons and flung them onto the roofs of houses. This wasn't wanton destruction. The more confusion and fear they could create the better. Ideally the villagers would flee and hamper the progress of any of their lord's men who were rushing to meet the invaders. Authun knew that success depended on getting to the child before significant resistance could be mustered. West Men nobles were a different proposition to farmers. They were raised as warriors from their earliest years and he didn't want to have to cut his way through such men to get what he wanted.

Up the hill they rushed. Here and there farmers armed with clubs and spears would stand taunting them for a few breaths, screaming defiance, but they would always run before the raiders came through them.

'You promised us death, lord!' shouted Eyvind. 'These cowards will keep me waiting for ever to begin my feasting!'

'You will be drunk with your father and his father before the night is out!' shouted Authun.

The church – though the Norsemen didn't know it by that name - was a squat wooden building like the rest in the village, though a solid one. Authun tried the door. It was shut fast. He nodded to the roof. Sigur and Egil crouched, their hands improvising a stirrup. Young Eyvind ran at the side of the building and the two bigger men thrust him up onto the thatch. In three bounds he was at the smoke vent, his formidable axe free from its strap.

'Kill no children!' shouted the king.

Eyvind disappeared from view through the hole at the apex of the roof. Ten heartbeats later the door was open and the other raiders were inside.

Authun looked around, his eyes almost blind from the transition between the blazing village and the dark of the church. He could see virtually nothing until Varrin came in with a brand.

It was a large windowless space with the hearth that had allowed them access in the centre and an altar at the back. Behind the altar cowered two of the enemy holy men, trying to make magic by gesturing from their foreheads to their chests. One was clutching one of their precious books inlaid with jewels.

'Find the boy,' said Authun. 'He will be here – it is foreseen.'

Varrin made a quick circuit of the room with his torch but found nothing. The only people in there were the cowering priests, who seemed determined to die like children rather than face their enemies as men.

'He has to be here somewhere,' said Authun. 'Burn the place and see who comes out.' He'd hoped to avoid this simply because it would take too long.

Varrin walked to where the thatch met the wall. As he applied his brand there was the sound from above of a child crying. Authun looked up. Hanging from the rafters was a basket secured by a rope tied to a post.

'Get it down,' said Authun.

The rope was untied and the basket was lowered to the floor.

Authun looked inside the basket, expecting to see the destiny of his race. He was unprepared for what was within. There, pressed together, were two naked baby boys, each with a wisp of dark hair exactly as in the vision of the witches. But he had only seen one boy. This was something the king had not counted on. The boys were clearly twins – small, dark and wiry, almost identical. Which one was he supposed to take? Would it matter to the prophecy's fulfilment if he was to take both? Still, Authun was a leader and knew that any decision is better than none.

'Take them both,' he said.

Authun killed the holy men and took their book. He didn't have time to prise the gems out of it right there so he tucked it under his shield arm. Then he had his second surprise. Close up, he could see the altar was just a table covered with a sheet. Authun lifted the cloth. He thought he heard a noise from inside, though he could see nothing without a light.

'Varrin,' said the king, gesturing for the big man to come forward. He did and passed the king the brand. Authun peered beneath the table. Shrinking away from him was a small woman. The king had seen her race before on raids. She was a Celt, from the furthest reaches of the West Men's country. She was beautiful, pale and dark. He pulled her to her feet. Even though he wasn't seeking slaves she would command a reasonable price, he thought, after he had tried the goods himself. But as she stood up, he took a step back. Only the left side of her face was pretty; the right had been burned terribly, and an awful scar ran from her brow to her chin. Authun, veteran of so many battles, was taken aback by her eye. It was terribly swollen with a pinprick pupil just visible in the torchlight, the rest blood red where it should have been white. It seemed to bore straight into him.

He dropped her arm – she was valueless. He then registered her alarm as she saw the basket with the children in it. She wailed and dived towards Varrin. Authun in an instant realised – she was the children's mother.

'Catch her.' Authun's command had no explanation, as orders in battle do not. The huge Varrin dropped his left arm and lifted her off her feet to pin her squirming at his side.

It hadn't occurred to Authun how he would feed two newborns on the three-week voyage back, and he almost laughed as he saw how nearly his plans had come to failure from such an oversight. The fates had dropped the woman into his lap.

'With us,' said Authun, striding outside. The church was already burning but he pitched the torch onto the roof for good measure.

Varrin shouldered the basket, the children crying and the tiny woman under his other arm still struggling. The raiders set off down the hill. The West Men were finally sorting out their defence and had managed to find some more skilful bowmen. Arrows flew past the Norsemen, one even glancing off Kol's helmet as they retreated down the slope. They quickly moved their shields to their backs as they ran. Making the boat would be the most perilous part, as they had to cross the open beach. Authun had an answer to that.

'Kol, Eyvind,' he said, 'harry our pursuers. Hide here and when they pass attack them from the rear. Take the bowmen first.'

Both men discarded their spears and took out their axes. Then they were gone, inside a house to set their ambush. Against the burning church, Authun picked up a different pattern of movement. A rider. The lord's bodyguard were arriving – trained fighters. Authun had heard traders call these men by many names – gesith, thegns and even, like his own retainers, housecarls. Authun was not a sentimental man and knew they were every bit as good as his own warriors.

There couldn't be many assembled so quickly but, squinting through the smoke and firelight, he could see at least three horses now. When more arrived, they would dismount to attack. The weapon of fear would be useless against them. It would be spear against spear, with the mob at the thegns' backs. He had no time to waste.

'The ship! The ship!'

The remaining six raiders ran through the village. Authun left four to lie in wait in the shadows of the last houses before the beach and shouted to the two on the ship to come up and defend the gap in the staves. Only he and Varrin pressed on, his kinsman carrying the basket, the king now driving the mother.

On the hill Eyvind and Kol died bravely. Kol split a bowman's skull with his axe from behind with his first blow and knocked a thegn unconscious through his helmet with his second. His third strike cleft a bowman from shoulder to chest. He never made a fourth — two spearmen came at his flank and struck him in the head and belly. He fell to the ground and a farmer cut off his head with a hand scythe. Eyvind broke a bowman's arm with a poor stroke from his battleaxe. He made up for his slack work with his second blow, taking a spearman's jaw clean off and managing to continue the arc of his axe so it embedded itself in another's arm. Four thegns were on him then with axes, and though he landed a solid blow on the shoulder of one warrior it was at too great a cost. The axe jammed momentarily in the man's collarbone, and another West Man had a free swipe at Eyvind's arm. Eyvind saw his right hand come off at the wrist. He tried to draw his knife with his remaining hand but the enemy were too quick for him. An axe split his temple, another bit into his neck, a third sank into his thigh — the blows were rapid, tight as a drum roll. Eyvind was dead but he and Kol had done their job, and the West Men moved more warily through the remaining houses — until they saw the pair guarding the entrance to the beach. Brimming with their success in taking down two of the raiders, the farmers were deaf to the commands of the warriors to hold their position until archers could be brought to bear on the Norsemen. There was a scream from the villagers as they rushed the men at the gap. Stabbing wildly with their spears or slashing with their knives, they were no match for the discipline of Arngeir and Vigi, whose spears hardly seemed to move, yet two opponents were down. Then two more. The West Men screamed and jabbered and rattled their weapons but the raiders kept their movements tight, the economy of their thrusts taking a heavy toll.

The five thegns cursed but felt duty bound to go to the aid of the peasants. Any one of them would have cut down a farmer for as much as a misplaced word, but faced with invaders it was their duty to defend the men that put food on their lord's table. As they rushed in, the courage of the farmers broke and they ran out. The four raiders who had been hiding burst into this confusion. In the maelstrom of flailing limbs and weapons one thegn was felled by a peasant who mistook him for a raider. West Men stumbled and slipped and blocked their comrades' blows as the Norsemen's axes bit and spears stabbed. Some of the farmers managed to get away, but the warriors, beset on both sides, stood and died.

Authun swung the basket with the boys in it onto the longship and Varrin heaved their mother after them. The big man ached to join the fight. He had his orders but still held himself a coward for minding children while his kinsmen fought for their lives. Varrin looked at the woman. She had one of the boys out of the basket and was comforting him. As he watched, a feeling of disquiet came over him. It was as if the woods around the village had begun to seethe. Somehow he could sense the forest coming alive, that the foxes, the birds and above all the wolves had caught the scent of slaughter on the breeze and were hurrying to the feast. From deep in the trees he heard their howling, the dissonant call of welcome for the dead. He turned back towards the village, itching to go to his kinsmen's aid. From somewhere above him, even over the din of battle, he heard a call, a sound, he thought, like the sky cracking. He glanced up to see a pair of ravens circling.

'My lord!' he said. 'An omen. Odin is with us – he sends his intelligencers. Our men have carried the day, they will make the ship.' His voice was full of admiration. What other leader could hack a victory from such unpromising odds?

Authun looked at him. 'They will enter legend here.'

'Leave them?'

'Leave them.'

Varrin was stunned but he did as he was told, helping the king shove the boat out into the river. The two men leaped aboard.

On the river beach their kinsmen leaned on their axes. Hella bore a deep cut on his cheek, Arngeir a wound on his chest that stained his tunic red, but otherwise they were in good fighting shape.

'He's going,' said Grani.

'He has said we must die,' said Vigi. 'It's foreseen.'

'Varrin and the king are no poets,' said Arngeir.

'They will tell the tale to a poet,' said Vigi. 'The words will fit our glory.'

Down the grassy hill behind the houses horsemen were pouring. It was nearly an hour since the lord had seen the village beacons and he and his bodyguard had ridden hard. There were around twenty of them, at least two armoured in byrnies, four carrying swords, the rest spears and axes. The thegns had come, and in numbers.

'They can begin work on our saga very shortly, I think,' said Arngeir.

'We will be remembered for ever,' said Vigi.

A bowshot away from the raiders, the peasants had cut through the staves and five horses jumped down the small cliff onto the beach. The Norsemen's advantage from holding the gap was gone and now they had enemies on two sides.

King Authun hailed his men from the ship. 'You have played your part in the destiny of the world. You die as heroes.'

The raiders saluted him with their axes as three horsemen dismounted and drew their weapons. Two stayed in the saddle, charging into the river after the departing boat. One tried to jump onboard but lost his seat and crashed into the water, the other was forced to pull up by Authun's flashing sword.

Caught by the turning tide, the boat rounded a bend and the beach drifted out of sight. Then the king and Varrin heard the sound of the thegns' charge.

'There will be many widows in this country tonight,' said Authun.

'And eight more in our own,' said Varrin.

The king lowered his head. Before the end of the journey, he knew, there would be nine. Still, the fate of his entire race was in his hands. When he returned his wife would fall into a coma and the false pregnancy the witches had laid upon her would end. When she awoke she would have a son, the magic child, the wyrd child who would lead his people to conquer the earth. Authun would have a poet sing of the death of his warriors and then he could go into his next battle ready to die. He would face his kinsmen in Odin's halls and they would know he had done the right thing. He had secured the futures of all their descendants. All he had to do was work out which child he needed to present to his wife.

Authun turned his attention to the boys in the basket. Their mother was bending over them, fussing. He wanted to look at them again but couldn't bring himself to pull her away. There would be time enough to examine them, he thought.

He sat back in the boat and took off his byrnie as Varrin steered out to sea on the outgoing tide. Which child? The witches would know; they had always known so far. The witch queen would cast her magic and the true heir would be revealed. How much would that cost him? He took out the priests' book and began to pick apart the jewels and precious metal with his knife. He had that and two ornate candlesticks. Would that be enough? The witch had an insatiable appetite for gold.

Authun was not just a fighter; a successful king needs to be a politician too. His whole experience and upbringing as a man, a king and a warrior, however, made it impossible for him to recognise his blind spot. He considered only how to fight, persuade, cajole and manage men. He might be skilled and subtle in his schemes, practised at bending others to his will – but so were the women of the mountain.

2 A Mercy

The dead had never meant anything to Authun before. Their separation from the living seemed to him so slight that mourning or grief had never come to him. Death was just life in another place.

The manner of death was a different thing. Varrin needed to die but he should die like a warrior. The secret of Authun's new heir must be absolute, and while anyone who was party to it lived there was the risk that the truth might seep out to whisper from the shadows of the feasting halls, hum through the markets, sing with the wind beneath the sails of raiding ships. Authun, though, would not kill his friend. The king had been raised to believe that a kinslayer is cursed eternally. It wasn't that he thought of killing Varrin and then discounted the idea. It didn't even occur to him.

Varrin's death was a problem that he would solve the only way he knew how – in consultation. The Norsemen placed great faith in the power of talk.

The land was in sight and the ship laboured across a current. Progress would have been difficult with a full haul of oars. With only the sail and a partly co-operative wind the going was very hard. It was Authun's last chance, though. Varrin had to die now so his body would be taken down the whale road out to the north or there was a risk it could wash up on friendly shores, raising difficult questions.

'Varrin.'

'Lord, I know I cannot return.' The old warrior knew his king well and, even facing death, sought to lift the burden from his shoulders.

Authun lowered his head.

Varrin said, 'What shall they say of me, lord?'

17

'Your friends loved you and your enemies feared you. Of all men on the earth, you were raised the least cowardly. Who could hope for more?'

'Will they sing songs?'

'They already sing songs of you, Varrin. In death they will unlock a word hoard to your memory.'

Varrin stood and breathed the air like a man waking on a fine morning. He peered out to sea.

'Lord, I see a sea serpent, a beast of venom and fury that could devour the world snake himself. Allow me the glory of testing my spear upon it.' As death approached, it seemed Varrin was already writing himself into a saga: his language became finer, emulating the songs of the skalds. Authun joined in, to honour his friend.

'You are right, brave Varrin. Fight and win honour. You will need strong armour against such a serpent. On you I bestow this byrnie, this sheltering roof of blows.'

Authun took his mail coat from its barrel and held it up. Varrin bowed, humbled by the honour, and allowed the king to dress him. When the byrnie was tight about him, the king took out the golden wolf helm, its ruby eyes part of a trove of plunder taken from the Franks of the south. He placed it on his friend's head and knotted the straps. Then he tied on his rich cloak. Finally he put Varrin's spear in his hand.

'Tell my wife she was as fine a woman who ever kept a key,' said Varrin. 'Though she was given to me, I loved her. May my sons serve you as I have served you. Dispose of my daughters in marriage as if they were your own.'

By the prow, the woman slept with her boys in her arms.

'You will dine at my right hand in Odin's hall,' said Authun.

'We shall be drunk for all time,' said Varrin.

Varrin turned to the side of the boat and put one foot on the rail. 'Now, serpent!' he said, his voice low with determination. Without a look left or right he dived from the longship, stabbing into the waves as he leaped. In Authun's splendid byrnie and helmet there was no swimming, and in an instant he was gone. The king swallowed and turned away. Varrin's death had been necessary; no more to think about it.

In the prow the woman and the babies stirred, though Authun was surprised to see she hadn't woken. She had hardly closed her eyes during the voyage but it was as if she felt some comfort and security coming from the land and had finally given in to sleep.

Authun, in all his wars, had never killed a woman before. They were too valuable as slaves was the reason he gave himself. But there was something else.

He stood above her watching the two children sharing her sleep at her breast. He had his hand on his knife. Soon he would use it to kill her, he thought, perhaps when they met the witches, perhaps just before he returned to his wife. Whenever, it would be by the knife. The Moonsword had only ever killed warriors and he wouldn't stain it with the blood of a woman. And yet he felt it wrong to finish her with the same implement he would use to gut a fish. She was a mother and, to him, that deserved some respect. He had seen his wife go through labour five times and had wondered how many of his men would stand such pain.

There seemed something precious and worth preserving in the bond between the mother and her children, a warmth that seemed to spread from her. Authun the Pitiless felt something stir in his breast that, had he known it, was the first faint flickering intimation of his doom.

The woman had a charm given to her by the boys' father, a curious, wandering man in an age when lonely wanderers were rare. Few would dare to walk the land alone, at the prey of hostile villagers, offended lords, bandits, wild men, trolls, elves and wolf men. But the boys' father had dared. The amulet – just a wolf's head scratched on a pebble – would offer her protection, he had said, and left. So far it had offered her none at all but she clutched it to her in her sleep. When Authun the Wolf, slayer of the giant Geat, pillager of the east, feared lord of the white wastes, touched his knife and looked down at her he felt pity. It was a new emotion for him but who is to say it was the stranger's charm? A man has to become tired of slaughter eventually. Only the gods have an endless appetite for that.

The ship, under no direction, had turned across the waves and made a sudden violent jar. Authun kept his balance but the woman and the babies were shaken and slid against a chest. They awoke in a confusion of screaming, and for an instant the woman stared at Authun with that penetrating bloody eye. The king, who could face down any enemy, turned quickly to steady the boat. Action, as always, kept reflection at bay.

The woman watched him tie the rudder and work the sail and thought him the second most terrible thing she had ever seen. She recognised him for what he was, a belligerent self-seeker who had taken all the fears he had in him and thrown them at his enemies, a snatcher, a killer and a hero.

The children's father had said he was bored by heroes but Authun seemed anything but boring – terrible, murderous, almost divine. As he'd taken her from the church, the arrows flying, the fires blazing and the villagers screaming, he had seemed a point of unnatural calm, a rock in the eddying currents of violence. It was as if, for him, that situation was normal. If she ever met the god of war, she thought, Authun is how he would look.

The gods, however, had been much closer in her life.

3   Night Caller

The mother's name was Saitada and she had been very beautiful, sold as a young child when she was captured from her own people. Then her name had been Badb. As she had grown she had attracted the sexual attention of her owner – a smith. He was a generous man and liked to share her with his friends. At the age of thirteen she had cursed her good looks, taken a hot iron from the forge and applied it to her face.

The smith had been furious. He had tried to beat her but for some reason couldn't bring himself to do it. He wanted to hold her, to kiss her, tell her he would make things all right, but he knew the girl would never come near him any more except by force. For as long as he'd owned her he had been convinced there was some bond between them – that despite her tears and her protestations, her eventual sullen withdrawal, that she felt something for him, even that he was special to her. There on her face he confronted the damage he had done and, as a coward, could not bear to look at it in his home. So he'd just taken her to market. Though she had been delirious with pain from her wound, she remembered that place, where she had stood alongside goats and pigs in the shit and the stink to be prodded and inspected and sold on.

'This one,' said the farmer's wife, who could have been mistaken for an upright pig in the wrong light. 'This one I think is very suitable.'

The farmer, whose advancing years had neither increased his discernment nor reduced his lust, had been delighted. If he positioned her right then he would have a rare beauty to enjoy. Then he had looked into that eye and the idea had seemed impossible. He felt bad for having had such lewd thoughts and took pity on the girl.

'Yes,' he said, 'she will make a fine maid.'

They had asked her what she was called and she, wishing to leave the sullied little girl with the pretty face behind, had chosen another of her people's names. Saitada.

The farmer's wife had picked her for her horrible looks, fearing to lose her husband's affections to a prettier girl. The wound, she knew, would not put a man off because a man in passion is a beast that no small deformity can deter. It was the bloody eye that seemed to look through you and expose your sins to shame that would keep her husband true. No man, she thought, could have that look upon him and feel his misdeeds would go unpunished.

The farmer's wife was a healer and had dressed and cared for the girl's wounds with presses of comfrey and chamomile. Lacking children of her own, she lavished attention on her, combed and plaited her hair, made her a pretty dress and even gave her a bed. Saitada was as happy there as she had ever been, though she swore she would never take another man. And she never did, until she was seventeen.

On the day that she was to go back on that vow a neighbouring farmer had visited to warn that, very unusually, there was a wolf in the area. Three of his sheep had been killed the night before. In such a tight community of small farms wolves were rare, put off by the number of men. Hence the local farmers had little experience of dealing with them.

So Saitada, the farmer and his wife drove their livestock into the pen by the pigsty and waited the night with the dogs and a spear. You have two ways to go with a wolf, unless you are an experienced trapper. One is to light your torches and sing your songs, hoping that the noise will drive him away. The second is to lie in wait to spear him and kill him. Neither will work but both courses of action will provide the comfort of doing something. If you come in force he will slip away and try again tomorrow. If you wait, he can wait longer, until you are tired and sleep takes you. To catch a wolf, you need a trick and a trap, things the farmer did not have.

The farmer was eager for sleep and wanted to get things over with, so he commanded silence from the women. Still, he could not quite keep quiet himself, so impressed was he with the weight of his spear. Men who have never had to fight love a weapon. They love to hold it in their hands, feel its balance and speculate on the damage they might do, were they called to do it. There is a killer in every cowardly man, waiting for the right set of circumstances when the time has been drained of the possibility of reprisals and he feels free to act. The farmer was no different and began, as he sat in the warm night, to feel the importance the spear bestowed upon him and, despite himself, to talk.

'When I was a boy it was said no one threw a spear better than I.'

The farmer's wife rolled her eyes because she had heard this story before many times when he was in drink.

'I thought we were being quiet for this wolf,' she said.

'I'm just saying,' said the farmer, 'had I been born higher I would have made a mighty warrior. As a boy I had quite the feel for weapons. The carl himself saw me one day and said he wished half his warriors could shoot a bow as well as I. I was quite the—'

Suddenly he was quiet. In the trees by the farm two gigantic eyes seemed to burn, less a wolf than some fiend from hell.

He moved smoothly behind the slave girl. She did not flinch, having endured worse than a wolf had to offer her.

'That is no ordinary wolf,' said the farmer's wife.

'Sound the alarm,' said the farmer. 'Fetch aid, fetch aid!'

'You fetch aid,' said his wife; 'you're the man.'

'If I move it might see me,' hissed the farmer.

'If I move it might see me,' hissed his wife.

'I am needed to till the land. Who will provide for poor Saitada?' said the farmer.

'I will go for aid,' said Saitada.

'Too late. The wolf is among you,' said a voice close at their ears.

The three turned but couldn't for a moment see anyone. Suddenly, so bright and white in the starlit night that they wondered how ever they could have missed him, a young man of around twenty was there. He was strikingly handsome, long-legged and lithe. He seemed to draw the moonlight to him, and beneath it his muscles rippled as if under some silvery sea. For a breath it didn't seem remarkable that he was almost completely naked. All he had to cover his modesty was a huge and bloody wolfskin draped across his back, a rear paw cheekily positioned by his hand over that part the nuns shun. His hair was bright red and stood up in a shock.

'Christ's wounds!' said the farmer. 'You nearly made me jump out of my skin.'

'Well, I did jump out of mine,' said the man, sliding away the paw that concealed his shame and then whipping it back again.

'How dare you appear in front of my wife like that!' said the farmer, who was a pious man when it suited him.

'The wolf behind you?' said the strange man.

'Where?' said the farmer. 'Oh Lord, the eyes.'

The farmer turned to run but he had those grim burning eyes in front of him in the wood and the strange and terrible young man behind. He had nowhere to go and, his brain running out of ideas for what to do with his body, he simply flopped to the floor.

'Not eyes,' said the man, 'just torches left by some kind traveller.'

The farmer squinted into the darkness. Now it was obvious: they were just brands.

'As I thought,' said the farmer.

'Fire,' said the pale man. 'That is the way to keep the wolf at bay.' He walked to the wood and returned with the two burning torches. Now he had tied the wolf skin's back paws around his midsection.

'I have covered that serpent that tempted Eve,' he said.

The man held the torches up and looked at the peasants. 'A farmer, his pretty piggy wife and who is this rare beauty? No wonder you panic, old man, to see such a face.'

'I wasn't panicking I was ... taking advantage of the terrain, that is why I got down.'

'It seems this one knows better than you that fire keeps the wolf at bay,' said the man, holding up his hand to Saitada's chin and studying the scar on her face.

Saitada did not flinch to hear his words because the scorn of a man meant nothing to her. He gently turned the undamaged side of her face towards him.

'Such beauty is a terrible thing,' said the man, 'for no shield can deflect its dart, and even the most nimble of warriors can no more dodge it than you can, old man.'

'You are mocking me,' said Saitada, 'but I am glad of it if it means you will not lay your hands upon me.'

'No, lady,' said the man. 'You are far more beautiful to me than any woman on earth. You have snatched the spool of destiny from the hands of the fates and woven a skein yourself.'

'You speak fine words, sir,' said the farmer.

'High praise from such a judge,' said the traveller with a bow.

'And now you're mocking me!' said the farmer, who like most old men tended to hear only those parts of the conversation that concerned himself. 'I once threw a spear the length of a laine. And it stuck in the mud properly too.'

'Don't worry, ma'am,' said the man to the farmer's wife. 'I shall mock you when I have finished with your husband, but, oh, shall I ever finish with such an example? No, ma'am, you are quite safe, I shall never finish with him.'

'What of that wolf?' said the farmer, whose head had become a little disordered since the stranger's appearance, though he had drunk little.

'I have slain that night-time caller, that freeman of the forests, that furry sir, oh farmer, my manure mangler, my seedy serf, my shit smith. But he tore my clothes,' said the man. 'Will you lend me some of yours so that I might cover the splendour the priests would call our shame?' He went to pull the wolf skin away but stopped at the last instant.

'If you have killed the wolf, as I see you have, then I owe you a cloak,' said the old man. 'Here in the house I have one that has served me many winters.'

'I prefer the expensive one you're wearing,' said the man. 'It was woven by the finest hand that ever picked up a distaff.'

'It was woven by me,' said Saitada.

'I know it, lady,' said the man and bowed deeply.

'She is not a lady, she is a slave,' said the farmer.

'She's freer than you will ever be,' said the man. 'Now get me your cloak before I tear the skin from your back and wrap myself in that instead.'

The stranger's words seemed to sizzle through the farmer's mind. He felt as though he was frying in the juice of all his boasts, all his pretensions and weaknesses. He did as he was bid. The pale fellow stretched out his hand to Saitada and it seemed to her that little points of light began to dance around her, tiny silver orbs no bigger than seeds, glinting in a shimmering web. He put on the cloak she had made, drew it around him and began to sing.

> Half beautiful is she, like the moon
> And from her shall spring the moon taker
> Oh the sun it grows dark at the noon
> And the wolf in his dreams is a waker

This last line seemed to amuse the fellow no end and he burst out in giggles, which Saitada could only share, as if she was a child learning some naughty secret. Her giggling seemed to grow and grow in her until she thought it might never stop.

And then it did stop and the night was silent. Everything had changed and for ever. It seemed to Saitada that she stood in the middle of a glade that was bathed in the silvery light of a flaming moon.

'See the beauty of the garment you have made,' said the man.

He was in front of her, but the cloak was not her cloak but a cloak of feathers that might not have been feathers but silvery flames or just points of light. It engulfed him and lifted him so he seemed to hover a stool's height above the ground. The farmer and his wife were nowhere to be seen.

'You have never been loved,' said the traveller.

'Sir, I have not,' she said.

'And you have not known until this moment that you could be loved,' he said.

'I have not.'

'I can only love your kind,' he said. 'Who could love the princes and the heroes with their murders and their wars?'

'I know no princes or heroes, sir.'

'Bide your time,' he said. 'You'll be sick to your back teeth of them before you're done.' He smiled at her. 'You, my dear, are perfect.'

'My face is not, sir.'

'You chose imperfection – what could be more perfect? You saw your imperfection was perfection and therefore remedied it by imposing an imperfection on yourself thereby becoming perfect again. The logic is imperfectly flawless.'

He descended to the earth, and the cloak he had been wearing became a carpet of white feathers that covered the glade, deep as midwinter snow. She lay down upon it and, having only ever known straw before, was overwhelmed by its comfort.

The stranger spoke. 'To strive to be the best, to excel and have the skalds sing your praises. They're all at it. What better than to spit at what the gods gave you and spite your fate?'

'I did it because I would not give them a moment's more pleasure from me.'

'They will have no pleasure ever again. Would you know their fate?'

'If it is a bad one.'

'I have repaid them,' said the burning beautiful god, for now Saitada was sure this was not a mortal before her. 'You should have seen the smith's face when I spoke to him from the fire and he knocked that smelting pot onto his bollocks. He's got his cock out of his breeks for a different reason now, I can tell you. Are you grateful?'

'It is not enough,' said Saitada.

He stretched out his hand and she saw the smith asleep in his bed. He was drawn and pale but something obscured her vision. It was smoke. The thatch was on fire. The smith woke and tried to move but his wounds wouldn't allow him to. She saw him panic as the fire took hold.

Saitada smiled as she watched.

'You are a power, lady, a power,' said the god. 'The elves sing your fame and the dwarfs of the earth despair for they know that in all their art they will never make anything to compare to your depthless beauty.'

'I would know your name, sir,' said Saitada. She felt something strange sweeping over her, something she had never felt from a man before: love as more than an idea, as something present and intense, like her forgotten mother might have cherished her baby girl.

'My name?' said the traveller. 'Name? Lady, like you my magnificence cannot be contained by just one. First, you must know me better. You must see what I am up against.'

The odour of blood and fire filled the glade. There was a clamour and a hammering like the sound of the smith's shop increased a thousand-fold, metal on metal, metal on wood. Saitada knew it by instinct – the noise of battle. At the edge of the glade stood a tall grey man with a beard, wearing a wide-brimmed hat. He had a patch over one eye and two huge wolves lay panting at his feet, their teeth as big as knives. The expression on the man's face was terrible. Saitada had seen it before. It was the look men wore at cock fights or when cheering two dogs to rip into each other, the look the smith's friends had worn as they'd held her down – a look of delight in violence and lust for more.

'See Odin, the king of the gods in his hungers,' said the traveller. 'See how he would know and consume and control. Father, let go!'

The old man said nothing, just stood there frozen in his expression of malicious joy. The traveller went across and flicked the old man on the nose, but he did not respond.

'He would eat the world!' said the traveller. 'He would know it all, devour every mystery until the whole of creation came at his call. He's mad, you know. He drank so deeply of the knowledge well but the waters splashed on that burning hunger and boiled all his brains. Yet still he wants to know, ever more, ever more.'

'I would forget,' said Saitada.

'Of course you would. It's the only sane thing to do. Not knowing is what gives the world its beauty. Who would know why the sun on the dew on a May morning makes the heart sing? That pervert would. Would you have no love, old man Odin, would you snaffle down even a girl's secret heart's desires for a gorgeous flame-haired fellow and spew them out on a table in maps and runes? Would you chart the very stir-rings of the heart? Well, lady, I think we should give this greedy knowledge glutton, this filthy wisdom hog, a right royal bite on the bum, don't you?'

'Yes, sir,' said Saitada, though she didn't really understand what he meant. She only knew she wanted to please him.

'That's where you and I come in,' said the traveller. 'Would you know my imperfections, lady?'

'I know all I need to know of the imperfections of men,' she said, 'though I think you are not a man.'

'Whatever gave you that idea?' he said as the fiery moon turned green and points of emerald light began to dance around the glade. The old man disappeared, then one wolf, then another, its body first, then its head apart from the mouth. Finally the tongue snapped back into the teeth and lips and the glade was empty in a blink.

'I want you,' she said.

'Well, that'd be a clue, wouldn't it? You could never love a man, and yet you love me.'

'I do,' she said.

The pale god took her in his arms and kissed her. She felt at one with the moonlight, with the stars in the heavens and, stranger than that, she felt all her fears and dreams consumed by the strange traveller and then fed back to her, sweet as honey on his lips.

She took him to her and held him, and as their bodies joined it seemed that so did their minds. A searing laughter filled her up, somewhere between malice and wild delight. But there was love there too. She felt connected to every living thing on earth, felt the earthworms moving beneath her, the forests teeming, the cold spaces of the stars delicious and beautiful above her. The world felt precious and the gods, who she sensed like a pressure at the back of her head, the gods with their bloodlust and their battles, seemed ridiculous, terrible and contemptible.

She stroked his skin, and it was wet with the blood of the wolf pelt. She found the crimson on the white of his flesh fascinating. Her hand was red with the wolf's blood. She licked it and the taste of it seemed to fizz through her, as if tiny bubbles went popping all the way down inside her from her mouth to her knees.

The god now had the wolf's head over his face. He peered through the animal's bloodied lids with cold eyes. The tongue that slithered from between the dead wolf's teeth was long and lascivious.

'What is your name?' she asked.

'Names are like clothes, lady. I have many.'

'And which one do you wear tonight?'

The god smiled. She could see he liked her words. He pulled

30

her to him, pressed his wolf lips to hers and said, 'My name is Misery, and would you know yet more?'

'Yes,' said the girl, breathing in his scent, the scent of something beautiful, strange and burned. 'I would know more.'

He flicked at her lips with his tongue and whispered, 'So is yours.'

The next morning the traveller was gone, along with the fine wolf pelt. Around Saitada's neck, tied in a strip of leather, was a strange stone. It was a token, the night caller had said, of his affection and protection. It didn't seem to do her much good.

The livestock had been slaughtered. The dogs were dead and Saitada was blamed for lying with a stranger while the wolf devoured the pigs. The farmer's wife wanted to forgive her, to comb her hair and call her daughter again, but the farmer, brave in the wolfless light of day, wanted revenge.

She was sold with only the clothes she stood up in and the pebble charm the strange fellow had given her to her name. The priests had bought her and told her to make a virtue of her suffering. When they discovered she was pregnant they set to chastise her but found they could not. Something about her, maybe the charm, maybe that eye that seemed to see all their sins, stopped them, and they let her live among them unpunished.

Then Authun had come.

So what stopped Authun's thoughts of murder on the ship? The stone at her neck was no more than a pebble with the head of a wolf scratched on it. Perhaps he had seen the rough little picture – his family sign – and felt some deep-seated fear that this foreign woman was kin. Or perhaps he just felt sorry for her.

He looked north, up into the white-capped peaks where he would meet Gullveig, witch queen of the mountains, that mind-blown child. She had been no more than ten years old when he'd first faced her the summer before. Authun knew the stories surrounding her. As the old witch queen was dying, she had appeared to Gullveig's father, a warrior at the court of King Halfdan the Just. She had told him to take his pregnant wife to the Troll Wall to give birth. He knew better than to refuse, surrendered the girl child and gave thanks for the luck the sacrifice would bring the family. Gullveig had been a decade in the dark of the mountain caves, breathing in magic like a fisherman's children breathe sea salt on the wind.

Authun looked at the mother cradling her twins. No, he couldn't kill her. He'd give her to the witches, he thought. The chosen boy would survive the journey from the Wall to his wife without feeding. The girl couldn't even speak Authun's language, would never know what had happened to her children. What harm could she do waiting on the witches? It wasn't as if she was going to escape them: no one could even find their way in and out of their caves without a guide. In this way Authun the Pitiless, burner of the five towns, allowed the privilege of life to a deformed slave that he would not allow to his kinsmen, and in so doing sealed his fate.

When they came ashore, the summer valley was pleasant and hummed with fertility but Authun could take no pleasure from the scenery. All his life he was a man of the necessary, someone who did what needed to be done and thought no more about it. He was pitiless but as a means to an end. The fouler the fate of his enemies, the more tribute he could exact from others without having to lift a spear. But, as the woman's strange eye seemed to watch him wherever he went, he could not rid himself of the image of Varrin's face as he'd faced death and spoken of his wife. He would, he decided, carry the message to the widow as his first priority after he had given the child to his wife.

There was a river between the coast and the Troll Wall and Authun would have liked to have sailed up it. Single-handed, however, it would be impossible. And anyway the witches had called down enough rocks to make, it impassable even with a full crew. So they walked.

The woman went in front of Authun, where he could see her. Her hair hung loose, as the wimple the priests had made her wear was now in the North Sea. In her tatty fifth-hand nun's habit and the overlong cloak that had once belonged to Hella she looked like a beggar. The king did too, in his salt-stained cloak and sea furs. Authun carried the Moonsword tied on his back, hidden away. The hills, he knew, were full of trolls and bandits, and he didn't want to go advertising his wealth.

They faced no supernatural opponents on their journey from the sea but on the second day saw three riders approaching in the distance. The girl looked for cover, which Authun thought a very reasonable course of action – for a woman. The king himself simply stood where he was. The men dismounted and approached, which Authun took as a sure signal of violent intent.

When taking on a warrior such as Authun the Wolf the best plan is to stalk him and cut him down in his sleep. Taunting him from afar and then approaching with 'What have we here?' is ill-advised. Still Authun, who was in a curiously melancholy mood, would have let the three pass had the first not attempted to shake him by the shoulder. Authun grasped the man's hand so he couldn't let go of his intended victim, took a pace back with his left foot to expose the arm and, in one movement, drew the Moonsword from his back and cut the limb in two. Before the bandit could realise what had happened, Authun struck him again, this time hard to the leg. Authun had no intention of killing him; already he was thinking how he might use him. His leg damaged, the man had sought to steady himself but had instinctively put his weight onto the missing hand at Authun's collar. He fell forward at the king's feet, bleeding heavily. The remaining two robbers stared in disbelief at the Moonsword. They knew now exactly who they were facing – they had heard so many stories of Authun the Wolf it was almost as if they knew him personally. One thing was clear in their minds. Fighting him was certain death.

They tried to flee, but Authun, even at thirty-five, was too fast for them. The king had noticed as soon as the men appeared that both were wearing costly byrnies. Thus encumbered, they died before they had run twenty paces.

He cleaned his sword on the fallen men's clothes and returned to Saitada and the bleeding bandit. Working quickly, he took out a length of walrus cord from his pouch and tied off the man's arm to stop the bleeding. The bandit was unconscious, which suited Authun. Saitada looked at the two bodies and then at the king. He found himself explaining.

'If I'd let them go they would have come back when we were sleeping, perhaps in numbers,' he said, though he knew she couldn't understand. 'They're scavengers. They never paid for those horses. See the byrnies? They're taken from the bodies of brave fools who came to steal the witches' treasure, treasure that is only there to draw fools on to death. They use them in their magic then they throw them from the rock.'

The rock. In the distance they could see it, already huge three days' march away. It was their destination: the Troll Wall, as tall as a thousand men standing on each other's shoulders. It was a monstrous overhanging cliff, like something from a dream, an obstacle which blocks all further progress, something symbolic, with a resonance far beyond its daunting physical mass. He looked up at it. It was impossible, he thought, to imagine climbing it, though he had done so before. It was the only way into the witches' caves that the sisters were willing to reveal to outsiders. The back of the mountain was even more impassable, swathed in permanent ice and perilous loose boulders, and defended by hill tribes under the witches' thrall.

So they would have to climb – almost to the top of the Wall and then into it, to the caves. Authun knew, though, that the Wall would not be the greatest impediment to seeing the witch queen. That would be the witches themselves.

4   The Troll Wall

Between the hour of the dog
And the hour of the wolf
Between waking and sleeping
Between the light and the dark
Is the doorway of shadows
Step on, traveller,
Do not tarry on that grim threshold.

Authun read the runes someone had carved into a boulder. He was below the dizzying overhang of the Troll Wall, a cliff so high that the top was invisible in clouds. Human bones and rotting clothing lay about him but it was the inscription that made him shiver. Mundane perils of bandits and falling rocks were bad enough without thinking of what other horrors waited in the dark.

The Wall would take even the fittest warrior two weeks to climb, even if he found one of the shifting routes around the overhang at the first attempt. But no one was that lucky. It was impossible to reach the caves in one go. Rock slides moved old paths, opened new ones and closed others in a blink. You could climb almost to within touching distance of the top and then have to turn, your way impassable, another route needed. The paths were becoming fewer too, as if the mountain begrudged them and sought to shrug them off. How long would it be before there were none? Would the witches eventually be marooned and left to rot in their caves? Or were there other, hidden entrances that the sisters and their servants used?

The climb, though, wasn't the biggest problem. The problem was, as the runes warned, sleep. For that tiny fall between

35

waking and unconsciousness was where the witches were. People came to steal their treasure and died; people came to seek their advice and died. Very few, armed with charms and acceptable tribute, ever came back alive, and of those no one was ever stupid enough to seek a second audience. No one but Authun and his ancestors, who by divine right, it was said, could hold regular counsel with the witches. Even to the wolf king though, the prospect was daunting. This was his second visit, and he hoped he would never have to make a third.

They would have to wait for a guide, he knew, dangerous as that might be. Authun saw no point in exhausting himself and the woman by attempting the climb unaided. At the base there was the risk of bandits, but better that than the children should fall to their deaths. He made a fire, drank water from a skin, fed bread and salted fish to Saitada and made sure the bandit was just about alive.

Then he lay down and pretended to sleep for a bit to see what the woman would do. She fed her children and settled down to sleep herself. She was, as he guessed, no idiot. She wasn't going to kill her only protector in a strange and hostile wilderness or even run away from him. The bandit was too badly injured to attempt anything. Authun wanted to take the precaution of breaking his remaining arm but feared that the shock might kill him. So instead he just tied him with walrus cord to a tree. Then he prepared for sleep properly and waited for the witch to come.

If it was the witch queen, all well and good. If it was one of the stranger sisters, well ... Authun was a warrior so he concentrated on what he would *do* if the worst came to the worst, not what would become of him. He would try to give her the bandit, then the woman, after that himself. With luck the witch queen would appear in time to save the children.

But sleep wouldn't come for him. The night was fine and temperate, and he was warm in his cloak, but little irritations seemed to keep him awake: a cold nose, a pebble in the small of the back, the smell of the moss on the rock, the taste of the rock even. Then he realised he was not awake but neither was he dreaming. Some of his senses seemed heightened – he could taste the cold on the air like iron, smell the difference between the flowers and the grasses; he could smell the tar and the dirt of a puddle. It was as if his hearing was slightly muted, his vision reattuned so that in the bright moon glare he could see new colours – deep metalled blues, sparkling dark greens and seams of gold on the side of the rock. He was where the witches were, he knew, in that place between waking and sleeping. He went to the tree and cut loose the bandit in preparation for what was to come.

Cries in the dark like a baby wailing. Authun wanted to prepare the woman for the arrival of the witch but they shared no language. She would just have to suffer it. He heard a voice through the rain. Where had the rain come from? He tasted it on his lips – more iron, like the way the hand smells after handling a sword, like blood.

> *Mother in the pen,*
> *Mother in the pen.*

It was a child's voice, high and piping but clearly audible.

Authun didn't want to look but knew that he must. If it was the witch queen then she would have to see him. He pulled the semi-conscious bandit to him, ready to throw him to the witch.

Down along the rock face he could see a young woman bent over as she tried to shield herself from the driving rain. She had something in her arms. It was a baby. Authun turned to Saitada. She was holding both her children close to her.

The woman staggered out from the cliff face with the baby and laid it on the ground. She took off its swaddling clothes and exposed it naked to the elements. Then she ran off into the night.

Authun stayed where he was. The witches had all sorts of tricks and he wasn't about to fall for one so easily.

He watched as the child died. After a short while it stopped moving and then seemed to disappear. So this was magic. Authun kept his hand on his sword.

And then the rain stopped and it seemed that it was a lovely summer evening. The same woman who had left the baby appeared but this time dressed in farm girl's finery, as if she was going to a dance. A man, also in his country best, walked past her, kissed her hand and seemed to tell her not to be late. Authun recognised the story. It was a fairy tale about an unmarried woman who had exposed her child to die rather than face the hardship of raising it. How did the story end? He couldn't remember.

The woman smiled and sat on a stool that had appeared from somewhere. She was combing her hair. She finished and got up. Authun recalled that the story told she had gone to check on the pigs before leaving for the dance. She looked into a trough and from within it took something cold and blue. It was a baby, and Authun knew it was dead. The woman held the dead child up and looked at it as it began to move, kicking out its legs as if attempting a jig. And then the rhyme began, a rhyme that seemed to come from inside his head.

> *Mother in the pen,*
> *Mother in the pen,*
> *Primp and preen to charm the men*
> *Take my swaddling clothes and dance in them.*

As the rhyme split its way through his mind all he could see was Varrin's face, bloated, white and drowned. What had he done? What had he done? The rain came down again, straight and hard in the windless evening.

Suddenly it was night, pitch black, and the young woman, her face pale with madness, clasping the dead child to her, was at Authun's side. Even the king screamed, though he didn't forget to push the wounded bandit towards the witch. It was as if the man's body was swallowed by the night. The king knew that he wasn't facing the witch queen. She would have recognised him. It was a patrolling witch mistaking him for another plunderer, or worse it was one of the truly terrible sisters, her mind simmering with magic, some half-demon who leaked delusions and madness to those around her and who could kill them without even noticing they were there.

'Gullveig, Gullveig!' shouted Authun at the top of his voice. 'Help us, lady!'

The Moonsword was out, and he looked around for whatever would come next. The light was so inconstant, one instant flat dark, the next the pale washed-out murk of a rain-soaked dusk. He wanted to find Saitada, to throw her to the witch, but she was not there.

'Authun the Wolf,' said a child's voice in his head, 'mightiest warrior in Midgard, is there no one who can defeat you in arms?'

'Gullveig! Gullveig!' Authun screamed, trying to make the witch queen hear him. He must not reply, he knew. He must not accept the delusion, enter into it and become consumed by it.

> I know one who can lay you low,
> I know one who can prick you so.
> If you defeat this one I know
> Then, King Wolf, I will let you go.

No mortal had ever challenged him and lived. He did what he had sworn not to: he answered the voice. 'Bring forth your champion!'

Behind the veil of rain there was a shimmering and the shape of a man took form. It seemed to Authun that the witch had underestimated him. His opponent was a man of near forty with long white hair and a straggly beard. He looked careworn and beaten by his years but there was something in his hand that shone with a cold fire. It was a sword, curved, slim and wicked. Even in the dullness of the rain it gleamed.

Authun recognised it at the same time he recognised his opponent. It was the Moonsword. His opponent was himself.

As the realisation hit him something very strange happened. He saw himself with his back to the rock and he saw himself advancing towards the rock. He seemed to be both warriors at the same time, looking out through both men's eyes. He could see a white figure with a woman and two babies at his back but at the same time he could see the same white figure advancing from the rock and hear the cry of the boys behind him. Authun did not know which warrior he was and in some way he was both.

More reflective men might have wondered what to do, but Authun, both Authuns, had been brought up to value swift action. The kings closed with each other and began to fight. It was a hopeless struggle, each man guessing the other's moves, each anticipating blows and ducking beneath them or stepping away so their swords sliced through thin air. All things being equal they could have fought like that for ever. But all things are not equal. What we do and how we react is not the same when we are facing up a slope as when we are facing down. Authun might instinctively know his opposing self might offer three feints and then a strike to the legs, but he couldn't know by how much the ground had raised one of his attacker's legs higher than the other, where the disposition of his weight lay – largely on one foot, largely on the other or spread. He could not guess when the rain would blind his eyes or when it would clear from his opponent's. Also, what you do facing a rock, looking only at blackness, is different to what you do facing a man with a moving background of trees. We are not the same people facing north as we are facing south: humans are a inconstant and contingent race. So the king did strike himself, a glancing blow to his flank.

Authun felt pleased he had drawn first blood but was also alarmed that he had been wounded. But then the king who struck the blow felt something in his side. An identical wound to the one he had inflicted had appeared. The king could not stop, could not back down, he was incapable of even having such an idea. So he struck again and hit again and both kings took a wound to the forearm. Then one to the ear, then the hand. Who hit and who received the blows became unclear, but Authun kept fighting because that was the only option for someone raised to believe the sword was the answer to everything.

One thing was plain to Saitada, though: if the fight went on she was about to lose her children's guardian.

Clinging to the boys – she wouldn't leave them – she sprang out into the rain to interpose herself between the warriors.

'No!' she shouted. 'Enough!' But her words, incomprehensible to the kings, were lost in the rain, and suddenly it was as if a giant hand had lifted her from the ground and she was shooting up through the sodden air, up the cliff, up and up and up. Then she heard a strange childish voice speak to her.

'Die,' it said.

She was falling, squeezing her babies to her. Then it was light and quiet and the same voice spoke again.

'Forgive me, Lord Loki,' it said.

'Sister, we all make mistakes. Forget the error, and forget me too,' said Saitada, though it wasn't her voice. It was the voice of the strange traveller, the boys' father. And then she was on the ground below the rock, and Authun, bloodstained and panting, was standing over her. It was dawn and the sun warmed her face.

'They have sent a boy to guide us,' said the king. 'See to the children and then we'll get going.' Strangely, she understood him, though he was still speaking his own language.

A pale child of about eight was in front of them, laden with protective charms, arm rings, amulets and talismans.

'Follow,' he said.

And they set off, on the arduous journey across the Troll Wall and up to the witches' realm.

5 The Loss of Sons

The cliff was perilous and it was becoming clear to Authun that they would not reach the top. The woman had finally yielded her children and they were strapped wriggling and squalling to the king, the mother checking their bindings with irritating regularity.

Authun still shivered to look at her but he could not yet cast her aside. He shivered still more when he thought of the ordeal that faced him in meeting the witch queen.

'Do you know where you are going, child?' he asked the boy.

The boy just kept on climbing.

It had been a still day at the bottom, but here, an inexorable ten days up, along winding paths, down others, braving terrible scrambles and awful jumps, the wind almost flattened the climbers to the rock. Authun had thought the slave girl would never make it. There was a path, not that you would see it from the bottom, but it was so narrow in places that even Authun, who had stared down death so many times without blinking, felt a tightness in his stomach as he trusted his life to a root or a fingerhold. He did not look down.

They slept tied on to the cliff with ropes and pegs the boy had with him, and surrounded by charms. The child seemed not to sleep but spent the night chanting a strange song to a broken tune in a language Authun did not understand. The only thing that troubled the king's dreams was the anticipation of what was to come.

And then the overhang became serious. Impassable. How had he reached the witches before? Authun couldn't remember. He remembered only the prophecy, the witch queen's presence and the dark.

Inside the clouds, visibility down to a few paces, the path finally gave out. The child guide seemed to have missed the entrance to the caves. Authun felt the fear drying his mouth. He was weak, the girl was weaker. They wouldn't survive the climb down, even if the boy agreed to guide them. The boy clambered back around Authun, back around Saitada and then, just visible in the clinging mist, he beckoned them. There in the rock was a gap, no more than a crack. It was only a shoulder's width and scarcely as tall as a man. Authun would not be able to pass through it with the children, and even without them would have to turn sideways and wriggle his way in. He peered into the blackness and smelled the deep earth. He could see nothing at all but he had to go on. He untied the infants and gave them to their mother. Then he slid inside after the boy. There was only the weak light from outside to see by. He could see an arm's length, maybe a little more, in front of his face but after that nothing. The mother passed her wailing children in. She was committed to Authun now, whether she liked it or not, and had no other option than to follow.

Authun tied the infants to him and watched the girl climb through. He had come to admire her and had certainly known men with less resolve. She needed no coaxing, morale building or bullying. She just followed.

The child guide stood very close to them and unwound a long cord from his waist. He passed it to the king, and gestured for him to tie it to himself and allow Saitada to take it too. She did. Then they went down into the dark.

Thoughts came and went in the blackness, as Authun fought to keep his footing and protect the children. The entrance on the Wall, he thought, must be how the witches admitted their few guests. It was too impractical as an everyday access. How did they eat? How did they come forth to visit in the night, to sit at the end of a stunned farmer's bed and barter magic for children? There must be other ways in and out, thought Authun, unless they could fly – as was the rumour.

In the dark he became acutely aware of his breathing, of that of the children and the woman behind him, and of his footfalls, heavy and uncertain. He lost purchase on time. At one point he heard water and felt the boy take his hand and thrust it into a stream. He drank and helped Saitada do the same.

They rested a while and he passed the babies to the girl to be fed. He was aware of how young and fragile they felt as he gave them over. How had the girl endured this journey so soon after giving birth? He admired her. Then the descent continued, sightless. His hands scraped on rock; he stumbled; he felt the boy push him back as they slowed to clamber over a rock fall or squeeze through a bone-crushing passageway. Authun felt terribly vulnerable and hated it. The dark was an enemy he couldn't fight; there a child could maroon him and he would be doomed. On they went, down and down, first cold then hot. They rested again, and then again. Had they been inside a day? Authun thought so. Down, down, down through galleries blind and cold, crawling into tiny fissures that scraped his face and arms as he wriggled through them. Standing room could have been just out of reach to his left or right and he wouldn't have known. And still down, the children's wails echoing through vast chambers or deadened by long coffins of rock.

How long now? Two days? Perhaps. Breathing became difficult; balance had to be fought for. The air itself seemed weak and lifeless. And then Authun felt the rope go slack to his front and heard childish footsteps going away. He pulled the taught end towards him and held Saitada to him with a tenderness that had never come as naturally before. He heard his own voice shaking.

'We will overcome. Do not let go of the rope.' He felt to see that she had tied it to her wrist. She had. 'Sleep,' he said. He didn't expect her to understand but she did – not just his words but his feelings of concern and tenderness. She sat down. What else was there to do? Moisture clung to

Authun's skin; he was sweating and then he was shivering. He felt around where he was sitting, aware that he could be a step away from a terrible drop. He pulled the girl to him, presenting her children to her. The terrible danger of their situation made them seem even more precious to him. The girl fed the babies and Authun struggled with the fixings of his scabbard, releasing the cords. When the mother passed the children back he tied their feet to his belt, stowing his sword under the boots he used for a pillow. For the first time in his life he valued something more than his weapon in a time of danger.

It seemed to Authun that sleep came – but what is waking and what is sleeping in such darkness? The body has its rhythms of hunger and excretion, but when hunger is constant and water scarce these cease to mark time. The woman's milk failed and the children's wailing became constant. Then, after a while, it ceased.

'Who?'

A voice was close in the dark, the word like a note on a flute.

'Lady?'

'Who?' Again, like the hoot of an owl, its breath near to him, foul and hot.

Authun imagined some giant bird next to him in the dark, picking him over in its claws.

'I am Authun, king of the Horda. I bring tribute of gold and slaves to the palace of the witch queen.'

'Who?'

Authun felt something climb over him. It was a human form, frail and light but still the king had to restrain himself from reaching for the sword. No. Whatever it was, they were at its mercy.

'Who?'

Authun breathed in. Would the Valkyries find him down here, he wondered, to take him to Valhalla to feast for ever? Or would it be just that damp dark, always. He reached to his side. Then he realised the cords on his belt were loose and the children were gone.

A guttering flame burned the king's eyes and he moved to shield them. In a glimpse he saw, leaning over Saitada and the babies, a tiny old woman in a white shift. Above her, in a flicker of gold, almost like a flame herself in that light, stood the witch queen, that grim child, pale and beautiful, crowned in an impossible tangle of golden cables, rubies, emeralds, diamonds and sapphires, like a dragon's hoard in miniature.

At her throat was a rich necklace whose jewels burned with a light familiar to Authun. It was the light he'd seen as he sacked the five towns, the light of the burning village from which he'd taken the child, the light of destruction. Then it was gone, and he could see nothing.

A baby was thrust into Authun's hands. Then some sort of object. It was a small leather bottle, half full with liquid, he could feel. No one spoke, though he understood what it was – medicine to give his wife, to complete the deception.

'The mother will come with me?' said the king.

'Who?' The older woman's idiot hoot again.

Authun must have been dreaming because all around him tiny lights came on and went out, the faces of the strange sisters appearing for an instant and then vanishing again. Wherever they were, it seemed, was wreathed in gold – arms and armour, cups and plates, fine arm rings and gilded chests of coins. The king used the light to locate his sword. His hand closed on it and he had to will the tension from his fingers. If he was going to fight he would need to be relaxed: too tight a grip would rob him of speed.

'The mother?'

'Who?'

Authun was finding his ordeal almost unbearable. He longed for the real light, for the feel of the breeze and the taste of rain. And then it was dark again and he didn't know for how long.

He awoke by the bank of a river. The Moonsword was

gone but the baby was at his side. He was terribly thirsty and plunged his head into the water and drank like a dog. Then he turned to the child. It was filthy but looked well enough. It was crying, at least, which Authun took for a sign of health. He looked at the Troll Wall, far in the distance, still immense. He washed the child and thought of all the sorrow that had surrounded it up until that point, the deaths and the deception that had brought them to where they were. Even the death of the bandits played on his mind. There were his kinsmen left on the river beach; Varrin, weighed down by the byrnie, swallowed by the sea; that poor girl with her hideous face – what had become of her? At the very best she had lost one of her babies. At the worst? Still alive and alone in that awful dark for as long as it took for thirst to kill her. On any other day of his life Authun would have regarded these things as simply the way of fate, unpleasant briars he'd had to pick through to get to the clear path ahead. But though he didn't know her name, he thought of Saitada and, alone by the water, Authun the Pitiless wept.

Then he wrapped the child in his cloak and headed for the cabin, five days away at a comfortable pace, where his wife lay supposedly pregnant. He looked at the baby. It needed a wet nurse and wouldn't last that long. He would need to do the journey in much less than that. Never mind. After the stagnant air of the cave it would be good to feel the exhaustion of movement. By the water's edge on his way he saw hoof prints, maybe two riders. He only had his knife, but if he could kill a horseman then he could be at the cabin in perhaps a couple of days, maybe less if he could get a second horse. More deaths would be needed before he reached his homeland.

6 Wolfsangel

Had Authun been of a more reflective nature, he might have wondered why the witches had been so generous as to grant him the son he longed for. He would have suspected unasked-for generosity in any rival king and expected it as a right from a visiting ambassador, but the witches belonged to another realm entirely. They were in the sphere of the supernatural, the unguessable, similar to providence or fate, and he didn't question their gift any more than he would have a whale beaching on his shores, or a good wind for his longships on a raid.

It would have surprised him to learn that the witches were acting from something as mundane as fear.

Though the women of the Troll Wall were considered monsters by the people and kings from whom they took their tribute, they were really not so very different to the terrified farmers, jarls and thralls who left their gifts of food, drink and children on the mountainside.

The fisherman who had lost his boy, for instance, thought of the witches as monsters. He couldn't say if he had been waking or dreaming that midnight when the air in his house had seemed as tight and cold as a compress on his skin and the thing he had glimpsed from the side of his eye vanished when he turned to look at it properly. The lad had woken in the morning and said the women had called to him, so the fisherman had taken him to the mountain. There was no other way, he knew. The consequences of refusal would be visited on all his people, not just his own family.

The man had watched trembling as his son walked away and was swallowed by the fog. He couldn't have imagined that the witches felt anything at all, least of all fear. But the women were afraid.

What is prophecy? It is a wide thing of many forms. We don't call a person who anticipates a cat will knock over a cup and moves to catch it a prophet. We don't maintain that the ability to look at the clouds and say it will rain makes you a seer. Even in the summer we know the cold of winter will come, but no one claims magic powers for that. These predictions are part of our everyday experience of the future, not a veiled and mysterious thing but something that connects directly to the present.

In the crags and caves of the Troll Wall, behind that door in the face of the cliff that you would not see, could not see, if you were not invited there, the witch queen's powers of prophecy were not unrelated to those possessed by us all. The boundaries between the present and the future are not as strong as we imagine, and the witch queen had sweated, frozen, starved and hallucinated until hers were not strong at all.

Prophecies were not something external to her, something she made or said; they were part of her consciousness, the way she saw the world. They were like a language she spoke. And for a year before the queen had sent Authun on his mission, that language had hissed softly of a threat. It did not arrive wholly formed one day, but rather started like a suspicion or even a rumour – a whisper beneath the rush of the cave streams or a cold that crept too far into the earth and left her shivering even in the wolf chamber, where the breath of a fettered god heated the rock so it was painful to touch.

The feeling grew in her as she sat in the dark, and it grew in the other sisters. As the witches eroded the distinction between today and tomorrow, they blurred the lines between me, you, she and it. Their experiences were like possessions that could be lent, borrowed or shared.

Minor magics were used to clarify the sense of foreboding. The sisters lit a whale-blubber candle and asked it for a vision. They could have asked anything to direct them but they chose the candle because it had once been a living thing and so its connections to the outside world were more solid than those of the rocks of the caves. First the candle revealed its past, as it would to anyone, the fish stink filling the cave. The sisters, though, could sense more. They breathed in the stress that had seeped into the fat with the whale's beaching, its discovery by hunters and its killing. The candle burned on, and they began to see that, for the prophecy, the quality of its light was the important thing.

Then a sister, because it felt right, reached forward and snuffed out the flame. The light disappeared but the thought of the light, its residue, filled the witches' minds. Underneath the sickly yellow of the flame, they thought, was a darker colour, a bright slate, the colour of the sky before a storm. The link was followed, and rainwater was brought down in a cup from the top of the Wall, and it was noticed that the water felt heavier than normal water, or rather it held a sentiment, a wish. The water, thought the sisters, still wanted to fall, to be rain again. The smell of it too was sharp, like ozone. The link to the coming storm seemed stronger.

A witch went to the top of the Wall to observe the birds. They had moved from the north face of the mountain and come around to the south. In the valley, she could sense, other animals were moving to shelter. The gulls had come inland and insects were burrowing into the earth. Why were these things happening? Because the witches were looking. The animals didn't move to offer auguries to the ordinary people of the mountains.

The portent was clear then – a storm, a magical storm. In the winter the message became clearer. The smoke on the wind bore the scent of funeral fires; the rats that ran through the caves seemed to carry an excitement and an expectation; more ravens than gulls were seen in the sky; a vision of the hangman's tree seemed to resonate in the witches' minds, day and night, the creaking of the rope waking them from their dreams, intruding on rituals where it had no place. Death was all around them, they knew, waiting for its moment to touch them. The time for subtlety was over.

A rune would need to be carved. The ordinary people knew runes, scratched symbols that allowed them to record simple messages or list things. But to the witches they were much more than that, more even than charms for amulets or to guard a chest, as some of the healers and wise women of the farmsteads knew them to be. They were living things that took root in the mind and grew within it, changing it utterly, feeding on sanity and blossoming into magic.

Rune carving was not something the witches took lightly. Runes were powerful sources of magic given by Odin – or rather taken in pain and anguish and wilful madness from the dark god by the earliest women who had retreated to the mountain.

Generations before, there had been just one witch. She had sat alone in the caves, her mind falling through the dark, until her pain had matched the dead lord's when he hung on the tree for nine days and nights pierced by the spear and chilled by the moon at the well of wisdom. Her reward was a rune that meant daylight and, though it had no name, it shone in her mind and warmed her bones like the sun on a summer's afternoon. The presence of the rune inside her gave her the power to heal the people of the mountain and the ability to reveal glimpses of the future to them. In return, they had sent her three girls to train.

One of them, drowned, starved and frozen for year after year, met the dead god by the deep pool and was given a rune that sparkled like bright water. The minds of men fell open to her and she began to dream the dreams of children in faraway places, hear jealous whispers flowing through the mountain passes and feel the coursing currents of love and hate that washed over the farmsteads.

Another took a different path to knowledge. She dug her own grave and the sisters sealed her in with a rock. As her sanity collapsed she had felt the god lying next to her in that tiny space, touched the rope at the god's neck and felt his body cold and lifeless next to her. Her rune seemed to grow and wither in her mind, now obscured by earth and weeds, now exhumed and vibrant. When she was lifted from the ground she was scarcely breathing, but she had won the most valuable rune of all. Now she knew the secrets of inheritance and how magic can be given as a gift.

From that moment on, death could not take the power of the runes from the sisters. Each could build on the knowledge of her teachers. Progress was possible. The witches grew more powerful, generation after generation keeping what they had and building on their knowledge until there were twenty-four sisters of the inner circle, each the guardian, nurturer and expression of a different rune.

Now, though, there was a twentyfifth witch. She was known to Authun as Gullveig, the witch queen, and to some of the local people as Huldra, but the sisters never called her that, or anything. She had been brought to the tunnels as a baby, destined – according to divination – to take on the rune of daylight. But when the witches started to work with the girl it became plain it was already within her, seeming to shine from the darkness from her first meditations, to rustle like the wind in a full-leafed tree in the minds of all the witches who looked at her. This was a puzzle for the sisters because it normally took years of suffering and denial to make the rune manifest – that and the death of the sister within whom it currently dwelled. At two years old the girl was put to further agonies and observed. A rune seemed to spill from her – silver like the sea on a moonlit night – then another, which twinkled like ice in the morning sun, and then a third, which seemed more a feeling than a vision, harsh prickles on the skin with a deep, blustery cold, and a fourth, with the scent of wild fruit, a fifth, like hunger, a sixth with the glint of gold, a seventh that smelled of roses and blood, and an eighth with the sound of the wind in sails. By the end of the girl's third year all the twenty-four runes that the sisters spent their lives expressing, dreaming and using for their power were in the girl.

She represented a new stage in the witches' evolution. Previously the queen had only held the daylight rune, that of the first witch. Gullveig had them all. Through her early years her ritual sufferings had propelled her mind on travels with the hanged god through dry tombs in arid lands where the dead seemed to claw at her from their crumbling graves, to mires and peat bogs where she had seen the fresh pink skin of the newly drowned whose faces seemed to implore her for help her as they sank, to battles where she heard the whispered names of lovers and children on the lips of dying men and where she picked the shrieking runes from their fingers. It was said she was mad, but had the farmers and warriors of the valleys known what she had been through, they would have marvelled she stayed so sane.

Reading the portents of rock, wind and water, Gullveig knew something extraordinary was happening. The foreboding that filled the caves, the heavy air, the sense of frustration waiting to break, told her she had no choice. She had to carve a rune, to force the future into the physical realm, to make it something that could be handled, discussed and, ultimately, manipulated.

For this she descended to the lower caves, where the rocks were stained glowing reds and greens and the damp and the cold gave way to a heat that seemed to pour from the earth. She took with her a small piece of cured leather that had once been a chieftain's belt and a pin that had held his cloak at his neck. Then she stayed on her own for a season. No one brought her food; the water she had was only what she licked from the cave walls; there was no light except the phosphorescence of the rock and no presence but her own. At the end of her ordeal the sisters came and carried her from the cave. She had written nothing and it was clear a greater trial was needed.

The sink hole at the bottom of the ghost caves was not a

natural phenomenon, though no one could recall who had dug it. It was about an armspan wide at the top but narrowed as it descended ten or twelve times the height of a man until anyone falling into it would have been stuck fast like a stopper in a bottle. The shaft cut across a powerful underground stream which entered through a fissure as wide as an fist at the top and left through another at the bottom. The result was that, when the witch was lowered by rope into the hole, she was immersed in flowing water up to her neck.

She knew that, for the ritual to succeed, she would need to spend nine days there.

The first three days had been dark and agonising. She was, after all, human. No one who had grown up without her training could have endured it. Since she was a tiny girl she had been subjected to terrible long fasts and meditations, she had consumed strange mushrooms and been confined and buried like the dead, spent nights naked beneath the moon on frozen hillsides when only the power of the mind stands between life and death. So the witch queen did endure it, clawing her way out of her humanity in pain and anguish. On the fourth day the torture had divorced her mind from her physical body and the lights had come on. Dwarfs stood in the darkness, offering her gold and jewels and a ship that seemed built of something like pearl but was, she knew, made of dead men's nails. It was all hers, if only she would call to the sisters to pull her from the water. On the fifth day the walls around her flamed with green and purple lights and the spirits of the rock tried to lift her from the pool, but she remained. On the sixth day her ancestors were at her side, the ghosts who gave the caves their name, one hundred queens all less powerful than her but all part of her. She was the sum of the whole, she knew. All the dead queens were there, some naked and smeared in muds and vegetable dyes, some finer than she was, calling, jabbering, singing and weeping in the dark. They begged her to give up, spat at her, tried to rip her from the water, but she would not relent. The witch queen was on the way to her answer. On the seventh day there were voices and she knew the gods were near. On the eighth day there was just blackness, an absence of thought, nothing, as she stood on the edge of death. Then, on the ninth day, she was back in the pool, just as she had been the moment she went in.

The flowing water had stopped and she felt warm. None of the other sisters was around her, nor any of the servant boys, but the phosphorescence of the rocks seemed even brighter. In the cave it was like daylight.

A voice came echoing from tunnels that stretched away from her.

'Do you know what they did to me? Do you know what they did?' Though the witch queen rarely spoke, she could understand these words that resonated as much in her mind as in her ears.

An odour of burning seeped into her consciousness, not a pleasant smell at all, nothing like wood or straw on fire. It was closer to hair.

'See what they did to me, see what they did!'

She climbed out of the sink hole and walked down to the lower caves, and then lower still, following the burning smell and the voice.

'I am blind, I am blind!' The voice spoke again.

The witch moved on down. The caves became smaller. She had never been in them before and sensed they were not part of the real world, but some place accessible only by magic. She could taste the smoke in her throat, thick and bitter, and the voice became louder. Then in the dim light she could make out a figure. At first she thought he was shrouded in mist, but as she drew nearer she could see something between steam and smoke hissing from his thrashing body.

The man was naked and tied to a rock with bloody and glutinous ropes, while above him snakes of vivid purple, green and yellow writhed, dripping venom onto his face and into his eyes. His features were swollen, bruised and black. His tongue was mottled blue and white and the poison sizzled on his flesh. His pale skin was burned into welts and his red hair singed to patches. He was screaming and howling, tearing at his bonds, but he couldn't get them off. The witch had practised enough minor magics to recognise the fetters for what they were. They were entrails.

Suddenly, for the first time since before she had joined her sisters underground when she was small, the witch queen felt like the child she was. The presence of this tormented man terrified her. This, she knew, was a creature even the gods feared.

Next to him was a silver bowl. The witch came forward and picked it up, collecting the venom before it fell onto the god's face. She knew now who it was – Loki, lord of lies, betrayer of the gods, bane of heroes but sometimes, occasionally, friend of man.

'I send my mind forth in torment. I travel the nine worlds in agony, witch. Do you see what they did to me, the slaughter-fond gods, they who have taken numberless heads in battle, just because I took one little life? Who could love Baldur, the perfect god, the stinking lickspittle? Not so perfect he couldn't die, eh?'

The witch had hardly spoken since she had been a girl, her only language what she picked up from initiates and servants who came to the caves late – aged seven or eight at the oldest. So she said nothing now.

'You have given me something, you have granted me respite. What is it you want?'

He turned his head to hers. Even during her long training, in her conversations with the rock spirits, with the dwarfs and the elves, she had never seen such a terrible sight. His whole face resembled a blood blister ready to burst. The bowl was overflowing, her fingers swelling as the venom splashed on them. She flung the steaming liquid to the floor, but before she could return the bowl to its place, the venom of the snakes fell once more on Loki, singeing and blackening his flesh. The god screamed and vomited and the witch shoved the bowl back under the flow of poison.

'Twice you've given me respite from this torment. What is it you want? For the first respite you gave me, I will tell you that you and your sisters are not long from death. You have grown too strong in magic and knowledge and he, the lore-jealous lord Odin, will strike at you. Odin is coming for you in your realm on earth. He has taken human form and is upon you, in the flesh, mighty in his corrosive magics.'

This puzzled the witch. She was close to Odin. She had looked for the god many times, and it was he she had expected to find through the ordeal of water.

Loki went on, coughing and retching from the effects of the poison. 'For the second respite you granted me, I will tell you that you have it in your hands to avoid this fate. He does not yet sense himself. The god is not yet awake; he does not know who he is. Act quickly and strike at him. There are two boys, Fire and Frost. One to live, one to die.'

The bowl overflowed again, Gullveig cast aside the poison and replaced it above the screaming god. Now her own arms were swollen and burned, her fingers numb. Only her training helped her ignore the pain.

'No one has ever stayed to offer me three bowls of respite,' said Loki, 'and for this service I grant you your answer. At the end of the world Odin will fight with the wolf and die. You must bring the wolf to earth as Odin is on earth. Make the spirit of the wolf come to flesh in a man as the god has come to flesh. This is your rune and your guide. It will kill a god. Take it from one who knows.'

A thought sprang into the witch's mind: 'Show me my enemy.' But then the steam of the venom obscured her sight, the acrid smell choked her and she dropped the bowl. Darkness descended. For the first time in nine days she cried out, and the boys threw down a loop of rope to pull her from the stream.

The witch hacked and coughed out the water from her

lungs as she was hauled from the sink hole. The boys moved back and the sisters came to her. They didn't bring food, fire, blankets or medicine but the scrap of belt and the brooch pin. The witch looked down at her fingers. They were swollen and blackened. Despite her pain, she took up the brooch and carved a rune into the leather, then she threw it to the floor and collapsed onto her hands and knees, panting and retching.

The circle of sisters looked down at the rune and felt a muttering thought of disquiet pass among them. Half of them saw this.

It was not one of the twenty-four runes given by Odin that they had expected to see. It was a new rune, something that hadn't been given to a witch queen for eight generations.

These witches knew it was something special, though they struggled to grasp its importance.

To some the resonance of the symbol was only slightly clearer than their existing forewarning of momentous change, which had come to them in the idea of a storm. It signified a thunderbolt. They took the feeling of the rune into their minds and turned it over. Then one saw the mouth of a river between two hills. Another saw a church on a hill and knew something important was inside it: two boys, each in his way important to them. A long magic was needed, taking years to make but lasting years too. What were the boys? One was the subject of the spell, the other something else. What? They couldn't see. A helper? No. A sacrifice? No. Something different. The other boy was like the extinguished candle, like the bowl of rainwater, like a hundred other things the witches used to work their magic. A medium for something? Not quite. Then they saw it. He was an ingredient.

Others saw a different meaning in the rune, one that it would bear down the centuries until one day someone gave it a name. Wolfsangel. This was not a word the sisters would have recognised, though its sense was clear to them – wolf trap. They saw themselves flying beneath a heavy moon as a smudge of starlings to settle at midnight on the roof of King Authun's hall, to call to the sleeping king and tell him that his wife would never give him a boy and that, if he needed counsel, then the witches would receive him. They saw the further future too. A girl on a hillside. She had bright blonde hair. She was important too, they could tell but none of them could see how.

Some of the witches who huddled around the rune saw the symbol on its side.

These sisters felt a chill, as ordinary people do when they hear wolves in the hills. The rune's resonance went through their minds like a hungry howl. It said 'werewolf'.

That was the point of the magic, what the two brothers were for: so that the wolf god could take form inside a man.

The witch queen was at the point of blacking out, unable to connect to her sisters in her normal way. Exhausted, her consciousness balled in on itself like a child left alone in the dark.

She tapped at the rune and, her voice cracking, she spoke.

'Protector,' she said.

7 What Was Lost

The beauty of the summer seemed to fill him to bursting, the fjord sparkling with a light that was almost painful to look at, the meadow flowers among the green grass like flames beneath the sun. Away over the hillside a man was calling.

'Vali! Vali! Where are you? You goat!'

'He's supposed to be hunting murmuring birds with me but he can't even find where I am,' said Vali, looking at the man from a hollow in the ground. He was about thirteen, ready to go to raiding almost, but still laughing like a little child.

'You'll be beaten,' said the girl with him. She was the same age, in a full skirt. She was pale, had long blonde plaits and in her hair was a whalebone comb. Next to her was a basket of herbs that she'd been collecting for her mother.

'It'll be worth it,' he said, and kissed her. It was the first time, just a peck.

'Get off me!' said Adisla, standing up. 'Bragi! Bragi, he's over here!'

And the big man had come running.

'Prince Vali,' he said, 'you make things very difficult for me at times. Where is your spear? Where is your bow?'

'I'm sure they're around here somewhere,' said Vali. 'I left them down by the stream when I saw Adisla.'

Bragi, a battle-scarred old warrior of around thirty-five, shook his head.

'Those weapons must never leave your side, you know that. When the time comes for you to go raiding, and it is awful soon, what are you going to do? Leave your shield and sword in the ship as soon as you see a pretty girl?'

'I think that highly likely,' said Adisla.

'You, young lady, can keep your mouth shut. Look at you,

pale as a princess. A farm girl like you should show more signs of honest toil.'

'This conversation could be regarded as toil enough for a lifetime,' said Adisla.

'I've had enough of this,' said Bragi. 'I'm going to speak to your mother.'

The girl shrugged in a do-what-you-like way.

Bragi pointed his finger at her.

'I make no bones about it,' he said. 'I blame you for what has happened to him. Before he started ignoring the court and spending his time with farmers' daughters, he showed some promise at arms. Now his weapons lie neglected and he spends his days at your mother's house, whittling away his time in games and talk. The son of Authun the White Wolf a cinder biter!'

Vali laughed. He had always wondered about that particular expression. Did cinder biters really bite cinders? If so, he wasn't one. But if it meant he was happiest at the hearth, sitting beside Adisla and listening to the stories of the farmers, then it was true, he was a cinder biter.

'I haven't cast a spell on him,' said Adisla.

'No,' said Bragi, 'but you may as well have. Come on, we're going to see your ma.'

It was a stiff walk up the valley to Adisla's farm and hot work in the sun. Bragi made Vali carry both packs and all their weapons as punishment for running off while hunting, and when he saw the prince wasn't encumbered enough added a few rocks to the bags for good measure.

Adisla's mother was Disa, a noted healer who lived in a house above the growing port of Eikund in Rogaland, home of the Rygir people. In Vali's time there it had blossomed from eight to twelve houses and so was considered a large settlement. Vali had been sent to Eikund by his father Authun five years before to guarantee the treaty between the Horda and the Rygir that had ended a bloody war.

Bragi had been sent with him to see to his training in hunting and swordsmanship but it had become apparent very quickly that the old retainer and the prince were temperamentally un-suited. The only time they seemed to get on was sailing Vali's little skute around the coast, hunting for seals and fishing. Neither ever said much on these trips. Vali was too engrossed in the sun and the water, the feel of the small boat as it moved with the wind like an animal. Bragi didn't speak because he had a superstition that it drove the fish away.

Vali was sweating by the time he reached the house, which was no more than a large hut. He was glad that it was high summer, where time began to lose definition and night was just a sliver of darkness in the broad wash of the day. Even though it was late, the sun was still high and down in the river that skirted the farms people were still bathing, as they did every Saturday. As soon as he got the chance, he would join them.

He laughed as he remembered the first time he'd met Adisla. He'd been at Eikund a week when he'd heard a commotion. She had gone to the bottom of the river and held her breath until her mother had plunged in after her on a mission of rescue only for Adisla to pop up behind her, giggling wildly. Even then, five summers before, no one could swim like Adisla. Her brothers called her 'The Seal', the first of a series of ever-evolving nicknames they had for her, not all of which were particularly flattering. Seals were known as 'dogs of the sea', so she had been called Garm for a while, after the hound that lives in Hel, and then – after Disa had objected to that – Woofy. Vali sometimes called her that himself when he was with her family, but he always used her real name when they were alone.

Vali loved this place – the smoke with its promise of food issuing from the vent on the roof, chickens running around his feet and dogs coming out to bark at him in greeting, not warning.

He had a place in the long hall of King Forkbeard in the port below but, since he'd come to Rogaland, this was where

Vali had always felt most at home and he'd spent as much time at Ma Disa's as he had at the court.

'Hello, Ma!' Vali shouted, and a woman taking drying herbs from the low roof of the hut turned to see them approach.

'Been up to your usual tricks, I see,' said Disa. Unlike her daughter, she was as brown as a baked barleycorn, having given up applying the lotions that kept her pretty and pale at about the same time she had ceased caring if she was attractive to men. Disa had divorced her husband and, since he was heavy with his fists, the assembly had voted that she be allowed to keep his farm. He'd died the next year on a raid that was intended to restore his fortune, and she hadn't been sorry. Now she was queen of her house, which teemed with her own children and those of the surrounding small farms.

On the summer evenings Vali would sit outside with Adisla and her family, playing the board game King's Table, telling and listening to stories and eating the food from Disa's incomparable hearth. He even managed something of an education there. Old man Barth, Disa's only thrall, had been captured in a skirmish with the Danes. Vali was fascinated to learn his language and spent a long time talking to the slave about his homeland and customs. Barth had been a slave in Denmark and, it turned out, regarded Disa as a better mistress than the Danish jarl who had owned him before.

In the winter everyone would cram into the tiny smoky hut, eating baked roots, salted fish and laughing until they couldn't laugh any more. Her brothers, particularly Leikr and the youngest, Manni, were very dear to him and were his friends in hunting, play and conversation.

'Ma,' said Bragi, 'I need to talk to you about your daughter.'

'Oh yes?'

'I want you to forbid her from seeing the prince.'

'I'm not in the habit of forbidding my children anything,' said Disa, 'but I'll talk to her.'

'You can't call her a child – she's thirteen years old at least.

There are girls of her age a year married and all the better for it.'

'What appears to be the problem?'

Bragi threw his hands into the air and gave a sound like a hiss, as if the bubbling cauldron of complaint he kept inside himself had finally boiled over. Still, he tried to maintain a grip on his politeness, to temper his language and to use fine words to emphasise the difference between himself and the farmers around him.

'The problem is this. I am an oath-sworn retainer of King Authun the White Wolf. I am a veteran of twenty-three raids. I stood side by side with the king as we faced the Geats at the Orestrond, hopelessly outnumbered, ready for death. With that dread lord I cut my way through twenty of the enemy and made the ocean red with sword sweat to reach our boats...'

Disa was having to suppress a smile. Behind Bragi, Vali was miming the story. He'd heard it all a hundred times and in a hundred ways – boasted before the drinking hall, whispered around a campfire, shouted at him as an example to greater effort. He knew the words by heart.

'I am a warrior, and I was honoured and delighted to be offered the post of bodyguard and tutor to this boy. I find, however, that it is increasingly a burden of loathsome proportions. Loathsome proportions. I feel like Loki, tied to the rock and my eyes filled with venom. He is ungovernable, madam, and your daughter is to blame.'

'In what way?'

'I curse the day he laid eyes on her. At first it was an innocent friendship of children, but in the last year he has had no time for hunting, none for weapons training. His father had the very unusual idea of allowing him work in the smithy, in order that he should know everything about weapons from their time as rocks of the earth to their effect on an enemy shield. He is absent from the forge. He is absent from the assembly meetings where Forkbeard was to teach him statecraft.

He is absent when I call for him to test him with sword and spear. He is absent everywhere, madam, other than at your daughter's side, where he is, very annoyingly, present.'

Disa shrugged exactly the same shrug as her daughter had made earlier.

'I can't tell her who she can and can't see. Nothing can come of it – he's already spoken for, isn't he?'

'Not by me,' said Vali.

Bragi gave him a look very similar, thought Vali, to the one he must have given Geat number twenty on the way to the ships.

'He is betrothed to Forkbeard's daughter,' said Disa, as if that ended all debate.

'The fact that I don't want to marry her seeming of very little consequence in the arrangement,' said Vali.

'Not very little,' said Bragi. 'None. Madam, Ma, this dalliance between your daughter and the prince must stop.'

Disa just spread her arms out. 'What do you expect me to do? He's come here since he was a little boy.'

'He is a little boy no longer. Have you any idea how the king would feel if any issue should emerge from this?'

'He's never touched me!' said Adisla.

'Not through want of trying,' said Bragi. 'Look, madam, forbid this association. If you do not, I could have the king command it.'

Now Ma Disa frowned. 'All I owe the king is a portion of my income and my sons in the wars. I'm not a member of his sworn bodyguard to be bossed and bullied. Who me and mine choose as our friends is none of his business.'

'Everything is the king's business.'

Disa took the last of the herbs from the roof and wiped a hand on her pinafore.

'Not so. The law supports no interference from him in the affairs of free people. He won't tell me who my children can have as friends.'

'These are not children, madam. Vali is a man of thirteen

summers and is likely to become king in his own right soon.'

'Then who can tell him what to do?' said Disa.

Bragi let out a growl, collected his weapons and headed back down the hill.

The old man was a figure of fun to Vali, but the following week he would be glad Bragi was at his side when for the first time he went raiding.

8 Fury

The ship had been in the great hall for repair and they'd had
to pull it down to the water. Everything had seemed more
intense than normal to him that morning – the creak of the
cords, the rumbling of the keel on the logs, the acrid smell of
the pitch on the hull, the heaving song of the warriors.

> *Bend your backs, boys, don't be slow*
> *Over and over the ocean we go*
> *Where our swords will dance on our enemies' shields*
> *Like the glimmering fish on the sea's blue fields*
> *So bend your backs, boys, don't be slow*
> *Over and over the ocean we go.*

He pulled as hard as he could. 'Don't leave all your strength
on the shore,' an old man said to him, and Vali had to smile to
himself. He saw himself as he was, a young boy trying to show
himself manly through his effort, frightened of the greater test
of battle to come. The self-knowledge, though, did nothing to
lessen the overwhelming nature of the experience.

The morning cold was sharp, the blue of the ocean dazzling
and the cries of the sea birds made an echoing cavern of his
mind. She had been there then, and this time he hadn't needed
to steal a kiss from her.

She fixed a bright purple sprig of betony to his cloak. 'It
fights evil,' she said, 'and it will keep you safe.'

'I'll still take my shield,' he said.

'It might be wise.'

'Adisla.'

'Yes, Vali.'

'I . . .'

She put her hand to his lips.

'Don't say it,' she said.

'Why?'

'It brings bad luck. If you let the gods know you value something they will take it away from you. Come back to me. You don't need to tell me how you feel.'

King Forkbeard had not missed their intimacies but chose to pretend to. His daughter Ragna stood at his side, six years old and playing with a distaff. Vali looked at Forkbeard and then back to Adisla.

'He's hoping I'm killed,' he said.

'But in a nice way,' said Adisla. 'He'd prefer Authun had sent him a different sort of prince. Tougher, more manly, more bad-tempered, that sort of thing.'

'Let's hope I'm alive to disappoint him.'

'If you're not you'll be in Odin's halls, drunk for all time in the company of heroes.'

Vali rolled his eyes.. 'Listening to the likes of Bragi banging on about their exalted deeds of slaughter. Drunk for all time? You'd need to be to stand that.'

'That's sacrilege,' she said, laughing.

'Who cares? The gods are afraid of us – that's what my father says.'

'Everyone's afraid of your father,' she said.

'Can you imagine it? Sozzled, with him glowering at me across the mead bench for ever. I'll die a coward if it means I can be with you.'

Adisla blushed. 'Don't go soppy on me just because you're scared,' she said. 'I shall be your Valkyrie, urging you on. Win glory, my darling, win glory! Return in triumph or not at all!'

She had put on an upper-class accent and pretended to dab at her eye with a cloth, just as the noblewomen did when their husbands went raiding. Vali knew her very well and understood that her light-hearted mood was for show. He smiled at her and touched her hair. The tears came into her eyes and he could not face them down.

Now he turned to the boat, splashing out into the water, shouldering the small chest that would be his seat for the journey. He heaved it into the longship, then climbed on board and picked it up. His feet stumbled on the spars and ballast stones of the undecked vessel as he looked for his oar place, trying to look calm, trying to look as though he knew what he was doing. There was no one he knew on the boat, and no one he even recognised.

He had a place on the drakkar, a sleek and slim warship with a carved bear's head snarling from the prow, as befitted his status as one of the warrior class. Alongside were two fat-bellied knarrs, trading vessels that, empty, sat much higher in the water. They were for the plunder. On those boats were the farmers Vali knew. This made him slightly nervous. Normally, the way men recognised friend from enemy in battle was that they were put into groups from the same area who knew each other by sight. Among strangers and in the heat of a fight, he might be mistaken for a foe.

He looked around him as he moved down the ship, determined that he at least would recognise the faces of the men he was fighting with. Each man at an oar was huge, his hair and beard unkempt and shaggy, his clothes dirty, with a stale smell coming off him. Many bore so many tattoos they seemed almost blue. Vali glanced at them and tried not to use their shoulders to balance as he went forward. There were mutterings. Vali couldn't tell if they were directed at him, at each other or were just ravings. It was an under-breath babble – the words were half formed; he could only just make them out. When he did, he wished he hadn't.

'Unmanly ... frightened ... Kill the cowards. I kill, smite, shit and piss. Know they've been in a fight. Kill all. None alive. Burn the earth, burn the earth.'

He glanced at their eyes. They seemed focused on nothing, red-rimmed like people who hadn't slept for days, staring balefully ahead. Some of the men wore the pelts of animals about them or on their heads, and some were near naked, despite the dawn cold. Vali didn't care for their company at all.

At the back of the boat, being sealed into barrels or tied to the stern, were their weapons – axes and spears. He'd seen only one sword. These were not rich men. Unlike themselves, however, the weapons were well cared for, the axe heads honed to brilliant silver, the spears as sharp as bodkins.

There was a hand on his shoulder.

'Here's your oar, son.' Bragi had come up behind him, and Vali was glad to see him.

Vali put his chest down and sat on it. Bragi climbed in across from him, put down his chest too, sat on it sideways and lightly punched the prince's arm.

'Now you might wish you'd paid attention to what I had to say about sword, shield and spear.'

Vali, his flippancy driven off by nerves, just smiled back.

Bragi put his hand on Vali's shoulder. 'Don't worry, prince, you'll be fine. Though if you'd listened to me more, you'd be finer. I got you a place on the best boat.'

Vali, leaned away, resenting the intimacy.

'None of my kinsmen are here.'

'No, but you are among the best warriors in twenty kingdoms,' said Bragi.

'These men?'

'Yes.'

'Berserks?'

'Yes, from the northern cult of Odin the Frenzied, working solely for transport.'

'And the plunder they can take,' said Vali.

'Only up to a point. They'll take plunder for sure, but it's not their main aim,' said Bragi. 'It might be better if it was.'

'What do they fight for?'

'To fight. Look at them. Each man here has been on many

raids but are they rich? No. Do they have many slaves? No. They aren't concerned by such things.'

'They want no plunder?'

'Yes, a little, but this is why they're useful to Forkbeard. Their reward is the scrap itself. He gets some good fighters and they don't bother too much about the booty.'

'They sound insane,' said Vali.

'Maybe they are, but you can learn from them nevertheless. You'll see how a man conducts himself in war.'

Vali said nothing. To him it was as important how a man conducted himself in peace. To sit muttering curses while bleary-eyed through who knew what concoctions of mushrooms and herbs was the act of an idiot, not a hero. They were three days from the fight, according to Bragi. The berserks were simmering before they had set off. What would they be like in sight of the enemy spears? Still, he was interested to see if they lived up to their reputation as invulnerable and fearless. Could it really be true that weapons didn't injure them? Looking around the ship, he was glad he was fighting with them rather than against them.

The wind was up, which was why they were sailing. The longship's sail billowed and snapped as it was unfurled, as if impatient to get going. Its design had been chosen in his honour − black with a snarling wolf's head picked out in white. Vali looked up at his father's symbol − the symbol, of everything he was supposed to become, in fact everything he was supposed already to be. It made him shiver to think of the weight of responsibility he carried.

His musings were interrupted by a boot in the back.

'Move your arse. I need to stretch my legs.'

He turned around to see a huge man in a thick tunic, a white bear skin over his arm. A deep groove ran from the top of his head, over his eye socket and down into his cheek. Clearly he had been on the wrong end of an axe at some time in his life. Every inch of his body seemed covered in thickly drawn tattoos: scenes of destruction and battle, the coiling world serpent around his right arm, the wolf fighting Odin on his left, the three interlocking triangles that made up that god's symbol below his left eye, and many other illustrations of animal figures, gallows and weapons all over his face and upper body.

Vali's knife and sword were at the bottom of his travelling chest and he knew the berserk would attack him if he saw him go to take them out. He had to act, though. This was a slight to his honour in front of everyone and he couldn't let it go unpunished, even if he was sure he'd receive more in return than he was capable of handing out.

He had only one course of action, one possible response. He swung a fist at the man's head. The man enveloped the blow under his arm and came up to join his hands at Vali's throat. The boy's arm was locked and he was forced down, feet skidding for purchase on the ballast stones but finding none. The berserk snarled into Vali's face and tightened his grip on his windpipe. Confrontation has a way of peeling back illusions and self-deceptions. Vali was no longer a man on his first raid, a prince of the sword-Horda, son of Authun the Pitiless, who could trace his ancestry back to Odin himself, and the hope of a nation. He was a frightened boy, caught by a much bigger and stronger man.

All he could focus on was the man's face, which seemed contorted with hate. He was choking Vali and the boy's whole consciousness seemed to condense into trying to remove the hands from his neck, but he couldn't budge them. His vision seemed to contract to a tunnel, his head seemed ready to burst. Then a broad-bladed knife came into Vali's line of sight, but it was at such an angle that the berserk could not have been holding it. Something else came into view – a large pole with three iron rings fixed loosely about it by pegs. Both were interposed between him and the berserk.

'Save it for the enemy, Bodvar Bjarki,' said a voice.

The berserk released his grip and Vali lay back gasping, his vision blurred. When he recovered his sight he saw Bragi staring down the scarred man, the old warrior's knife pointing at the berserk's throat. There was the rattle of metal on metal and a huge berserk in a brown bear pelt shoved that odd pole between the men. Bodvar Bjarki and Bragi said nothing, as hard men often don't in such circumstances. They just continued looking into each other's eyes. The brown bear berserk gently pushed Bjarki back down into his seat with the pole. The big man put his hands onto his oar. Bragi gave a short, amused snort and slid his knife back into its sheath. Then he sat back at his oar. Vali stood and climbed in across from him.

Bragi turned to Vali, making no effort to keep his voice down so the berserk wouldn't hear.

'I told you the value of keeping your weapons close. If you'd had your knife you could have gutted him.'

Vali nodded. Embarrassment mingled with relief, but still, he thought, hadn't the situation resolved itself without anyone being gutted – for the moment anyway? If he'd had his knife then the result might have been one dead berserk and a blood feud. Or, worse, the berserk might have got the knife off him. Vali was aware that his strength in no way compared to that of the giant behind him. He glanced at the shore. Adisla was looking anxiously towards him. He inclined his head towards the big berserk and shrugged. Adisla mouthed, 'Be careful,' and he nodded in acknowledgement.

After that, the men said nothing at all, just began to row out to sea, more for show than for effect, as the lines on the great sail were tightened and it pulled them out of the bay at an exhilarating pace. Vali raised his hand in goodbye to the people on the shore, saw the figures becoming smaller and smaller and lost himself in the rhythm of the oars.

The ship, which the skalds called the stallion of the waves, really did feel like that, a living force straining to get forward. For a moment Vali almost forgot the brooding presence at his back. Then, against himself, he gave half a glance behind him. The disfigured man was staring directly at him. Or was he being silly? There wasn't really anywhere else for him to look.

Bragi saw Vali's glance and turned to wink at the boy.

'Don't show me the man with the scars; show me the man who put them there,' he said. Vali smiled. Bragi was a good man, he thought, who had his interests at heart. He was honest, big-hearted, straightforward and courageous. Vali just wished he found him less boring.

The journey was to take three days – three days of dull stories, homely advice and excruciating jokes from the old boy. In rescuing him from the berserk, Bragi had achieved a small victory. Vali should have had a knife on him, granted. But it was that, a small victory. It didn't imply, as Bragi seemed to with his told-you-so smile, that *everything* the old man said and believed was correct, and that he now had the right to patronise him for the foreseeable future.

Vali thought of a trader he'd met two years before, Veles Libor from Reric in the east, who was travelling up to see the Whale People. Now *he* would have made a better mentor, had he stayed. He knew so much, had travelled the world in peace not slaughter and survived off his wits. With him, Vali felt inspired and eager to learn. He had spread out his scrolls, and Vali had been amazed to see the beautiful colourful pictures and intriguing squiggly writing. He had longed to find out how to read it, how to put down his thoughts in long waves of ink that rose, fell and broke like the surf. Bragi, though, had nothing to teach him that he wanted to learn.

The journey had been scouted the summer before. They skirted the coast north up nearly as far as the Whale People and then across west to the Islands at the World's Edge – which were no longer at the world's edge but simply a staging post to the richer lands to the west. From there they sailed south and picked up the coast of the West Men's land. Vali slept on the bottom of the boat, wedged in among the other men, listening to the mutterings and cursings of the berserks, looking up at the stars and thinking of Adisla.

The berserks never bothered to speak to him, and he was glad of that, as it allowed him to remain in his own thoughts. His people saw no beauty in the sea. He thought of the names they gave it: roarer, empty place, devourer, rager. To them it was an obstacle, a place of production and a killer. They turned the backs of their houses to the water, not wishing to look at it when they opened their doors. But Vali was enchanted by it, the sparkling greens and blues, the movement of the clouds on the horizon, the delight when a wave broke over the side of the ship and a mackerel landed in his lap.

Then: 'The island! This is where it happens, boys!'

Vali glanced over his shoulder but could see nothing, no land, no enemy. Bragi put a hand on his arm. 'Stick to the oar, lord; don't worry about what's waiting for us when we get off the boat.'

Vali nodded, aware that soon he would be killing his first enemy, or being killed himself. He wished he'd unpacked his sword already. He felt the need to piss and stood to do so. He wasn't the only one. It was almost a comical sight, ten men weeing over the side in one go, a like number on both accompanying knarrs, as if it was some sort of ritual.

Vali scanned for land. All he could see was open sea. No, there was something, a flat dark patch in the hazy distance. 'This is it,' he told himself. 'This is it.'

The men pulled in their oars and laid them flat in the bottom of the longship. The berserks' leader, the man with the strange staff, piled up ballast stones. Then he took out some twigs and kindling, and got a fire going on top of them. When it was established, he hung a cooking pot above it from a tripod and added water from a skin. Then he began throwing in things from a pouch.

Vali went to the back of the ship and took his weapon from a barrel, along with his helmet. He was intensely nervous and every movement felt unnatural, scrutinised by the men around him and found wanting. Other men were breaking open barrels and strapping on their war gear. There was no conversation. None of the berserks spoke to each other but just mumbled into their beards, cursing and issuing threats to non-existent opponents.

The contents of the fire pot were poured into a large bowl, which was passed around, drained dry and refreshed. It came to Vali and he looked inside to see a gritty soup. In it floated shrivelled, spotty mushrooms that looked to him like human ears. He passed the bowl on to the berserk next to him without drinking and watched as the man gulped at the brew.

When each of the berserks had taken the soup, they took up their oars again.

The war band leader made his way to the front of the ship, carrying the staff with the iron rings. He steadied himself by the prow as his men rowed and began to bang the staff on the boards of the ship, thumping out a clanging beat. The berserks responded to the rhythm by stamping their feet as they worked the oars.

'Odin!' shouted the leader.

As one, the berserks replied, 'That means fury!'

'Odin!'

'That means war!'

'All Father!' screamed the leader.

'Mighty in battle!' came the reply.

'All Father!'

'Make red our swords!'

'Odin!'

'That means frenzy!'

'Odin!'

'That means death!'

The berserks howled and smashed their heads into their oars, spat and swore as they powered the boat towards the shore. The war band leader beat the rail of the ship with his rattle, screaming and shrieking out his words.

'Odin's men!' he shouted.

'We are men of Odin!' the berserks screamed back at him.

'Men of Odin!'

'We are Odin's men!'

The chanting seemed to go on for ever, and the berserks seemed to have an endless supply of words spilling out in chants as fast as a fighter's heartbeat. They went wild, punching at the oars as they rowed, slapping themselves and screaming the words into each other's faces. The beat became faster.

'Odin!' shouted the leader, hammering his rattle into the rail.

'Man maddener, all hater, war screamer!'

'Odin!'

'Wolf fighter, spear shaker, corpse maker!'

'Odin!'

'Great wrecker, down thrower, foe slayer!'

'Odin!'

'Berserker, berserker, berserker!'

Now some of the men stood, punching their chests and arms. The ship lurched as one man in his frenzy forgot his oar, and the blade caught in the water.

'Odin!'

'Berserker, berserker, berserker!'

'So they call me!' shouted the man with the rattle.

'Odin!' howled the oarsmen.

'So they call me!'

'Odin!'

In his fear and excitement the words came to Vali as impressions. They seemed more than names. It was as if the wild chanting gave them a life, as if he could see the images they conjured – Odin fighting the Fenris Wolf, a spear flying through a clear blue sky, gallows and slaughter, fire and blood. The beat of the oars never slackened, though Vali was sure the men could not sustain the pace for much longer. Instead they got faster, hardly missing a stroke, despite many of them swigging from drinking horns which were regularly refilled from a huge jug carried by a boy. Vali wondered that anyone could even lift such a pitcher, never mind pour it without spilling it on a longship as it crashed through the surf.

As the jug passed, Bragi shouted across to him, though panting with exertion, 'I'd have a drink if I were you. Ale waters the courage inside you and makes it grow!'

Vali did as Bragi suggested, taking his horn off his belt to have it filled and swigging down a couple of mouthfuls. He could drink no more, beginning to feel sick with the anticipation of what was to come rather than the movement of the ship. The berserks were baying now, screaming obscenities and promises to their god.

He glanced over his shoulder again and got the impression of the blue giving way to green behind him. Then white joined the blue and green. A beach. There was a judder and Vali was thrown back off his chest to sprawl onto the ballast.

Propelled by the frenzied rowing, the boat grounded on the beach far harder than it needed to. Vali thought they'd been lucky not to tear out the hull. He had to roll aside as a stampede swept over him, the berserks howling in their mania to get off the boat. Not one bore a shield, none even armour or a helmet, just spears, axes and, in the case of the leader, a sword in one hand and the huge rattle in the other.

Vali turned to see who they were charging at but saw nothing, just a pleasant broad beach of light sand, the sunny day, birds over the meadows and deep green grass. There was no enemy there at all.

The berserks were off and running across the island, the more conventional warriors disembarking from the other two boats behind them.

'Come on,' said Bragi. 'We've attacked from the rear of the island for surprise. You go ahead of me; I'm too old to run all the way. Remember, pretty women, fit men, they're the slaves you're looking for. The rest, kill 'em for the fear it'll bring next time.'

Vali stepped from the boat and had the strange sensation of setting foot on foreign soil for the first time in his life. He was inclined to stop and look around him, to see how the place differed from his home, but he knew he couldn't.

He pressed on in the throng of helmeted warriors from the knarrs, all of them carrying shields, chasing the fast-moving unarmoured berserks inland. The island was flat and not too long, but he could see no buildings on it. They moved quickly and, as they crested a small ridge, found the first bodies, four old men dead in a furrowed field. He could tell they were old by their white hair; their features gave no clue to their age. The men had been mutilated, their heads cut and cut again, stamped on and kicked.

Vali took them for slaves, as they were dressed very plainly and the two heads that were still anything like intact were shaved completely at the front, the hair left long behind, which he thought must be the sign of the lowest rank, a mark of their subjugation. There were farm implements lying discarded around them, rakes and hoes, but more than could be used by just four. Vali wondered why they hadn't simply sat down and been taken prisoner. Why should a slave fight for his owner? Then he realised what had happened. He thought of the chanting of the men on the boat and the consumption of those mushrooms, the frenzy of the dash for the shore. There would be no surrendering to the berserks. There were three paths of action available to the people on the island, run, fight or die. The other slaves had fled, leaving only these old ones behind. Vali shook his head. If the berserks were on a killing rampage it greatly reduced the chances of them getting anything valuable from the raid. A slave was worth as much as gold in some ways.

He ran on, up a long incline. There was some sort of sound. At first he took it for the crying of gulls, but then, as he got nearer, it became easier to identify. Human screaming. It was high-pitched and desperate, counterpointed with low roars of aggression. Smoke was already in the air.

There, towards the beach below him, was a settlement of around fifteen houses. He was struck that they were the wrong shape. There were a couple of big halls like a king might own but the huts that surrounded them were all tiny and circular.

That was wrong, he thought – huts should be square, perhaps with bowed sides but not round. He had never seen anything like them. He found them very exotic and exciting, and he very much wanted to go inside one to see what it was like.

Then there were the people. Vali had rarely seen so many in one place, all men too, panicking under the axes of the berserks. Only a few were making an effort at resistance; most were running for their lives.

He stood watching the attack for some time, watching the huts burn, watching the berserks hack down the men. All the enemy, thought Vali, appeared to be slaves, all with that strange shaved head at the front, the hair long at the rear. Vali couldn't help noticing that none of the berserks had actually bothered to take any plunder. With that in mind, he looked down the hill towards the biggest building, the one with the cross on the roof, which he took for a temple. If anything was to be retrieved, he thought, he had better do it before the whole settlement was reduced to ashes.

Bragi had made the top of the hill and put his hand to Vali's shoulder.

'Draw your weapon, prince,' he said.

'I hardly think that's going to be necessary,' said Vali. 'There's no resistance at all.'

'Best to have something in your hand in case our men of Odin run out of West Men to spear,' he said. 'Nothing like the sight of a sword to remind them whose side they're on.'

Vali shook his head – he could hardly believe what he was hearing. Still, he unsheathed his sword. It was a good one, a single-edged seax sent to him by his father, more a very large knife than a true sword but strong, short and straight with a whalebone pommel. He felt embarrassed by it and wished he had a plainer weapon. Still, he left his shield at the top of the hill. He didn't see any point carrying it because, even from this distant vantage point, he knew he was at more risk fighting with staves with Adisla's brothers than he was here.

It was, he thought, instructive what panic could do. Some of the West Men had managed to make off down the beach, but others, their wits frightened away by the shock of the raid, had just run into the sea and were attempting to swim for it. Vali didn't fancy their chances. He had a good sailor's eye, and the water between the island and the mainland looked a prime spot for currents.

He came down to the big building. It was even taller than he had thought from far away, with long thin windows cut into overlapping logs. On the ground outside lay the remains of a stone carving that the berserks had smashed. It was finely wrought cross within a wheel, about two handspans across. It was beautiful, thought Vali, and he almost felt like taking it home with him.

The berserks were hammering at the door of the temple, unable to get in, screaming and jabbering. From a burning hut, one brought a brand, cursing and muttering as he did.

'Tell him to forget that,' said Vali to Bragi.

Bragi gave a little start. He was unused to Vali expressing a view on anything. The boy's manner, thought the bodyguard, was not unlike his father's.

'Put that down!' said Bragi. The berserk took no notice and threw the torch up onto the thatch. Luckily, it was high and steep, and the brand tumbled off.

Bragi looked at Vali and shrugged. Some of the farmers from Eikund came up. They had caught one of the shaven-headed men, and had stripped him naked, booting him towards the temple.

'Tell them to open it!' said one.

The man was old and terrified. He just sank to his knees, put his hands together and jabbered.

'Open it, you girl, or I'll cut your throat.'

The voice was Hrolleifr's, a farmer from up on the hill behind Disa. Vali had thought of him as a gentle man. He often helped Disa take things to market and was skilled at carving. Here he was, though, with the same knife that produced tiny ships, little men, even Vali's own King's Table pieces, thrust at the side of a man's neck.

'He can't open it; they'll have secured it from the inside,' said Vali.

Hrolleifr shrugged and cut the man's throat. A thick spray of blood pulsed into the air, soaking the farmer, and the man fell forward, kicking and squealing on the floor.

Hrolleifr turned to the other raiders and shouted, 'See me in my battle sweat. See how I spread the slaughter dew among the warriors of the enemy.'

Everyone else laughed and clapped. Vali couldn't believe that he was boasting about what he had done. The man had been old. It was harder, much harder, to stick a pig. Was this what they amounted to, all those tales of glory? Killing old men who were begging for their lives. Vali wanted this to end, and quickly, the quicker to return to the boats. He needed to get into the temple as fast as possible. The prospect of plunder might prevent further pointless murder.

The screams were becoming more distant. Everyone on the island who could run had run, and most of the berserks were pursuing them. A brief silence descended over the houses. Vali breathed in. The odour of smoke against the chill of the summer morning was wonderful to him.

The roof was too high to reach, the doors were impregnable. If they had long enough, it would be possible to dig under the walls. There was a chance though, that he could get in at a window. It was too narrow for any of the bigger men, but he was so much smaller.

'Bragi,' he said, gesturing with his eyes to the window, 'make sure no idiot burns it while I'm inside.' He took off his sword belt and stripped off all three tunics he was wearing as armour.

Bragi helped him onto his shoulders. Vali could reach the narrow slit of the window but couldn't gain any proper purchase on it.

'Stand on my head,' said Bragi, straightening his helmet.

Vali did so, and managed to get a second hand into the gap and lever himself up.

He forced one shoulder in, wriggled and pushed, and finally he was through, dropping onto a table directly beneath him.

There were four windows in the building and their light made it easy to see. At first his impression was just colour – silvers and golds, a large embroidery on the wall to his right, the door with its bar to the left. His eyes adjusted and he saw the men. There were four of them, with shaven heads, two with large candlesticks, one with a weighty silver cross. Only one, a man of his age, thirteen or so, was unarmed. It was then that Vali realised – he had forgotten his weapon.

The men didn't charge him, which he thought stupid, because he would open the door if not knocked down. They just stood shouting at him. He recognised some familiar words in their odd language.

'God, redeemer, help.' The man with the cross thrust it forward, shook it at him, and said something Vali didn't understand at all.

'*Helsceada, Helsceada, Helsceada*. Satan!'

Then the man said something else he could make out, although the accent was heavy and strange. 'Flee me!'

Were they casting a spell on him? Vali didn't feel like he was being enchanted. There was a renewed clamour at the door and some more snatches of sentences came through.

'Burn, Odin! Blood swan! Inciter!'

Vali stood up from his crouch. He didn't get off the table because he wanted to appear tall to emphasise his royal status. There were four men, all of working age, and a reasonable quantity of silver. That wasn't a bad haul. First, though, he had to subdue them unarmed. All he had was words, and he knew only half of those would be understood.

'I think it's you who should have fled,' said Vali. 'There are wolves and bears outside this door. Shall I feed you to them?'

He dropped off the table, went to the door and made to open it.

The men jabbered but didn't rush him. There was a clang. His seax had been thrown through the window.

Vali looked at the weapon. He made a gesture of refusal towards it.

'No need for that,' he said, 'if you're sensible. Better a slave than a dead man, I think.'

One of the men spoke. Vali understood some of the words.

'Inroad from the sea. The hand of —' and there was that word again '— Satan in this.'

'Just a good ship and the blessing of the gods,' said Vali.

'One god,' said the man. 'Christ Jesus.' He pointed to the embroidery.

Vali looked at it. It was a strange but beautiful representation of Odin suspended from a tree, a spear piercing his side. It was a depiction, he felt, of the god's quest for wisdom at the well of Mimir, where he had given up his eye for knowledge. But if these men were Odin's, where was their fury and their fight? He couldn't imagine walking into a place holy to the berserks and coming away alive.

'He is on our side, not yours,' said Vali. 'Lay down your weapons and submit. I offer you my protection. On oath.'

The one word seemed to get through. 'Protection.'

The men looked at each other. Then they put down the heavy silver and sank to their knees, pressing their hands together and muttering. The banging at the door became even louder. He walked up to the men in front of him.

One of them held a strange oblong object, like a slab of leather. Vali went to take it from him but the man held on. Vali wondered what it was that he should cling to it more dearly than silver. He went to the table, where there was another of these slabs. He picked it up and looked at it. It was paler on three sides than it was on the fourth. The pale edges seemed to be pressed together in layers. He went to put it back down but, as he did so, it fell open. Inside were lots of papers, like he'd seen Veles Libor carrying. The squiggly writing was all over them, along with some beautiful pictures. Then Vali saw it – these slaves could teach him to write. They valued these papers so they must be able to read them.

'Lord!'

There was a face at the window.

'Bragi!'

'Yes, lord. '

'How did you get up there?'

'A ladder, lord.'

Vali laughed. 'You could've saved your head, if we'd thought to look. I'm going to open the doors. Make sure no one, and I mean no one, harms the slaves I've taken. They're my property. Can you make those Odin-blind idiots understand?'

'I can try, lord.'

'Three knocks when you're ready.'

Vali knew the challenge he would face once the doors were open and so, making gestures of calm, he picked up his seax and took the old man with the slab of leather by the arm. He was the least useful as a slave and the most at risk.

After a short time he heard the three knocks and removed the bar.

Light flooded the church as the doors opened. Two berserks rushed past him carrying spears and burning brands.

'No!' said Vali, but it was too late. Two of the slaves were stabbed and fell; one other – the young man of Vali's age – ran for it, dragging the old man with him.

'No killing!' shouted Vali. Luckily the men fell into the hands of Bragi and the farmers and were merely smashed to the floor with pommel blows.

'Silver!' shouted Vali, and that was enough: the rest of the men poured into the church.

Vali didn't know what to do to save his captives. Acting on instinct, he pushed them both up the hill at sword point, back towards the longship. It occurred to him to let them go but he was fascinated to learn how to write and saw it as a key to developing and maintaining his kingdom, when he came to rule it. Also Vali had met very few foreigners before and was interested to talk to them. These men, he thought, might have something interesting to teach him.

As they got back to the top of the hill, he picked up his shield and looked down. Now the church and the little huts were all on fire. Livestock was being rounded up and driven towards them. The men with Vali began to weep. Vali looked at them properly for the first time. They were clearly slaves, he thought, as their rough clothes and shaven heads denoted. Even slaves develop a bond with a place though. Again he noticed how enchanting the island looked: the sparkle of the sun on the ocean, the thick line of smoke stretching out over the sea to the mainland beyond like an enchanted causeway, the fires themselves. In the face of such beauty, it was difficult to remember that it was a scene of destruction.

He pressed on to the ships and, when he got to them, was the first back apart from five or six guards.

'Good plunder?' asked one as he arrived.

Vali just gestured to the slaves with his seax.

The guard nodded. 'One of them's a bit old, but the other one'll be worth a bit at Kaupangen.'

He was talking about the big southern market. Vali had heard of it but never visited it. These captives weren't going there; he had plans for them.

'They're mine,' he said.

The guard shrugged. 'Depending on the split,' he said.

'They're mine,' said Vali. 'I'm the one who made the effort to save them, the others are more interested in easy kills than taking prisoners.' The guard shrugged again and sat down on the shore.

'See what the berserks say,' he said.

It was nightfall before everyone returned. Vali sat by the fire and watched as herds of sheep and cows were driven to the ships. There were no slaves. Vali could hardly believe how wasteful the raid had been. All the loot from the church was piled up, along with flagons of wine that didn't remain untouched for long. Some men even came with bales of hay they had stolen, more than would be needed to feed the animals on the short journey back. Vali was thankful that there were pebbles on the beach at home, otherwise he felt sure they'd be returning with a full haul of those too.

The berserks had taken no prisoners, though they had a quantity of coin and some silver plates, along with about ten slaughtered geese.

A change came over these men with the end of the day. They were no longer the baying animals he had seen get off the boat. Instead, they seemed listless, weak even, hardly talking, just crouching by the fires and staring into the flames through red and angry eyes.

'Lord.'

'Yes?'

It was Bragi's hand on his shoulder.

'Did you not hear me? We are to put out to sea. This island is linked to the mainland by a causeway that is open at low tide. We should leave. The burning buildings may have drawn attention to us and we risk counter-attack if we stay here.'

'Why burn them then?' said Vali.

'What?'

'If the fires give away our position then why light them? Surely it would've been better to plunder the place in secrecy.'

'The berserks will have their fires,' said Bragi.

The animals were loaded onto the ships, thrown in, roped in, hauled in, until the vessels were perilously low in the water. Some of the bigger creatures couldn't be fitted in and were slaughtered at the beach and tied behind the ships. They would be dragged back, as long as the ropes didn't break.

Vali waited with his slaves to take his place in the drakkar.

The helmsman was counting.

'No room for those two,' he said.

Vali looked at him. 'You'll make room. I want them for my slaves.'

'Lord, it would mean offloading valuable animals. The boy is sickly and the man's old and not much good for work.'

Vali could, he supposed, just let them go. The raiders would be long gone before they could help any pursuers. Still, he reminded himself of who he was. He'd spent so long at Adisla's hearth among farm children that he sometimes forgot.

'Princes need different work to common men.'

'Lord, I—'

There was a scream and the old man fell to the ground.

In the firelight Vali saw the gleam of a knife and the red eyes of Bodvar Bjarki, the scarred berserk who had attacked him. Then there was a sudden movement and the boy cried out and fell too.

'Debate over, prince,' said the berserk. He could hardly stand. He seemed torpid and sluggish but had still stabbed both men in an instant.

For the first time in Vali's life he felt genuinely angry, violent even, and as that emotion touched him he felt a chill go through him. This wasn't the sort of rage that explodes in fury but an insidious, crawling thing, as present and real as the smell of smoke across a summer meadow. Vali was frightened by the intensity of the feeling. He would, he thought, have his revenge. It came to him not as an intention but as a fact, as real and unavoidable as the engulfing night, the endless stars and the cold dark sea. It was the first time in his life he could remember feeling hatred, and the sensation was almost intoxicating.

The raiders were around him, their faces expectant. Vali, though, would not give them what they were asking for – a demand for compensation, a challenge to a duel. Instead he smiled at the berserk and said, 'I will not forget you.'

Bodvar Bjarki just grunted, huddled into his cloak and made his way onto the ship.

Vali bent to the old man. Dead. Then he went to the boy. He was breathing but Vali could see he was dreadfully pale and close to death. He held him in his arms to give him comfort. The boy looked up. Vali had expected to see blame or hatred. Instead, he saw something else. Understanding, sympathy, pity even. He found it chilling.

The boy looked at Vali and said a word he recognised: 'God.'

Well, he doesn't seem to have done you much good, does he? thought Vali, but he said nothing. In a few moments the boy had stopped breathing.

Vali climbed aboard a knarr. He had no intention of spending the journey home with the berserks.

He took an oar without a word, listening to the men around him swapping stories of the raid. Farmer Hrolleifr told how he had faced the enemy's leader and cut him to the floor. He omitted to say that the man was naked, kneeling and begging for his life at the time. Others told tales of taking on two or three enemies at once, leaving out inconvenient facts such as that their opponents had been unarmed. The most remarkable thing about the stories of the returning warriors was that they seemed to believe them themselves.

He looked over to the drakkar as the ships pulled away from the beach. The one West Man the berserks had saved had been hanged, sacrificed to Odin in thanks for their safe return. As Vali watched the man dangling from the mast, his legs kicking as if in a useless attempt to run away, he made up his mind that he would never seek that god's help. His followers, he thought, dishonoured him.

'I hate you, Odin,' he said, 'and I will oppose you in all your works.'

For some reason that made him feel better and he bent his back to the oar, losing himself in the rhythm of the rowing, thought banished by effort.

9 Varieties of Darkness

Some grow in light and others in darkness. Feileg – the boy the witches had taken – was not raised on the sunlit coast but on the mountaintops with the wild men and the wolves.

The witch queen sensed that the boy she had taken needed to be prepared in a different sort of magic to the one she practised. Her magic was known by the ordinary people as Seid. It was a wholly female art – a magic of the mind. Gullveig had blurred the division between past and future, she had travelled entranced as the shadow of a hare or a wolf to enter the nightmare of a dozing king, but the arts of physical magic were unknown to her. Her trances and meditations would leave her weak for days afterwards, near to death even, and the toll on her was enormous. Her limbs were wasted and her body emaciated. She seemed no more than a rune herself, an arrangement of lines rather than a human figure. As the years went by, the change that other girls knew did not come to her. It would never come. The witch queen accepted the cost of her knowledge was that she would remain in a child's body her whole life – small, weak and undeveloped. The werewolf could not follow that path. Odin, she knew, would come as a warrior, dispensing death at the end of his spear. Her protector couldn't be weak, so Gullveig could only do part of what was needed.

To create her werewolf, his body would need to be strengthened and conditioned by the berserks, the ulfhednar who lived as wolves and fought as wolves, gaining unnatural strength and ferocity from their training and their magic. The witch spoke to a berserker chieftain in a dream and the man took the baby, along with a payment of medicines, from a boy servant at the bottom of the Troll Wall.

Until Feileg was seven he lived on the lower slopes of the mountains with a small berserker clan, who cared for him, fed him, taught him trance dances and beat him. On his seventh birthday the berserk chieftain who had taken him from the Wall woke him before dawn and led him back up into the mountains. It was early winter and the going was hard. The berserk took him over the snow fields, waiting for him when he fell, driving him on when he tired, shouting when he tried to use his little spear as a staff, warning him not to abuse something on which his life could depend.

Most of the way the snow was shallow and they didn't need their snowshoes, but as they got higher it deepened and they had to stop to tie them on. They climbed up through stark lines of spruce and pine that towered out of the fields of white like an army of giants until the trees began to lose their fight with the altitude and grow smaller and thinner, eventually shrinking to the size of shrubs.

In a small valley next to a waterfall turning to ice the berserk stopped.

'I am to leave you here,' he said. The berserk was a rough man but even he gave a sad smile. 'Take care, little Feileg. We will miss you. You have enough to eat to last you until tomorrow. You know how to climb a tree with your rope, and remember the wolves will not want to risk injury. If they come, attack them and make them look for something weaker.'

The child said nothing, but as the berserk turned down the slope, he followed him.

'You are to stay here,' said the man. 'Your time with us is over.'

He turned to go once more, but the child followed him again. The berserk, though rough and given to beating him, was the only father he'd known, his wife his only mother. He wanted to go back to the cooking pot and his brothers and sisters, to help his father at his forge and lie next to his mother in the cold nights, warm and protected.

'You stay,' said the berserk. He didn't have to say what

would come next. He'd already asked once more than he normally would. There would be no third request, just the lash of his belt.

Feileg felt frightened and very alone. He clutched his spear and said, 'One day I will come back and kill you.'

The berserk smiled. 'It truly is a shame to lose you, Feileg. I believe you will. When you are a man you'll be a great warrior, and I'll be old, should I live so long. It will be an honour to die by your hand. Don't be frightened. Your destiny is already woven and it doesn't end today.'

He turned again down the slope and in moments he was gone.

Feileg looked about him through the slit in the cloth he had tied around his face to shield his eyes from the glare. It had begun to snow lightly. Above him was a ridge, below him the valley. He saw the footprints that had brought them there but he had hunted for long enough to know that the snow would have already obscured the rest of the way home.

He didn't know what to do, so he just stood wondering why he been brought to such a desolate place and what he had done to offend the people he considered his family. Presently his feet began to feel cold and he decided it would be good to find shelter. The days were short and already the sun was low in the sky.

Feileg had never been treated as a child and so had never thought as a child. He had hunted almost from when he could walk and had been expected to sharpen weapons, cook food, make fires and clean himself from the moment he had been able to understand what to do. Raised to self-reliance, he came up with a plan. He would do what his father did when caught by a blizzard – dig a pit beneath a tree, build a platform of branches within the pit and sleep there. The next day he would head down and see if he could find someone who would take him, maybe even sneak home and tell his mother he was sorry and beg to be taken back.

He went back down the slope and found a suitable tree

near a small cliff that he thought would provide wind protection. He had been scraping away with a rock for about half an hour when he heard the howling. A single wolf, somewhere above the trees, towards the sinking sun, he thought, but it was difficult to tell in the mountains. He checked his spear was near and carried on digging. An answering call came from down the valley. He carried on digging. A third call, this time closer. He looked up to see a large white wolf, much bigger than he was, sitting on the ridge above him. The animal was just visible against a large rock. A heartbeat later it had moved, vanishing into the snow. Feileg kept digging. Life with the berserks had taught him never to think too much on consequences. He needed a shelter; it was getting late; he had to dig. If the wolves came for him, he would die. If he was outside without a shelter, he would die. Climb the tree and die, so dig and hope the wolves do not come.

But they did come, soundlessly assembling on the ridge. The howls had been to locate each other. There was now no need for any more noise, no need to alert rival packs. As the weak sun dipped behind the ridge and the dusk turned the sky to a metalled purple, eight wolves watched the digging boy. As soon as the first one moved, Feileg grabbed his spear and gave a shout.

The largest wolf was darker than the first he had seen. It had dirty red and grey fur, was as tall as the child at the shoulder and looked much heavier. It halted halfway down the slope at Feileg's cry. The berserk had been right. Wolves in the wild are scavengers first, killers second and fighters only as a last resort. In the snowy woods getting injured means limited mobility, which means starvation and death. Like all animals, humans included, wolves prefer their prey weak, preferably defenceless.

Feileg fixed the animal with a stare and forwarded his spear. The light was dropping and flattening the perspective. His vision swam and he fought to maintain concentration on what was in front of him. From the corner of his eye he saw a wolf

93

insinuating its way around to his right. A glance to his left confirmed the same was happening on the other side. Feileg wasn't scared.

'I am deserted and ready to die!' he shouted. 'Which one of you, my lords of the forest, wants to do the same? When I am in Odin's halls and you are at his feet, how I shall kick you!'

One of the wolves was behind him now, he could sense, and more were filing left and right. Still he fixed the dirty red-grey wolf with his spear. That was the biggest and would die, which would make a good tale at the feast table in the all-father's halls.

The big wolf ambled towards him through the floating light. For the first time Feileg felt fear rise in him. There was something strange about its movements, something wrong. The other wolves had seemed to glide on the snow. This one, he could see, was very powerful but more uncomfortable in its gait. Was it injured? The dusk was falling, vision difficult. What was wrong with it? It was huge. What he had thought was merely a large animal he could now see was of truly terrifying proportions. It was as big as a man, bigger. His father was the biggest man he had seen but this creature was taller by a head.

Ten paces away, the wolf stopped and looked at the boy through the greying dusk. Feileg, who had been raised to regard his life as a trifle, to believe that the noblest destiny lay in death in battle, who coveted that fate like others might covet gold or a fine house, began to tremble. This wasn't an ordinary wolf, he was sure, but a creature of myth.

The animal lowered its head to the snow. 'Kin,' said the wolf.

The word seemed to judder into Feileg's mind. He looked into the creature's eyes.

Then he realised – it was a man, peering out from under a wolf skin. He was huge and powerful, and awfully weather-beaten with frost in his blond beard. He had no fur on his arms and legs, just a long reindeer coat of the sort you could see on any winter hunter, though he carried no bow or spear and wore no snowshoes or skis.

Suddenly all the fear that Feileg had been holding in flooded over him, and he felt terribly cold. The night seemed to collapse upon him and the stars awoke like the eyes of a million wolves all hungry for his blood.

'Help me,' said Feileg, unable to stop his tears.

The man said nothing – as he would never say anything again – but turned and walked up the slope. The boy followed him, with the pack trailing behind. The berserk had done as the witches had asked – given the child over to Kveld Ulf, the Evening Wolf, the shape-shifter of the hills. He was not a werewolf as Feileg would later come to understand it, but a man who had become by instinct and thought half animal.

The boy grew up as much in the dark as in the light. This was not the solid, tomb dark of the witches but the northern dark that bristles with stars and is shot with stripes of light, where morning brings mirages of cities floating in the distance and evening falls under a wide silence. There was no fire, just a cave den and the bodies of the pack close about him. He would warm his hands by plunging them into the carcass of a reindeer the pack had taken, use the moon for light and learn to love the taste of uncooked meat.

In the short days of winter he fed well – animals were weak and easy to catch. Summer was the spirit time, perpetually light and the pickings more scarce. Feileg would push on in fruitless hunts, hardly sleeping, never speaking, his thoughts freeing themselves from the anchor of language in years of silence, his mind ever more animal, his body ever tougher. In the weak dark of the summer night Kveld Ulf would beat his drum and sing discordant chants. They would cut out the bladders of reindeer that had eaten strange mushrooms and drink the piss, and the boy would be transported to the spirit kingdoms where he ran through dark passageways and dripping caves, drank from subterranean streams and felt the darkness of the underground world widen his mind. He had a sense, as powerful as the smell of reindeer musk, of something alive in those tunnels. The caves, he thought, were hungry.

When he came back to himself it seemed his body could feed on the dreams, making him unnaturally strong and fast. By the age of twelve he could kill a reindeer with only his hands, his spear having long since broken and Kveld Ulf refusing to allow him another. At fourteen he began raiding, but not as Vali did. His prey were travellers through the land, merchants heading north with goods for the Whale People or the king's men travelling south on sleds and skis with tribute taken from them. He and Kveld Ulf stole from them as they slept and attacked them if they woke to challenge them, tearing flesh with their teeth and nails, breaking limbs and snapping necks, dashing swords to the floor and pulling spears from hands. He still understood the cries of the men in the camps but their real meaning – of fear, anguish, longing for loved ones – was becoming lost to him.

They kept the plunder in their dens high in the mountains. It meant nothing to Feileg – you couldn't eat it and it wouldn't keep you warm – but Kveld Ulf knew that the fine walrus ivory combs, the gold arm rings and good swords would one day be useful to the boy. He would be going back to the witches, and it would not hurt to have some gifts for the witch queen. Kveld Ulf knew from his own dealings with the witches that a gift of some sort could distract the sisters long enough for them to remember that he wasn't an intruder and they had, in fact, sent for him.

By the age of fifteen Feileg saw as a wolf and thought as a wolf, his body hard, his teeth a weapon. The mountain winds tearing through his mind, past-less and future-less, he lived caught in the moment with no more thought than a snowflake on the breeze. That summer the hunting was thin, and he found himself down in the foothills, ghosting around the farmsteads to try to take a duck or a pig. He was wary of being discovered because the farms were a tight network. One blow on a horn could very quickly bring twenty or thirty armed men.

That was when he had come to the ruin. It was a small long-house, the roof broken in by the weather. It was raining and he decided to seek shelter there. He went inside. Scavengers – animal and human – had taken everything of value, but there were some signs of the former occupants – a broken distaff on the floor, a worn-out shoe, even a small rickety stool. There was better shelter at the back of the house but he decided to stay near the centre, next to where the smoke vent would have been. He didn't know why but instinct made him pick up the stool and sit on it – something he hadn't done in nearly ten years. And then he saw them in his mind: his sisters by the fire, his father, massive and silent on the bench at the back of the room, drinking, his mother patching clothes. It was his house, where he had lived until he was seven. He hadn't known what to make of the feelings the memories stirred inside him and he had gone out into the rain. He had never returned.

At sixteen he awoke in the dusk of the cave mouth and stood up ready to hunt. Kveld Ulf tapped him on the chest and let him know with his eyes that today would be different. He led him across two valleys to where the pack's oldest wolf had fallen down a gully and lay dying at the bottom. The men descended to sit beside it. The wolf's eyes were cloudy and its breath shallow. Kveld Ulf looked at Feileg, and Feileg understood that the wolf's spirit was to join with his own.

For two days the men sat and chanted, beat the drum and shook their rattles. On the third day the wolves came and added their voices to the music. They sat in the galleries of frost and howled out a strange chorus of exultation and lament. Feileg, his head buzzing with tiredness and the noise, took the creature's head in his lap and stroked its ears as it died.

His body trembled and there was a taste of blood in his mouth. Strange longings coursed through him and, where the world had seemed wide beneath the stars, now it narrowed to a thin stream of hunger raging through his mind. He stripped the skin from his fallen brother with a sharp stone, tore out his entrails, ate his heart and liver. Then he placed the bloody pelt around him, looking out from behind the wolf's face, as the wolf had done, as the wolf.

After that, Feileg had no story, no progression of events from day to day. He hunted and he fed and he slept and sat howling beneath the stars. He was part of nature, moving beneath the wind and the sun as heedless of his identity as the foam upon the surf.

And then, at midsummer, when the sun never dipped beyond the suggestion of dusk, his double came and his life changed again and for ever.

10 The Dead God's Bride

'What did you say?' Vali turned to face the person who had spoken. It was Ageirr, one of Forkbeard's sworn bodyguard, a man of around nineteen, two years older than Vali though not much taller.

It was over three years since the raid – three years in which Vali had gone no further than half a day's travel from the farms. He had asked Forkbeard to let him go trading, asked him even to allow him to command his own raids, but the king was adamant. Vali would go and fight as a common warrior or not travel at all. So Vali did not go.

There were many reasons for his refusal. One was that he would not take part in needless slaughter when there were so many easier ways of extracting loot. He had calculated the profit that had been thrown away on the raid on what he now knew was a monastery, and had concluded that the price of the slaves he'd lost to Bodvar Bjarki's brutality alone could have bought him ten head of cattle, before he even started considering how many possible captives had gone free because the berserks hadn't bothered to surround the island.

Another reason for his reluctance was that he thought his people had things to learn from the West Men. One of their priests – the men with the shaven heads – had visited Eikund when Vali was fifteen. To Vali's disappointment, Forkbeard had refused to even let him tell his stories. When the man showed him his writing and pointed out how useful it would be in the administration of his kingdom Forkbeard had torn it up in front of him and told him to go while he still had his life. It had been the talk of the village. Vali had learned the man was a member of the cannibalistic religion of Christ, whose followers ate flesh and drank blood.

The main reason he kept away from war, though – hardly acknowledged to himself – was that he wanted to be branded sword-shy. He hoped Forkbeard would not let his daughter marry such a man, which would leave him free to marry Adisla. But so far the king had refused to release him from his obligation. Vali had also got a merchant to carry a message to his father telling him point-blank that he would not marry the girl but there had been no reply. Vali took it as a rebuke and felt foolish. His father could hold him to his duty if he chose, his protestations and refusals were meaningless.

He had to accept he was a prince but, until he was forced to confront the fact and marry Ragna, he would indulge the fantasy that he was a farmer – a free man, as they were called. He gave Adisla's little brother Manni his seax and only attended training with Bragi to allow the old man to retain his self-respect. Without a valued task, he knew Bragi would wither. Out of gratitude for the kindness Bragi had shown in guiding him through the raid, he tried hard too. When he was beating Bragi's shield with the stave that stood in for a sword, he let the injustice of his inability to marry Adisla fuel his aggression.

For the rest of the time he helped Adisla and her mother around their farm or worked the flocks with her brothers and spent his evenings chatting in Danish with Barth. He would not go raiding though. That took all his courage. He knew that the gods hate nothing more than a coward, and only the knowledge that he was acting for the right reasons allowed him to keep up the pretence that he was.

The king didn't call Vali a coward to his face but there were plenty in his bodyguard who murmured the word as the prince passed. Ageirr was one of them. Vali would have preferred to take the insults, looking on them as helping him on the path that he wanted to travel, but he wasn't made like that and always reacted.

'I said, what did you say?'

'Nothing, prince, nothing at all.'

Vali had heard the word but he didn't want to press Ageirr to repeat it. If he did, Vali would be forced to challenge him to a duel. Ageirr was no keener. He wanted the fun of taunting Vali but didn't want to push it to a fight. Vali was still Authun's son and so valuable to King Forkbeard. The penalty for killing the prince, in a legal contest or not, would be severe. And besides, he had seen the way the prince split those staves against Bragi's helmet. He didn't want to find out what he could do with a sword.

Vali grunted and turned away.

'Are you looking forward to the wedding? We'll have a rare feast that night, I think,' Aegirr said as he did so.

'What wedding?'

'Adisla, the slut from the top farms, is to marry Drengi Half Troll from over the valley. What a union that will be!'

Vali was stunned. He even forgot the insult to Adisla.

'That is not so,' he said.

'I'm afraid that it is,' said Ageirr. 'I heard it from her brother this morning. Go and ask if you don't believe me.'

'If you're lying, you'll answer to me,' said Vali. Then he ran. He knew that Drengi had asked Adisla to marry him before and been refused. Drengi was a good man, strong and hard-working, but he was known as Half Troll because he was both ugly and not much given to talk. Adisla, thought Vali, could never agree to marry him, could she?

He made Disa's house at a sprint. Adisla wasn't there when he arrived, but her mother was sitting outside in the sunlight pulverising some acorns from her store with a large stone.

'Is it true?'

He saw by her eyes that it was.

'Why?'

Disa stopped her pounding.

'You are of a different rank, Vali, and sworn to a princess. My girl is three summers past the age she could have married. It's right that she should do so.'

'I love her, Ma. Is it right she should turn her back on that?'

Disa tapped the pounding stone on the edge of her wooden bowl.

'She hasn't said yes to him yet, though I think she intends to.'

'Don't let her. Make her refuse him.'

She pursed her lips. 'What life would it be as your concubine, Vali? You can't marry her so that's all she can ever be. What if you tire of her?'

'I will not tire of her.'

'Won't you? Forkbeard changes his concubines with every season.'

'I'm not Forkbeard,' he said.

Vali wanted to say more, to reason with Disa, but he was too shocked. He had never discussed it with Adisla but had always assumed he would have to marry Forkbeard's daughter, if that's what their peoples demanded. Then he would father a son and never have much to do with her again, taking Adisla as his wife in all but name. Once Adisla was married to another man, it became a different proposition. That brought spears, blood and feuds.

Vali glanced around, looking for Adisla's brothers to see if they could talk some reason into Disa. They weren't there, though – gone away to Nidarnes as part of Forkbeard's advance guard to prepare the way for the meeting of kings before midsummer.

'I won't let this happen,' said Vali to Disa.

'It's for the best. You love her now but will you offer her the security a husband can when she's old? Will you—'

He didn't wait for her to finish speaking. Forkbeard's hall was a good distance inland but he arrived there in a heartbeat. The king was hearing a dispute between two farmers when Vali burst in. The farmers recognised him and withdrew to the side of the room.

Another man, further down the hall, stood up as Vali

entered. He was tall, young and powerfully built. His clothes were out of the ordinary. He wore a bright white silk shirt, the like of which Vali had only ever seen in the possession of the trader Veles Libor. Vali thought that perhaps he recognised him, but the thought was fleeting. He approached the king and bowed. Forkbeard – one of those squat strong men who gives the impression of being wider than he is tall – was slurping at a bowl of soup and getting much of it down his beard. He was a tough man who'd come to kingship through fighting his way there. His court was not one of intrigue and debate but a place where, to carry an argument, you had to outfight or outdrink your opponent, preferably both.

'If, prince, you're here again with some fancy plan about how we can win battles without fighting, then save your breath. A man goes into war thinking only of his foe to his front and his friend at his side, not weighed down with schemes. Raid and fight or stay put, that's the deal. Take it or leave it and don't ask me again. We've been here too many times before, haven't we, lads?'

A couple of the bodyguard nodded and said that they had. Vali had repeatedly annoyed Forkbeard with his contention that planning could win a battle more effectively than direct attack. Forkbeard had always just asked him where glory fitted into his schemes.

'I have not come about that.'

'Then what is it?'

'I want you to release me from my marriage pact with your daughter. I am not the son you want, and the Rygir deserve a better, stronger prince than me.'

Forkbeard snorted. 'You're right there, son.'

Vali's heart skipped.

The king lifted his beard and licked the soup off it. He seemed to ponder for a moment.

'But forget it. Too many questions if I release you – half the kings along the coast would think I was planning to have a go at Authun. And, worst still, so might he. That is a war-loving fellow indeed. Ain't that right, lads?' The body-guard said that it was.

'My father will not take offence, and he has not raised a sword these ten years.' Even though Forkbeard was not given to niceties, Vali instinctively gave him the respect of high speech.

'Too long for a man like that,' said Forkbeard. 'I tell you, son, if I could think of a way to stop this marriage then I would. Your children will be weaklings, but what can I do?'

'Find another prince, lord.'

Forkbeard shook his head. 'Your old dad wouldn't like it,' he said, 'but, as it happens, there might be a way out after all. Hogni, get up here.'

The young man in the silk shirt came forward and bowed to Vali and Forkbeard.

'Hogni son of Morthi,' he said, 'messenger to King Authun.'

So that was where Vali had seen him, at Authun's court.

'Tell the prince what his father has said.'

The man bowed again and looked slightly nervous.

'Go on,' said Forkbeard. 'No one gets the chop here without my leave. It's me who's asked you to speak to him, so say what Authun told you. If the prince wants to pick a fight about it he can pick one with me, and that's a bit of trouble he won't want, I can tell you.'

'That's right!' said a bodyguard.

Hogni glanced at Forkbeard and then addressed Vali precisely and formally. 'Exalted King Forkbeard, terror of the south, mighty in battle, lord of the Rygir, know that it is my wish that my idle son be shaken from his life of ease. Reports tell me that he ignores arms, counsel and raiding in favour of conversation with women. Let him prove himself. The land to the north of our kingdoms is beset by bandits. Merchants, shepherds and farmers all fear attack from the savage men who plague the Troll Mountains. Truly these men are wolves, sorcerers able to assume the form of that monstrous animal, striking down with fury and viciousness all that cross them, invulnerable to weapons and murderous in intent. Seven of my own men have died trying to wipe out this scourge. My son will bring you the head of one before midsummer. If he does not, then I leave it to you to impose a meaningful penalty.'

Vali looked at the man and then back to Forkbeard.

'Why this? Why now?'

'Who are you whying?' said Forkbeard.

Vali ignored his belligerence. 'It makes no difference to my request. Release me from the pact with your daughter and allow Adisla to marry me, or at least forbid her from marrying anyone else.'

Forkbeard looked to the rafters. 'That farm girl is the cause of all the bother in my life. I have less problems with the bastard Danes than I do with her!' He lowered his eyes and stared straight at Vali. 'Return with a wolfman's head – no, better for proof, the whole man – or your Adisla is Odin's bride at the summer blöt. She'll hang to please the god.'

Vali went pale.

The bride of Odin was a tradition almost never celebrated in individual kingdoms. He had heard that on great feast days, when kings from all over the land met for a festival, a blöt, there were human sacrifices, but Forkbeard had never insisted on one before.

'You can't do this,' said Vali.

Forkbeard sipped from a jewelled drinking cup, booty from a raid. Vali thought of the Odin-blind berserks and the needless deaths they had caused, thought of the stupid frenzy that had exposed his kinsmen to danger and the valuable slave hanged on the returning boat. One day he would drink Odin's blood, tear that god down and make him pay for his corpse lust.

'Can't I?' said Forkbeard. He leaned forward and said in a forceful whisper, 'I might have to go running to the assembly to get my laws passed but religion is my turf and mine alone.'

Now he stood and shouted, 'I'm the king, the top boy, Odin's priest on earth, bargaining with the god, telling all you lot what he wants for his favours! Do you get that?' He sat again, but he was pointing at Vali. 'Well, he wants this girl for his bride unless you bring him the head of his enemy, the wolfman. Your father reckons you've got what it takes. I don't. We'll see who's right. I expect you'll die even before you get to the wolfman, which'll suit me down to the ground as I'll be able to get someone with a bit of balls about him for my daughter. And you'll have the consolation of knowing that your farm girl will be filling your cup in the halls of the slain.'

'You can't take a free-born woman and sacrifice her. The people will know she didn't volunteer,' said Vali.

Forkbeard shook his head.

'She's a threat to the kingdom, lad! And it's you who's made her one. The people will understand why she had to die. And if the gods want to stop it, then they'll bring you success. Seems straight enough to me. What don't you understand?'

Vali stood shaking. He wanted to shout that if Adisla died, it wouldn't be the head of the wolf that he presented to the people of Rogaland but that of Forkbeard himself, but he saw now how stupid he had been, how artless. He should have hidden his true thoughts from others, participated in their chaotic attacks, bragged about the slaughter of old men and boys. As a respected warrior he would be in a much better position. Forkbeard would treat him seriously, would ban Adisla's marriage at least. He wouldn't even need to ban it. If word of his displeasure reached the prospective groom's house, he would never go through with his suit. Now this. And what if he couldn't find the wolfman? His only option would be to challenge Forkbeard to single combat. He was confident he could survive on a battlefield but a one-on-one duel with a man who had cut his way to kingship was a different thing. Never mind. If Forkbeard tried to harm Adisla then Vali would defend her.

'This is a perilous course for all of us,' said Vali.

'Perilous courses are my favourite sort,' said Forkbeard. 'Remember, kings are made for glory, not long life.'

Vali tried to reply with something like he would have said to Bragi – 'If you have the wit, you can combine both' or 'You seem to have lived to a respectable age' – but the words seemed lodged in his throat.

'I'm up at the assembly of kings at Nidarnes until midsummer. It is a month. Return with the wolfman by then or watch your farm girl hang,' said Forkbeard.

'And then will you excuse me marrying your daughter?'

'Not a chance. You'll have proved yourself a great warrior. Your girl'll live, that's all. Now get out of here before I change my mind on that one too.'

Vali saw how he had been forced into a situation where the best he could hope for was that things would remain as they had been. The worst? Well, that wasn't going to happen. The chances of finding wolfmen, let alone capturing one, were terribly slim. A different plan was needed. Adisla would have to marry her farmer immediately. That would make it much more difficult for Forkbeard to take her as a sacrifice. It would mean they would never be together but she would live. And he would still have to go on his mission. He was sure he wouldn't return.

For the second time that day, he ran the distance between Forkbeard's hall and Adisla's house, pushing himself ever faster. Halfway there he heard hooves behind him – three riders of the king's bodyguard, their purpose clear. They were riding bareback, with only bridles on the horses. They hadn't had time to saddle up because they were trying to beat him to the farm.

The horses slowed as they approached. They were on a narrow track through trees and he moved to bar their path.

'You stop there!' shouted Vali. 'As a prince I command you to stop.'

The horses drew up. The riders were armed – one with a

sword and two with spears — but he felt sure they wouldn't attack him.

The swordsman drew his weapon and pointed it at Vali — it was Ageirr, who had told him the news of Adisla's marriage in the first place. 'Where are your arms, prince? Ah, but you are Vali the Swordless, hearth hugger and thrall friend, aren't you? How do you propose to stop us? With the words you learned from the women? Or are you going to speak our enemies' language at us?'

The other two laughed, though slightly nervously. Vali was after all a prince, and they knew very well that at some point he might have the power of life and death over them.

Vali was desperate. 'I'll pay you to let me go first. On oath, you'll have money if you do so.'

Where Vali would get this money from, he didn't know. Maybe he could sell the helmet his father had given him, if he could get it back off Bragi.

'We are sworn defenders of the king,' said a spearman. 'There is no money that can sway us from his orders.' He urged his horse forward at a trot.

As he came past, Vali lunged for him, grabbing his tunic and pulling him from the animal's back. The horse was spooked and bolted, streaming the reins behind it. The other two kicked their mounts forward and around the pair brawling on the ground. 'See you at the slut's house!' shouted Ageirr as he passed.

Vali jumped up in useless desperation.

The bodyguard followed him and dusted himself down.

'A fair smack, prince, weapon or no weapon, I grant you that,' he said. Then he looked to the ground. 'I'm sorry for what's to happen to her. She is a fine girl.'

'Save your words for your horse,' said Vali, turning to run through the trees to the farm.

She was gone, of course, when he arrived. Disa was waiting in the doorway. He had never seen her so angry.

'What have you done?' she said.

Vali felt hot and wretched. 'How is she? Where have they taken her?'

'She's at Forkbeard's hall. She's perfectly well and likely to remain so until they hang her. What are you going to do about it, boy? What are you going to do?'

Vali's body felt full of energy. He was bursting to go somewhere, to do something, to make it all go away, but even as he said the words, they sounded unconvincing. 'I'll do as Forkbeard demands – I'll find the wolfmen.'

'How?'

'I . . . I'll go north and walk around until they attack me.'

For the first time in his life Vali saw Disa's eyes fill with tears.

'You'll do nothing of the sort, you useless fool. That'll be two of you dead if you do.'

'Then I'll go to Forkbeard's hall and fight him for her.'

'You'll fight Forkbeard, a man who killed his first enemy at twelve and who has murdered more people than you have ever seen. You fight Forkbeard, you'll . . .'

She wiped her eyes. Bragi was watching from where he was sitting beneath a tree. He had decided long ago that the best way to keep an eye on the prince was to spend time at Disa's himself.

'You, old man, you go with him.'

'I was told the order yesterday, madam. The boy is to go alone.'

'You knew, and sat there drinking at my table?'

'I knew he was to go; I knew nothing of the fate of your girl, on my oath.'

Disa composed herself.

'Will you lend him your sword at least? It's the best blade in the kingdom.'

'It would be my dearest wish,' said Bragi.

'Then come on,' said Disa. 'We have no time to waste. Come inside.'

'I need to go now. I need to find this wolfman,' said Vali.

'That,' said Disa, 'is exactly what we are going to do. Get Ma Jodis; we have work to do.'

11 An Invitation

Word of what was happening spread throughout the little farmsteads and curiosity drew a crowd. They packed into Disa's house so tightly that she had to drive some of them outside.

While they waited for Jodis to come, Disa took a pack from her shelf and began to stuff it with food – bread, some cheese, honey in a pot sealed with cloth – and other things. She was talking, as much to herself as to Vali.

'You'll need food, for a little way at least, and something to light your fire. I'll put in some webs and yarrow for wounds. The honey's not to be eaten; you can put that on any cuts you get too. Long root will give strength to your blood and mint will keep you watchful. This,' she said, holding up a small flask, 'is to be taken in small quantities when you are well hidden and sure to be safe from enemies. It will help you sleep through the white nights, no matter how hard the bed, though you need no more than a drop. Five drops in a man's glass will see him sleep so soundly he cannot be woken for a day – you may need to resort to such measures if you are hard-pressed. Here is wolfsbane, to take away pain, again only a drop. Now, what else?'

As she scoured her shelves Bragi came in with his sword. Disa took it from him without a word and put it next to the pack. All the time Vali was stewing in his shame. He had condemned Adisla to death because he had considered only himself, not her.

'This,' said Ma Disa, holding open a small bag of mushrooms and dried flowers, 'is what the berserks use. Boil it with water and drink it as hot as you can bear.'

Vali was going to protest, to say he didn't want anything

to do with berserker magic. He couldn't really see a situation where he would have time for what amounted to cooking before a fight but, he thought, best take it and be grateful.

Jodis came in, smacking him hard over the back of the head.

'I heard. You're a fool, prince, and the gods help the Horda if you ever become their king.' Ma Jodis was a big bustling woman with arms like pork hams and the blow hurt. Vali accepted it, though. He'd known her since he was a small child and almost regarded it as her right to cuff him around the ears if she wanted to.

The women exchanged a long look.

'Begin?' said Jodis.

Disa nodded.

The women went to the centre of the room and started work, stoking up the fire, moving goats, chickens, benches and stools out of the way, pushing the curious to where they would cause least interference.

They brought in a table, which was positioned very close to the fire. On the table was placed a chest, pulled through the throng of onlookers. As this was done Disa shook down her hair. Jodis caught it up in her hands, tying it at the back in three tight knots. Vali shivered. He knew what they were – the hanging knots of the dead lord's necklace – symbol of Odin, the god he had come to hate.

The women's actions were accompanied by a whispered commentary, as those who could see passed news of what was happening to those who could not.

'She's tying her hair.'

'She's becoming the bride of Odin.'

'If she hangs herself then the god might save the girl.'

'That terrible fellow wants someone to swing, no mistake.'

'He is lord of the hanged, a mighty god indeed!'

'Don't be so stupid – Ma Disa's death won't save the girl.'

Some voices praised Odin almost ecstatically. Others were quieter but disapproving of what they saw. The poorer people, those who had the hard pasture and mean dwellings, thought that destiny lay in the hands of the gods. The richer farmers, or those who had enjoyed successful raiding, were more inclined to say they had made their own luck and put less trust in the divine.

Jodis pushed the chest to the front of the table and Disa sat on it, her head slightly above those of the standing crowd, her feet only just above the fire. Jodis took Vali by the arm and sat him on the floor on the other side of the fire, looking up at Disa.

Vali glanced around at the watching faces, long in the light of the flames. It was as if he was at the centre of some strange clearing in the forest, the people hanging over him like twisted trees.

'Them that don't have to be here, shouldn't be here for the next bit – you'll be in for a long night,' said Jodis, but no one moved. She pushed through the crowd, took a pot from a shelf at the back of the room, removed a stone serving as its lid and shook something into her hand that looked to Vali like kindling.

Jodis threw the stuff onto the fire and it began to burn, releasing an acrid and unpleasant smoke. Most of those nearest to it, Vali included, pulled their tunics up over their mouths and noses, but Disa breathed deeply and intoned in a strange high voice:

> I speak the rune of the spell god
> I howl the rune of the hanged god
> Odin, who lost his eye for lore
> Odin, waiting mind blown by the well.

Disa then produced a piece of wood and marked something on it – Vali couldn't see what – with three strokes of her knife. She put the wood on her knees and held the knife to her palm. She drew in breath, steeling herself, and then made the same three strokes in her hand, but much quicker. Vali recognised the Ansuz rune and was fascinated. He could carve runes himself and knew they were said to have magical properties. He'd asked Disa to tell him what they were, but she had just said that kings and warriors made their magic cutting runes on the bodies of their enemies and had no need for further knowledge.

The blood dripped from Disa's hand down onto the wood. She smeared it into what she had carved there and then threw it onto the fire.

'What am I? I am a woman. Where am I? At the hearth. What am I? I am a woman. Where am I? At the hearth. What am I? I am a woman. Where am I? At the hearth. What am I? I am a woman. Where am I? At the hearth.'

Jodis came to Disa's side and bound her hand, but she seemed not to notice. She continued to chant, eyes vacant and staring into space. Her voice seemed to deaden Vali's sense of time. He saw the fire restocked both with logs and with the strange herbs by Jodis and then old Ma Sefa returned with more of each.

'What am I? I am a woman. Where am I? At the hearth. What am I? I am a woman. Where am I? At the hearth.' Again and again she said the words, rocking slightly on the chest as Vali looked up at her through the fire and the smoke. Sometimes his mind wandered and he thought that she had stopped, but when he came back to himself she was still chanting, How long had he sat there? He couldn't tell but his legs were numb and his head was heavy.

The smoke filled up Vali's senses. Tiredness descended on him but he was not allowed to sleep. Every time he began to drift off, Jodis or Sefa would shake him, as they roused Disa. The purpose of her seat became clear. It was uncomfortable and precarious – virtually impossible to doze on. Then Vali noticed the room was lighter and colder. Some people had left; in fact many people had left. Looking over to the doorway, he realised he had completely missed the brief night and the light was that of the dawn.

Around them the farmers came and went: chatting, speculating on how Disa worked her art, wondering what enchantment she was laying on Vali. Some said that she was trying to make him invulnerable to weapons, some that she would turn him into a bird to scour the land for the wolfmen, some that she was pleased her daughter was going to Odin and would frustrate Vali in his quest. A couple began to play at dice; others picked up Vali's King's Table set and played that, bored by the ritual but afraid they might miss something if they went home. Two young men even started to mock Disa, repeating her words in silly high voices. Jodis sent them packing with a whack from a broom. Late arrivers, religious women of the outlying farms, came and joined in the chant, hoping to gain the blessing of the god Disa was seeking.

'What am I? I am a woman. Where am I? At the hearth. What am I? I am a woman. Where am I? At the hearth.'

The chanting never stopped. The light outside grew brighter. It was hot again and then it was cold again. More people came in. Others left. Jodis shook Vali awake, shook Disa awake, steadying her on her platform, throwing more herbs on the fire.

'What am I? I do not know. Where am I? In the dark. What am I? I am a raven. Where am I? On the field of the slain. What am I? I am ravens. Where am I? Where I can see.'

Was she really saying that? Vali wondered. The ground seemed to rock as if he was on a ship. The air seemed thick and clinging. The light outside was weakening once more. Neither Vali nor Disa had slept in three days. Disa's voice was cracked, hardly audible.

Something cut through the fug of his thoughts. Disa was coughing and spluttering, then she let out a scream and began to shiver violently. Jodis and Sefa leaped to her side, holding her on the chest. Disa's body went rigid – it seemed almost as if she would lift off her seat.

'These pins are so sharp in my skin.'

Disa had spoken but in a way that Vali had never heard

her speak before, slow and deliberate, much higher than her normal tone and with a strange accent.

Vali looked up at her, his legs stone with sitting, his mind like a boulder.

'A rune I took from the tormented god.'

It was a tremulous voice, almost like that of a child, thought Vali. On some sounds it seemed to draw and suck like the sea on shingle but on others cracked and choked like the noise of a dog with a chicken bone.

Disa threw herself back and sat down heavily on the table, the chest going crashing to the side. Her body convulsed but then the shivering subsided, and she became calm. Jodis and Sefa let her go and she stood on the table looking out across the room. The temperature in the room plummeted and Vali felt his skin prickle into goosebumps. His breath froze on the air in front of him. There was something in Ma Disa's manner that was quite unlike her. She stood tall and proud, surveying her surroundings like a queen. The people drew back from her, a couple giving involuntary cries. A patina of frost had formed at her feet. Vali was sure he was seeing magic working before his eyes. He was right. But it no longer had anything to do with Disa.

12 Enemies

The witch queen had sensed the first death like someone dozing on a summer day might sense a cloud go over the sun. Things had moved quickly then — candles had been lit to pierce the tomb dark of the caves, sisters disturbed from their ritual sufferings, boys dispatched to find the corpse.

Authun was not yet back home from the Wall with the infant Vali when Gullveig located the first body.

The girl was lying in the lower tunnels, close to the wet rocks, near the deep pool where the rite of the water rune was performed. She was hanged, a rough rope thrown over a jutting rock, a triple knot tied at the neck. The witch queen had touched the girl's cold smile and then the rope. She knew what those knots meant, the three tight interlocking triangles — the dead lord's necklace, sign of the god Odin, the berserk, the hanged, the drowned, the wise and the mad, the god to whom she had dedicated her life.

The witch queen touched the white of the girl's throat, her magic-widened senses drinking in the resonances of the child's death. The bruises had the sense of a delicious stain, she thought, blackberries and dark wine. She took up the girl's hair in her fingers and breathed in. Baked bread, cinders, straw bedding and dried flowers were the odours of her death. The girl had gone home. It was a suicide, Gullveig was sure.

The dead child had not been unhappy. She had been scared when she had first entered the caves, but the presence of the queen — at twelve years old a child herself — had reassured her and the witches had touched her mind to bring her calm. The pain and suffering of the rituals had not come easily to her, but she had endured, seen the aim, felt her mind widening as her grip on sanity loosened.

She was to have been the inheritor of the rune of water, to carry the resonance of that ancient symbol within her, to sustain it and be sustained by it. Two girls had been trained. When the old witch who was their mentor died it would be decided who would nurture the rune and who would participate in lesser rituals – to help, to fetch and carry. Now there was only one girl to continue the magic. If anything happened to her the rune would cease to manifest in the physical realm and the sisters' power would diminish.

There was something else Gullveig could sense in the magical signature of the girl's death, a feeling of heaviness – the heaviness someone drowning feels as their clothes fill with water, the heaviness of a downward current as it sucks the strength from a swimmer's limbs. There was a magical presence there, the witch could tell, and it had flowed from the rune the girl had been given to learn. That should not have happened. The witches had suffered losses before but they had been physical ones – sisters frozen, smothered or suffocated by smoke when a ritual had gone wrong. The runes had been within their control for generations. Until that day.

The witch leaned forward and tapped her tongue on the girl's cheek. The taste was of ocean depths, sightless and empty voids. Gullveig felt the pulling tides, the tug of groping blind sea beasts, the weight of waters above her, all seeming to say, 'Come lower. Descend, lose sight of the light and give yourself to this heavy darkness.' She shivered. There would be more of these deaths, she knew, as certain as people of lesser sensitivities know that one wave follows another.

The following years proved her right. Sometimes there were no deaths from one summer to the next; in others there might be two.

Knowledge of the girls' passing came to the witch queen in different ways. One death presented itself as a lurch in the consciousness, like when you suddenly pull back from the brink of sleep. Another came as a feeling of disquiet from a dream that didn't stop when she woke. Still another arrived like the taste of tar in the back of her mouth, a nausea that she could not shake until she saw the corpse.

Gullveig held their pale bodies in her arms, touched the bruises at their necks, put her fingers to their swollen lips, stroked their broken limbs and felt an unbearable pressure in her head.

Loki had told her the truth, she thought. Odin was acting against her, killing her sisters. She was certain of one thing – this creeping harvest was only a prelude. Odin would not be content taking one or two lives, nibbling away at her power from the shadows. He was coming, as himself and in force.

It had taken her nearly sixteen years to find him, which did not surprise her. If the god did not know himself then it would take a huge effort for a mortal to identify him. She had managed it, through the old and trusted ways – meditation, ritual and suffering. At first his presence had been elusive in her mind, glimpsed like the glimmer of a fish in water, gone almost as soon as it was there. But over weeks and months, in waking and sleeping she had tracked him, through her agony-induced trances.

She saw herself wandering under the empty spaces of the northern evening until, so startling they shook her from her trance, she saw a pair of pale blue eyes looking at her from a field of snow and heard the lonely howl of a wolf. It was him, the god, appearing in just a fleeting vision, but it was all that she needed. She was on his trail.

She did not see, and could only barely sense, the pale woman with the ruined face who watched her in her meditations. She knew though that there was a presence who walked at her side, hating her, just out of sight. It was that presence that guided her. All the queen could tell was that something travelled with her in her meditations and seemed to know what would harm her. She had sensed its excitement rising when she had caught sight of Odin. The witch did not find this particularly disturbing. She had lived all her life alongside strange entities, faces that flickered from the firelight, shadows on rock that seemed to glower with carnivorous intent. Sleeping or waking, she was never far from the suffocating spirits of the dark.

The thing that followed her now was at least useful. The closer its attention, the nearer she was to the greatest harm of all – Odin.

A year after she had seen the eyes looking at her from the snow, her unseen hater had lead her to Disa, and so back to him.

The witch queen had almost ignored Disa's call, she was so caught up in the search for her enemy, the god. It was the fourth day of her hanging ordeal – her flesh pierced by thick pins secured by cords to a slab overhanging a scree slope in a steep cave near the surface.

Disa's words had come to her on a wisp of smoke from the cold air at the top of the Wall. Entreaties from village healers and wise women were not common – such women knew the risks of invoking the witch's attention – but they were distracting when they came. But as Gullveig prepared to dismiss the call, she felt an interest from the thing at her side. Here, it seemed, was harm and therefore, perhaps, Odin.

The witch allowed her mind to float up over the grey rock, to mingle with the smoke and use it as a road to carry her back to its source.

In her house Disa breathed in the herb-laced fire and with it consciousness of the witch. She shook and trembled, throwing herself back off the chest. Then things became hazy, she felt terribly drowsy, and she had the sense that her body was not her own. There was an odd presence prowling through her head.

As Gullveig looked out through the healer's eyes, she could see the room with the faces of the villagers gaping back at her. She could also see the youth at her feet. She knew him straight away – the wolf's brother, the ingredient, the holy victim.

But there was someone else there too. At her side she saw a woman who she thought she remembered, beautiful but with a terribly burned face. In front of her, his form insubstantial and spectral in the firelight, was the god. He was beating a shallow drum with a bone stick, his eyes were piercing and on his head he wore a four-cornered blue hat. The drum was painted with runes, and as he beat it they seemed to fall from it, shaking to the floor and collecting at his feet before disappearing like snowflakes on warm autumn ground.

'Lord Odin,' said the witch.

She knew exactly where she was – that space that wasn't a space, a nexus called into being by ritual, where sorcerers and spirits from remote and distant locations could allow their consciousnesses to assemble. The physical form of the woman with the burned face and that of the sorcerer might be miles from the house but their magical selves were there.

The woman with the burned face extended her hand towards her and Gullveig took it, as if for reassurance.

The god spoke to her. His language was strange, as was the name he called her, but she understood him perfectly. 'Jabbmeaaakka, the wolf is ours. We have seen your intent and you will not prevail.'

There was a murmur of assent but it didn't come from the people in the room. Others were collaborating with the god, she thought. The witch was terrified by his presence but she thought she had a chance. If the god did not know he was a god then he may not yet have come to his full power. That meant he could be defeated in magic, or at least beaten back.

She sent her mind like a belch towards the blue-eyed man, a poisonous stink of rot, mould, worms and the crawling things of the earth that spewed forward to engulf him. It wasn't even really a spell, just an opening of her consciousness, a little glimpse of the places she had been and what she had seen there, enough to cook the brain of anyone who had not walked at least some of those paths themselves.

But something came back, a rhythm, an insistent beat that clouded her thoughts and made her long for sleep. She heard a strange rough singing, felt a blast of cold, saw white fields of snow, creatures thin as runes moving across them, and she longed to step into that cold.

Gullveig, however, was not a wise woman with potions and chants, a village seer or ragged prophet. She was the witch queen of the Troll Wall, lady of the shrieking runes, a creature born and raised to magic. She did not step into the cold; instead, her mind on the edge of disaster, a rune expressed itself in her, a rune like the point of a spear, its steel tip gleaming as it flew across a clear blue sky.

The drumming burst to a frenzy; raised voices became shouting; she had a taste in her throat, ash and sour milk, the smell of funeral fires, and when she looked again the blue-eyed man was gone. Had she killed him? She doubted it, but there were others about him and she sensed they had suffered from her attack.

Odin had felt weak to her, far from his full power. So he could not yet move against her. So what had he done? The girl with the ravaged face who sat by her side in the hanging cave stroked her hand and the answer came to Gullveig in an instant. He hadn't the power yet to take on any of the witches directly so he was working where he could – at the girls who were being prepared to inherit the runes. If they died then there would be no women to continue the witches' traditions. Gullveig would eventually be left alone and isolated. While his strength grew, hers would diminish.

She saw it was time to accelerate the pace of the magic. The wolfboy had been prepared. Now he had to meet his holy victim – the prince.

What is magic? Disa had sought to unite the wolfman with the prince so had called the witch. The witch had decided it was time to begin the spell to make her werewolf and so to bring the wolfman and the prince together. Was that a coincidence? Had this conjunction been caused by Disa's ritual or was it an expression of the witch's far more powerful magic, which worked away in her deep mind without needing to come to consciousness? Or had it come about through the strongest magic of all – that woven by the fates?

Whatever it was, Gullveig's desire was now in harmony with Disa's and it found expression in a spell. Gullveig reached through Disa to touch Vali.

Vali forced his heavy eyes open to watch as Disa's body convulsed again. She coughed and shook, shivered and growled. Then she dropped onto the floor by Vali and crouched in front of him. She leaned forward, taking his face in her hands. Vali looked into her eyes and was afraid. It wasn't Disa looking at him, he knew, but something far stranger, and whatever it was exuded cold. Vali felt her hands freezing on his face.

The witch, hanging from the torture rock, tried to work her spell, but Disa's mind was inadequate to channelling her magic, too fastened to everyday reality. The healer needed to be sent somewhere that would banish her day-to-day consciousness completely and allow Gullveig to work through her.

Vali looked into Disa's eyes. He could smell something. Burning. Disa, he realised, had pushed the edge of her skirt into the fire, almost surreptitiously, trying to avoid detection until the last moment.

The material caught and the room filled with light and movement and noise. Jodis pulled Disa from the fire, then people were on her, beating at her skirts, trying to extinguish the flames, but Disa was holding them off with one hand, extending the other towards Vali and hissing something under her breath. Two of the men got her down, someone else threw water, but still Disa fixed her eyes on Vali.

Vali felt a cold enter his mind, a creeping feeling of damp and dark. He fell back. Something had gone into him: it felt as though he had a toad stuck in his throat, a clammy, writhing thing that would not be coughed out. The only way to get rid of the hideous feeling was to stand, to go. He was overwhelmed by tiredness but not sleepy. He got to his feet.

His sympathy for Disa was like something on the tip of his tongue, known but distant beneath the nausea he was feeling. He had to move, he knew that. It was like the frustration of being trapped indoors through a long winter storm – dying to get outside but knowing it is impossible – but magnified many times.

He went to the back of the room, where Bragi had hung his sword next to his pack. He picked up both and left. No one followed him; they were all attending to Disa or watching her being attended to.

It was the long twilight of the northern summer. The sky was a pale silver and a big moon hung alongside a single bright star. Already, Vali noticed, the moon was not quite full. He had less than a month to save Adisla.

A large crow flapped from one tree to another and Vali's body seemed to respond to the movement. Tired beyond thought, he saw himself start walking and noticed that he was going east along the shore of the fjord. Only his forward movement seemed to stop the nausea inside him. After that, he seemed to forget that he was travelling at all.

His movements seemed automatic, unconscious and un-guided as he took the road from the village, only dimly aware of his surroundings. He was lost in a trance of thoughts of Adisla, of Disa, of the cold eyes of whatever had looked through her, and he didn't really notice where he was until he woke.

He stood up, shook the moisture from himself and looked around. There was a depression in the grass. He had slept there, it seemed. It was dusk again. He checked his pack and his sword and looked to the distance. A dark blue range of mountains split the horizon, and he knew that was where he needed to go. The feeling of sickness was still with him and he thought that he wouldn't bother with food, just go on until he found his wolfman.

He was high up on one side of a steep valley on a slope that, within yards of where he had woken, fell away as a cliff. He moved to the edge and peered down. There were two riders below him and they had made a camp. The men had laid blankets beneath a heavily leafed alder tree and made a small fire. They were preparing to sleep, he thought, taking advantage of the shelter of the tree.

One of them was Authun's messenger, Hogni. Vali looked up at the mountains. A horse would halve his journey time. He dimly sensed he was enchanted and wondered if that was why his thoughts had suddenly come to clarity. Did the spell, or whatever was controlling the spell, want him to take a horse to speed him forward?

The men hadn't seen him. It occurred to him to simply walk down the hill and command them to give him their horses. They were, after all, his father's retainers and so owed him a duty of obedience. But his father had ordered that he should be tested against the wolfmen. Would they agree to give up their animals? And what was to stop them killing him right there if they felt like it? There were other people, cousins and uncles, with claims to Authun's throne. If one of these men was of their party, Vali thought, they could run a spear through him and go home with no one any the wiser.

His hand instinctively went to his sword. Then he lay flat and waited for the men to sleep.

13 The King's Men

An hour after the men lay down Vali felt it safe to move. It was just dark, that splinter of night that pricks the long days of the northern summer. A bright moon, full save a slice of darkness on its right-hand side, shone down from a sky of deep stars. He imagined it as the eye of a sleepy god. By the time it had closed to nothing and opened to fullness again, Adisla would be dead, unless he could succeed.

His task wasn't straightforward. He needed to steal at least one saddle and a bridle from the sleeping men without waking them up, then he had to get to the horses. Catching them would be easy because resting travellers always hobbled their horses by tying a foreleg to a back leg, which prevented the animals from moving faster than a walk, but he knew well that a horse might object – and noisily – to being saddled by a strange rider.

He made his way down the slope as quietly as he could. There was no cover and the glaring moon caught him in its bare light, so he had to rely on the men remaining asleep.

Vali recognised the other sleeper when he got closer – Orri, one of his father's retainers, who he had seen on his rare visits to Authun's court. His mind was emerging from the effects of the tiredness and the smoke he had inhaled, and he wondered why the men were travelling by land during summer. Merchants seeking to avoid pirates made the journey overland sometimes, and so did herders and those who needed to travel but couldn't afford a boat, but nearly everyone who had the choice went by sea. Only when the rivers and lakes froze did the land offer a quicker journey than the water. You'd have to be mad, or enchanted, to walk if you could sail.

Vali crept past the the smouldering campfire and found a

saddle and bridle. He had never quite considered just how much metal was on these items before, or the row they made when they moved. They made such a clinking and creaking that they seemed less like horse tack and more like musical instruments. If he was a real thief he would have found it easier just to kill the men in their sleep, he thought. With great care, he withdrew to where the horses were grazing.

The animals were well trained and he had no difficulty approaching one of them, a squat and sturdy beast that looked up to a long ride. He saddled it up as quickly as he could, with half an eye on the sleeping men. The horse made no sound beyond a brief cough of complaint as he tightened the girth on its out breath. Then he bent to undo the rope that connected the horse's left legs. It was when he stood that he felt the hand on his shoulder.

'You'll be mistaken for a wolfman, prowling around like that, prince.'

He span round to see the face of Hogni grinning into his.

For a moment he didn't know what to say.

The man broke the silence with a laugh and called out, 'Orri, fetch Prince Vali a drink; he must be parched after his long walk.'

By the fire, which he was stirring to life, Orri waved and picked up a wineskin. Nausea swept over Vali, the taste of Disa's smoke herbs returning to his throat. He wanted to be away, desperately, but it was more than a natural desire to get on with his mission. It was all he could do not to run northwards. He was certain he was under some spell.

'A drink isn't necessary; I'll just take the horse,' said Vali.

'Relax, prince. I have good news for you: your father doesn't require you to kill any wolfmen.'

'That wasn't what you said at Forkbeard's hall.'

'No. But what is said in a hall is not always matched by what happens outside it.'

'I don't understand you.'

'It was a deception.'

'Call it by its name, a lie. It is not manly to lie.' Vali's head was swimming. The desire to leave was becoming overwhelming.

'I was delivering a message, and the message was not sent by your father; it was sent by your mother, Queen Yrsa, so indeed it wasn't manly, being of a woman.'

Vali focused his eyes on Hogni's face, trying to make his thoughts do the same. 'Since when does my mother handle my father's affairs?'

'For about four years now,' said Hogni. He shifted from foot to foot and said, as if afraid the grass would hear him and carry the secret out down the valley, 'Your father is sick.'

'In what way?' Vali's heart leaped. Was he about to inherit his kingdom? If so, he would send these men back to Forkbeard with a message that he should release Adisla immediately or see Horda longships on his shores before winter.

Hogni didn't reply.

'Likely to die?' The taste of the herbs was strong in his mouth, the tickle in his throat vile.

'Unlikely to die.'

Vali guessed at the meaning behind the man's brief reply. 'Madness?'

Again, no answer. So, it was madness. Vali had heard rumours but he had taken them for just that – things said by the men of Rogaland to make them feel more comfortable with their warlike neighbour. You could hear stories like that about any king, should you bother to enquire.

Vali thought for a moment and then said, 'So what is required of me? What would my mother have me do?'

'Simply come home to the court.'

'She only had to send for me.'

'This way raises the least suspicion,' said Hogni.

'Suspicion of what?'

'Things are under way that I have no right to discuss. It's for the queen to speak to you. We meet a ship half a day west of here, and on that we will bring you home.'

Vali nodded. He still wanted the horse but knew that there was no way of getting it other than by deception.

'Good,' he said. 'I'll be glad to come. Here, let me sit by your fire and share a drink for a while.'

He moved to the fire, sat down and the men offered him the remains of a cooked hare with thick bread. He still had that horrid feeling of sickness in him but he forced himself to eat and to suppress the 'Thank you' that Disa had drummed into him. Gratitude was fine for farmers, not for princes. He would rule these men one day and he knew very well that kings took such things as a right.

They ate and the men's manners and customs seemed faintly strange to Vali. He had been raised among the Rygir, and to him the way Hogni and Orri spoke was slightly odd. He had known, for instance, that the Horda called a cooking pot a hot cup, but it still felt strange to hear it described that way, as if it could never have been called anything else. When the men had finished their meal, they took a tiny pinch of salt, spat, and threw it to the ground, saying, 'For Loki's eyes.'

The words struck him as strange. Of all the gods, thought Vali, Loki was the most interesting. He was the sly god, the one who fooled the others, and Vali still loved to hear tales of his cunning. It even struck him as funny that he had killed the beautiful god Baldur for no other reason, it seemed to Vali, than that the perfect one had bored him. When Vali had been a young child, Bragi had beaten him when he laughed at how Loki had contrived to make Baldur stay in the underworld after death by refusing to mourn for him.

'You like that naughty fellow so much perhaps you would like to share his torments. They lashed him to a rock for his crimes. Shall I so lash you?' he had said.

Disa had taken Vali in and consoled him. 'Not everything funny is to be laughed at,' she said. 'Well, not out loud anyway.'

He wondered how Disa was. He couldn't believe that he hadn't stayed to help her and hoped she was all right. Had the ritual been worth it? The question seemed to crumble in his mind as he felt the need to look behind him, to the north. That was the direction he had been travelling and where he instinctively felt that he wanted to go. He had to get there. But first he needed to concentrate on his deceit, make these men confident of him.

'How did you find me here?' Vali asked Orri.

Orri laughed. 'There is only one road north in the summer and it's hardly used, as the merchants prefer the sea. In the winter, when the rivers freeze, then there are a hundred quick paths this way, and your wolfman would be harder to find. In summer, one road, one opportunity for ambush, few travellers. You'd have more difficulty avoiding them than digging them out.'

'If wolfmen are so easy to find it's a wonder Lord Authun hasn't done so yet,' said Vali.

Hogni waved his hand. 'The king has other concerns,' he said.

Vali said nothing more. He knew that the summer would be an easy time to draw down the wolfmen. The reindeer were well fed and energetic, as were all the animals, and their tracks were not so easy to follow. Hunting without a bow or snares – as the wolfmen were said to do – would be very difficult. It was well known the peril they offered was greatest to summer travellers, and this was one of the reasons they had remained unmolested for so long. Kings went by boat in fine weather. Only the poor, the foolish and outlaws suffered from their attacks.

Nausea suddenly took him, as if the toad he had imagined in his throat was alive and kicking to get out. He put down the bone he'd been picking at and tried to stop himself from vomiting. He managed it, just.

'You are pale, lord. Does our meal disagree with you?' asked Orri.

Vali composed himself. 'We will continue to my homeland now,' he said.

'We have not slept, lord.'

'I have,' said Vali. 'We will go now.'

The two men made no complaint, got up and put the tack on the horses. As they did, Vali fought down the rising sickness inside him and kept up a stream of questions about Hordaland. Was it true that his father kept wolves as pets (he knew this to be false)? Did traders from the east still come to the Horda? Were the girls of the Horda still pretty?'

'The rumour is, lord, that you only have eyes for that farm girl.'

Vali made himself laugh. He had turned the conversation just the way he wanted it.

'She is a useful piece in my strategy with Forkbeard. The weaker he thinks my passion for his daughter, the greater will be her dowry.'

'You are a cunning man, sir,' said Hogni, laughing. 'They say no one in the north is your better at king's table.'

'No southern man would beat me either,' said Vali, mindful that such men as these respected bravado. 'Now bring me my horse.'

Hogni gave up his mount for his prince without question.

Vali looked across at Orri, who was swinging himself into his saddle. He was a lean man, lightly dressed, no armour, only his spear and helmet. Could he outrun him on a strange and potentially unreliable horse? No.

Vali turned to him. 'This animal stinks. Give me yours, Orri.'

Orri looked oddly at the prince. 'This one stinks the same, sir.'

'I want the horse, not a debate. Get down.'

Vali looked into Orri's eyes and the warrior thought that he glimpsed a little of King Authun in the prince. Orri dismounted, and as he did so Vali brought his own animal's hindquarters into the flank of Orri's horse. The beast stepped sideways, knocking Orri to the ground. Vali snatched the reins, put his heels into his own horse's flanks and shot forward, taking both animals with him. He was clear of the men in an instant, not even bothering to look back as he urged the creatures on.

They shouted after him.

'You have sentenced us to death, sir!'

'We cannot return without you.'

'The Rygir's fate is sealed.'

'They are as the dead!'

He didn't turn, just kept driving on up the valley, the feeling of sickness leaving him as he moved. He had, he thought, a good chance of getting away. He had two horses, was well rested and would be pursued on foot by men needing sleep.

He reached the top of the valley and found himself on a broad ridge above hills that stretched away to distant mountains skirted by trees, a fjord just beneath him. Did he follow the ridge or drop down to the east? He rode a few steps east, then north. Did he feel any more sick going in one direction than another? He couldn't really tell.

He allowed the horses to slow at the top of the hill and his mind turned back to the house and Ma Disa.

Ansuz was the rune she had carved, the rune in which she had put her faith. Vali visualised the rune in his mind, even moving his hands in the air to mark out its three lines, one vertical, the others on a slant. He tried the rhyme Disa had used.

'Who I am? I am a man. Where am I? In the hills of the north.'

He only succeeded in making himself feel ridiculous. But something did happen. His horse stumbled. He looked down at it. The animal was in a great sweat. At first he thought he might be in the presence of some supernatural thing – they were said to frighten animals – but the other horse was not sweating nearly as much. He looked around him. The light was subtly different. The ridge was coming into trees. Then he realised he had travelled a great way. The animal desperately needed rest. He dismounted and led the horses to a stream. There was plenty enough grass for pasture, though he had no food himself. Never mind, he thought. The feeling of nausea was faint but surprisingly welcome. It was a lucky coincidence to be off your food if you had none.

A fire was out of the question with pursuers on his back, so he watered the horses, removed the tack, hobbled them and waited. He didn't attempt to sleep, nor to take his mind off the cold and, beneath that, his nausea and hunger. It was as if he was driven by some instinct that told him suffering was something he could offer the gods. He had never seen the point of sacrifice, of stuffing funeral ships with gold or slaughtering animals and slaves, but here, in tiredness and discomfort, he felt connected to something fundamental inside him. His bodily pain was nothing to what he felt for her. He could endure far worse, he knew, and his love would sustain him.

The next morning he set off again, picturing that rune in his mind. He saw Disa carving it, first on the wood and then on her hand. He saw the blood drip and fall, and where it fell it ran again into the shape of the rune. Then he was aware of the warmth of the horse under him. By the position of the sun he had clearly been riding for hours. It was a peculiar feeling – driving forward with great purpose but not really knowing where he was going. The horses allowed him to travel much more quickly than he would have managed on foot. Vali found himself riding across high passes, dropping down perilous slopes of scree, fording rivers and skirting fjords, but always as a passenger, rather than as someone choosing his way. He seemed to instruct the horses without thinking about it. There were signs he was on the right route – broken and discarded footwear by the side of a trail, the occasional marks of wagon wheels and hooves.

He saw next to no one, just far-off shepherds and the occasional homestead. He took care to sound his horn as he passed, to avoid being mistaken for an outlaw, but did not stop. Only the needs of the animals slowed him down, and though sometimes he drank when they drank, he never ate and rarely slept. Thinking about Disa's rune seemed to have wakened something deep inside him, but thirst, hunger and tiredness combined to dull his conscious mind.

It was hardly surprising then that he did not hear the approach of the wolfman.

14 The Prince and the Wolf

Feileg had been watching the rider for days, assessing the man's strength. Lone horsemen in the inland mountains were never seen, and to the large part of Feileg's mind that had become wolf this was suspicious. Also, the traveller was not on the trading route. He was two days north of that, in the backcountry, just above the treeline in a narrow dark gorge, following a tiny stream. All animals are wary of things they haven't seen before and Feileg was no different. But there was something uniquely threatening about the man in the valley.

In other circumstances he would have called across the mountains to Kveld Ulf, but the shape-shifter had been gone for days, as he sometimes was, leaving Feileg to hunt with only three of the pack for company. The wolves, and Feileg, of course, wanted the horses and knew that the easiest way to get them was to wait for the man to sleep. Without Feileg's help, the wolves would have had to wait for one of the animals to wander off at night, which might not happen.

Stories of wolfmen attacking camps of travellers were sometimes true but it wasn't something they did by choice and usually only in summer. In the hungry hot months, when the animals ran swiftly and the berries were not yet on the trees, Kveld Ulf and Feileg had to take their food where they could get it.

Native traders wondered why the Whale People of the northern edge managed to travel by land without trouble from the wolfmen and imagined that they had some charm or spell that kept them safe. It was simpler than that. The Whale People lived among bears and stored their food well away from their camps, hanging it in packs from the thinnest possible branches of trees. The wolfmen would only fight if travellers caught them stealing their food and animals. The Whale People sometimes lost their dinners but always kept their lives.

Feileg waited for the rider to sleep, but the rider did not sleep, or at least Feileg could not be sure he was sleeping. When the pale grey of the long dusk came down, the man just dismounted and saw to the horses, then sat on the ground, clinging to his sword and rocking back and forth. Feileg saw few people with black hair, fewer still who seemed to care for their animals better than they did themselves and none who never ate, but none of these things accounted for the feeling of disquiet he had when looking down from his hiding place at the figure below him.

Feileg had some remaining idea of magic from his time with the berserks, but having spent so long with Kveld Ulf he no longer saw it as something separate from any other way of being. It was no more incredible that he could send himself into a trance where he would track, move and fight as a wolf than it was that a stream fell down a mountainside or that birth and death came to man and animals – no more incredible than breath, the rising and sinking of the sun and moon, the movement of the tides. To Feileg, creation seemed a rhythm that he connected to in ritual and meditation with rattle and drum. That man, there in the valley, was where the rhythm broke down, he felt. When he looked at him, he shivered. He had the wordless sense that the rider was a stumble in nature's beat.

The wolfman scented the wind. Nothing to learn there, just the smell of horses and rain coming from the dark mountain behind him. Then he realised what was strange. He wasn't interested in the rider for his horses or his food; he was curious about *him*. For some reason he wanted to see him closer. It was the sort of human feeling he had allowed to atrophy and its reawakening left him feeling puzzled and a little miserable. He put it to the back of his mind and concentrated on his hunger.

Vali's thoughts were elsewhere. He thought of Adisla, imprisoned by Forkbeard; he thought of Disa; mostly he just thought of that rune. Its image and, even more strangely, its sound as Vali imagined it, had been humming through his head for days. The rune seemed to bring with it a music that was related to how people said its name – Ansuz – but was more than that. He remembered the voice of the thing that had spoken through Disa sounding like the drawing and pushing of the surf. That was how the rune sounded.

Then, in an instant, all the human feelings he had ignored on his long ride came back. He was terribly hungry and thirsty, and tired as he had never been before. These feelings seemed important to him, to contain a message. No more nausea. He had arrived where he needed to be. He looked around, his eyes heavy and refusing to focus properly, his mind telling him that the most important task he had was sleep.

Vali pushed his face into a stream and drank. Then he opened his pack. He took out some hunks of salted bread along with some pickled fish. He ate the food quickly, drank again and then settled down. He had not made a proper bed the whole journey. Now he spread a walrus skin on the ground, put his cloak about him and used the pack as a pillow. His tiredness had not quite taken his reason away and he was careful to conceal himself with scrub beneath an overhang, but in the dwindling grey light of the midsummer dusk he could not make his eyes scan for enemies. He was simply too tired and he sank onto the comfort of his bed.

Feileg watched all this from above. Now he felt he could move. When he did, it was with liquid speed, dropping silently down the sides of the gorge to the shadows of the valley floor.

He went forward alone, the wolves watching him from the valley lip. Feileg kept to the same side of the gorge on which Vali was sleeping, slinking low but fast towards his target. The horses were past the sleeping man, and Feileg felt there was a chance he could take them without waking him. It was too big a risk, however. Who knew who was riding to meet the sleeper? Who knew if he was an experienced tracker or even a sorcerer? He would have to die. To Feileg's keen senses threat oozed from the sleeping man. It hummed like a nest of bees in a cave mouth, seeped into his consciousness like fire on the breeze. There was only one way to make it go away.

The quickest way to kill someone in their sleep depends on how they are lying. If he is on his front then it's relatively easy to break his neck with an arm around the head and a knee in the back. Feileg had done this two or three times and found that even if the neck didn't break he still had an effective stranglehold on his prey and could finish him very quickly. If the man was on his side or back then he might stamp him to death. Other times, when silence was necessary, he had power enough in his fingers to crush his throat.

Feileg — perhaps it is better to call him the wolfman because the hormonal surge he felt within him at the prospect of killing made his humanity seem a weak and withered thing — didn't make a sound as he reached the brush that concealed the sleeping man. The man was on his back and the wolfman decided to creep up on his victim and twist his neck.

There was a growl, low and guttural. The wolfman glanced around to see where it had come from. He hadn't made the noise himself. It was like nothing natural, and he felt a chill creep down his spine. Every pore seemed open and sweating, his body signalling danger with every sense. The growl came again, even lower, like rock on rock.

Feileg flattened himself to the ground. A third growl, this time like something coming from the lower earth, and a word: 'Adisla.' Feileg looked up. The noise was coming from the sleeping man. He was snoring. Feileg's mind went back to the hut of the berserks where he had been raised. His memories of that time were now just impressions: the dark of the hut, the smell of his mother's skirts, a glimpse of himself being chased in a game by the girls he considered his sisters. Only one incident stuck out. The man he had called father had snored like thunder, especially when drunk. The children had put feathers on his lips and hooted as he puffed them away. He remembered one of the girls putting one next to her father's behind to see if that moved when he farted. It *had* moved and Feileg had thought he would never stop laughing. Looking down at the sleeping Vali, he heard another strange noise, like the babble of a stream. It was, he realised, coming from himself. He was chuckling. He hadn't done that in a long time.

As he laughed, a glimpse of the meaning of human interaction returned to him, or rather a fleeting delight in inanities, and he felt a sort of fellowship with the snoring man, almost the desire to wake him and tell him how loud, how funny, he sounded. But Feileg had to kill him. The focus – those who didn't know wolfmen called it rage – that made this easier though had been carried away by his laughter. He looked hard at Vali. Feileg hadn't seen his own face since he was six and then only rarely. His image of himself had been mainly formed by looking into the shiny surfaces of the sword blades he had taken so he wasn't immediately struck by his resemblance to the man before him, but something within him made it difficult to murder him outright.

Feileg sat for a while at the man's feet. He studied him closely. He had – by ritual, the consumption of strange mushrooms, privation and lack of practice – lost the habit of thinking in words. So it was a shapeless, sliding thought that came to him as he looked at Vali's combed and clipped hair, the fine sword that lay at his side, the rich colour of his woollen coat. He could not have articulated what he felt but this made the sense no less powerful. There was himself, as he could have been, had the fates weaved him a different skein. The man had said a word: Adisla. Feileg instinctively recognised it for what it was – a girl's name. He did not feel unhappy, or at least he could not identify his emotion as unhappiness, but he did begin to feel uncomfortable about the path that the fates had chosen for him.

He breathed in, smelling something sweet and something rancid. He saw Vali's pack and felt his saliva rise. He opened it and, without pausing to examine what he found, began to eat. He ate the honey and the stale bread and the cheese. He ate the berserker mushrooms and the long root. He couldn't abide even the smell of the wolfsbane but the sleeping mixture was sweet and palatable so he sucked it down and pushed his tongue into the pot to get the last drops. Then he ate the mint and drained Vali's wineskin. He began to feel peaceful, warm and relaxed.

From up the valley the wolves began to howl, but he could not hear them to reply. Disa's white night potion had made the world soft. Feileg lay down on the grass and slept.

15 A Captive

Vali really did think he was dreaming. He came to himself with that strange sensation that you sometimes get when waking in unfamiliar surroundings, when reality makes a sudden lurch and you don't know where you are or how you got there.

At his feet, sleeping face down, was a powerfully built man dressed in little but a wolf pelt. The ruins of the pack were next to him, all food gone, and his wineskin lay flat as a blanket at his side. At first he thought it was dark but then he realised it was the shadow of the horses. They had pressed in as close as they could to him. No wonder. From down the valley he heard the call of a wolf.

Vali grabbed for his sword and drew it, pointing it at the sleeping figure. This had to be a wolfman. Vali didn't know what to do. He knew it would be far more impressive to take the bandit alive and – more than that it would be proof he had a wolfman and not some dressed-up slave. But the man – no older than he was was impressively muscled. Even the thralls who did most of the heavy labour on the farms were not made so powerfully. If he awoke while Vali was tying him up then the prince didn't fancy his chances in a wrestling competition.

Vali looked around him. The pack was completely empty, everything in it gone. There were the little cloth bags in which he'd carried Disa's herbs all torn; there was the empty honey pot and the one containing the sleeping draught.

He smiled to himself when he realised what had happened. Carefully, he pushed the tip of his sword into the wolfman's back, drawing a little blood. That was a relief, knowing that ordinary weapons could hurt him. The wolfman didn't even stir.

Vali took the cord from the saddle at his side. He had never actually needed to tie anyone up before and didn't quite know how to do it, so he erred on the side of caution, binding the man's hands behind his back, then his legs, then his hands again and his legs again.

He had never thought of himself as religious or superstitious but he was almost afraid to touch the wolfman and certainly didn't want to move the wolf pelt he wore over his head. It was a magical item, capable of transforming the man into a snarling half wolf. Even the merchant Veles Libor had taken those stories seriously.

Vali thought of the remedies for magic that he knew – not many, he'd had no reason or opportunity to learn them. However, he knew that magicians were supposed to be able to enchant you with their gaze and a way to negate this power was to blindfold them. He had nothing that would do for a blindfold; he did, however, have the bag that he had taken the rope from. But as he lifted the wolfman to slide the bag over his head, he caught a glimpse of something extraordinary.

The man was strikingly similar to Vali himself. His face was far more weatherbeaten and lean, and his hair was wild, but his beard was sparse and thin, like Vali's, his features virtually identical. Vali shivered. This was truly a shape-shifter.

He pulled the bag over the man's head, taking care not to touch the magical wolf pelt, breathed out heavily and told himself to be calm. Was this a shape-shifter? It was possible, he thought, that the man simply resembled him. He had seen very few dark-haired men. Perhaps they all looked the same. Bragi said the people of the far west islands had dark hair, and you couldn't tell one from another. He also said that they stank – and this man certainly did.

Vali thought on. He had heard rumours and stories brought back by traders of something called a fetch, an evil spirit that copied someone's appearance. He couldn't remember what it was meant to do but he was sure it wasn't very pleasant. He tried to regain his calm. He told himself he had been tired.

142

No wonder he was seeing things. The sooner he was back at Forkbeard's hall, the better, he thought. He tacked up the horses.

Vali didn't quite know the best way to transport the wolfman, so he improvised. He pulled the man up to a standing position and then shouldered him across the saddle of the horse. He tied the wolfman's hands to his feet around the animal and then looped a rope around his waist. He wound that around the pommel of the saddle at the front and the cantle at the rear. All the time the wolfman lolled and flopped as if he was dead. Vali pushed and tugged at him to make sure he was secure.

When he was satisfied with his work, the prince tied the reins of his captive's horse to his own saddle, mounted and kicked towards home. From somewhere up towards the black bulk of the mountain he heard the wolves call. He headed down the valley with the horses at a trot. The sooner he was out of this country, he thought, the better.

16 An Engagement

News of his arrival had spread from the outer farms and the people of Eikund were there in numbers to greet him as he arrived at Forkbeard's hall.

He had gone there by the most direct route, bypassing Disa's house. He'd asked the first person he'd met about her and had been told she was very poorly. Visiting her, he thought, would be too much for her at that moment and he decided to wait until the clamour that greeted his arrival had died down, though he sent her word of his success. Every child in the area was running ahead of him, shouting and whooping and calling him a hero. Some of them touched the wolfman as he passed, or threw mud and cursed him. Women too rained insults on the man, and hit him with sticks for good measure. Vali had to tell them to stop it, as they were frightening his horses. The men stood with their arms folded, shaking their heads and laughing to themselves. They had misjudged Vali, it seemed, and they were glad to have been mistaken. Finally, he had acted in a way they understood. One or two of the farmers came forward with knives, shouting that they would kill the wolfman there and then. Vali drew his sword and they backed off. They were glory thieves, he thought, and if they wanted to kill a wolfman they could go and get one of their own.

It had taken two weeks for Vali to make his way home. The return had been in some ways harder than his outward journey. Leaving Eikund, he had been in a trance and had had to make no decisions regarding his direction of travel. On his way back he had no such help and had to decide his way for himself. However, he did recognise the country he had travelled through, and in the lush northern summer his tracks were clear – hoofprints from his horses, the nibbled bushes and manure that showed he had made camp. He even managed to shorten his journey by getting fishermen to row him across a few of the fjords. They refused payment when they saw his captive, glad he had rid them of a dangerous bandit.

There were practical difficulties. The wolfman had woken up after a day and Vali had been forced to chase after his horse, which had been spooked by his kicking. Vali had talked to the man and he had become calmer, accepting his fate like an animal. The wolves had proved a disquieting presence. During the day he didn't see them, although he felt always that he was being watched, but in the long dusk he heard them in the hills. He had expected the wolfman to reply. Vali knew these sorcerers were said to command wolves. He decided that if the wolfman called for help he would have to kill him. His prisoner remained silent though.

There was the problem of untacking the horses at night, and of replacing the wolfman in the saddle every morning but, these difficulties aside, the journey had gone smoothly. They passed farmsteads and Vali asked for supplies. The farmers would have been generous to any traveller but, like the fishermen, when they saw the prince had a captured bandit, they were elated. They gave freely and Vali ate well.

At first Vali was almost pleased to see that the wolfman had developed sores from the chafing of the saddle on his side. He allowed him to drink, sparingly, once a day – though he never fully removed the bag – but he gave him no food. This meant that if he should work free of his bonds he would be less able to fight or run. Part of him was almost inclined to let him die. But Vali had finally begun to appreciate the merits of portraying himself as a hero. It might be a lie, but it gained him the respect of his fellows and made life easier. A week from home Vali had begun to feed the wolfman, to give him more water and to sit him upright on the horse. He wanted him to look fierce when he arrived back, the better to reflect on himself.

Vali's success, it was agreed, was spectacular. It had been thought the mission would take him a minimum of two months and that Adisla would hang. He had returned in less than one and she was free.

Adisla was not at the hall. With Forkbeard gone to the assembly at Nidarnes along with all the nobles and the rest of the court, enthusiasm for keeping her confined had waned. She had never been more than half a day's walk from her farm in her life so was unlikely to run off, reasoned her guards. Her habit of singing in a discordant voice during the evenings hadn't endeared her to them either, and they'd let her go back to her mother.

However, as Vali tied up his horses, he was led aside by Hogni and Orri, both in a fever of agitation.

'Prince Vali, Prince Vali,' said Hogni, 'I must talk to you.'

'You have nothing to say to me,' he said. 'Your animals are safe and you may take them back now.'

Hogni kept his voice as low as he could. 'You are in great danger.'

'Are you my vassals?'

'Yes, lord.'

'Then act like it: fetch me mead and be silent.'

'Lord, we must speak to you.'

Hogni grabbed at his arm. Vali glowered at him. 'Do you presume to touch your prince?'

'You must leave this place. You must leave now,' said Hogni.

'Why?'

'It is cursed. A calamity is about to befall these people.'

'What sort of calamity?'

'We have only heard whispers, lord. Some say it will be a plague, some say the Danes are coming, but your mother wants you out of here by the next full moon.'

'Tomorrow.' Vali smiled. 'Well, my mother can wait. You have a choice: stay here and share whatever fate befalls us, or go back to my father and do the dead lord's jig, should he

146

keep his temper long enough to hang you. Personally, I think your chances of survival are vastly better here.'

Hogni and Orri stood tall.

'We are warriors and not afraid to die.'

'Then prove it. Stay to the full moon and then I'll be happy to accompany you back to my father's court. You are dismissed.'

The Horda men walked away, overcome as much by the change in Vali as by his refusal to go with them. He was no longer the daydreaming sword-shy boy he had appeared before, but now acted in a way they would expect from the son of Authun the White Wolf.

Vali watched them go. The Rygir were beginning a celebration. A horn of mead was shoved into his hand and he drank it down. Something was happening, he didn't know what, but his mother would never have acted on hearsay. What was most likely? A plague? There was nothing he could do about that. His mother might have seen it through a witch's vision, he supposed, but Yrsa had a well-known dislike of magic. What else? He made himself think practically. Pipes were playing inside the hall; Jokull the Skald was already singing a song about him. The only eventuality he could do anything about was a raid. If that was going to happen then he should stay to defend the people who had raised him.

Vali looked down at the little port. It was empty save for a few fishing boats. Forkbeard had taken his three drakkars with him and the knarrs were all away on trading missions. He had chosen a bad time for glory, he thought.

He pulled the wolfman down from his horse and tied him to a birch tree near Forkbeard's hall. He called out in a loud voice, declaring the man his prisoner and warning that no one should do him any harm until Forkbeard had seen him. More mead was offered to him. He accepted. Then Adisla was there, running down the hillside, calling out his name. She was laughing, almost jumping with joy. Vali couldn't help but start laughing himself, the sort of laugh that comes from someone who bends to tie his shoe and feels a rock whizz past his head.

She fell on him and hugged him, and he kissed her as she clung to him.

'I have to say,' she said, 'I didn't have a great deal of faith you would make it back.'

'We're so alike,' said Vali. 'Neither did I.'

She laughed again, although when he looked down at her he could see she was crying.

'How did you do it?'

'I don't know. I'm waiting to hear what the skalds come up with. I'm going to say I challenged him to three competitions, eating, drinking and fighting, and made him so drunk with the drinking that I tied him up. What do you think?'

'They'll say you fought him.'

'Well,' said Vali, 'let them then. Who knows, maybe I did. I would have fought a score of wolfmen for you.'

'Only a score?' said Adisla.

'There has to be a limit,' said Vali, 'and a score is mine. One more than that and you'd be on your own.'

This joking and teasing was familiar to them but there was more to it now, something more insistent. Vali felt that his only way forward was with this girl, the only way he could see the future. He had to tell her what had been between them since the moment they met but neither of them had ever quite managed to say.

'I love you.'

She looked into his eyes. 'Yes.'

'You don't say you love me.'

'Because the feeling is too strong. If I speak it I would never be able to deny it.'

She hardly managed to get the end of the sentence out, stammering into sobs and putting her hand to her face to disguise her tears.

'Do you intend to deny it?'

She said nothing and turned her face away.

'You cannot forget me, Adisla.'

'I'll never forget you.' She threw her arms around him and wept into his shoulder.

'Will you marry him?'

Adisla stepped back from him, composed herself and looked directly into Vali's eyes. Even through her tears she looked so pretty, thought Vali. He wanted to stop her crying, to make it all all right for her, to see her smile and hear her laugh, but he knew that he was the cause of all her miseries. He was a hair's breadth from everything he had ever wanted – the girl he loved, a beautiful summer afternoon, the sun warm beneath the fresh breeze – but it may as well all have been an ocean away.

'You will?' he said.

'Vali, I will not be your concubine and I cannot be your wife. What choice do I have?'

Vali nodded. 'Drengi is a fine man. He's been a good friend to all of us. I wish you could have picked someone who I could have consoled myself by hating.'

'I didn't pick him, Vali. How many men are there to choose from? Five farmers' sons in the whole area, and three of those wouldn't look at me because I have such a skinny dowry. And I am old, Vali, three summers past the time most girls are married. Fate put us together.'

'No,' said Vali. 'Fate put *us* together. Our skein is woven into one cloth. The wolfman was given to me – I didn't need to lift a finger. The gods were on my side.'

'I've never heard you mention the gods before.'

'I've never needed them before. I swear, Lord Odin, give me this girl or I will move against you in whatever way I can.'

On a tree behind the hall two ravens alighted.

Adisla's eyes widened. 'Well,' she said, stroking Vali's cheek, 'he's heard you now.'

Vali felt tears come into his own eyes, though he chuckled. 'Well, listen to this then, you couple of mangy chickens. Tell your master that if I don't get what I want then I'm coming for him. He should keep his spear by his side because if he defies me the gods' final day starts here!' He tapped his sword.

The ravens took off again, moving low across the buildings, their black shapes rising up and over the hill like forgetful little pieces of the night flapping out of the day.

'Sshhh!' said Adisla, almost ducking. 'What if those are his intelligencers?' She laughed but Vali could see that she meant what she said.

He smiled. 'Let's hope they are,' he said, 'because I want him to hear the message.'

Vali wasn't sure at first if the blow had caught him on his chest or his back. It was so hard that it nearly knocked him into Adisla. He turned to see Bragi, the old man's face glowing and his arms wide.

'You did it, boy, you did it. I never had a moment's doubt. How could you fail with the training you've had? You did it.'

'Thank you, Bragi,' said Vali. 'I couldn't have done it without you.'

The old man almost danced a jig.

'Let me see the old girl,' he said, taking the sword from Vali's scabbard. 'I bet you had a good sup of wolf blood, didn't you, my lady?'

Vali looked at Adisla. There was the destiny he wanted – home, hearth and love – ready to walk away from him. He looked at Bragi, the destiny that had been thrust upon him, and for the first time saw it was useless to resist.

'I killed three of them,' said Vali. 'It was the crafty pommel strike you drilled into me that did for two.'

'Good lad, good lad! More mead, more mead!' said Bragi. 'This is a king, didn't I tell you, this is a king!'

17 Strange Meeting

Vali stayed in the hall, drinking away the raw emotions that were in him. Adisla did not join the party. She had said what she had to say and could see that her presence was causing him torment.

Vali collapsed with the others who had celebrated his return – a collection of old warriors, youths and the handful of unfavoured jarls who had stayed behind when Forkbeard sailed east. He became drunker and more unhappy with every sip he took. Eventually – he couldn't remember how it happened – he was fighting someone. His opponent was worse for wear than he was and collapsed on the floor under his blows, cold unconscious. All Vali could focus on was Bragi's face, red and roaring, holding up his arm and saying what a mighty man he had raised. The acclaim of the hall rang in his ears. He could drink no more and crawled beneath a bench, where he slept, his body restless but his mind dead.

Adisla, however, did not sleep. She returned to her mother and told her to accept the offer of marriage from Drengi. Disa, who had not been able to leave her bed since she was burned, hugged her daughter to her.

'You're sure. You'll leave your prince behind?'

'This is the fate that has been woven for me. The shore may as well wish to be the sea as I to marry him.'

Disa held the sobbing girl to her.

'Go on,' said Adisla. 'Let it be done quickly.' Disa let her go and sent Manni up to the hill farms.

Adisla could not sleep that night – though it wasn't the enduring sun that kept her awake but her thoughts. It was no use, her bed might have been made of nettles for all the chance she had of sleeping in it. She got up and wandered down to the sea. It was as near to night as the midsummer had to offer, a pale washed-out light like that of the pre-dawn rather than true deep darkness. She found herself by the hall, listening to the sounds of drunken laughter from inside. It was late but the drinking showed no signs of stopping.

Adisla couldn't bring herself to share in the fun, even though she had the most to celebrate. She felt hollow with misery but knew she had done the right thing. Her thoughts were like trolls, reaching at her from the darkness of her mind. She tried to lose herself in the beauty of the moon, low and huge against the sky of smoky silver. It was nearly full. For a month or more her destiny had been tied to it. Now, in days, she thought, Forkbeard would be home. She thought of the story of how the god of the moon had snatched two children while they drew water at a well, and how those children now rode with him in his chariot in the sky, pursued by a dreadful wolf called hate, who snapped at their heels. She had a wolf following her, one that had been set on her at birth – her station, her rank. She had seen what she wanted as if from across an impassable river.

Suddenly she felt very cold. She was, she noticed, sitting in the shadow of a pale birch tree. The darkness there seemed unnaturally deep and the air around her was very still, as if it had a weight to it, one that she would struggle to push away. And behind her she felt a presence, something quite unlike anything she had felt before, something that seemed born of cold waters and dark, damp spaces.

'Is there someone there?' She felt ridiculous saying this.

She stood and looked around. Like an arrow storm, starlings broke across the moon, wheeling in a shifting black cloud that turned and darted as one. The sudden changes in the birds' direction made Adisla think of a thousand tiny gates opening and closing in the sky and of a story Vali had told her, one he'd got from Arab merchants, of a djinn, a demon of smoke, towering over her.

As quickly as they had come the birds were gone and with

them the cold and oppressive feeling in the air. It was then she thought of the wolfman. She looked up past the last of the houses to the single birch where he was tied.

She was curious to see this strange bandit who had been forced to trade his life for hers, so she made her way up the hill. When she got to the birch, Tassi, the fat old man who had been charged with guarding him, was sitting on a low three-legged stool and looking very unhappy. Next to him was the wolfman, seated on the ground, leaning against the tree with his hands tied to it behind his back. He still had the bag on his head. The people of Eikund shared Vali's superstition about sorcerers and were not about to allow him to enchant them.

'Hello, Tassi,' said Adisla.

'You're not about to start singing, are you? He might be a wolfman but he doesn't deserve that. We draw the line at hanging 'em round here.'

'No,' said Adisla.

She looked at the wolfman. He was naked apart from a wolf pelt around his back and his body was smeared in a grey substance that she took to be chalk dust. The only places free of the grey were two red sores on his stomach and chest.

His muscles were remarkable, even to a farm girl who lived among people strong through toil. Even the berserks, with their potions and their constant drilling with weapons, their wrestling and their tests of strength, were not made like that. The man's muscles seemed almost twisted onto his bones, like willow roots around stone.

She was almost inclined to check he was securely tied – she wondered that a normal rope could hold him.

'Quite a specimen, isn't he?' said Tassi. 'Although I got tired of looking at him after about ten breaths and now I wouldn't mind just getting slaughtered.'

Adisla didn't reply. She was scared of the wolfman but intrigued by him. Was it true what people said – that he had the head of a wolf, or that only the best steel could cut him? The

153

man didn't look dangerous now. He was clearly exhausted and breathing heavily.

'I said,' said Tassi, 'that I wouldn't mind the chance to take a cup of ale.'

'So?'

'Well, if you are going to be here for a while, couldn't you watch him and if he tries to get away just come and get me?'

'Couldn't you have paid one of the children to do that?' Then she remembered: Tassi was notoriously mean. He didn't pay for anything if he could help it.

He shrugged as if she had made a ludicrous suggestion.

'Go and have a drink,' she said, 'but don't be too long, I want to go home to bed soon.'

'Make sure you don't take him with you,' said Tassi, smiling and getting up.

'What?'

'I see the way you look at him,' he said. 'He's out of bounds but, should you be in the mood . . .'

'Go and have your drink,' said Adisla.

'As you like,' said Tassi. He slouched off towards the hall.

Adisla didn't like to admit it but Tassi had been right to a point. She did find the wolfman fascinating, but she couldn't find a man like that attractive. He stank for a start, a musty smell more animal than human. She sat down on the stool. She wanted to say something sympathetic, something to make him feel better, but couldn't think of anything. Instead, she heard herself ask: 'Are you sorry for your crimes now?'

The wolfman said nothing. A shadow flitted across her and Adisla looked up to see what it was. There was nothing there, though the speed of its passing made her think of the starlings. She was possessed by a sudden urge to see what he looked like. She thought that if he tried to enchant her then she would just look away.

There was no one about and the riotous sounds from the hall were as loud as ever. She leaned forward and touched his arm. It was just as it looked, hard as a tree. Some of the grey came off on her fingers. She licked at it. As she had thought, it was some sort of chalk. The wolfman had not flinched when she touched him and this made her bolder. She lifted up the hood on his head. Now he did move, his head lolling forward. At first she thought he really did have an animal's head. Then she realised it was the pelt of a large wolf, which had slipped down to cover his face. He coughed, and stretched his neck. Gingerly she lifted the pelt and was so surprised she sat back down on the stool. Vali was looking straight at her.

'You *are* a sorcerer!' The implications of what she saw began to sink in. If this was a shape-shifter, if he could appear exactly as Vali, then – if he got free – he could take the prince's place, eat with them, play and who knows what more? Perhaps they would have climbed the hills and lain kissing on the grass together. Perhaps they would have gone out in the little boat, as she and Vali often did. And then what? Murder, as wolves always murdered.

The man blinked at her. He cleared his throat and said slowly, 'Not a sorcerer.' His voice was low and cracked, with a strange accent. He produced his words carefully, as if they were fragile things that might break if he let them out too quickly. It was as if he was unused to speaking.

'Then what are you?'

'I am a wolf.'

Adisla was careful not to look at him directly for too long, in case he cast a spell on her.

'You've stolen the face of the prince.'

'This face was given me by a brother. I am proud to wear it. I look through his eyes and he sees again through me. I wear his fur and he runs again, through me.'

Adisla realised he was talking about the wolf pelt.

'You are a fetch,' she said, 'a subtle, scheming shape-changer. Who sent you here?'

'I stole the food of a black-hued man. He enchanted me and brought me to this place.'

Now Adisla did laugh. Vali, she well knew, was more

interested in playing king's table and mooning about the hills than he was in magic.

'You're black-hued yourself, no need for insults.'

'It is true,' he said. 'I am a wolf.'

'And now what is to happen to you, wolf?'

He said nothing, just looked into her eyes.

'They will hang you,' she said.

Still he didn't speak but she couldn't shake his gaze. Was this what it was like, she wondered, to be enchanted?

'You don't seem too concerned about it.'

'I am a wolf.'

She thought that he didn't understand the trouble he was in. Or did death not mean the same to him as it did to her?

'You are the Fenris Wolf,' she said, 'fettered and chained.'

'Fenrisulfr will break his fetters one day, say the prophecies.'

Adisla felt a chill go through her. She had always found that myth disturbing. The god Loki had had monstrous children, one of which was the gigantic Fenris Wolf. The gods had been so afraid of Fenrisulfr that they tricked it into fetters. Lashed by a cord called Thin to a rock called Scream, a sword thrust into its jaws to keep them open, its saliva ran out to become a river called Hope. The tale said the wolf would lie there until the twilight of the gods – Ragnarok – when it would break its bonds and kill the All-Father Odin. It would usher in a new age, ruled by beautiful, just, fair spirits, not the corrupt, battle-mad, vengeful and deceitful gods they called the Aesir, of which Odin was the chief.

The rhyme from the prophecy went through her head.

The fetters shall burst and the wolf run free
Much do I know and more can see.

Her mother had told her the story when she was a child and Adisla had been thrilled and scared.

'But you are not the Fenris Wolf,' she said, 'or you would break your fetters.'

'No,' said the wolfman. He seemed very sad.

'Would you like some food or drink?' said Adisla.

'Yes,' said the wolfman.

Adisla went over to the hall. Everyone was too drunk to notice her, everyone except Vali, who caught her eye and then looked away. She took some bread and butter from the mead bench, along with a cup. On her way back she drew water from the well and dipped the cup into the bucket. Then she approached the wolfman again.

She fed him the bread, pushing it into his mouth, almost afraid he might bite her. He ate it slowly, not gulping it like an animal as she had expected him to do. Still he held her gaze. He's showing me he's human, she thought. He says he's a wolf but that's not really what he wants me to see. Then she held the cup to his lips.

'More?'

'Yes.'

She refilled the cup three or four times. The man did not seem like a savage or a sorcerer. His eyes were not furious; he didn't spit at her or curse her. Adisla studied him closely. She could see he was very like Vali indeed, although his face was more weather-beaten and leaner. She reached forward and touched his hair — it was like Vali's too. But he wasn't exactly the same, only very similar. Did she still think he was a sorcerer? She didn't know.

'I didn't think wolfmen could speak,' she said.

'I only know two,' he said. 'One doesn't, but I do, when I must.'

'When is that?'

'Not much,' said the wolfman.

'Is your mother a wolfwoman. Or a wolf?' she said.

'My family are like you. I lost them when I was young.'

'They died?'

'No, I lost them, on a hillside. My wolf father looked after me from then.'

He was more like Vali than Adisla had thought. He too had

been effectively orphaned at an early age. Why did she feel so sorry for this bandit, so fascinated by him?

'You were given to a wizard?'

'Not a wizard, a wolf.'

'A wolf like you?'

'Yes.'

They said nothing for a while; she just helped him eat and drink.

Then the wolfman said, 'Why are you helping me?'

'I don't know.'

'Your kinsmen beat me and tied me here. Are you a traitor to them?'

'I am true to myself,' said Adisla. 'I am a free woman and no one commands me.'

The wolfman was watching her very intently now.

'What is your name?' she said.

'I am a wolf.'

'Don't wolves have names?'

'No.'

'Well, wolf, I am Adisla,' she said.

For the first time he broke from staring at her to look at the ground.

'My family called me Feileg,' he said, 'but I lost my name when I lost them.'

'You seem unused to kindness, Feileg.'

'I am a wolf,' he said. She found herself looking into his eyes again. They were like Vali's, without the humour but also without the discomfort that so often radiated from the prince.

She sensed he wanted to ask her something. Was this it? The spell that enchanters work, was it coming over her?

'What?' said Adisla.

'Marry me,' said the wolfman.

If it was a spell, that broke it. Adisla burst out laughing. 'I'm afraid, sir, that your prospects seem a little bleak for that right now.'

158

'I will escape,' said the wolfman. 'Marry me. We have spoken, we have exchanged kindnesses. Then you go to your kin and they arrange it. My mother said this is how it is done. I have many treasures in the hills and I will spread them before you. Go to your kin.'

Adisla stood.

'I'm afraid it's a bit more complicated than that,' she said. 'I will not marry you, but I'll stay here and protect you for the night, so you'll come to no harm until the great harm that awaits you on the full moon. And I shall sing to you.'

And Adisla did sing, not in the discordant way she had used to torment her captors, but as she could, clear and high, a song about a farmer's boy who risked his life for the love of a princess, and was killed by her brothers as he slept next to his beloved.

'Do your people allow women to sing such things?' said the wolfman when she was finished.

'No,' said Adisla, 'but there are none here to hear it. And I am not an enchantress, as you are not a sorcerer.' She looked down at the cup in her hands. 'There's no one here to bewitch anyway, even if we were.' And then she sat with him and watched the moon climb in the sky.

18 The Raid

Vali woke with a jolt as if on a beaching ship. At first he wondered where he was and then he remembered – Forkbeard's hall. He had a thick tongue and a thicker head. He needed desperately to puke. He looked around him. Everywhere people were slumped at the benches, some with drinks still in their hands. He wanted to piss, to be sick, to do everything to get rid of the tight humming feeling in his head.

'Ale, boss?' said Bragi, proffering him a horn. The man was still awake, still drinking, despite the fact that everyone around him had collapsed.

'I'll take my next one in Valhalla,' said Vali. Just looking at the drink made him want to be ill. He staggered outside the hall and down to the moorings, where he did what he had to do.

It was hot. The sun was high and felt like it was boiling his head. He had to get cooler so he waded deep into the water and then just lay back. The cold seemed to restore him and by the time he came out of the sea he felt better. He looked around. No one. He went to the well, drew up the bucket and poured it over himself, drinking as he did so. He glanced over to the wolfman. Someone had spread a cloth over him to protect him from the sun. Who would have done that? There was someone sleeping on the ground behind him, almost completely wrapped up in a cloak. Vali's eyes were full of sleep and moisture, and he could neither make them focus nor force his befouled brain think about anything beyond his thirst.

He took another drink and looked out to sea. On the horizon he saw a smudge of grey in the sky. At first he didn't recognise it for what it was. He rubbed his eyes. He was hungry and thought he'd return to the hall to see if there were any leftovers from the night before.

And then it dawned on him. That smudge was smoke. It was the fire on a ship. Longships carried rock ballast for stability, and it was possible to cook on top of it. Someone, just over the horizon, was cooking something. Why cook so close to land? Merchants could be in the village in no time, where they could ingratiate themselves with their hosts by buying food, along with the ale to wash it down. Then he remembered the raid on the abbey. Berserks cooked before they went into battle, stewing up their herbs and their frenzying mushrooms.

'Don't be silly,' he told himself.

Then the truth of the situation struck him like a fist. Of course! It was an attack.

Forkbeard had gone to the regional assembly, taking sixty of his best fighting men with him. If any enemy had discovered that then they would know the Rygir village was virtually undefended. Who was left? Farmers, old warriors, women and children. What better time to attack?

It all fell into place. That was why Vali had been called away. His mother hadn't wanted him there when the raid took place. Why hadn't his mother sent aid? Because Authun was mad but still in command. She could buy grain, marry her daughters and send for her son, but the White Wolf's warriors moved only for him while he was alive. Without Authun to lead the Horda, she couldn't act to help friends or strike enemies. And hadn't Vali's sister Dalla married the Dane Ingwar? That had happened because the Horda were powerless − they needed marriage alliances to protect them. As long as no one knew of Authun's illness the Danish kings would gladly offer their sons − they thought they were buying protection. In fact, they had been deceived into offering it. But why hadn't Yrsa sent word to Forkbeard? Because she feared Vali would not marry his daughter. His message saying that he would refuse to marry Ragna had reached the Horda court. If Yrsa could not be sure that Vali would go through with the marriage then she might fear the treaty with the Rygir would fail. The queen wanted to keep her neighbours occupied with another enemy. So why had the Rygir been left unwarned? Because, in a moment of stupidity, Vali had said he would not do his duty. He had visited this calamity on the Rygir and he felt ashamed for it.

Vali ran into the hall.

'Get up, get up! The enemy is here. Get up, get up!' he shouted.

There were still some coals burning in the fire. He scooped several onto a bread plate, gathered some straw from the floor and ran out to the beacon, which seemed to take an age to light.

'Hurry up, hurry up! Get your arms and shields, we've got a fight on!'

Bragi strolled out like a man surveying his land on a fine morning. 'What, lord?'

'Look, the horizon – smoke. It's warships, I know it.'

'That or a trader cooking up some mackerel,' said Bragi. He was calm.

'He's either coming here, in which case he'd eat here, or he's going past, in which case he'd never risk alerting our ships. When have you seen smoke like that before?'

'Not here, but—'

'Who am I?'

'Vali, prince of the sword-Horda,' said Bragi.

'Whose son am I?'

'Authun, lord of battle.'

'Then respect me and call to arms. Call to arms!'

Bragi shrugged but took a horn from his belt. One of the endearing things about the old warrior was that he was almost permanently dressed for a fight. He even carried his helmet with him much of the time, though he drew the line at wearing his byrnie. He had been known to take his shield if he wasn't going far, however.

Bragi blew three blasts on his horn, then walked into the hall and started rousing the men. At first few believed him and thought it a prank but, urged on by Vali, they stumbled outside and saw the beacon burning. That was never lit as a joke. Up on the hill another one answered it. Behind that, they knew, would be others, calling the men of the farms down to defend the shore.

Vali looked at what he had. Forty men, or rather boys and grandfathers, some still half drunk. He shouted and kicked at them to arm themselves. Hungover and red-faced, they opened chests in the hall, taking out weapons, padded jackets, a couple of byrnies and helmets. Shields and spears were found in a separate storeroom. Men stumbled and tripped as they pulled on their gear, clattered into each other as they reached for the weapons.

'Sails!' shouted Bragi from outside. Despite being clearly very drunk, the old man had his byrnie on and had taken up two spears, one stout and long, the other shorter and thinner, for throwing.

Vali didn't bother putting on a byrnie, though he had a right to one. He grabbed a seax, a shield and a helmet, and gave them all to Bragi.

'Shield wall at the top of the hill, the Hogsback, on the cart track at the side of the copse,' he said. 'They won't get round the back of us through the wood, not in a hurry anyway. Have these for me there behind it. Put five archers in the woods and tell them not to fire until I give the order. Nothing as the enemy advance. Nothing, do you understand?'

'Yes, lord, but will they come to the top of the hill? Surely they'll plunder here and be gone.'

'They have berserks aboard. They'll come,' said Vali. 'I'll ensure it. Our only chance is to fight them there. Get to the hill and set your wall, though be ready to receive me – I'll be coming through it at speed.'

Bragi had been amazed when Vali appeared with the wolf-man. He was even more amazed at the transformation in him now.

Hogni and Orri appeared from the hall.

'Ah, Horda – good men,' said Vali. 'You'll go with the

archers into the woods to cover the front of the shield wall. You'll see that they do not fire until my command. Then, and you'll know the time, you'll attack the enemy from the back.'

'Yes, lord.' Hogni and Orri were too hungover to argue, to point out that they were veterans of five raids each. Anyway, Vali was a prince. In battle, that is what princes are for, if nothing else – they give the orders.

The longships were closer now. They could hear the baying of the berserks, the sound of them beating their shields and their bodies, the oaths to Odin and the curses on the enemy. The voices were indistinct, but if you had heard the chanting before you would know what it said.

'Odin!'

'That means fury!'

'Odin!'

'That means war!'

'They speak our language, sir,' said Orri.

Bragi shook his head. 'Look at the ships; they sit so shallow in the water. These bastards are Danes – their ships do no more than kiss the waves. I saw them at Kaupangen. They've hired a few pirates from near here, no doubt, but these are Danes.'

Vali turned to his band. 'I am Vali, son of Authun the White Wolf, plunderer of the five towns, peerless in battle. As the prince here, I assume command, as there are no princes of your own to lead you. There are three ships there, eighty warriors at least. It is beyond us to fight so many. Yet we will make them pay so dear a price for what they take that they will curse the day they set sail for our shores. Until I arrive at the top of the hill, Bragi is in command. Offer a prayer to your gods and tell them to prepare to receive you.'

Bragi nodded and beckoned the men after him. They streamed through the village, women, children and dogs chasing after them.

*

Adisla woke at the commotion. She looked around her. She had slept in the open, a borrowed cloak over her, and her hair was wet with dew.

There was shouting and screaming and the smell of fire. Children were wailing, men and women crying out. She looked over to where Vali was marshalling his force and then out to sea. Three sails. Chanting. She knew what was coming. So did the wolfman. For the first time he strained against his bonds.

She had heard what Vali had said: they were all to die. It seemed wrong that someone who had lived his life so free should die tied like a pig for slaughter. She took the bag from Feileg's head.

The first thing the wolfman saw after Adisla was Vali. He let out a low snarl of such fury that Adisla stepped back. Feileg had remembered the face of the sleeping man and guessed who had taken him prisoner.

She looked at him. 'I intend to let you go,' she said, 'but first you must swear that you will not harm me or mine.'

'I will protect you. I will serve you.'

'Swear it, on whatever gods you have.'

'I swear it on the sky and the land,' said Feileg.

'Then this is the only service I require of you: that you will not harm him, my love, who brought you here,' said Adisla. 'I hold you to your oath. Can you keep it?'

'Yes.'

She took a knife from her belt and cut through his bonds. The ships were closer now, the men almost individually visible. She sawed and cut. The wolfman was bound at the hands and at the neck. No one noticed what she was doing in the panic. Eventually he was free.

Feileg stood, moving like an old man getting out of bed.

'Now go. You are in danger from both sides. Go!'

'I will stay with you.'

'No,' said Adisla. 'I forbid it. Go. You swore me your service now do as I say and run.'

The wolfman stared at her. In some ways he reminded her of an animal, a dog, craning its head in curiosity at hearing an unfamiliar sound.

'The wolfman is free, sir!'

'Adisla, stay still; I'm coming!'

Vali was a bowshot away but coming towards them at a run, a seax in his hand. The wolfman saw his advance and bared his teeth.

'Your oath!' said Adisla.

The wolfman took her by the shoulders. 'I will not forget you,' he said.

And then he kissed her – a child's kiss, no more than pushing his lips into hers – and was gone. Adisla was rigid with shock as Vali arrived at her side.

'Adisla, are you all right? How did he get free? Are you all right? Darling, are you all right? Where is Drengi? Where is he? Where is your betrothed?'

'I think he went with the other men to the hill.'

Vali frowned. 'Well, he should be looking for you. You should be his first concern.'

'What shall I do?'

'Go to the farm and get your mother out into the fields. You must hide – you know the places. I'll look for you when it's done.'

Adisla hugged him and for the first time in her life understood the feelings of the women on the quayside as they wished their husbands off to war, and she knew what a man wants at such times – not reminders of the love he's leaving, not adjurations to keep safe or wishes for luck. A man in battle needs courage, no thought that his death will inconvenience or upset anyone but himself. So Adisla kissed him and said the traditional parting words from a wife to a warrior setting out for battle.

'Kill a hundred of them for me.'

He nodded, squeezed her to him and then let her go.

'Run,' he said. 'Run for your life.'

166

She did, tearing up the hill towards her farm.

Vali looked back to the sea. By the quay he saw the most extraordinary thing. The wolfman was facing the three long-ships alone. He stood on the little beach growling and beating his chest, standing tall and upright one instant, crouching low to the sand the next. The berserks were baying to attack, but the ruddermen had brought the boats about to get a better look at him. To the sober men in charge of the ships it seemed they were confronted by a werewolf and they wanted a clear sight of him before rushing in.

Feileg was delaying the landing and that gave Vali time to act. He had no idea where Forkbeard stored his treasure – that secret was known only by a very few people indeed – but in the hall there were enough fine cups and wall hangings to suit Vali's purpose. He tore a couple of hangings down and wrapped as many of the metal plates and cups as he could inside them. Then he tied them loosely and ran outside. He knew the berserks would follow him simply if he taunted them but he wanted to give the rest of the warriors a reason to chase him too.

Now he really could see the enemy clearly. The longships were only a short distance from the shore and parallel to it. The warriors were screaming, howling like wolves and roaring like bears, some jabbering incoherently, some even fighting each other. Berserks, definitely. Vali swallowed. Good. That was what he wanted.

The ruddermen now evidently decided that one wolfman, no matter how magical, would not stand in their way. Turned by their oars, the prows of the boats swung towards the shore. Picking up the pace, the rowers sped the longships in to attack.

The wolfman had done what he wanted, given Adisla more time to get away. Now he too ran, and Vali was the only one left in the settlement, just a couple of scouts watching him from up the hill.

He waved to them and they waved back. He got onto his

horse, swinging the clanking bundles up beside him. It wasn't easy to balance the load but he managed it, dropping a couple of plates as he did so. That didn't matter; in fact, it was all to the good. Vali wheeled his horse towards the shore, trotting towards the onrushing Danes.

A couple of berserks couldn't contain their desire to get at him and leaped into the water, half drowning as they tried to stay afloat without letting go of their weapons.

Vali turned the horse side on to the approaching boats and screamed at them, 'Too late, you cowards. Can't you see? Forkbeard's treasure is flying from you!'

A few arrows flew from the nearest longship and Vali instinctively pulled back on the reins. Not one arrow struck him but the animal took fright, staggering sideways, bucking and kicking him off. Vali landed in the water and the tapestries spilled open, showering cups and plates into the sea. The clatter spooked the horse even more and it bolted.

A roar went up from the incoming boats. Vali was badly winded but had no time to recover. He gathered up what he could in his arms and staggered up the beach towards another horse.

Behind him he heard a heavy crunch as the ships grounded.

'Odin, slayer! Odin, madman! Odin, war-drunk! Odin! Odin! Odin!'

The berserks didn't even stop for the plates and cups, just charged at him. Vali made the other horse, untied it and mounted. He had one silver cup left from the hoard he had bundled into the tapestries. He raised it towards the berserks. As he did so, he saw a familiar face. At the front of the charge was a massive man in a white bear skin, a cleft right down the front of his forehead. It was the berserk who had killed the monks, Bodvar Bjarki. He had a throwing spear in one hand and the huge iron rattle in the other. So now he was their leader.

It had been three years and Vali was a stronger man than he had been then, but he reminded himself of his plan. Still, he called to the berserk: 'Remember me, you half-witted coward? Have you come to pay me for my slaves you killed?'

The berserk heaved the spear at Vali but the prince dropped his head flat to the horse and it sailed over him.

'I'm afraid I'm going to require a little more than a spear. That can't be worth much, even after we've scraped your shit off it.'

The berserk became even more enraged, charging up the beach without drawing his weapons. Vali was sorely tempted to ride him down but reminded himself that he had faith in the merits of organisation and a cool head on the battlefield. One of the reasons he'd given his gear to Bragi was that he didn't even want the option to fight. This battle, he thought, would be won in the mind, like a game of king's table, and he had to stick to his plan. He urged his horse a little way up the hill and then turned to see what was happening. The more sober warriors were disembarking, and he saw the banner of Haarik, king of the northern Danes of Aggersborg – the black dragon. As he'd thought: Danes fronted by local berserks. He wondered if the berserks had suggested the raid. No time to think though. He kicked the horse off at a fast walk, careful to stay out of range of the spears but not far enough away so he couldn't be seen.

He heard the shouts behind him.

'We will have your blood.'

'Catch him!'

Good. He had their attention. Already Forkbeard's hall was burning but the berserks were chasing him. Would they lead the rest of the raiders? He stopped as he left the settlement, holding up the cup again. He saw the man holding Haarik's standard point at him, then a group of around forty warriors began to follow the berserks up the hill at the trot.

He rode away, the taunts of the enemy at his back. The most dangerous part of his plan was about to unfold. As he approached the woods he had to let the berserks catch him. He dismounted and held up the cup.

'Cowards!' he shouted. 'Cowards!' There was no point in finer insults on the battlefield; they would not be heard. The horse panicked and ran off. Now Vali had no means of escape. He would succeed or he would die, he knew.

A scrum of six or eight berserks was following Bjarki up the hill. They were near and a couple of spears thudded into the bank beside the track. Vali turned to see them screaming and posturing, pointing at him and howling. They'd stopped following, though. Vali pulled one of the spears out and threw it back, heaving it far too far as the heat of battle filled him. Never mind, he'd achieved his goal. The berserks came charging after him again.

He ran as fast as he could, aware that he was in a narrow sunken lane and that the advantage he hoped to give to his own force could now work against him, cutting down his scope for weaving and giving his enemies a clear target.

He was lightly dressed, but so were the berserks. They were bigger, heavier men though, and he was faster than them down the lane. Another spear thunked into the track beside him, then a hand axe hit him on the back, but luckily not with its cutting edge. He knew they were close – the effective range of the axe was nowhere near that of the spear. He hoped the shield wall would be in place as he came to the crest of the hill.

It was, thirty men in four ranks crammed tight into the lane. It was then he realised he had nowhere to go. He didn't want to tell the wall to part because he wasn't sure it would close again in time. He glanced behind him. The berserks were no more than twenty paces away.

'Spears down!' he shouted, sprinting towards the wall.

Bragi was at the front. He slapped down four or five spears so they were pointing at the ground.

Vali pulled one last effort from his legs and ran flat out. Then he spotted a tree root sticking out from the bank and veered towards the side of the lane. He hit it with one foot and thrust himself up over the heads of his men, missing his footing on the bank on the way down, crashing into the back rank and sending three men tumbling.

'Spears up!' shouted Bragi. 'Spears up!'

The men levelled their spears as the berserks came loping and howling towards them. One of the boys at the front fainted at the sight of the enemy. The men behind pulled him back by the legs. Vali's sword was nowhere but there was no time to think about that. He shoved on his helmet, snatched up his shield and bundled forward through the line, moving to fill the gap. It was tight-packed at the front, no room to swing a weapon, which hardly mattered as Vali didn't have one.

'Spear! Spear!' shouted Vali, but no one heard him. He'd have to make do with just the shield until he got a chance to find his seax or another weapon. He gripped the straps behind the boss tight in his fist. Bragi could actually punch with a shield but Vali had never got the knack. The point, said the old man, was not to swing it but to drop your weight behind your hand in a quick jolt, the whole forward movement being no more than the width of a fist. He'd regularly seen Bragi fell men with the move for a bet when the old man was in drink, and now he wished he'd tried harder to learn the trick.

The women and the children behind him were screaming, the berserks were howling, his own men were shrieking curses and clattering their weapons. The noise alone was dizzying. The back rank, though disordered by Vali's arrival, got some missiles away. Two spears, a hand axe and a couple of rocks flew towards the enemy. A spear took a berserk in the leg and, though he tried to run on, he was hopelessly encumbered. As the butt end of the spear dug into the bank, he screamed, stumbled and fell. The axe missed and the rocks too.

The berserks had no shields, just spears or rocks in one hand, huge axes in the other. Vali ducked behind his shield as a volley of missiles came in and was glad that he had. A spear tip punched straight through the front of his shield and stuck there, though it caused him no harm. No one around him seemed injured, and for the moment it seemed the wall had done its job.

Some of the spears had done theirs too. Vali's shield was now heavy and unwieldy and he knew he would have to let it go if an enemy pulled at the spear and it didn't come free. The berserks crashed into the wall, less hard than he had anticipated. They had to clear the opposing spears first, hacking them down with their axes or just grabbing them and pulling them aside. The thump that Vali had expected never came, just a squabble of weapons as each side fought for advantage. Then his own men attacked from the back rank, long spears reaching over him to stab at the attackers. One berserk got through, driving his axe into a shield deep through the rim into the wood. Then another berserk did the same, and another. Vali saw that there was more method to their attack than he'd credited them with. They were battering down the shields, or sticking weapons into them, gaining levers by which they could pull them away, with the owner attached ideally, or making them so unwieldy they were unusable.

A berserk in front of Vali hurled his axe into the wall and then took hold of the spear that was through Vali's shield, simultaneously drawing his knife. He clearly intended to rip aside the shield and then do for Vali in close. The spear pulled free though, and he fell back. Vali did not press his advantage by coming forward to stamp on him.

'Hold the wall!' screamed Vali. 'Hold the wall!'

Then he was struck again. Bjarki sank his huge axe into Vali's shield and tore it down. His strength was so great that Vali was pulled from the line. Bjarki's axe was briefly useless but the berserk sank a heavy kick into Vali's belly as he ripped away his shield, sending the prince crashing to the ground. Bodvar Bjarki was not so delirious he didn't know who he was fighting but his speech was incoherent and nonsensical.

'Death, prince. Blood, prince.'

Someone jabbed a spear at the berserk and that took his attention. He shook Vali's shield free of his axe and battered into the wall, knocking men to the ground. The defence collapsed. The berserk killed one man, then another, the axe taking half a farmer's head away. Vali saw Bragi put his sword clean through an opponent but he was the only one who seemed to be retaliating. Now Vali could see the value of the berserks and was pleased there were no conventional warriors following them in. The shield wall had fallen in on itself and a charge by a second wave of attackers would be decisive. Vali recovered his wind and got to his feet. Bjarki drove his axe into another shield, ripping it away, but lost his grip on the weapon, which went clattering onto the track behind him.

Vali had no weapon, no shield and no choice. He couldn't allow the berserk to draw his sword. He leaped at him, striking forward and with both hands at his enemy's chin, trying to snap back his neck. Here, his attention to Bragi's lessons stood him in good stead. He hit his man hard, pushing up with his legs to deliver a powerful two-handed blow. The berserk took a step back, tripped over a body and fell, his head slamming down against the bank, where he lay absolutely still.

Vali could allow himself no self-congratulation. 'Attack! Attack!' he screamed.

Bragi had got four men side by side with shields and they re-engaged the remaining berserks. There were three still fighting, tearing at the shields, beating away the spear points, stabbing and yelling. Vali picked up a spear that had been broken to an arm's length and drove it into the neck of his nearest enemy. The weapon stuck. He had no knife to draw so just jumped at the second berserk, grabbing him around the waist and driving him to the ground. Bragi's sword snicked past his shoulder to impale the berserk in the chest, though Vali took a couple of punches and a bite to the arm as the man died.

There was only one attacker left and he was quickly overwhelmed. A great cheer went up from his men. They'd killed seven berserks for the loss of three themselves. Bodvar Bjarki was trying to get to his feet but he was still hopelessly disoriented. Bragi came forward with his sword.

'No!' said Vali. 'I want this one as my slave. Take him behind the ranks and tie him up. And make sure the women don't kill him; I want him alive.' The berserk was bundled away.

Then he saw Drengi, the man who – Vali had to think it – was betrothed to Adisla. 'Hello, Drengi.' Vali tried to keep his temper. He was furious that Drengi had not tried to find Adisla.

'Lord.' The man couldn't meet Vali's gaze. He knew what Adisla meant to Vali, and though this hadn't stopped him pursuing her, it did mean that he found the prince's presence disconcerting.

'Go and find Adisla and her mother. Help them to safety.'

Drengi nodded and turned to run down the back of the hill, as glad to be spared further conversation with Vali as another attack.

'Die for them!' shouted Vali after him. Then he called up into the woods, 'You did well, Hogni. Stay your hand until my command, or if I die, until our foes are about to overwhelm us. Take them at their thickest press. Our wall will stay here, behind the bodies. They can walk to us on a road of their own dead.' He turned. 'Bragi, where's my seax?'

Bragi shook his head, said, 'Vali the swordless,' under his breath and went to the back of the line while Vali retrieved his shield. The old warrior came back with the weapon, which Vali stuffed into his belt.

There was a knocking sound. Two men fell. Then the sound again. Another man fell.

'Arrows!' shouted Bragi. 'Shields up.'

'Reform the wall!' screamed Vali. 'Reform the wall!' He pulled and pushed men into position.

Vali snatched up a spear as the men packed back in, bunching to shelter under their shields. Vali knew this was far from ideal. The best formation to receive arrow fire was spread out

174

and separate, but to resist an infantry charge they needed to be together. Never mind. He pushed the men in, raising his shield to meet the angle of the incoming arrows. The arrows made a scrabbling sound as they glanced off the shields, like rats running over boards, thought Vali. The noise came again, and again, and he crouched low. He realised that they were safe beneath their shields. Few of the arrows penetrated and those that did had been slowed beyond harm.

The noise stopped. Vali risked peeking out from over the top of his shield. Seventy warriors at least, all with shields, the men at the front in byrnies and helmets, carrying spears. The dragon standard was brought to the front of the line. This is it, thought Vali: this is where it ends. He had thought his wit and cleverness could triumph, but as he looked at the ranks of the enemy he realised the crushing power of numbers. He had only half believed it when he had told his men they'd die that day. It had been meant to encourage them, to remove the anxiety of battle. If you are certain of death then fear becomes pointless. Looking at the Danes – the strong jarl warriors at the front in their armour, helmets and swords, the young men behind them with their caps and spears – then looking at his own old men and boys, he knew the game was up. Still he'd done his best and maybe bought Adisla some time.

'The back ranks must push forward at the moment they hit us,' shouted Bragi. 'That was why we got flattened by the berserk – you didn't push. You must push. If you don't they will overrun us.'

The Danish king looked relaxed and confident beneath his banner, jovial almost, more like a man about to welcome guests on a feast day than a warrior in the field. He was talking to someone – an odd figure. Vali had never seen anyone like him before. Clearly a foreigner, the man was dressed in a blue tunic, skirt and trousers, all edged with red. On his head he wore a blue cap, the top of which took the form of a four-pointed star drooping down over his head. Who was he? What was he doing with the Danes? Vali thought he matched descriptions of the northern Whale People, who were noted sorcerers.

The king was pointing left and right, weighing up options.

'He must charge,' muttered Vali. 'He must charge.' He knew very well that Haarik had time to cook a meal, sleep even, and then outflank them the next morning. One of the Danish jarls was sweeping his arms, gesturing around to the back of the hill. If he came around the back or even sent ten men that way, they were done for. They were likely done for whatever happened, but if they were to have a glimmer of a chance, head-on confrontation was it. Then Vali saw a beautiful sight. The Danish king shook his head, laughed and patted the jarl on his shoulder. He was too proud to do it the sensible way: he was going to charge the wall down.

The king put on his helmet and took up a spear.

'Come on,' said Vali. 'Come on.'

But then he saw some men split off. One group of warriors went left, another right, leaving around fifty. Where was the king? His banner was there but he had disappeared. Vali had no time to think about that. The numbers were more even but Vali faced being attacked from the back in very short order. What to do? In king's table they talked of 'getting the run'. This meant that though your opponent might be in a better position, you had the advantage of time. If you didn't let it slip away, he would never get the chance to bring his most threatening pieces to bear. It was the same here – no time for fancy tactics or movement. They just had to kill the enemy at the front before the enemy behind arrived.

Bragi, crushed in by Vali's side, saw the significance of what had happened.

'Looks like we'll have to fight quick, lord.'

Vali nodded. He would still rather be captured by the Danes, sold into slavery and killed than spend another evening in Bragi's company, but the man's loyalty and, more than that, his competence, impressed him. He'd weighed up the situation

176

immediately, not by thinking about it, as Vali had done, but as an instinctive reaction.

Bragi spoke: 'You're your father's son. I never thought I'd say it, but you are. There was a rumour for years that he'd bought you in the Isle to the West, and not got much for his money either.'

'Your charm is effortless,' said Vali, but the smile he gave Bragi was genuine enough.

'You can see why people thought that, with you being an ugly black-haired bastard and all,' said Bragi.

Vali looked at the enemy. The swords of the men at the front were drawn. It was about to begin.

'Bragi,' he said.

'Yes, lord.'

'If we make it to Valhalla ...'

'Yes, lord.'

'Don't sit next to me.'

The old man laughed until tears came down his face. 'You are a king, sir, a king,' he said.

Bragi had once told him it was a fine thing to die and Vali had thought it more homespun nonsense, but for just an instant he could feel the warmth of the sun on his face, smell the smoke of the burning village, take the weight of the spear in his hand and believe him. There was a comradeship here that he had never felt before, a bond with his fellows that went beyond any small consideration of actually liking them.

There was a roar like a landslide, and the enemy were charging, screaming oaths to Thor, the thunder god, and Tyr, god of war. The name of Odin was not on their lips. These were not berserks, and the hanged god was too peculiar, mysterious and mad for the average farmer or bodyguard.

Vali felt curiously disconnected from the scene and wondered who he should call on for help. None of the gods had ever appealed to him at all. All apart from one.

'Lord Loki,' he said, 'prince of lies, friend to man, let me endure. Let me endure.'

Vali was not religious but for a heartbeat he realised the truth of the gods of his people. Every one was a god of death – of war: Freya, goddess of fertility and war, Thor, god of thunder and war, Freyr, god of pleasure and prosperity but battle bold. Only Loki was not a fighter. Only Loki stood at the sides and laughed, a laughter more deadly to the self-important gods than any sword or spear. No wonder they had chained him.

The sound of the enemy's feet in the little lane vibrated through the ground. Now they would throw their missiles. Vali felt confident. His men were cheek by jowl, the front rank of shields locked tight into each other. The enemy were coming on in a mass somewhere between close order and spread out. They were too far apart to offer each other protection with their shields but not spaced enough to dilute the effect of an incoming volley of missiles.

Vali turned to the man on his other side and thought he had never seen him before. He was a tall pale red-haired fellow in a long brown feathery cloak. Vali wanted to shout at him for being such an idiot as to wear a something like that in the line but found he couldn't. He struggled for words, desperate to say something to this stranger. In the end he managed it.

'Are you with us?' he said.

The man, who seemed able to find some space to move in the press of the wall, touched his arm and said, 'I have been with you since the beginning.'

'And now you're here at the end.'

'No end for you,' said the man. 'None, ever. You are always and eternal, Fenrisulfr, and soon you will see that. The gods, in their dreams, now walk the earth.'

'What?' said Vali.

Spears, axes and stones hammered down. Vali ducked into his shield. A man behind him fell. When he looked up, the red-haired stranger was gone and he had no time to think about how odd that was.

'Loose!' screamed Vali, and the ranks behind him hurled

their spears. Three of the Danes fell, one in the front rank. The jarl impeded the men behind him as he fell to his hands and knees, the others spinning and leaping to get past him. Vali gripped his spear, his hands wet with the sweat of fear.

Bang! The wave of warriors hit the line. The Danes slid their shields into the spears, trying to push them up or aside or snag them, then to release their shields and hack in with sword and axe. Vali found his spear torn from his hand as a Dane came steaming in to him with his shield and struck at him with his axe. Again Vali could not draw his seax and was glad of his helmet as the axe knocked it off with a glancing blow but without hurting him. The press was so tight that it didn't fall to the ground but wedged at the back of his shield. Then a spear was pushed over his shoulder from behind and the warrior was driven back. The helmet dropped and Vali kicked it towards the enemy. The Danes rushed forward again, under the defenders' spears. More men pushed in by his side, still more behind him. It was shield to shield in the crush with no room to swing a sword. Those in the front rank became spectators at the fight, shoving forward and hoping not to be stabbed by spears wielded by opponents they had no hope of reaching. A Dane slipped on the body of another but Vali couldn't move to draw his weapon. No need. The man went down under the feet of his friends.

More warriors joined the back of the Danish push, throwing weapons and heaving their shoulders into their comrades' backs in a bid to force the defenders down the lane. Vali shoved, was shoved. He strained forward with every sinew but he felt his line giving ground. Even though the Danes were stumbling and slipping on fallen bodies, there were many more of them than the Rygir. Vali went a pace back, then two. The faces of the enemy were right in his, hurling insults, promising death, spitting, trying to bite even, but there was almost nothing the men in the front could do to hurt each other. They were too close to even kick. Behind Vali someone fell, then another, and it seemed that, in a breath, the wall would be overwhelmed.

'Now, Hogni, now!' screamed Vali. Hogni couldn't hear him but the Horda was an attentive and experienced warrior who had listened well to what Vali had told him. 'Now and quietly,' he told his archers.

They came forward out of the woods, five of them, and released a volley of arrows from above at the back of the Danish press at a range of five paces. Then another, and another. Two Danes fell, then three, then two more before they even realised they had been outflanked.

'Push,' screamed Vali. 'Push!'

Danes were trying to scramble up the bank to get at the archers, slipping on the bodies of their comrades, sliding and falling. The archers shot again and again. Vali stuck his shoulder into his shield and shoved as hard as he could. The Dane in front of him lost his footing, grabbing out and taking a companion with him. The Rygir began to gather momentum and stamped forward over the fallen men, driving down with boots, spears and axes.

The enemy broke and ran. Hogni's archers continued shooting, though he commanded them to stop. He wanted some of the glory for himself and leaped into the lane to pursue the fleeing invaders.

Vali's men streamed past him after the enemy. Vali shouted at them to halt. About twenty Danes had gone off on a flanking movement and he felt sure they were about to attack from the rear. But there was no hope of controlling his men, who sprinted after the Danes, followed down the lane by most of the women and many of the children, waving sticks and house knives as they ran.

Pushing back through them, Vali then ran to the end of the lane and stared down into the valley behind the hill. No Danes. Instinctively he looked over to Disa's farm. A pall of smoke hung over it. He gave a shiver. Had Disa been able to run with her burned legs? Had Adisla managed to get her away? Her daughter would not have abandoned her, he knew that.

He glanced around for help but the only warrior near him was Bjarki, still barely conscious, tied up to the point of strangulation with a couple of small children hitting him with sticks. Vali shooed them away from the berserk, all the time looking around for any of his men who had remained.

'Bragi, with me!' he shouted, as loud as he could. But Bragi was gone, down to the Danes' boats, planning to take them out to sea and deny the attackers their escape. Vali was on his own. Dread swamped his exhaustion and he ran towards the burning farm faster than he had ever run in his life.

19 Endings

Drengi had arrived in time to at least face the invaders. He was a farmer not a fighter though, and he was lying by a feed trough with his own axe embedded in his chest. The old Dane Barth had been shown no mercy by his countrymen and was slumped next to him as if dozing in the sun. Little Manni was dead at the doorway of Disa's house, Vali's old seax still in his hand.

Vali closed his eyes and tried to compose himself. He had no time for mourning; he needed to find what had happened to Adisla and her mother. He ran into the smouldering building. The Danes had tried to set it alight but the turf roof would not burn well and the smoke looked more like that from a dung heap than a fire. Disa had been murdered in her bed. Blood was everywhere, a grisly scarf of red extending down the front of her white smock. He approached and saw that her throat was cut. He could imagine all too well what else had happened to her.

Vali knelt beside her and took her hand. She had been his mother, or the nearest he had to one. He said nothing. So far that day he had learned what it was to believe in a fight and take up arms in a cause that was beyond plunder. Looking into Disa's eyes, it seemed impossible that he would ever do anything else. He did not cry, which surprised him. There was something inside him too cold for tears. It was a certainty that seemed to lodge in his throat like a bolus, stopping up any emotion. He would have vengeance for this. Adisla had told him to kill a hundred of them. He wouldn't stop there. He would kill the Danish king and all his stinking race, tear down his halls and burn his lands to ashes. The Danes had unleashed a wolf by what they had done. He had never known such purpose in all his life. But first he had something else to do.

He went to the top of the bed and kissed Disa on the forehead.

'I will find her,' he said and then left the house. As he did so he passed the boy's body. He ruffled his hair and kissed him. He went to take the seax but thought better of it. Instead, he just squeezed the child's fingers onto the weapon's handle. 'You keep it,' he said, 'use it in the afterlife. Go to Freya's halls, not Odin's.'

Vali heard a groan. He looked up. Drengi was still alive. He ran over to the fallen man.

'Drengi, it's me, Vali.'

Drengi was just about breathing, the axe had caused a terrible wound in his chest and his mouth bubbled with blood.

Vali didn't know what to do. Disa or Jodis might have known, but one was dead and the other who knows where.

'Drengi, you'll live. I've seen men with worse wounds survive. You will live.'

This was not true and they both knew it.

'They came for her, Vali; they came for her.'

'I know.'

'No, they came for her. No treasure, no plunder, *her*.' He let out an awful cough, fighting to suck in breath. Vali's mind was too disordered to take in what Drengi was saying.

'You'll be fine, Drengi. I'll fetch Ma Jodis and she'll patch you up. You see, you'll be fine.'

'Vali, they were looking for *her*. They asked for the healer's daughter.'

Vali couldn't understand why that would be at all.

'Asked who?'

'They had taken the boy Loptr prisoner. He led them here and told them who to look for. They were shouting her name.' He coughed and blood flowed over his lips.

'Is the boy dead too?'

'No, he ran away. Remove the axe, Vali. Take the axe away. It is a blight to me.'

'Yes.'

Vali put two hands to the shaft near the head. He pulled and Drengi screamed. He pulled again and the axe came free. Drengi coughed and spluttered, hacked and wheezed. Then he was quiet. Vali took his hand. He was dead.

Vali became aware he was being watched. He looked up to see Loptr peering out from behind a pig shelter.

'You can come out now, child. They've gone,' said Vali.

The boy didn't move. He looked very scared.

'Did they take her? Did they take Adisla?'

The boy nodded.

'Which way?'

The child pointed at the track heading south out of the farmstead that led to several broad beaches. If the Danes had got their ships away from the harbour, they might pick up stragglers there.

'Go back down to the harbour,' said Vali. 'If you encounter any of our warriors, tell them I've gone down to Selstrond to find these pirates. And tell them to come and help me. Quick. Go on!'

The boy didn't move, just stared at him. It was no use, Vali decided. Loptr was too shocked by what he'd seen to do anything. 'Well, don't go into Ma Disa's house,' said Vali, and he set off for the beach.

When he arrived, the shoe told him all he needed to know. It was where the track petered out in the sand, just at the point that anyone coming onto the beach would find it. It was hers, one of the green leather best she had been wearing to greet him back from his journey. Clearly she had kicked it off.

He was only just too late – the longship was close offshore. He couldn't see Adisla but there were around twenty warriors visible on the boat. Still he didn't really absorb Drengi's words: 'Vali, they were looking for *her*.' His brain was hot with hatred and he didn't even recall what Drengi had said.

'Come back, you cowards!' he screamed. 'I am one and you are twenty. Are the odds not enough in your favour?'

There was no reply from the ship; the Danes were too busy with their sail. But then, for a heatbeat, he saw her, struggling to dive overboard and swim to freedom. She was pulled roughly back onto the boat.

'I'll find you!' he screamed as he splashed out into the water. 'And know, Danes, that if she is harmed I'll visit a thousand times worse on you and your kinsmen! I am Vali, son of Authun. I am death to you!'

Vali felt utterly hopeless. There was no prospect of pursuit. Forkbeard's longships were away down the coast at the regional assembly; all they had were a few faerings – four-oared inshore boats – and he couldn't chase a warship in one of those.

How would he find her? He'd try Haithabyr, he thought, the market where any slave brought to Denmark ended up. He could buy her, if he could raise the money from his father or borrow it from Forkbeard. Then he remembered: he had the berserk. He would get what he wanted to know out of him. He turned back towards the site of the battle.

When he found Bjarki he was in no fit state to answer questions. The drugs, drink and the bang on the head had rendered him almost insensible. All he could do was curse and drool. He was safe for the time being but Vali wondered how long he would last if any of the townspeople got hold of him. Preserving the berserk's life was his only key to finding Adisla. The man was too big to drag anywhere without help. Luckily, up the hill at that moment came Bragi with two farmers, Gudfastr and Baugr, Loptr beside them. So he had done his job after all.

'How does it go?' said Vali.

'They're routed. One ship captured – a good day's work.' Bragi didn't look quite as jubilant as Vali might have expected.

'They've taken Adisla. Ma Disa's dead, and the rest of them at the house from what I can tell.'

Bragi's mouth fell open. 'Anyone else?'

'I don't know. They were quick so I think it unlikely. They didn't take him, did they?' He nodded to the boy, who was still looking at Vali with wide terrified eyes.

'They were being quick, for sure, or they wouldn't have left the boy. He'd have got a good price at market. You'll want vengeance, won't you, Loptr?' said Bragi.

The boy said nothing, just withdrew behind Baugr.

'Get that berserk down into the village,' said Vali. 'He's got some questions to answer. As soon as he recovers, let me know. Tell the people that by my command there will be no celebration until Forkbeard returns. Make them keep a watch. Two drakkars escaped and may well return if they think we imagine the danger is past.'

He turned away down the hill, towards the valley.

'Where are you going?' said Bragi.

'To see Ma Jodis,' said Vali.

20   A Hard Road Forward

'Ma, it's me. Ma.'

Jodis's house was much smaller than Disa's – not much more than a hut sunk into the earth, its walls just waist high. With its flat turf roof you could hardly see it until you were right on it.

Vali knocked at the door. 'Ma, it's me, Vali. Ma, it's all right, they've gone.'

The door opened and Jodis peered out. She was trembling though trying not to show it.

'How many dead?'

'I don't know. It could have been worse. We beat them. They've gone, Ma.'

Jodis wiped the tears from her eyes. 'Adisla? Ma Disa?'

'That's why I'm here,' he said. 'I—'

'O Freya, guard them,' said Jodis, who had guessed no good had come to the women. 'What?'

'Ma Disa is dead and Adisla taken,' said Vali.

Jodis could no longer hold on to her tears.

'I'll avenge the first and find the second,' said Vali.

She gave him that look again, the one she'd given him when she'd heard that Forkbeard had planned to hang Adisla, but then she tempered it. She was very fond of Vali but regarded him as something of an idiot. The capture of the wolfman had shown that he wasn't.

'Do you even know where they've gone or who they were?'

'I suspect they'll go to Haithabyr, at least eventually. They were Danes – Haarik and his men.'

'They could take her to his court or sell her in the east, or do many other things with her. She could be anywhere.'

'Which is why I'm here,' said Vali.

Jodis looked blankly at him.

'I want you to work Ma Disa's magic. It took me to the wolfman; it can take me to her.'

She shook her head. 'I've never done it. Ma Disa had a gift for that. I just helped her.'

'Then you know how it's done?'

'Yes, but it's not possible, even if I wanted to. The fire herbs are all gone. They grow only in the spring and they're very rare. We won't be able to harvest any for months.'

'Those herbs are entirely necessary?'

'Yes.'

Vali breathed out heavily. He had no faith at all that the berserk would yield information under torture, though that wouldn't stop him trying. Did the berserk know anything anyway? He was a hired hand. Vali knew that when Forkbeard went on raids with berserks he kept the target secret until they were at sea, to prevent them going it alone. As much as it would please him to try to beat information out of Bjarki, Vali doubted he actually had any.

'There is no other way?'

Jodis shrugged.

'What?' said Vali.

'There is, but it will kill you.'

'What is it?'

'You go to Odin at the mire,' said Jodis.

'Meaning?'

'It's not been done since I was a girl, but if the prophecy is important enough to you then it's worth it. You go to Grimnir's Mire and present yourself to the god of the hanged, the god of the drowned, and you ask him what you want to know.'

'How do I do this?'

'By drowning,' said Ma Jodis.

'How can the prophecy be any good to me if I die?'

'You go to the edge of death, and there you bargain with the gods for your life. You offer them what you can, and if it pleases them they take it and tell you what you need to know.'

'What can I offer a god?'

'Your suffering,' she said.

Vali stiffened his jaw and gave a short nod. 'Have you done this?'

'No, but I have seen it done. It was many years ago now. Princess Heithr went to the mire.'

'I thought that was just a story. Was it a success?'

'She revealed four traitors in her father's court and the location of the Thjalfi hoard.'

'They found the hoard?'

'They did. Though she never got to see it. The ordeal killed her.'

Vali put his hand on the low roof and thought for a moment. What was his life without Adisla anyway? Everyone has to die, it's just a matter of when. Only a fool would throw his life away, though.

'Can you do it? I don't want to die for nothing, Ma.'

'It's straightforward but more a question of whether you can do it. You drown at the sacred mire, the place between land and water. It's a gateway that leads to other places in the nine worlds. The force of your will is all you'll have to help you find the path. You need no more preparation than a warrior dying in battle does to make it to Valhalla.'

Vali gave a curt nod. 'How long will it take?'

'Who knows? You must drown and revive, drown and revive, until the vision comes to you or you drown and do not revive. It could happen the first time; it could happen the tenth or never. And it's not easy to force yourself back to those waters, no matter how much you're burning for an answer. You'll fight it, so you'll need to be tied.'

Vali had vowed to ask Odin for nothing but his was a circumstance he had not foreseen.

'I'll do it,' said Vali.

'There is one other thing,' said Jodis. 'The gods aren't the

189

only things waiting in the nine worlds. We'll put a noose on you. It's a symbol so the god can find you, but if you snap your bonds or begin to speak as a giant or witch, or worse, then we'll use it to kill you. Don't converse with giants, Vali, nor with the other monsters you may see down there.'

'Bring your rope,' said Vali. 'If this is the only way, then this is the only way.'

'You'll need men to help you in and out of the water. Even in your bonds you'll need to be held down,' said Jodis, 'and I haven't the strength to strangle you or the sureness to shorten your suffering with a knife.'

'Is your grandson in there?'

'He is.'

'Then send him to Hogni and Orri,' said Vali. 'Come on. We need to begin.'

21　The Drowning Pool

He had been at the drowning pool before, of course. It was in a sunken hollow on a natural shelf in the low hills that led up from Jodis's farm. Prisoners and sacrifices had been sent to the gods in Grimnir's Mire in years gone by, but no one had died there since the princess had sought her answer all those years before. The children knew its reputation though, and it was said that the ghosts of long-dead kings and warriors haunted the waters at night.

Vali felt a chill go through him as he sat waiting for Hogni and Orri. Was it the breeze cutting in from the sea or was it some deeper feeling? How many had died there and to what purpose? Did places such as the mire really carry an imprint of the deaths they had seen or was it just childish memories that set his flesh creeping, the echoes of stories told to frighten and thrill the long winter nights away?

He felt very cold. Clouds had rolled in off the sea, turning the sky to iron and spitting the air with rain. He wished he had brought his cloak with him but then realised he was going to be a lot colder soon. And what did his discomfort matter? Did Adisla have a cloak to shelter her from the rain out on that boat? What was happening to her? He couldn't bring himself to think on that. For every discomfort or abuse she suffered, he vowed to himself, those who inflicted it on her would suffer one hundred times worse. Until he met her again, he swore, no pain would daunt him. He had suffered as much as it is possible to suffer when he saw her on that longship.

'Lord, a great victory.' A hand was on his shoulder. It was Hogni.

'The Danes have taken flight,' said Orri, 'and the win is yours to claim.'

'My glory must wait a while,' said Vali. 'I have another battle to fight.' He nodded towards the water.

It was just a pool, he told himself, something he would use for a purpose, like a plough or a sword.

Hogni and Orri looked at the noose Jodis was tying, the symbol of Odin, the triple slip knot – if that's what you could call it. The dead lord's necklace only slipped one way. Once it was on, you took it off with a knife or not at all. The men glanced at each other.

'You are seeking answers from the gods?' said Orri.

'I want to find where Adisla has gone. Do you have a better way?'

'They'll take her to Haarik's court.'

'Maybe, and maybe not. They could sell her in Haithabyr or in any market along the way. She could be given to a mercenary as payment, and besides ...' He didn't want to say it, the thought seemed too bizarre. He recalled that strange man in the four-cornered hat. What had he been doing there? Drengi's words had sunk in too.

'They came for her; they were looking for her. They called her name,' said Vali.

'Why?'

Vali shrugged. Whatever Adisla's fate, it was surely not to be a straightforward slave. He was beyond explanation. He just knew that he had very little time and no scope to make a mistake.

'This is the best way,' said Vali.

Hogni nodded. 'I performed this office for your father,' he said.

'What?'

'There is a place in the Iron Woods, four days from his hall. Like this, it's a pool of prophecy. Your father asked questions of it.'

'How?'

'In the same way that you will,' he said. He looked at the coil of rope.

'Did he find answers?'

'It was when his difficulties began in earnest,' said Hogni.

'When was this?'

'Four years ago. He hadn't been well for years but ...'

Hogni looked like he was too ashamed to finish his sentence.

'He never came back from the woods,' said Orri.

'I don't understand,' said Vali.

'Your father lives alone in the Iron Woods,' said Hogni. 'He has taken up the life of a mystic.'

It began to rain harder, a sudden sea squall coming in over them as fast as a bird.

'The people say that Odin speaks to him in the woods, that he is granting the king his power.'

'Do the people say that or does my mother?'

The two men did not reply. Things were worse than Vali had thought. If anyone suspected that Authun had lost his mind it would be a disaster for the Horda. The king had more enemies than any man alive. No time to think on that. Vali looked into the dark waters and stretched his neck forward, steeling himself.

'Begin,' said Vali.

Jodis told Orri to bind Vali by his hands and feet, while she put the noose over his head.

'Is this the way Lord Authun went about it?' said Vali. Jodis seemed confident how to perform the ritual but Vali's nervousness made him look for reassurance.

'He offered a dedication to Odin before he went in,' said Orri.

Vali smiled. 'Well then, since I'm bound, perhaps I should offer a dedication to a bound god. Lord Loki, who the gods tormented, guide me to the vision I need.'

'You shouldn't invoke that fellow, lord,' said Orri.

'Is Odin any more reliable?'

'Nor him,' said Orri. 'Freyr for a fuck, Tyr for a fight and

Thor for a fuck, a fight and the rain to wash you afterwards – you don't need any more gods than that.'

'Odin is the god of kings,' said Vali, 'isn't that what we're told?'

'And berserk madmen,' said Orri. 'Sorry, sir, but it's true. When I go into a scrap I want to know my god's on my side, not likely to desert me if the fancy takes him. Odin is a treacherous god; it is in his nature. I respect Lord Odin, and his kings and lunatics, but I wouldn't call on him, or the other one you mentioned.'

Orri wound the rope around Vali's feet.

'Loki is an enemy of the gods, not of people,' said Vali. 'When did you ever hear of him acting against men? He kills giants, he kills gods, but men he helps or leaves alone.'

Jodis spoke: 'This is Odin's ceremony. He's lord of the hanged, the god who gave his eye for wisdom in the waters of the well. If you want help, it's him you'll call for. If you don't now, you will when you're in there, believe me.'

She put the noose over his neck.

'I've sworn never to ask that god for anything,' said Vali.

'You will ask or you will die,' said Jodis.

She adjusted the rope at his neck, almost like she would straighten her child's tunic before allowing him to go to market. 'Let's hope we don't need this. Stay away from dark things,' she said. 'Only speak to the god himself.'

'How will I know the difference?' said Vali.

'I have no idea,' said Jodis. 'Magic is a puzzle not a recipe, so Ma Disa used to say.' Vali nodded. His hands and his feet were secure and he couldn't even balance to stand. She finished adjusting the noose and kissed him on the forehead. 'Take him to the middle of the mire.'

Hogni and Orri lifted him but found him cumbersome to carry between them. In the end Hogni put him over his shoulder and walked across the squelching ground and into the water, Orri in front of him to test the way. In the middle they stopped. Hogni let Vali slide down and supported the prince as he stood precariously. The water was freezing, and it came up to their belts. Vali shivered.

'Should I call for Odin?' said Hogni.

Jodis shook her head.

'The prince should call. You should save your breath. If he comes, you might need it to beg him to leave. Are you ready, Vali?'

'Yes.'

'Put him under and hold him there until I tell you to bring him up,' said Jodis. 'Hogni, hold him down; Orri, keep hold of the rope. And both of you stand by with your knives. He is going to the gates of Hel, and if something claims him there it can't be allowed to live in this world. This is how the swamp monsters are born.'

The three men glanced at each other.

'If you have to kill me, kill me,' said Vali. 'I won't consider you kinslayers – Ma Jodis is a witness to that.'

'Then sit down, lord,' said Hogni.

The first time was the easiest. Vali just let his legs go soft and leaned back into the mire as if into the sea on a summer's day. He closed his eyes and did not see the dark waters close over him. The panic kept away for a few heartbeats. At first it was as if he was not himself but an observer – the danger of his situation was not clear and he still thought he could just stand up. Then fear broke over him like a wave. He desperately needed air. He tried to stand, and when he couldn't, he tried to sit up. Someone had a boot on the centre of his chest. He could hear distorted voices from the surface and had to resist the desire to cry out to them. He wriggled free of the foot, tried to get onto his knees and then felt a push at his side. It turned him over. Someone was pulling at his hands, then they were kneeling or sitting on him, he couldn't tell which. Hogni and Orri were doing what they had promised – helping him to stay below the water.

He struggled to hold his breath. Dread overwhelmed him, he felt that he was drowning in fear as much as water. The bonds would not come off, the weight on his back and on his legs felt immense, almost part of him, as if he were some enormous giant too heavy to lift itself.

He couldn't get the ropes off, couldn't get free. Vali tried to remember that he had chosen to be here, that he wanted this, but it was no good. An instinct, animal and undeniable, rose up in him and he fought for the surface. He opened his eyes to look for the light and could see no more in the muddy waters than when they were closed. Then his will burst and he breathed in. He spat and coughed and then felt his throat clench shut. He had the desire to move his body but he could no longer do so, though he was kicking with his mind. His longing for the air seemed like something trapped in his head, thumping to get free. Still he struggled, the panic swamping even the emotions of despair.

Then, as suddenly as it had come on, the terror was gone and he felt peaceful, as if any cares he had, any frustrations and fears, were just silly things, almost incomprehensible under the calm that came down on him like a parent's kiss on a sleepy child.

Light. And noise, hard blows and a sensation of movement. The grass felt cold. Someone was slapping him across the back of the head. He tried to defend himself but his hands were tied. A face came into focus. It was Jodis.

'Nothing?' she said.

Vali coughed, spluttering out water and mucus from his nose and mouth.

'Nothing.'

'Do you need a rest?'

Vali thought of Adisla, of what she would be enduring on the Danes' drakkar. 'No rest,' he said. He could hardly get the words out. His throat was dry and sore from where it had constricted in the water and his muscles writhed on his bones in a deep shiver.

'Put him back,' said Jodis.

Time became flexible to Vali, a malleable thing, like a piece of hide to be stretched or shrunk, a smith's ingot heated and cooled, bent and straightened. When he was in the water every heartbeat seemed a year. When he was out the sun seemed to dip and rise like a skimmed stone. Even though his will was strong, Vali couldn't help but take rests. At first they untied him when he did so. Eventually they did not. He could say, 'Put me back in the water,' but he couldn't make his body allow it, and the more times he went in, the harder he struggled. At first he could control himself until he reached the centre of the mire. After a day he began to fight as they led him to the edge. It was a place of horror to him now, though no visions came, no insight or revelation, just the awful black water closing in on him, the pressures from within as the air struggled to burst from his lungs, and without as the water rushed to get in. A weighty black mass seemed to pull at his brain, heavier on the left than the right, the asymmetry giving him a headache like he had never known. His throat was raw and he could hardly speak.

There was no crowd there to see the magic. The Danes had gone and the Rygir were at home, sitting in groups remembering the dead, tending the wounded or just keeping their children close and the door shut. Adisla was the only one taken but ten others had died and still more were wounded. People drank, though not in celebration, hoping to damp down the misery and accentuate the glory of the violent day. Only Jodis's children and Bragi came to watch Vali suffer.

Jodis sent her girl away to bring soup, but Vali couldn't drink it. His throat had clamped shut, so he shivered out the interludes between his ordeals starving and cold. On the first day he managed twelve trips to the water. On the second he did four. The third day, lack of sleep blunting the reality of what he was doing, he managed eight. And, towards the evening, he did begin to see.

Drowning beneath the dark waters, he was somewhere else other than the mire, somewhere equally cold but not wet or dark. At that turning point, the moment between the panic and the calm of drowning, he was in a confined space, a tunnel that seemed to glow, the rocks emitting a soft and alien light. Someone was there, he was sure, though he couldn't say who. He could feel their presence as a tone, a mood or a pattern of thought. He had never known anything like it. It was a mind that seemed like a river – always moving, always the same – and, like a river, it had currents that might drag you down.

And when he was lifted from the water, he didn't see Orri and Hogni but that strange red-haired man in the cloak of hawk feathers, taking him up and out into the clean cold air. He heard a voice that seemed familiar.

'Give yourself completely.' Then the man was gone and Vali could stand it no more. He knew what was required. You cannot go to the gates of death if you are still looking back at life. He needed to step forward boldly. The idea didn't come to him in words but as a feeling of want, like a prisoner wants freedom. He was fettered by something and the fetters needed to break.

The men pulled him up and he lay back in their arms, limp as pondweed.

'Lord,' said Orri, 'you have tried. There is nothing there for you.'

'No,' said Vali, though the word was more of a cough than anything understandable. The men started towards the bank.

'No.'

They stopped.

'What, lord?'

Vali made himself speak, forcing his aching lungs to expel the air through the constriction of his throat to frame the words. He was weak and tired and he needed to end this suffering whatever the cost. From behind the hillside, towards the sea, there came the sound of horns and a clamour. Forkbeard was returning. It meant nothing to Vali.

'Do not pull me out,' he said.

'You mean to die?'

'The water,' said Vali, pointing into the mire. He was beyond explanation. The sky was a cave, black with rain, the light unnatural, a subterranean glow, like that tunnel. His senses seemed muted and dull, as if the darkness of the mire still clung to him.

'You are raving, lord,' said Hogni. 'Ma Jodis, the prince says we are to put him in again.'

Jodis tapped the ground with her foot in thought. She looked back over her shoulder in the direction of the sea, thinking of the girl on the Danish ship. Of course, the prince would be taken out of the mire but perhaps it was time to give it longer. Much longer.

'Do as he says,' she said.

Now it was Hogni and Orri who hesitated, but Vali took the decision from their hands. With the last of his strength he kicked his feet away from under him and cast himself back into the water.

22 Magical Thinking

The witch queen was working on the Moonsword when she realised that the sorcerer had found Vali. She had taken Authun's weapon on an impulse, not a whim like an ordinary human might have but in response to a magical feeling. She knew it was important and, in the years since the king had come to the cave, she had realised how. The wolf would kill Odin but then it would need to die. Ancient prophecy was clear on how this would happen. Odin would fall, and then another, kinder, more humane god would kill the wolf. If the pre-echo of that conflict really was to be played out in her lifetime then that god would need a weapon. The wolf could not be killed by any normal blade, otherwise it would not be able to defeat the king of gods in battle. So the sword would need to be enchanted.

In the lower caves there was a narrow wedge of rock where the jagged ceiling met an uneven floor. She had always thought it looked like the jaws of a wolf. Now she wedged the sword into it, as the sword was wedged into the jaws of the Fenris Wolf, and for months she concentrated on seeing it as something that could harm the savage god.

The witch was so strong in magic that she was half a god herself, and her perceptions were not like those of humans, things that flicker into being for an instant and then cease to exist when attention shifts. They were more like living things, spider thoughts that crawled from the egg of her mind over the object of her meditation – the sword – and waited to ensnare whatever encountered the weapon in future. She convinced herself that the weapon would kill the wolf, and the sisters sat with her, sharing that belief. At the end of their period of meditation that idea had entered the Moonsword and would warp the perceptions of all who encountered it in future, including the wolf himself.

Gullveig knew that anything that could defeat Odin would not be killed by a lesser magic, and all magics were less than that possessed by the king of gods, but she saw one hope. The prince, she knew, had been raised on tales of his father's battles and had grown up hearing stories of the magical lost sword. When he was eaten by the wolf, his consciousness would mingle with his brother's. That, she believed, provided the key to the wolf's death. The magic would not need to batter down the wolf's defences; it would enter through a crack provided by the man who had given his life to bring the Fenris Wolf to earth.

The meditation was finishing when the witches felt a brief pause in the flow of things, like someone sleeping in a cart might suddenly become aware that it had stopped. Vali, in the mire, had stepped into the magic space of visions and prophecy where the witches lived, and it was as if they had heard his footfalls at its threshold.

The witch queen was aware of someone else too. She heard chanting and drums and saw the eyes of the sorcerer. Then she felt the delicious pull of cold waters, felt her throat constricting, the desperation for air, a thick despair in her head, and she fell into Vali's mind.

She had known before that male magic was weak. The rituals that the wolf shaman Kveld Ulf practised, for instance, could influence the physical realm but were scarcely recognisable as magic at all to the sisters of the Troll Wall. They were performed without the aid or understanding of the runes and to the witch queen were as strong as a house built without foundations. The blue-eyed sorcerer's presence was almost fragile to her.

She saw images pulsing from his drum, running wolves, reindeer, bears, all moving from the skin as little stick figures, dancing their way into the mire. What was he trying to do? She allowed herself to sink into the rhythm of the drum, turning it over in her head. After a time she understood it, owned it. The rhythm was hers to command now. The sorcerer was concentrating too much on the man in the mire and didn't realise she was there, that the beat coming from his drum had been altered and was spilling his secrets into the web of the witch queen's mind. His thoughts fell open to her. He had been seeking the twin who had become a prince, had insight into his importance but had no real idea how to proceed, she could tell.

The witch queen was pleased. She had her enemy at her mercy, distracted, not aware of her, his limited magic ensnared in an attempt to influence the young man in the mire. She felt the runes rising in her as a sharp thorn to prick him with, fire to burn him, ice to freeze him, water or earth to stop up his breath.

In the darkness of her cave she felt a hand take hers. She turned in the weak glow of a whale-fat candle to see a woman with a ruined face sitting beside her, smiling. Then a realisation came to the witch's mind and she forgot her odd companion.

The witch knew that the sorcerer, no matter how weak he appeared, was the god Odin. Therefore any vulnerability he expressed was a strength in disguise. She might attack him but he would survive, and, in surviving, he might realise who he was, awake to his powers and crush her.

The candle guttered and the shadows seemed to stretch across her sight as she sensed her murder-minded ancestors looking at her from the rocks around her. In their sudden presence was a message, she knew.

Magical thinking can appear close to insanity but, like some forms of insanity, it has aspects of genius. The first witches had known Odin had taken up female magic. He alone among men was a master of the women's art – Seid, as it was called. Loki had told Gullveig that the god was lore-jealous, that he was striking at her because she had become too wise in magic. So the god hated powerful sorcerers in the earthly realm and would come to kill them. Very good, she thought. Then, if the god himself came to the earthly realm and was made to recognise himself as the most powerful sorcerer, he would strike at himself. The god could be tricked into killing his own incarnation. Odin was known as the all-hater. Would he exempt himself from that hate? No.

She would help the sorcerer, strengthen him and weaken herself, and in so doing she would shrink from the notice of the dead god and make him focus his attention on his own earthly self. He had seen enough to embark on that path anyway, she could tell. His visions had shown him the wolf and the boys and now he was trying to summon the creature to be his protector. He was using the girl. The Wolfsangel showed the witch that the healer's girl was bound to the brothers and to their eventual transformation. So Gullveig's enemy had nearly everything in place to summon the wolf. And yet, without her help, he would never do it.

The death of the girls in the Witch Caves had not been an attack. It had been a sort of prophecy, guidance, even perhaps a manifestation of her own magic, telling her what to do. The keys to magic, the witches had always known, were pain and shock. Now she saw the key to survival was weakness. She would diminish the power of her sisterhood, bolster that of her enemy and help him perform the magic that would destroy him. She had thought that she would call the wolf to destroy the god. Now she knew better. The god could call the wolf himself.

The sorcerer had achieved a great deal without the runes. With them, she thought, he would rush to his fate. Gullveig decided, she would send her enemy a gift.

One of the older sisters, the one who held the rune that shone like a lamp in the dark and brought insight and clarity to the witches' visions, was dying, lying in the upper caves. Her inheritor was at her feet, deep in the trance that would enable her to receive the rune. That, thought Gullveig, could not happen.

Disa had been right about magic. A spell is not a recipe as

such, though many have their ingredients, their methods of mixing and baking in the dark oven of the mind. It is more like a puzzle, where constituent parts must first be identified and then assembled into a whole, or even like embroidery, but formed from pain and denial rather than needle and thread.

At its higher reaches magic is a matter of feel. The witch queen, who had trained her instincts in years in the dark, knew that cold thought yielded nothing in sorcery. The way to achieve what she wanted was simply to begin, to take those invisible threads in her hands – the one called agony, the one called despair – and weave them into something more than the sum of their parts.

As she allowed herself to fall into a trance, Gullveig thought of the dying witch and her breathing became shallow, her limbs feeling weak in sympathy. Rot was in the witch queen's mind – disease, the burst corpses of fever victims, the stink on the breath of old women dying. The smell seemed to cling to the witch queen and she knew that the old witch's was a rightful death, a fine and beautiful thing.

The witch queen walked with the woman through her deathbed memories. She saw how the old witch had been brought to the caves as a girl, felt her fear of the darkness, her anguish as she was trained and her elation as the rune finally lit up in her and bonded her fast to her sisters. She sensed the other witches too, spectral presences in the old woman's mind, and she went to them, telling them it was time to leave and to bid their sister goodbye. The witches melted away and the queen felt the dying woman's thoughts shrivelling in on themselves. When the sisters were gone, Gullveig sat with her in the dimness of her mind. Her rune was shining in the murk like a lantern.

Gullveig took it and the witch died. She saw the girl who was to receive it waiting in the dark. In her trance, the witch queen held up her hand and the girl fell dead. Then she returned to Vali in the mire and sent it spinning towards the sorcerer.

She heard a cry, heard the rhythm of the drums falter as

the rune entered him. The witch smiled to herself. Now he would have insight and clarity like he had never had before. He would understand what to do when she sent him the next rune. She took out her small piece of leather, ran her thumb around the outline of the Wolfsangel rune. The sorcerer could sense her now, she could tell. She thought of the Wolfsangel and opened her consciousness like a deadly flower, exposing the dark nectar of the rune within. Something reached hungrily into her head, tearing and ripping. The witch fought to stop herself retaliating, to keep her defences down. Her eyes felt as though they would burst as the sorcerer's drumbeat seemed to chisel the rune from inside her. She fell forward, bleeding at the nose and at the mouth, biting at her fingers to try to distract herself from the pain in her head. She felt her enemy's exultation and agony as the rune wound its tendrils into his mind. The witch was satisfied. The god's manifestation was on the way to where he needed to be to destroy himself. Now he really could call the wolf, which meant he would die. She withdrew from her trance and shivered.

The experience of having killed one of her own buzzed through her mind like an angry wasp through a summer's day. She had stepped deeper into insanity but even that felt right. She got up to go to her dead sister. She would sit with her a while, she thought. It would be useful to confront what she had done, feel its impact, stroke the old witch's hair, stay with her in the darkness while she rotted. Murder, regret and grief were tools she could work with to dig new tunnels through the labyrinth of her magical mind.

She stood, not noticing the hand that helped her to her feet.

23 Running Wolf

To Vali, the panic seemed dimmer this time, smudged by tiredness. His endurance was gone and he breathed in, then felt the clamping of his throat, the involuntary spasm of the muscles as he tried to propel himself to the surface. He tried to relax, to let what had to happen, happen. Then the fear fell away from him, disappearing like a ballast stone dropped from a ship.

'He's still,' said Hogni.

Orri just shook his head and looked down. The rain had set in properly, unrelenting sheets sweeping off the ocean. The whole world seemed made of water, the mire and the hillside that held it just smears of grey against a storm-black sky.

Vali felt the certainty of death, calm and comforting, bringing with it the promise of an end to cares. Death felt like a warm bed he could climb into, like meat to the hungry.

There were entities in his mind – hostile presences, he thought. He felt displaced in his own consciousness, a tenant in his own head. There was a man, his presence felt fragile and he was fighting a woman whose mind seemed as deep and dangerous as the ocean. But the man was winning. He had taken something from the woman. Vali's normal senses and thoughts could not understand what that thing was. It came to him as a shape, a cut in things, a cut in everything, a jagged slash in the fabric of creation.

Vali was in that tunnel again, the glow of the rocks like light through water, the air cold and heavy. The floor was flooded up to his knees. He looked to his side and saw a strange figure. It was a man in a stiff wolf mask, something constructed of wood and fur. In his hand was a shallow drum.

'Why am I here?' Vali's voice sounded curiously muted.

The man in the mask began to beat the drum. Vali instinctively understood it was intended to summon something, something within him. The light seemed to ripple and he became aware of the shape again. It seemed to tremble from the skin of the drum, to hover, shake and pulse in front of his eyes. Destinies, he knew, were set at birth. The future was a path between mountains and you could not deviate from it. The legend of the Norns, the three women who sit beneath the world tree spinning out the fate of each human, had been impressed upon him since his earliest years. But now something was being offered to him. That shape, that awful, awful shape, something between a knife and a needle, to cut the thread of his life and restitch it, something hooked and sharp yet incorporeal – an idea more than a thing. The strange shape was a disturbance in the world that caused other disturbances. It was a rune. He could not see it now, but the thought of it seemed to float at the edge of his consciousness, like an idea remembered from a dream.

The rhythm of the drum seemed to command Vali and he had the strong urge to lie down in the water of the tunnel. He gave into it, leaning back and stretching out his arms, bending back his legs and sticking his head forward. Vali's body contorted into the shape that seemed to capture his whole being, his whole destiny. The Wolfsangel. He now seemed just an expression of its meaning.

He understood that he was being offered a choice: this shape or no shape, the rune or death. And then, in his mind, he wasn't the rune at all. He stood. The rune was the wolfman he had captured in the hills, floating there in the water of the tunnel. And then it was someone else. Adisla. She lay flat, her dress spread out around her, her arms wide and her legs bent in the same posture he had been. He seemed to be floating above her, or she beneath him, as if they were turning.

'Darling, where are you?'

'I am—'

'This is the place.' It was another voice. He had heard it

before, he was sure. Yes, it was how that man in the shield wall had spoken, the strange pale fellow in the hawk-feather cloak. Had he been called by the drumbeat too?

'What place?'

'The place where you are lost.'

The drum seemed to shake him, to call forth something inside him. It had set something in motion, like the footstep that starts a landslide. A roar. It was a voice like he had never heard before – a choking, rasping expression of a wild hate.

Suddenly he was on the ground, and where Adisla had been was a huge, slavering wolf, much bigger than he was. The creature was tethered to a rock, lashed by thin cords that cut into its flesh tight as twine on a joint of meat. It struggled and thrashed to stand but couldn't, like an animal trapped in the moment of its birth, the legs inadequate to its weight. Worse was its mouth, a gaping bloody wound kept open by a dull metal spar that dug into the flesh above and below.

A voice went skittering through his head, dry and quick as pebbles across rock: 'When the gods knew that Fenrisulfr was fully bound, they took a cord called Thin and tied it to a rock called Scream. When the beast tried to bite the gods they took a certain sword and thrust it into its mouth so its jaws could not close. There the Fenris Wolf will lie between waking agony and tormented sleep until the last days. Then the fetters will break and the gods will be torn.'

The creature strained against its bonds, half rose, collapsed, staggered up and pushed forward again, the huge head gasping towards him. The sound of its torment was like iron on a smith's stone but magnified a thousand-fold, a scraping, discordant note of anguish.

Vali felt a strong impulse of fear, not the fear of the shield wall or of battle – that can be bargained with, told that it will be listened to if only, just for a heartbeat, it will stand back. This was like the fear of drowning, of being buried alive, when the terror of extinction, of the hand of death blotting out the senses and stopping the breath, clamps down on you.

All reason smothered by those constricting coils of panic, you will claw and tear towards anything, anything at all, your mind's only ambition, your only coherent thought, 'Not this, not this.'

Vali turned to run but the walls were now close about him. He was trapped in a little pocket of dim light within a smothering dark. The wolf's agonies were like his own. He felt its yearning for freedom like stifling air sweeping over his face; felt its hatred of the tourniquet-tight bonds, the stabbing pain in his jaws. It was as if he was drowning, not in water but in the anguish of the wolf; as if the creature was consuming him, not with its teeth but with its mind.

He had to get out – to breathe, to live. His blood beat in his ears, or was it the drum? He looked up. The drummer was standing over him, the bone with which he beat the skin now in the shape of the jagged rune.

'Help me,' said Vali.

The drummer stopped drumming. Then he threw the rune towards Vali.

'Become,' he said. And Vali went wild.

Standing in the mire, Hogni was taken off his feet by a sudden kick of Vali's legs.

'He's broken his bonds!' shouted Orri to Jodis.

'Then take up the rope and kill him!'

Hogni pulled tight on the noose, but it was too late. Vali had it in his hands and stood to pull hard on it. Hogni had coiled the rope about his body and was dragged towards the prince through the water, fighting to untangle himself. He was too slow. Vali was on top of him, howling and spitting, biting and punching. Bragi was on the bank and he leaped into the mire towards the fight.

Orri drew his knife and went for Vali's back but hesitated for a fatal breath. This was the heir of his lord, after all. The prince seemed to sense the threat and turned to break Orri's neck with a blow.

Jodis screamed as Vali went for Hogni again but now Bragi

was on his back. Hogni got Vali's legs and together the warriors bundled his thrashing body from the mire. Then there were others there, jumping on Vali, pinning him, holding him and choking him. They were Forkbeard's men, and there, behind them, glowering in his full war gear of byrnie, helm, shield and sword, was Forkbeard.

Vali was hallucinating. He still saw the Rygir in arms but to him they were not understandable as men, just ciphers for pain and murder. It was as if he could taste their suspicion of him, their jealousies and their fears, as if all their emotions hung around them. Their feelings were like a scent he could breathe in; their many and several emotions, from larger hatreds to tiny animosities, were his to sense and name, as real and as many as the cooking smells on a feast day.

He struggled again and felt the noose go tight at his neck. He began to come back to himself, to realise who he was. Then everything vanished, and there was a different kind of blackness, a different cold at his back. He blinked, vomited water and opened his eyes. There was Hogni looking down at him.

He blacked out again for an instant.

'Get him to his feet. Get this dirty murderer and kinslayer to his feet.'

He was pulled upright. Vali's bones felt terribly heavy, like things excavated rather than lifted. Then he was staring into a familiar and furious face.

'You'll pay for this,' said Forkbeard. 'I should have known never to trust the Horda. No wonder they sent you, their most useless son. Well, we'll have your blood anyway. The prince wants death. Well, we'll oblige him, won't we, boys? Take the weapons from the other spies.'

Five spears were pointed at Bragi as Vali's arms were pinned behind his back.

'Get him down to the hall. I want the assembly there in short order. He can't die without their say-so. This is not just an execution – make sure everyone knows that – it's an act of war.'

Vali was kicked forward up the hill, still gasping and retching. His mind was full of what he had seen beneath the waters: the wolf, the cave, but most of all the memory of Adisla, himself and the wolfman, all twisted and misshapen under the influence of that dreadful rune. Their destinies were linked, he knew that, and the knowledge brought him comfort as well as dread.

24 Trial

There were voices raised against Vali's execution. Arnhvatr said how he had organised the defence; Hakir spoke of his bravery in the line. But Forkbeard's charges were strong ones.

The assembly took place two days after Vali had been taken from the pool, but the summons had travelled quickly and only those from the most distant farms did not attend. People were drawn into Eikund to hear of the Danish attack and to see the spy Forkbeard had caught.

The king was a blunt man and laid out his case bluntly. First, Vali had known of the raid and had called in the attackers when Forkbeard was away. Second, he had killed Drengi because of his jealousy over Adisla. That could not be denied, as the boy Loptr had seen him with the axe in his hand, standing over the body. He had also been heard on the Hogsback telling Drengi he should die. Third, when the enemy attacked he had tried to make off with a quantity of plate, a plan undone by the very people he was seeking to help. He knew that, though he had brought the berserks to Eikund, they would not recognise him in their rage and, fearful of their swords, he had fled. Fourth, in the wall he had refused to take up weapons and had even saved one of the invaders from death. When it became obvious his crimes would be uncovered, he had gone to the drowning pool to try to conjure magic to save his skin. An additional point, if additional points were needed, was that the traitor could even speak the language of the enemy. Why had he bothered to learn that, if not to trade with hostile powers?

Vali could not speak. His throat had clamped shut after his ordeal in the pool, and his mind with it. He had taken something with him from those waters, a pressure in his skull, a weight that seemed to make his head too heavy for his body. He had stepped close to something, he felt, something hidden within him, and had pushed the normal world away.

The assembly seemed to pass as in a dream, its significance not quite graspable. There were faces, some familiar, some unknown: hard-eyed farmers' wives staring at him in accusation, warriors, some friendly, some inscrutable, some hostile. Many people were sympathetic to him but a battle is a crucible of confusion. Those at the port when the raiders arrived had no coherent picture of exactly what had happened. Forkbeard made sense of it for them – interpreted the actions of the day, named the heroes and the cowards.

Vali's thoughts seemed obscured, glimpsed only in blurs, like the light of the day through the waters of a mire. He had never been so cold. He shivered and his flesh was pale and blotchy. The voices around him said it showed his weak-hearted nature.

Each man who had been with Forkbeard at the regional assembly said Vali was a coward and a turncoat. The warriors' shame at being absent when the Danes attacked redoubled the venom of their accusations.

Forkbeard knew he had let his people down, been too easily deceived, lured into complacency by years of peace. He needed a scapegoat, and Vali – an outsider and a man who didn't fit the heroic mould – provided him with one. Vali's mistake had been that he hadn't realised it wasn't enough to act heroically. You needed to talk heroically too, show relish for arms and slaughter, not laugh at heroes and spend your time chattering with women at the hearth. When Vali had led the defence, deceived the berserks and won the victory, many could hardly believe the evidence of their own eyes. By the time Forkbeard had finished bludgeoning his message home, they didn't.

Queen Yrsa had unwittingly endangered her son too. She made a mistake that Authun in his right mind would never have committed. Wary of the Danes' capacity for deception, she had not gone to the regional assembly and doubled the watch on her shores. She had known there would be an attack on the Rygir but suspected the Danes might have more than one target or, if they were successful in Rogaland, would push on to Horda territory. The Horda's absence at the assembly – not even a jarl was sent to represent them – was all the evidence Forkbeard needed.

Vali was a spy, said the king, a spy who had been placed in his court from his earliest years, accompanied and tutored in deceit by the scheming Bragi.

Vali's old tutor was next to him, beaten and bound. Bragi shouted his denials but Forkbeard had him struck down. The vote was taken. It went badly. Vali was seized by Forkbeard's guards and dragged outside.

A pit had been dug up on the hill, twice as deep as a man is tall and just wide enough to stop anyone wedging themselves against the walls and climbing out. Vali noticed none of this as he was thrown into it – just the fall and a sensation of breathlessness. The pit was wet. The rain had stopped but there was two fingers' depth of water at the bottom. His clothes had been torn to nothing during his struggles in the mire and he was cold. Still he was exhausted and he fell into a dead sleep, dreamless.

Vali heard voices at the top of the pit. Argument and struggle. Then something large and heavy landed across him with a thump.

'Bastards,' said Bragi. Vali shoved the old man off him and he rolled away, cursing. 'I have demanded a trial,' said Bragi. He was fuming. He was indifferent to anything but the injustice he had suffered and, it seemed to Vali, had been complaining of it almost as he fell.

Vali glanced up at the square of stars above him and looked around him at the walls of the pit. He swallowed. There was an awful ache in his throat and one in his head to keep it company. He remembered how he had once stood on Bragi's shoulders to gain access to the church. That was their way out of the pit. He was sure he could reach the lip to pull himself up. Did he have enough strength, though? A face appeared against the moonlit sky, almost as if on cue to render his question meaningless. There were guards. All he would get for trying to climb out was the butt of a spear in his face.

'A trial is the least I am owed.' Bragi was actually thumping the walls.

'A trial?' said Vali. His voice was rough and it was painful to speak.

'Not that thing in the hall,' said Bragi. 'A trial by combat – holmgang, the proper way.'

'You can't challenge the king to fight. The assembly has decided.' The prince spoke slowly and quietly to save his throat.

'I have challenged him and he will provide a champion,' said Bragi.

Vali leaned back against the wall. There was an acrid scent in his nostrils. He recognised it. Down on the beach they were burning the dead. Glimpses of what he had done came back to him.

'I killed Orri,' he said.

'Yes.'

'Then I am a kinslayer.'

'You were bewitched by the mire. And he attacked you, remember. He was coming for you with a knife at the time.'

'You would make a good advocate before the lawspeaker,' said Vali. 'I killed him. He was my kin.'

They sat for a while. Vali tried to come to terms with his crime. He couldn't. He deserved to die for that alone. Then he said, 'If you win, you'll be free. I suppose it's as logical a way out of this mess as any.'

'I knew you would see it that way, lord,' said Bragi, 'and I am pleased to say I have issued a challenge on your behalf, as your trusted vassal.'

Vali almost laughed but the effort hurt.

'Which of the king's champions am I to face?'

'Leikr,' said Bragi. Vali swallowed. Forkbeard knew his business. He meant him to fight Adisla's brother.

'And you?'

'The berserk in the pay of the Danes.'

'He lived then?'

'Yes. Forkbeard has promised him his freedom if he defeats me.'

Vali looked at Bragi. He was an old man, really, still useful in a shield wall or on a raid because of his experience; in personal combat he would be no match for the berserk. Bragi had his tricks, his skills and his willpower. The berserk was in his prime, a giant and a war leader. Still, Vali was pleased for Bragi. He would die the way he would have wanted.

Bragi read what was on Vali's mind.

'It was the best I could do. Better this way than the rope, eh?'

'I won't fight Adisla's brother,' said Vali.

'Then he'll kill you.'

'Yes. I deserve that for what I've done.'

'And she?'

'He'll look for her.'

'No. Forkbeard won't let him. He's declared her nithing, a sorceress and a force for evil, for the bad luck she has brought.'

'Adisla is no more a sorceress than I am.'

'Forkbeard says she is, that she was so envious of his daughter that she bewitched you and turned you against the people who have been your hosts for so many years. Do you know she killed her mother? It was seen, as the Danes approached their farm. She cut her mother's throat.'

Vali breathed out and leaned back. What must it have taken for Adisla to do that? Her mother must have asked her to do it to deny the Danes the satisfaction of her rape and murder. Again Vali felt no tears, just that hollow empty feeling that he knew he could only fill with Danish blood. He imagined little Manni with his seax at the door, trying to defend his mother and sister, struck down by people who could easily have disarmed him and sent him on his way with a kick up the backside. Vali had never known such a cold fury inside him.

'Ma Disa couldn't be moved and Adisla looked to spare her,' said Vali.

'That's not how Forkbeard sees it. Or her brothers. They've forsworn her and are pledged to kill her, if ever she's found. The girl's hopes rest with you, which is to say she has none at all.'

Vali nodded. 'Then I,' he said, 'must find a way to live.'

25 Escape

It was the brief night and the lonely voice of a wolf was in the hills, far away over the dark valleys, its howl testing the emptiness. It was almost as if Vali could understand what it was saying. 'I am here,' it said. 'Where are you?' A bright full moon lit the night sky, turning Vali's skin to silver, even in the pit.

'They sound hungry, don't they? Don't worry, little wolf, you won't starve for long. We've got two juicy hunks of traitor flesh here in the pit for you.'

It was the voice of Ageirr, the rider who had taken Adisla, come to taunt him. Her brothers had come before of course, but they had said nothing. Leikr had looked down at him, and Vali had felt his friend's anger and pain. He'd tried to talk to him, not to defend himself but to tell him his little brother had died a heroic death, but Leikr had just walked away.

Ageirr was not angry; he was there for fun. He pulled down his trousers and took a heavy piss into the dark of the pit. Neither Bragi nor Vali gave him the satisfaction of complaining.

'I did it with your little girl, you know, Vali. She asked me to. She said you couldn't do it properly and would a real man please her.'

'You'll have the same pox as me then,' said Vali with difficulty. 'I thought your piss smelled like mine.'

Bragi laughed like he might shake something loose. The old man's arm-thumping appreciation of Vali's wit almost made the prince wish he hadn't bothered.

Ageirr chuckled under his breath. There was movement beside him. He had someone with him, it seemed, most likely some of his cronies from Forkbeard's bodyguard. He poked his head over the side of the pit.

'You don't seem bothered by what I did. Is she such a slut?'

'Adisla wouldn't look at you, Jarl Ageirr; she prefers high-born men.'

Ageirr set his jaw. 'I am a jarl and the same as you,' he said.

'Is a jarl the same as a prince of the line of Odin? Tell me, did your father grant your mother her freedom before or after he knocked her up with you? Or is it true what they say, that she loved the thrall Kobbi and that you are his child?'

'Which Danish pig's bastard will Adisla be fathering?' said Ageirr. 'She'll have been ridden from here to Haithabyr by now, and when they sell her on she'll be ridden from there to wherever she's going.'

Vali had been trying to keep Adisla's likely fate from his mind since she had been taken.

'If you've anything behind those words, step into the pit and let's debate them in the old-fashioned way,' said Bragi.

'Oh, do be quiet,' said Ageirr. 'I wouldn't want you alerting anyone to the little present we've brought for you. No no, you're far enough away that no one will hear.'

'Where are the guards?'

'We are the guards.'

There was a sound of dragging and then some conversation between Ageirr and the other man at the top.

'Take the bag off its head as you throw it in. No, you idiot. Cut the ties on the legs but hold the muzzle, I don't want the thing biting me.'

There was a low note of distress that Vali had heard before. He knew what they had. It was a wolf.

'Forkbeard will want to know how that got in with us,' said Vali.

'It just fell in, I suppose. You know what wolves are like,' said Ageirr. 'They sneak up on even the most vigilant guards.

If you kill it, we'll just say it fell in. He's hardly likely to believe a kinslayer.'

The word felt sharp as a spear to Vali. Ageirr could try to humiliate him in any way and he would ignore it as the spiteful rantings of a fool, but nothing was more bitter to him than the truth that he had murdered one of his own.

Vali heard a scrabbling at the side of the pit, saw a flicker as something moved across the sky above him, and then a body hit him, hard. Instinctively he flinched back, throwing up his hands to defend his face from the attack of the wolf, but nothing came.

He heard a shout and the sound of a sword coming free from a scabbard.

'Who's there? Who's there? No, no! No!'

Something else, wetter, hit him.

The light was dim in the pit but Vali could see perfectly well. It was just that his mind was having difficulty coming to terms with what was in front of him. Across his legs was the body of Ageirr. He was dead.

With them in the pit was another body. It was Signiuti, one of Forkbeard's bodyguards, pulsing blood from a huge wound at his neck. He had fallen flat on his back onto Bragi, his sword still in his hand. Vali saw he had no throat; it had been torn clean away. Vali pushed Aegirr's corpse off him, the blood black and shiny on the white of his hands, light on darkness, life on death.

Then Bragi was on his feet, taking the sword from the corpse's hand. A face looked down at them. At first Vali thought it was a wolf. Then his eyes adjusted to the light. It was his own face, framed by a wolf's pelt.

'Do you mind stopping throwing bodies at us?' said Bragi, 'second thoughts, chuck a few more down and we'll climb out on 'em.'

A ladder was lowered into the pit and neither man needed a second invitation. Bragi was up first. Vali untied Signiuti's sword from his belt and followed.

When he put his head over the lip of the pit, he could see Bragi looking uncertainly at the wolfman. Feileg was freeing the wolf. He untied the animal's front paws, then took off the bag. The wolf snapped and bit but Feileg made a low noise, inclined his head and scratched at the dirt. The animal became calmer. It looked about it, first at Feileg, then at Bragi and Vali. Then it ran and was gone.

Vali pulled himself up to face the wolfman in the moonlight. His instinct was to attack him but he had seen where that had got Aegirr and Signiuti. The bandit's hands and face were covered with blood and Vali didn't need to be told where it had come from.

The wolfman fixed him with a stare. His eyes seemed to go right into Vali. The prince recognised the look – cold murder.

'Where is she?' said the wolfman.

'Who?'

'The girl. Adisla.'

'I don't know. I want to find her. Why does it concern you?'

'I love her.'

'What?'

'I love her. She was kind to me. It means she loves me too.'

This was too much for Vali to take in, so he concentrated on more immediate concerns. 'We have to leave. Now,' he said.

'You do what you like,' said Bragi. 'I'm going to find the berserk. To back down is to admit my guilt.'

Vali looked up at the stars. He couldn't believe what Bragi was saying. 'Who to? Forkbeard? You know he plans to make war on my father. That is your enemy, down there in those farms. The gods have proved you right by rescuing you from this pit. Don't spite your fate by throwing your life away. I'll need your sword where we are going, old friend.'

Vali's reasoning did nothing to sway Bragi, but the declaration of friendship was unexpected. He had wanted that from the prince ever since they had been together.

'Very well,' said Bragi. He went to the ladder and started to climb back into the pit.

'What are you doing?'

'Getting us some clothes for wherever we're going,' he said. 'We don't want to freeze to death and I think we'd cause a stir if we turn up in Haithabyr on market day naked.'

Ageirr and Signiuti had a good deal of gear on them. Since his return Forkbeard had insisted on his warriors being fully armed at all times in case of another Danish attack. Aegirr, the richest man in the area after Forkbeard, had a good byrnie over a padded jacket, a helmet, sword, shield and axe. The poorer but still affluent Signiuti had no byrnie but a good coat, a fine knife with a whalebone handle, the sword Bragi had already taken and also a shield. Vali let Bragi take the byrnie. The old man also took Aegirr's helmet and his other weapons. Vali took Signiuti's stuff. He wasn't sure how useful the shield would be but he knew its value as a shelter from the wind at sea. And it was to sea that he was going.

'Old Brunn has a faering on the coast just a vika from here,' said Vali. 'It's half a morning to get there, maybe more as we'll have to be careful.'

'That's our surest way home,' said Bragi. 'We could be at Hordaheim within the week.'

Vali shook his head. 'Forkbeard's longships would run us down long before that,' he said. 'We're going in another direction entirely.' He turned to the wolfman. 'Thank you. I don't really see how I can pay you but, should you come to the court of my father, tell this story and say Vali the Swordless bids them receive you as they would himself.'

The wolfman just stood looking at Vali.

'What?' said Vali.

'Is the girl there?'

'No, not there. We don't know where she is – that's what I intend to find out.'

'Then I am coming with you,' said the wolfman.

'No,' said Vali. 'I don't know you.'

'I swore to protect her. You are going to her. I will go with you.' He said this as if it was an uncontestable chain of reasoning.

'She doesn't need your protection,' said Vali.

'Sir, I think we should move before much longer. They may come to relieve the guards,' said Bragi.

'Yes.'

Vali said no more. He just pulled Signiuti's cloak – half soaked from the pit – about him and made his way to the path towards Brunn's house. The wolfman went to follow but Vali turned and drew his sword, more in anger than cold reason. The images of the two dead men in the pit came to him as he did so.

'I said no,' said Vali. The prince couldn't quite put his finger on why he didn't want the wolfman along with him. He had no reason to mistrust him; he had after all rescued him. But still he didn't want to take him. His talk of having sworn an oath to Adisla bothered him. Who had covered the wolfman from the sun when he was tied to the tree? Who had released him? Vali couldn't recognise the feeling within himself because he had never had it before. He had never questioned Adisla's love for him, nor did he now. Inside him though something had sparked to life – not quite jealousy, yet not far removed from that emotion either. He knew that Adisla could not feel affection for this man, but something seemed to shift within him at a deeper level than rational thought. It was just that there were too many uncertainties in his life at that moment. The presence of the wolfman would add more than it took away. Yes, that was it.

A look of blind fury passed over Feileg's face. Then he composed himself. He looked from Bragi to Vali and said, 'I will follow.'

Then he was gone, lost in the rolling country towards the beach.

Bragi and Vali watched him leave.

'He would have made a brute of an ally, sir,' said Bragi.

'Or a liability,' said Vali. 'He's strange and he's noticeable. Where we're going we'll already stand out as foreigners. With him we might receive an even harder welcome.'

Bragi nodded. 'But he'd be some back-up in a scrap. Ageirr and Signiuti might have been idiots but they were as good a pair of swordsmen as you're likely to meet. He did for both of them with his bare hands. You have to respect that level of raw violence.'

'If we survive then it'll be wit not fighting that brings us through,' said Vali. 'Come on, let's get to the boat.'

Vali had been concerned that it would be dangerous to use the path between the farms because it increased the chances of them being seen. However, he now reasoned that most of the warriors were down in the main settlement and that, if they did meet anyone on the path, chances were they would have fought with him against the Danes and be well disposed towards him. That said, they would be duty bound to go to Forkbeard and tell the king what they had seen. The only difference between friends and those who wished him harm would be how quickly they reported seeing him. They would take the path for the sake of speed.

They moved off, up the hill that led away from the sea, down the side of the copse where the battle had occurred. There was very little sign that anything had taken place there. Everything of value – from broken axe heads and spear tips to the clothes of the dead – had been looted. Only a pile of naked dead raiders had been left for the ravens and the crows.

They made their way down the back of the hill into the valley behind the port. Smoke was rising from the farmsteads, from cooking fires and dung heaps. The sun was creeping up, though the valley was still cast in a long shadow. Only one figure stirred among the houses, a wife off to tend her husband's flock. Most of the men were still at the hall. The farm animals were braying themselves awake, though the dogs still lay asleep in the doorways.

Vali looked back and thought that he loved this place and

that this was the last time he would ever see it. They climbed again. The path, as he knew it would, took them past Adisla's house. He saw the destiny he wanted – there together with her, he to guard the flock, she to make the butter. No battles to trouble them, no concerns of kingship or inheritance. If he ever got her back, he would renounce his claim to the throne and take up a farm. Perhaps then he would be allowed to marry her.

As they ascended the other side of the valley, they were seen. It was only a girl, nine years old and chasing with her dog along the path, but Vali knew her and he had seen her at the assembly where he had been condemned. She was Solveig, a noted mischief, doubtless on some errand from her mother as a way of stopping her waking everyone in the house.

Her face told him that she understood the implications of seeing him and, as artless as she was, she exclaimed, 'Outlaws!'

Bragi and Vali exchanged glances but neither did anything and let the girl run. Both felt that there had been enough killing in Rogaland for one summer.

'Can you go faster?' said Vali.

'You run on and I'll catch you if I can.'

Vali smiled. 'I'll never sail a faering without your help,' he said. 'Unfortunately it's a job for two, minimum, or I'd leave you to cut Forkbeard in two for me. Do you need the byrnie?'

Bragi slapped Vali on the shoulder. Vali could see the old fighter's offer had been sincere but could also see that Bragi was pleased it had been refused.

'It doesn't slow me down,' said Bragi.

This almost made Vali laugh. He had heard Bragi swear that he could move faster drunk in his war gear than he could sober in a tunic and trousers.

'Then you must have been rare slow to begin with,' said Vali.

They could hear the alarm going up in the farms behind

them – shouting, the barking of dogs and the excited voices of children.

'We'll have one chance when we get there,' said Vali. 'As soon as they realise we're taking a boat they'll be back to the port for a drakkar. There's a good wind, so we'll sail out of sight of land then take the sail down and hope they can't find us. Do you think we can make it?'

Bragi was puffing and blowing beside him. 'I haven't got a better plan.'

The sky was giving way to cloud coming down fast from the inland hills. Rain began and Vali was pleased. Anything that lowered visibility was to be welcomed. He'd planned to make for Haithabyr, against what Forkbeard would assume – that he would run for Hordaland. There he'd try to pick up word of the ship that had escaped with Adisla, to buy her back or if necessary steal her. If she wasn't there ... He couldn't think about that. Haithabyr was his only hope and, though it was a slim one, he clung to it.

Brunn's farm was just two huts on a sheltered inlet. He made most of his living by fishing in his one little boat. Vali had no choice though: he had to take it.

It was pouring by the time they got there. The smoke rising from the vent in Brunn's low hut made Vali wish he could stay for some food. Ma Brunn was at the door shaking out a cloth when they arrived. Her face went white when she saw them.

'Lord Vali, Jarl Bragi,' she said, nodding tight-lipped at them, 'this is a surprise.'

'Is your husband here?' said Vali.

'He's down tending the boat,' said Ma Brunn.

'Are your sons at home?'

Ma Brunn's hand went to her throat. 'They are at the court, as you know. Men of fighting age have been there this last week.'

Vali nodded. At least he wouldn't have to kill them. They were boys of twelve and fourteen, strong from years on the sea, but they wouldn't stand against two swordsmen, let alone one of Bragi's experience.

There was shouting and the barking of dogs.

'I expect your boys will be here presently,' said Vali and walked towards the shore.

He found Brunn pulling the boat down the beach towards the sea, oblivious to the rain. It was a well-built craft, high-sided to handle rough seas, four-oared and fat. On the beach it was unstable and leaned to one side like a gigantic mussel, gleaming black in the rain.

'Brunn,' said Vali.

'Lord,' said Brunn. The fisherman was a phlegmatic sort who, if he was shocked to see two named outlaws appear before him, didn't show it.

'Brunn,' said Vali, 'I have to trouble you, I'm afraid.'

'For what, sir?'

'For your boat.'

The clamour was becoming louder. Vali didn't have much time.

Brunn's eyes flicked up to see what was causing the noise. Then he looked at the weapons Vali and Bragi had by their sides.

'It seems I am not in much of a position to refuse it,' he said, 'though I doubt you'll get it out to sea in time.'

'Apply to my father in Hordaland for compensation,' said Vali, 'and if I return then I am yours for whatever service you ask. On my oath.'

Three skinny boys had made the top of the beach. They were all armed with sticks.

'If I starve this winter, then your boons will not do me much good, sir,' said Brunn. Vali did not have time to reply to him. He and Bragi began shoving the boat down the beach. It was not light but the slope was with them. Vali glanced over his shoulder. Two farmers from outlying farms had arrived next to the boys. They were only in Eikund to answer Forkbeard's summons and Vali hardly knew them.

'Are the thieves taking your boat, fisherman?'

Brunn said nothing. It was an unusual situation and he was a cautious man. To call a prince of the Horda a thief was a boldness too far for him.

More farmers and a few thralls arrived, though no warriors so far. Bragi and Vali kept pushing as the men made their way down the beach. When they came within eighty paces, the boat was still five lengths from the water's edge. Vali realised that they would not make it. He drew his sword and turned. 'There are ten of us, lord. Let's make this easy,' said a stout farmer who looked like a barrel with legs.

'There will not be ten go back,' said Vali. 'You know Bragi, trusted bondsman of Authun the Pitiless. The wolves howl his name, so often has he fed them.'

Vali was careful to use fine words, to impress the farmers.

It had some effect and the men paused. Vali could see their courage had reached a tipping point and could go one way or the other. He began to walk towards them, sword pointed. Unfortunately two of the men were drunk and, slapping their staves into the palms of their hands, came on.

What happened next was a blur. There was a scream from the farmstead as Ma Brunn saw what was coming. Across the beach, moving at speed, came the wolfman. He was not upright but running on all fours, his massive arms propelling him forward across the shingle. Suddenly he was between Vali and the mob, facing the farmers with a low growl. His face and hands were bloody, his eyes invisible beneath the wolf pelt. Truly he did appear to be a werewolf, a man-monster created by privation, ritual, blood and, most importantly, fear. Someone observing the scene from the safety of a boat might have simply seen a man with a wolf pelt on his head loping in a weird way towards the farmers. The farmers though, brought up on winter night stories of sorcerers who donned skins and ran as animals, saw something different entirely. Here was a creature of fireside tales come to life, staring them down beneath a black sky on a black beach, a fiend that could drag them down to Hel. The drink that had so emboldened the two men a moment before now reversed its effect, loosing unimaginable fears within them.

Feileg lowered his head and then threw it back, letting out an unearthly howl. The two drunks turned and fled. The others held their position but Vali could see they were ready to run. They seemed almost to dance upon the spot, taking a step forward, then to the side. Knives that were drawn were sheathed, and knives that were sheathed were drawn, weapons moved from hand to hand. The men glanced behind them to look for support. There was none.

'The boat!' It was Bragi.

Vali turned and resumed shoving as the wolfman stood seething and growling in front of the farmers.

The boat scraped and slid across the stones to the ocean's edge. Another push and it came upright in the water, floating. Vali and Bragi pushed for all they were worth and then jumped aboard, leaping to the oars.

Vali bent his back, rowing hard. Twenty paces from the shore, he looked back at the wolfman on the beach. He was now running for the water. The farmers took courage from his flight and gave chase. Vali heaved at the oars, no time to get the sail up, as the wolfman splashed after them, thrashing through the surf in extravagant swipes. It was then that Vali realised he couldn't swim.

Willpower alone was keeping him going but he was taking huge gulps of water with very little progress to show for it. The farmers were now raining stones at them. Vali ducked and turned to Bragi. He had been going to tell Bragi to pull them out of range of the farmers as quickly as he could but he heard his voice say something else. 'Get him.'

Bragi didn't hesitate, just rowed the boat around under the hail of missiles. A rock bounced off his helmet as they turned.

'That works then,' he said, tapping his helmet, but Vali could hardly hear him. They came alongside the wolfman not twenty yards from the shore. More stones crashed into the boat. Bragi had armed himself with pebbles for Ageirr's hunting sling but his attempts to balance in the boat and return fire were doomed to failure, so he opted to do one task well rather than two badly and put the sling away.

'I'll come back on that beach and shove those stones somewhere they're not meant to go!' shouted Bragi. He took up his shield and started insulting the men on the shore, to draw their fire while Vali worked.

Vali leaned over the side. The wolfman's legs were pumping to little effect, his arms thumping at the water. Bragi moved to the opposite side of the boat as Vali bent down to grab Feileg. Every part of his conscious mind told him this was stupid. He didn't know why he was rescuing this dangerous wildman. All he knew was that after the mire he would never be able to watch someone drown. But was it something even more fundamental? He remembered that rune, the floating body beneath him that he had seen in his visions – the body that was him, the wolfman and Adisla all at once. He grabbed the thrashing man.

The prince took a couple of blows on the shoulder and back from Feileg's flailing arms but then he had him. As he took the wolfman's weight all the tiredness of the last few days seemed to descend on him – the battle, the ordeal in the mire, the pit, the flight to the beach – but then he looked into his face. It was his own, looking back at him.

The stones suddenly stopped, which Vali thought strange. He hauled Feileg into the boat and regained his oar. As he and Bragi heaved on the oars to get themselves to a distance where it was safe to put up the sail, he looked back. Brunn the fisherman was standing in front of the stone throwers, begging them not to throw any more.

'He thinks they'll damage his boat!' said Bragi. 'You bastards throw one more rock and I'll chop it to bits and swim just to spite you!'

Vali felt guilty. He realised there was no hope of Brunn

applying to his father if a war broke out and his promises had been useless. He had made a poor man poorer. Still, Brunn wouldn't starve; the community would rally as it always did.

One hundred paces from shore, they fitted the mast into the socket sailors called the old lady and let the offshore wind take the sail. As the boat surged forward, Vali allowed himself a glance back at the land.

'We shan't see this place again,' he said.

Bragi was lost in practical concerns.

'There's no chest for this byrnie,' he said, stripping off the mail. 'It'll be a game keeping our war gear dry.' He was right. The seats for rowing were just strengthening spars across the ship. They kept the vessel sturdy but they offered no storage.

The wolfman lay coughing on the bottom of the boat, looking very ill.

'No sailor,' said Bragi, nodding towards him.

'Well,' said Vali, as the land receded, 'he won't be murdering us while we're at sea, at least.'

He looked down at the wolfman, as he had looked down on him in that vision in the mire. From now on, he knew, their destinies were inseparable.

26 Into the Unknown

Adisla sat shaking in the bottom of the ship. She'd had the courage to do what she needed to do to her mother but her resolve had failed her when it came to herself.

She had tried to get her mother out of the bed but it was no use. Disa was too heavy and in too much pain to be moved. Then they'd heard the Danes coming through the farms. Her mother had begged her to do it but the Dane had been grinning at her from the doorway of the house before she'd had the courage. He hadn't tried to stop her until her mother's throat was cut. Then she faced him with the knife. He was a jarl, a tough-looking man with a hard, lean face. He was wearing a byrnie and a helmet, carrying a shield and a long seax.

'Come boat, quick,' he said in bad Norse. 'Boat now, quick. Bad for me no time with you. Knife down, break arm. Choose.'

Adisla had heard his words and understood some of them but she could hardly make sense of what he was saying. She'd just stood sobbing, soaked in her mother's blood, the knife loose in her hand. The Dane had taken it from her and led her out.

She'd often wondered what it would be like to set out in a drakkar for one of the great markets, or to see the southern lands. Now she was going where she had dreamed of, but in the most horrible circumstances. She had feared what would happen to her on the ship but, numb with the horror of what she had done, real terror didn't bite at first. They had said things, of course — how she was going to get it across a week of ocean until she'd never be able to put her legs together again. Some had even come and drunkenly tried to talk to her, a cross between taunting and a strange sort of wooing.

There was one who chilled her even more than the rough warriors. He was a foreigner, she could see, wearing clothes of blue wool, trimmed with red. On his head was a four-cornered hat, he wore a thick sea cloak and on his back was a shallow round parcel, like a big disc, wrapped in seal skin. He came to her as soon as she was on the ship, examined her with his brilliant blue eyes as if she was a horse he was thinking of buying and then sat down next to her. Adisla looked back at the fires rising from her homeland and wept.

The ship pulled away and the king stood up, declared her his prisoner and told his men that anyone who touched her would find himself swimming home. The oars moved in a steady rhythm, the men drank as they rowed, and Adisla wondered how long the king would be able to control them. He said nothing to her, just threw her a heavy cloak and went back to the tiller.

Adisla resolved not to cry and tried to sleep, but every time she closed her eyes she heard the Danes at the door of her house, saw Manni, brave with his seax, heard her mother begging her to kill her, saw the blood and saw the fires. When she opened them, she saw only the strange savage in his odd clothes, staring at her from not two paces away. She didn't see lust in his expression, or anything in particular, just an implacable, constant observation.

After an hour at sea she allowed herself a look around. Haarik's remaining drakkar was alongside but land was nowhere. Her hands were shaking with anxiety. Adisla had never been more than half a day away from her own home but she knew that ships had to cling to the coast. What other way was there to navigate? It was possible to take to the open sea in times of dire emergency, but sailors avoided it whenever they could.

Thick cloud was rolling in and the sun was just a lighter patch on the grey horizon. She could see they were heading north. The rain came on, nagging at the sail in squalls so they moved forward in sudden lurches and drops, making

Adisla queasy. Then it really began to pour, curtains of water sweeping across the ship in the rising wind. The crew had abandoned their oars and were now employed in full-time bailing, using helmets, bowls and wooden pails.

Eventually Haarik shook his head. 'Sail down,' he shouted.

The problem was not the wind, nor even the swell, which was nothing to trouble an experienced sailor, but the rain. The mast was lowered quickly and soundings taken. Then the anchor was dropped and the sail lashed across the ship, providing shelter but turning the world dark.

'Join us beneath the blanket, darling?' shouted one of the warriors to Adisla.

She said nothing, just huddled into the side of the boat for shelter. The cloak at least kept her warm, and the sail kept her dry, though the stink of the men under the cover was terrible and the dark made her wonder how well Haarik would be able to guard her.

Now the motion of the ship was frightful, a regular and relentless rise and fall that seemed to leave her stomach at the bottom of the wave while her head was sent to the top. She couldn't help but retch and vomit. Her mouth felt dry and she was terribly thirsty, but she wouldn't ask for water.

Adisla lifted the side of the sail and looked out around her. The light was jellyfish grey, the sea a gentle but stomach-turning swell.

She thought of her mother, she thought of Vali – she knew she would never see him again – and she thought of the wolf-man. Had he survived the attack?

She tried to remember the words of the prayer to Freya: 'For the love I've known, lady, receive me.'

Adisla lifted back the edge of the sail and slipped over the side.

27 Haithabyr

The going was hard down the coast. Vali felt he couldn't risk stopping at any farmstead or fisherman's hut in case word went back to Forkbeard of the direction he had taken, so the men slept on beaches or in caves as they hugged the shore south. The advantage of the enduring daylight was that they could rest in shifts, Bragi working the sail for a time, Vali taking over when the warrior became tired. The wolfman could not sail or row, so he just sat, his head on his knees, staring at his feet and looking miserable.

Feileg proved a much better asset on land. He was an accomplished forager, bringing back seabird eggs and bitter plants to chew. So they ate well enough, supplementing the wolfman's food with seaweed and roots from the surrounding countryside. Water was easy to find; in fact, when it rained they had rather too much of it.

Vali wanted to get on, so he only stretched the sail across the boat as a shelter when the rain was at its heaviest. The rest of the time he just worked the bailing pan as hard as he could. They were frequently soaked but making progress, and that was the important thing.

This was hostile territory but their little fishing boat attracted less notice than a longship. Still, they had to be careful, rounding the lands of the Agder and the Westfold, sprinting across the bright broad bay of Vingulmarken and over to Alvheim.

Then it was threading their way through the islands to Denmark and their destination – the trading town of Haithabyr. This was where the Danes would have taken a slave. They were in constant peril. They had to keep the coast in sight for navigation but this meant they risked being seen.

Vali thought it would be a bored king who would launch a drakkar to catch some fishermen, but then again kings did get bored.

The weather was rough at times but they were prepared, beaching the little boat, inverting it to use as a shelter and sitting out the high winds for a few days until the going was safe again. Vali knew that even if Forkbeard had sent a long-ship after them, he'd be no keener to sail in bad weather. Longships could strike across the open sea but, given the choice, clung to the coast and beached if they saw a storm coming rather than risk swamping.

The boat seemed to crawl through the islands, though they were glad of them, the many coves and inlets providing good beaching and hiding places. And navigation was easy if circuitous at points as Bragi had travelled this way before. Once or twice they had to go west when their destination was south, but it was a small price to pay to avoid the open sea. Much of the journey was rowed, but they were following a trade route so the currents and the winds were favourable. From their final stop on a beach they could see a long promontory, a trail of smoke from a line of campfires stretching along it.

'Is this the town?' said Vali. 'It's no bigger than Eikund.'

Bragi laughed. 'That's just the bjorkey at the mouth. That's our first problem.'

Vali had never heard the expression before so he asked what a bjorkey was.

'It's a collecting point,' said Bragi. 'If two big ships want to exchange goods then there's no point them going all the way into port. They'll do it at the mouth of the inlet. Also, if a ship is on its way somewhere else it can just pick up or drop what it has to here without wasting time stopping.'

Vali found such haste difficult to believe. Who didn't have time to stop? What could be so urgent that you had to ply your trade routes as if pursued?

'Riches,' said Bragi as if reading his mind. 'The first sheep at the trough drinks deepest. You don't want to turn up at a port with a cargo of whetstones if someone else has done the same the day before. These merchants want us to beg for their wares.'

In other circumstances Vali might have found Bragi's words exciting – a glimpse into a world that he knew nothing about. As it was, they just added to the sense of uncertainty he was feeling – of going into a situation unprepared. The vulnerability he felt did not come from the immediate threat of the Danes. Ever since his time in the mire he had felt fragile, slightly removed from himself, not fully in the present. Still, he couldn't help wondering what else Bragi knew that he could tell him. Up till now the old man had only ever seemed to want to talk about battles, and Vali had made the mistake of assuming that was all he had to say.

'Do you want me to pick a few holes in your plan?' said Bragi as they got back into the boat and prepared to go across.

'Go on.'

'Well, we have stolen clothes of the Rygir nobility. The Danes have just attacked the Rygir and therefore could be considered to be at war with them. Haithabyr is in Denmark, which – the last time I checked – was full of Danes. Now I'm not a deep thinker like yourself but it strikes me that, should we turn up as we are, then we may as well put on the manacles ourselves, to save everybody the bother of a struggle. Do you see what I mean?'

'There are problems with what I'm proposing to do,' said Vali, 'but I don't think we'll have any trouble. They have quite a few separate kingdoms. We'll be all right as long as Haarik isn't there.'

'If he is?'

Vali shrugged. The wolfman said nothing, just sat staring at the sea as if he hated it.

Bragi said, 'Well, assuming we get past the being-cut-down-where-we-stand part, what then? They'll know that they can hold us for ransom or enslave us – both meaning a good profit. They may even think they can get the berserk back.'

'The berserk is a mercenary and also not a Dane,' said Vali. 'They won't bother about him.'

'So what are we going to do?'

'Make use of what we have.'

'Two fine swords, one byrnie, a sling and a good set of teeth on your fellow here,' said Bragi.

'You're missing the clothes,' said Vali, 'and this.' He held up a stubby black stick he had taken from the purse at Signiuti's belt. 'This is as good a piece of eye dark as I've ever seen.'

'What good will that do?'

'Well, if we're going to look like Rygir jarls, then I suppose we had better act like them. I'm going to ask for compensation for the raid.' He held out the stick. 'If you would be so good, Bragi, as to try to make me look as if I'm trying to please the vanities of a court, not like I've come to burn the place to the ground. Best not try it as we go across. I don't trust your hand on land; on water I would fear for my eyes. And when we get there treat me like a prince – a bit more bowing and scraping.'

'Let's hope we can make them understand us.'

'I speak their language,' said Vali. 'Not all my talk at Ma Disa's house was wasteful.'

Bragi shrugged and took the stick.

As Bragi applied the kohl Vali spoke to Feileg. 'And you just tell them you're our priest. It had occurred to me to sell you, but I should think the byrnie will be enough to buy her freedom – if she's there.'

'If the girl is there, I will take her,' said the wolfman.

'You might find it easier to pay,' said Vali. 'Haithabyr is a town of a thousand people, if what I hear is true. Even you can't fight that many, wolfman, though one day I will. We will come here and burn their lands from shore to shore for what they have done.'

Feileg just looked at him blankly.

The problem of turning up in a fishing boat when pretending to be an ambassador had occurred to Vali, but there was nothing he could do about it, so he decided not to let it worry him.

The wind was not entirely favourable and the men had to row their way across, which Vali thought no bad thing. It was good to get there at the oar, clearly vigorous, clearly in charge of his destiny.

As it turned out, the bjorkey was no problem. It was no more than two houses and a collection of barrels with a few people sitting around them. A couple of the men on the shore raised their arms in salute as the boat passed and Vali returned their greeting.

'That went smoothly,' said Vali.

'So far,' said Bragi.

The wolfman looked around him. Like Vali, he had never seen a place like this – small flat fields of green oats turning to gold where the dark clouds broke and the sun poured through. They were on a long narrow inlet which was much calmer than the open ocean, and for the first time since they had set off Vali saw the colour come back to Feileg's cheeks.

As they moved up the river, there were small camps. Children ran down to the shore, trying to attract their attention, shouting out words, one in four of which Vali recognised. That word was 'stew', and if he had been under any misapprehension as to what they were talking about, their mothers stood by fires, rattling earthenware pots and making eating gestures.

'What hospitality!' said Vali.

'Not quite,' said Bragi.

'They're offering us food.'

'Yes, and they won't be handing it over until we've paid for it. In coin.'

Vali laughed. 'It's a poor man indeed who takes payment for food from a traveller.'

'Well you'll find Haithabyr full of poor men then,' said Bragi, 'though you wouldn't know it by the silks they wear.'

Vali concentrated on his rowing after that. To him, it was

demeaning to ask guests to pay, no matter how many there were. Likewise, it was shameful for a guest who had made great claims on his host's hospitality to leave without offering a gift. The idea of paying for what you received had never even occurred to him until that moment, and it confirmed his view that Danes must be entirely lacking in honour. And he was going into a nest of them.

It was two hours before he saw Haithabyr. They rounded a bend in the inlet and there it was, crammed by the waterfront. He had never seen so many houses. They seemed to fill the gentle slope that led up from the river. There must have been a hundred altogether, not counting stables and wells, even a large church – as he now knew it to be – like he'd seen on the raid, marked by a cross on the roof.

It was as if the buildings were not properly anchored and had slid down to the harbour, pushing in on each other like cattle at a feed trough, shouldering each other aside in an attempt to get to – what? There were eight ships – two small snekkes, a fearsome drakkar and five merchant knarrs – moored a few yards off the wooden jetties. The narrow space between the houses and the water was devoted to boat repairs, large and small. Here was a longship taking a patch to the bottom of its hull; there were fishing boats stripped to almost nothing. The boats reminded Vali of the carcasses of beasts, half eaten by wild animals, their ribs showing.

Something strange was happening. Two of the knarrs were full of rocks and men were casting them overboard into the harbour. Vali realised that this must be some sort of defence they were building, a screening wall against sea attack. The idea was so simple and so brilliant that Vali wondered why his people or the Rygir had never thought of it.

People were on the waterfront, a knot of fifty or sixty cramming forwards shouting to them, some waving weapons, which made Vali feel he wanted to reach for his sword. Others brandished bizarre items: rich cloths, blocks of iron, necklaces and arm rings, clothes even.

'Do they mean us harm?' said Vali, eyeing one particularly large man waving a spear.

'Only to our pockets,' said Bragi. 'They're trying to trade with us.'

He heard calls again in uncertain languages, gibberish, some words in a weird Danish slang, followed by, 'Where you from? My friends, where you from?'

'We are Rygir!' shouted Bragi, which to all intents and purposes they were.

The gibberish ceased and everything became intelligible. 'See these silks, carried for three years from Serkland, glass from there too.' 'If you have furs I will buy them.' 'Best price, best price. Ale and mead for the weary traveller!' 'Hello, mates. Let's do business!' 'My father was Rygir, only the best deals for them!'

Men were virtually fighting each other to get to the front of the wooden jetty, some almost falling into the water. Vali realised why the houses were crammed so tight. They too were trying to be as near as they could to the source of trade – the inlet.

Now some of the traders were climbing into boats to row out, so Vali could see he needed to act quickly. Were they traders, though? One was very bizarrely dressed, with a wolf's mask on his face, not like Feileg's pelt but a stiff thing made of wicker and fur.

The prince stood up in his boat and shouted to the crowd, 'I am Vali, son of Authun the Pitiless, king of the sword-Horda, ward of Forkbeard, king of the Rygir. I am here to speak to your king, Hemming the Great, son of Godfred.'

'Greetings to the son of the White Wolf!' shouted the man with the mask on.

Three boats came towards them, two or three men in each. Vali realised he had little choice but to let them come alongside. When they did, he almost did reach for his sword. Not pausing for a breath, three men expertly stepped into his boat – one with iron ingots, another with a roll of carved daggers and the third in the wolf mask, a small fat man in many-coloured silks. Vali could see as he climbed aboard that his hair was black and as slick as a seal's back.

'Best iron in the world,' said the man with the ingots. 'We can deliver as much as you like to your homeland. Think of the swords your smiths could forge with this.'

Vali looked at the man. He actually did find his words persuasive and began thinking about how, when he was king, he would love to equip his bodyguards with fine weapons they could use on these Danes.

'This dagger was used to kill a dragon in the lands of the east. It will pierce even the strongest byrnie,' said the man with the knives.

'And what are you selling?' said Bragi to the man in the mask. Bragi had tried to drain the belligerence from his voice, which made him sound more threatening than if he'd just shouted.

The wolf-masked man let out a deep chuckle. 'Everything!' he said.

Feileg, who had watched all this with a kind of horror in his eyes, suddenly jumped up and roared at the man in the mask.

'No!' said Vali, gesturing for him to sit down, but the ingot seller and the dagger man had both instinctively leaped for their boats. The knife merchant managed to roll into his, but the other, in his panic to get away, missed his step and fell into the water, drawing a huge laugh from the crowd. Only the man in the mask remained. He seemed entirely unperturbed by Feileg's display and the sudden exit of his two friends.

'Sit down,' said Bragi, to Feileg.

The wolfman ignored him and stood glowering down at the remaining merchant. Bragi put his weight suddenly to the side of the boat, wobbling it and forcing Feileg to grab for the rail.

'I said sit down,' said Bragi.

The wolfman did as he was told.

'Berserks are such formidable bodyguards, are they not, prince? And yet never quite your men for a pleasant hello. I was brought up among them, if you can believe it. We call them the Vucari, men who live as wolves. First time in the big town for the boy, I bet.'

'Who are you?' said Vali.

'I am your smoother of the way in Haithabyr, your scythe in a forest of doubt, your beacon in darkness, your—'

'He asked who you were,' said Bragi. 'Unmask yourself and face us as man to man.'

The man took off his mask.

'Veles Libor,' he said, 'friend to the prince and to all who travel with him.'

'Veles!' said Bragi. 'Veles, is it you? What are you doing here?'

'Living here,' said Veles, 'at the invitation of the late King Godfred, may whatever gods you find appropriate guard him in the afterlife, and the good King Hemming, may the same gods... Well, you catch my drift.'

'You have abandoned your people?' said Vali.

'The good King Godfred abandoned them for me when he was so considerate as to burn down my home town of Reric. His generosity did not stop there though. He was kind enough to offer, nay insist, that we merchants transfer our business here. The chance to come to such a warm and pleasant land was far more welcome than the alternative, so here I am.'

'What was the alternative?' said Vali.

'An inventive, original and rare death,' said Veles. 'It was the easiest bargain I have ever struck.'

'So you're a thrall?' said Vali.

'But a comfortable one. If you're going to be a slave, why not be the king's slave? And besides, the price of my efficiency is a certain level of freedom.'

For the first time since he had returned to Eikund with the wolfman, Vali laughed. 'It's so good to see you,' he said.

'And you. You have grown mighty, my prince. You must

have killed many men by now.' Vali noticed he was looking strangely at the wolfman. Veles missed nothing, least of all something as obvious as the wolfman's resemblance to the prince. It didn't stop the merchant speaking. 'I have arranged everything for your stay here. You are guests at my house. Whatever you want to buy here, whatever you want to sell, I will be pleased to do it for you. It would be my honour to conduct your dealings for you and lend you my expertise.'

'We are a delegation.'

'From Forkbeard. Some business about Haarik's raid, no doubt.'

'How did you know about that? No one could have travelled here more quickly than us,' said Vali.

'You are a seer?' said Bragi.

'Hardly,' said Veles. 'I simply asked them when they passed through.'

'Which way?' said Vali.

Veles looked hard at Vali.

'Come on, man. It's an easy enough question to answer. Were they on their way or coming back from the raid?'

'On their way,' said Veles. 'They have something you value? A captive?'

'Magician!' said Feileg in a low growl.

'My skills are baser, I assure you,' said Veles. 'It is my business to recognise want when I see it. There has been a raid on Rogaland; the esteemed prince is dispatched to retrieve something that can be carried in such a small boat. Very wise way to travel. You need five drakkars or none in these waters nowadays. Believe me, the pirates have nearly broken me in two. I bleed coin to them. Bleed it!' He seemed on the verge of losing his temper but then caught himself. 'So it is a single captive. I can't think of anything else that needs diplomacy to retrieve. If it was gold I think you would come with war-paint on your eyes, not these fine lines fit to please a lady.' He gestured at the kohl that Bragi and Vali had applied to each other.

'Where is the girl?' said Feileg.

Veles smiled broadly.

'I do not have her here, but if she is to be found, then I can find her,' said Veles. 'A girl. A princess no doubt. Has little Ragna been taken? I will help find her and expect no payment; simply your thanks and whatever gift your generous people choose to bestow on me will be enough. '

'It is not Ragna, though the captive is no less dear to the king. No gift would suffice to thank you for her return,' said Vali.

'Well, let's talk about the exact sums later,' said Veles. 'I'm joking of course. But, please, come to my house, where you will be my guests. And you must see King Hemming. We should start by asking for compensation for the raid *and* the abduction of the girl. I'm sure he couldn't have sanctioned this, prince. He wouldn't want to risk your father's wrath. I will handle everything – the amount, whichever way it is paid, the form, the delivery. The details of mere trade are beneath princes, or at least that's what the Franks maintain, and their empire seems to thrive on it. You need only return to Rogaland and wait for the happy outcome.'

Vali felt his heart leap. If anyone could locate Adisla, he thought, Veles could.

28 Bargains

Haithabyr was as much a marvel close up as it had been from the sea. Logs had been split and laid on the ground so there was a solid path, firm underfoot. The houses huddled in so close that the thatches nearly touched at some points, blocking out the light. Each yard was fenced, some with individual wells. People shoved and bustled on the waterfront, and even in the alleys that led up from the jetties you could hardly take twenty paces without encountering someone coming the other way. Still, the place was filthy. Piles of rubbish lay everywhere and in places the wooden path was slick with shit.

Would it have hurt, thought Vali, to have carried some of the mess down to the water and thrown it in? Haithabyr stank, and he wondered that people could live in such fetid conditions.

'Danes,' said Bragi. 'They don't know the meaning of washing and cleaning.'

'They are a filthy people,' said Veles, 'say their enemies. However, I have always found them to be scrupulously clean, as such an opinion is more conducive to a long and happy life. This way, please.'

They moved up through the town, crossing a bridge over a small stream that ran down to the quay. Vali marvelled at that too – the stream had been cut into a channel and was as straight as an arrow. Was this stinking, teeming place the future? he asked himself.

Then, in a square not far from the channel, he saw it – the market. All around were open barns, which he could see contained livestock. One was smaller than the others, squat to the ground like a normal longhouse but without walls, the roof low and the space underneath it black. Vali went closer and saw ragged figures huddled in the darkness. Walking faster and faster, he ducked under the roof of the building and peered into the gloom. Pale faces looked back at him, some shrunken with starvation, others quite plump and healthy. All, however, were chained together. The smell was overwhelming.

His eyes went from face to face. There were two monks – as he now knew them to be – as he'd seen on the island, a mother and two children huddling together, a tall man who could only be a Swede, sitting upright and defiant, and, at the end, a girl of around seventeen, blonde-haired, pretty and staring blankly ahead. It wasn't Adisla though, not her at all.

'What is it you're looking for, sir? Market is two weeks from now, but if you offer the right price the goods are yours. Or do you have slaves to sell? I will buy the right material.'

Vali turned to see a well-dressed man in a dark cloak. He was carrying a long switch of hazel. Beside him was a red-haired woman he guessed was a freed slave because she did not look Danish. She was carrying a set of keys.

'I'm looking for a woman who might have been brought here, taken from the raid on Rogaland,' he said.

'The Rygir girls are cold,' said the man. 'Here, try this one at the end. She'll set your bed on fire, as long as you're willing to put up with a month of sulking while she gets used to you.'

The girl looked at him from the darkness. Her eyes didn't contain hope, or anything in particular.

'I want the Rygir girl,' said Vali.

'This one is from the western islands – that's as near as you're going to get to Rygir,' he said.

'So Haarik's men have not been here selling slaves?' said Vali.

'They left a month back,' said the slaver, 'and I haven't seen them since. Hey, you, pauper, come away from there.'

Vali turned to see Feileg inspecting the irons on one of the children. As the slaver ran across raising his switch, the wolf-man turned and let out a low snarl – a raw and angry sound, a boiling expression of animosity, a communication of the kind certain animals have sent to humans since earliest times. It was the sound the wolf and the bear make to their prey, a sound that speaks to the instincts, not the mind, and says only one thing: 'Run.'

Vali sensed the fear come off the slaver like the blast you feel when you pass the door of a smithy. The slaver dropped the switch and reversed direction, backing away from Feileg and falling back into some straw. The wolfman stepped forward and stood above him. Then Vali saw the knife. The slaver was a hard man and had recovered from the shock of Feileg's fury as he had fallen. He pulled a blade from his belt and as he stood drove it forward into Feileg's belly. There was a sound like a breaking branch, then another and then a thump. It all happened too fast for Vali to take in. A breath after the slaver fell back into the straw for the second time, Vali's mind finally caught up with what he'd witnessed. Feileg had broken the slaver's arm, snapped his knee joint and thrown him to the ground. His head flopped back into the mud with a squelch.

The wolfman dropped on top of his man, teeth bared. Vali instinctively knew what was about to happen and leaped forward to push Feileg off. It was one thing to get into a fight within a blink of coming into town – that might even be good for their reputation – but savaging someone with your teeth was a step too far. Vali pushed as hard as he could, but the wolfman just turned his body and Vali found himself face down in the mud. Feileg was tearing at the slaver's face with his nails, pulling the flesh from the bone. The noise he was making was unbearable, a demented, keyless howl. The slaver lost an eye.

The woman stood watching expressionlessly as her companion suffered.

'Feileg!' Vali got back up and shook the wolfman by his shoulders, staring into his face as if into a mirror.

And then the nature of things seemed different: his consciousness seemed a wide and inclusive thing. It was as if the

248

way of seeing things that he'd found in the mire had leaked into the day to day, as if the whole world was bathed in that dirty underwater light. Emotions pulled his head this way and that – the fear coming off the slaver and from Feileg a powerful sense of something trying to break out, something smothered under a blanket of pain. Vali forced himself to speak, though he didn't know where he got the words.

'Feileg, please,' said Vali. 'It's all right. Just leave him. Come on, you must be tired. Veles will have a fine bed, I'm sure – better than the ground, eh?'

The wolfman looked back into Vali's eyes and Vali sensed that he shared something fundamental with this man, something deeper than could be conveyed by any word. He was connected to him, more than that, the same as him. The feeling made him shiver.

The wolfman didn't move, just looked down at the man beneath him. The slaver was silent – blue at the lips.

'He's dead of fear,' said Bragi. 'I've seen it before.' Vali looked down at the body and it was as if its smells leaked memories. He tasted sour curds, sea and wood, sweat and blood, caught the scent of smoke and rain, saw piles of gold and wide bright skies. The sensations crowded upon him and then they were gone.

A crowd had been drawn by the noise.

The slaver woman now pulled at Vali's arm. She wasn't upset or angry. 'I want weregild. Compensation for my husband's death.'

Vali had the bearing of a prince, so she had naturally gone to him rather than the wild Feileg, who seemed in some sort of trance.

'I ...' Vali didn't know what to say. He was trying to think straight. The fight had registered in his mind on a level beyond the fact of its violence, terrible though that had been. The strength of the emotions had seemed to wake a new sense in him, something between smell and memory. He felt dizzy and his head began to ache. The wide consciousness of a breath before had retracted to a thin stream; there was a high-pitched ringing in his ears like the echo of a scream.

The woman spoke again. 'Some compensation is right. I saw you arrive. You have a fine boat. If I can have that, then the matter is forgotten.'

Veles put up his hand.

'I am the prince's representative in all such matters. You will get no weregild from us. Your husband attacked this man. The berserk did no more than shout at him and your husband drew a knife. It is you who owe us compensation.' He turned to the crowd, some of whom were now coming in to look at the body of the slaver.

'Is that not right?'

There were some murmurings, a few half-hearted jokes, which Veles acknowledged with a smile.

The woman seemed to weigh Veles' words in her mind.

'Give me two oars and we are even.'

Veles shook his head.

'My friends have a case against you. Give us all your slaves and it is forgotten.'

The woman looked at the crowd. She was not articulate and Veles was a popular man.

'Give him the slaves,' said a voice.

'The wolfman was wronged – I saw the knife,' said another. Others just shook their heads and laughed.

The woman looked to left and right, hoping for a friendly face. There were not many.

'I offer you the two children,' she said. There was a mild change in Veles' posture, almost like a hound taking a scent. The stink of the slave barn seemed terrible to Vali, who felt as though he couldn't move. He put his hand on the low roof for support.

'They are more a burden than a help,' said Veles. 'Include the parents and my friend's claim is done. Your man was no great loss. Look at your face – you didn't get that bruise from his kisses.'

The woman thought again for a moment. She walked to the corpse of her husband and spat at it.

'Take them,' she said. 'I thank Jesus for my release. Few people are freed twice in their lives.'

'Have them delivered,' said Veles. 'I have better things to do for the moment, and see that they're fed before they arrive. I don't want to start paying out until I've had at least a day's work.'

The woman nodded. 'Bread, no stew.'

'Stew,' said Veles, 'or we put it before the assembly, and I tell you, you'll lose more than slaves for this.'

The woman shrugged. 'Stew.'

'Come,' said Veles. 'We must away.'

Feileg still hadn't moved. Veles put his mask up to his face and looked at Feileg through it.

'Woof, woof. Come on,' he said. Some of the crowd laughed, though others were still craning over the corpse. Remarkably, the merchant's mockery seemed to break Feileg from his trance, and he looked up and followed his companions, Bragi patting him on the shoulder and congratulating him.

'That's how a man deals with people who pull knives on him, son,' he said. 'Ah, by Lord Tyr's holy stump, I could have done with you on a few raids. If I was ten years younger, we'd get some plunder between us, eh? If you could learn to use a sword there'd not be a man between here and Serkland who'd face you down.'

The wolfman said nothing.

Vali followed Veles through the streets. He wondered if his time in the mire had taken too great a toll on him, whether it had affected his mind. Looking into Feileg's eyes had been a disconcerting experience, the violence worse still. There had been something intoxicating about it.

Bragi was now in conversation with Veles.

'I thought that was going to cost us a helmet at least. You really are a magician, Veles,' he said.

'I have my talents,' Veles replied. 'She had already been

paid by your wolfman. She's a rich widow now. I think she probably wanted to give howling boy a gift; I just showed her how it could be done.'

'What is Feileg going to do with slaves,' said Bragi, 'other than eat them?'

'Give them to me,' said Veles.

Veles's house was a big longhouse with bulging walls in the Haithabyr style. It had a fenced area outside it, within which, on a stool, sat a Dane in a padded coat, carrying a large seax. Vali instinctively checked his sword was still at his belt.

'No need, no need,' said Veles, putting his hand on Vali's. 'This is my bodyguard, not a robber. He is paid to be here.'

This shocked Vali. Why would anyone need a personal bodyguard? Couldn't the community guard itself against outsiders who might come to rob? Forkbeard's plunder sat in the open air for days after a raid so the people could see his success and reflect on his power. His kin would never steal from him. Also, bodyguards worked for loyalty and honour not pay, and only nobles had them. Veles was a commoner, a thrall even. The whole thing struck the prince as immoral.

Vali eyed the man suspiciously and went inside. The house was built around a big single room, with separate pens for goats and small cattle leading off it. Vali thought this luxurious. In Disa's house the goats had shared the same space as the humans. Veles did not seem quite as prepared as he had said at the quay. There was no food for a feast and not much in the way of ale, though the merchant had dispatched a boy and assured them that these things were on their way.

The main living space was richly appointed with furs on the floors, the smell of sweet herbs masking the stink of the town outside and animals within, and the walls were hung with strange embroideries of wool and linen. One showed a woman surrounded by winged men, another the god Vali had seen at the raid on the island, again impaled like Odin on a tree.

Veles saw Vali looking at them.

'Bought for warmth and beauty rather than from religious fervour,' said Veles, 'one god being much like another, I find.'

A small dark woman, the same race as Veles, came in, along with a gaggle of three boys, their hair black and shiny. One of the children had a bear mask, like the wolf mask Veles now had in his hand. He held it to his face and chased the others, growling.

'You see what I mean,' Veles said. 'These objects are sacred to the Whale People of the north. A brother people to my own, the Neuri, have similar things. With a mask, a Neuri man or a northern sorcerer can transform himself into a beast. Here, they are playthings for my children.'

Feileg stretched out his hand for the mask that Veles was holding and the merchant gave it to him.

'Why do you wear that?' said Vali.

'To attract attention at the quay,' said Veles. 'Here a merchant needs to be seen. The Christians have a saying – a wolf in sheep's clothing. I, as you see, am rather the reverse.'

Feileg was looking at the children and the woman through the mask. When he took it down, Vali could see that tears had come to his eyes. The wolfman was unselfconscious and made no attempt to wipe them away.

'The fire bothers you?' said Veles.

Feileg shook his head. 'I am sad because I am remembering my own family,' he said.

'How can you tear a man's face off in one breath and be crying for your mummy with the next?' said Bragi.

'I am a wolf,' said Feileg, and continued staring at the playing boys.

Veles raised his eyebrows and shrugged his shoulders. Then he clapped his hands and spoke to the eldest boy. 'Jarilo, you are too old to be chasing around like that. Here, go and slaughter a goat – we have esteemed guests.'

The boy picked up a knife and headed towards the pens, keenly pursued by his brothers.

'Woman, fetch wine from Geiri as quick as you can. Tell him payment will be his within the week. Is this how you prepare when I tell you the prince of all the north is a guest in our house?'

Now it was the woman's turn to look to the heavens, as she put down her broom and made her way outside.

'You ought to beat her more,' said Bragi.

'I couldn't beat her more if I made it my only occupation,' said Veles in a low voice, craning his head to make sure his wife was out of earshot, 'but still she doesn't obey.'

'She bears no bruises,' said Bragi.

'Obotrite women do not bruise easily,' said Veles. 'They also kick like cows and bite like sows. Come, have some ale while we wait for the wine.'

There was a large bowl of the murky beer under a cloth on the side and he passed it among them.

The men drank and, as they did, visitors came and went. There were other merchants with their wares, there were curious children and there were friends of Veles, come to meet the new arrivals.

The butchered goat was brought in, and when Veles' wife returned she grilled the meat over the fire, which Vali thought a strange choice when there was a stew pot within hand's reach. He wondered if this was some Obotrite custom. Still, he had to admit it was delicious and that the wine went very well with it. After the long journey eating fish and whatever plants they could find near the shore the meal was lovely, and Vali began to feel light-headed. In drink, Bragi could not be prevented from telling the tale of the defence against the Danes, at several points holding Vali's arm in the air as he related some particularly momentous aspect of the victory.

Eventually, Vali found himself seated next to Veles on a low stool near the fire. In the smoke and the glow of the flames the easterner resembled some sort of strange spirit, sparks flying around him as he spoke, the jewels he had put on in the safety of his house – amber and jet attached to his ears, gold arm rings and brooches – sparkling in the firelight.

Perhaps this was Lord Loki he had prayed to, taken human form to help him, Vali thought. And perhaps not, though Veles was certainly a different sort of man, as Loki was a different sort of god. Vali knew no one else who dropped eastern poems from his lips or who talked always of markets and gold rather than battles. Veles had no means of support, as far as Vali could see – no herds or fields, or even a trade beyond buying and selling. Vali found his company exhilarating but at the same time unsettling. He thought of Adisla. Was she even alive? A crowd of emotions came in on him: anger, concern and desperation.

'You are thinking of the girl,' said Veles. 'I can see she is more than a princess to you – your face betrays you. What is her name?'

The wine and the food, the warmth of the fire and the feeling of being among friends lessened Vali's caution. 'Adisla,' he said.

'Adisla?' said Veles. Vali had not been able to imagine what would break Veles' mask of urbanity. That did. His voice dropped as if he was about to say something he needed to conceal from the others. 'I remember her from my visit to you when you were a child. She's a pretty thing, I'll grant you, but tell me you haven't come all this way for a farmer's daughter. Have you?'

Vali swilled the dregs of the wine in the bottom of his cup and said, 'She is everything to me.'

Veles rolled his eyes to the rafters. 'You sound like an Arab!' he said. 'They're always banging on about love. "Mine is the religion of love! Wherever God's caravans turn, the religion of love shall be my religion and my faith!"'

'It seems a better choice than a religion of war.'

'Really?' said Veles with mock shock. 'And you descended from Odin as well.'

'I am sick of that fellow,' said Vali. 'If there are gods, I would prefer one of love.'

'You should speak to the Christians,' said Veles. 'King Charles of the Franks piously follows the god Christ, who is a god of love. The king has so much love in his heart that he turns the rivers red with the blood of his god's enemies. That's a rare love indeed.'

'I'll be wary of that sort of love,' said Vali.

'You should — and of the sort you seem possessed by. It does not do to love women too much, don't all your people say that? An Umayyad merchant told me one story of a caliph, a king of many lands, who fell in love with a slave girl. He could demand from her anything he wanted but that wasn't enough for the idiot. She had to give it freely. He saw the wrong sort of look in her eye one night when they were in bed together and threw himself off a tower.'

'What is a tower?' said Vali.

'A high building, too high to jump off, big as a cliff. They have them in the east, like a fort but not for war.'

'What's a fort not for war?' said Vali.

Veles laughed. 'A woman's heart, it seems, at least according to our friend the caliph. There are plenty of women who will love you. If one doesn't, through inclination or circumstance, find one who will. Better that than chase half around the world to have what you could get for thirty silver at a slave market.'

Vali looked into the fire. 'I won't abandon her. Neither you with jokes nor Forkbeard with threats will shake me from my purpose.'

A look of dawning realisation came over the merchant's face and Vali knew he had said too much.

Veles spoke in a hush. 'One moment. Did Forkbeard approve of this little trip of yours? He didn't, did he? No wonder he didn't give you a drakkar.' Then his look turned to one of mild horror. 'Have you Forkbeard's permission to be here at all?' he said.

'I am a prince of the Horda, not the Rygir.'

Veles shook his head. 'That sounds as good as a no to me. Oh dear, oh dear. What did you think you were going to do about Hemming? Sit there and broker some peace you couldn't deliver?'

Vali saw there was no use in pretending to the merchant.

'I could think of no other excuse for being here.'

'Is that in itself not an indication that you shouldn't have come? Go back to Rogaland. Now. Have you any idea of the danger you've placed yourself in? Hemming sits at the centre of a web of competing interests. If you don't have Forkbeard's blessing, he'll be almost bound to take you as a hostage whether he wants to or not. He'll say you're here as his guest, but you'll be lucky if you see Rogaland ever again.'

Vali couldn't tell if it was the wine or just the need to un-burden himself to someone he respected, to gain the benefit of Veles' advice. He decided to tell the truth.

'I will never see Rogaland again.'

'Why not?'

'We are outlaws,' said Vali.

Veles almost ducked as if anticipating a blow.

'What in the name of nine kinds of devil have you done?'

Vali shrugged. 'It was more to do with politics than actions.'

Veles had to restrain himself from plucking the wine cup out of Vali's fingers and shoving him through the door.

'Are you an outlaw in Hordaland?'

'No,' said Vali.

'So you've still some connections.' Veles thought for a moment. 'Look, you must leave here tonight and go with one of my men to a place of safety. You can take your boat down the coast and wait in the forest. It is too dangerous for you here. Hemming will soon discover you've been outlawed – he has men in all the kingdoms. He may even want to ransom you to your father or Forkbeard. If Haarik comes back here he will sue to have you killed.'

'I'm going after the girl,' said Vali.

'I will send out for word of her, but you must come away. Immediately.' He actually took the wine cup from Vali's lips.

Vali could see his old friend was serious. 'Now?' he said. He eyed the luxurious piles of furs used for beds.

'Now.'

Vali went to the others and they gathered their few possessions. Bragi was drunk and complained loudly about going back to a freezing boat but Feileg said nothing, just followed on.

'Six bends of the river, the opposite way to where you came in. I'll meet you there,' said Veles. 'I can't go with you. It's bad enough that I've entertained you here. Why didn't you tell me your situation from the beginning? We could have done all this very differently. Just follow the hill down to the water. Your boat will be where you left it.'

'Thank you,' said Vali. 'I won't forget this.'

'Forget it – just not before you've sent me a large gift,' said Veles. He kissed Vali on the cheeks in the Obotrite way and pushed him out into the night.

The men made their way down to the quay. Haithabyr at night was beautiful: a deep field of stars shining down on the town, a thousand tiny flames of hearth and candle flickering out as if in response. It seemed friendly, the country around something hostile. The dark beyond the town seemed to bristle with unseen malevolent forces: mountainsides with their murderous drops, sucking mires, trackless moors and above all a vast emptiness that meant that, should you need help, there was no one to reach out to. That, though, was where they were going. In the distance he heard a wolf howl. It set the town's dogs grumbling from unseen shelters. Their noise, almost human in its complaint, made him wish he could stay in Haithabyr, safe by the fire, rather than venturing out onto unknown waters.

But then a figure stepped across his path. At first he thought nothing of it, but the man didn't move. Someone else joined him, then a third and a fourth. Vali looked behind him. In silhouette he could see the shape of shields and spears. There must have been twenty men. He looked at Bragi and the wolfman. He glanced left. Another dark shape crossed the alleyway and stopped. So right then. There was no need for words. The three set off as one. They ran parallel to the water, up a slight slope along a narrow lane through the houses. At points Vali had to duck as the roofs came low, nearly touching each other. He could hardly see and blundered forward in the dark, slipping on the slick planks of the path in an uncomfortable compromise between caution and haste. Never mind. If he couldn't see well, neither could their pursuers.

The lights of candles and fires from open doorways trailed past him, golden smears in the dark, and then, to his left, a light of a different colour and size a gleam of silver there and then gone, like a blade flashing from the scabbard of the dark. The water.

'Here,' he said, hoping Bragi and Feileg were still behind him. They ran up the hill, quick as they could on the slippery logs, but there were shadows about them again, moving across the path. Vali turned across the slope once more, but their way was blocked, not by warriors but by a wall of earth. The town had ramparts. They were surrounded on all sides. The figures didn't close on them but remained at a distance.

Bragi was at his ear. 'Get ready to take your place with your ancestors in Odin's halls,' he said.

'I'll ask no one there to make space at the bench for me yet,' said Vali. There were people all around him now, some with burning torches. They were nobles, he could see. Some had spears but there were swords too – one of them drawn. 'If there was ever a time to play the prince, this is it,' said Vali.

He drew himself up to his full height and strode towards the men in front of him.

'My word, I thought you were pirates. What are you men doing skulking about in the dark?'

'We are kinsman to Hemming, king of Denmark, mighty ruler whose ships are numberless,' said a voice.

'At last you come. So slow a welcome does King Hemming bring that I betook myself to mount my wave steed once more. Truly, it seems that I shall eat sooner at my father's table ten days hence, following the mackerel's backs to Hordaland, than wait on Danish hospitality.' Vali tried to speak like a prince, to be received like one.

A voice spoke back. 'We are sorry for our tardiness. The king does not reside here, and it took time for word of your arrival to reach us. We are as apologetic as Geirroth when to Odin he did refuse the gift of mead.'

'Didn't Geirroth fall on his sword?' said Bragi under his breath.

'Your words are sweet as Idun's apples,' said Vali. 'We greet you, Hemming's men, brave spear Danes and sons of honour.'

Vali was now face to face with the man who had first blocked his path. The warrior was richly dressed, a gold brooch glinting like another candle in the dark and at his waist a fine sword, its scabbard picked out in gemstones. He was tall and thin, and by his bearing a formidable warrior.

'I am Skardi, son of Hrolf,' said the man, 'trusted adviser to Hemming the Great, foe of the Franks and protector of the Danes, he who takes tribute from eight kingdoms and whose glory shall last until the gods destroy us.'

'I am Vali, son of Authun the Pitiless, scourge of the north, most feared lord in this Middle Earth. I am ward to Forkbeard, king of the Rygir, whose name resounds everywhere beneath the skull of the sky god.'

Vali glanced to his left. Bragi had the wolfman by the arm and was speaking into his ear. Feileg's eyes were wild as they had been at the slave market and he looked ready to attack. Vali remembered what he had thought of berserks the first time he had seen them operate and wondered how he had found himself with this man, next to whom the followers of the cult of Odin seemed models of restraint.

'Forgive my retainer,' said Vali. 'He seeks only to protect me in a strange land.'

Skardi pursed his lips. 'Tell him he will find my men harder work than any slaver. They have fed the eagles until they are too fat to fly.'

Reports of the slaver's death had clearly reached Hemming's court. There was nothing to do but stick with his original plan. How long would he have before word from Rogaland arrived? A month at the most, maybe a lot less. If Hemming detained him too long then his future looked very uncertain.

'Our bearing and our deeds shall cause those birds to starve,' said Vali. 'We come as friends, with kind words and respect for your far-famed king.'

'Then welcome, friends. Allow us to bring you to the halls of our high lord.'

The two men embraced and this seemed to calm Feileg.

'We have a boat at the river's mouth. If you would do us the honour of accompanying us ...' said Skardi.

Vali knew this was hard hospitality, the sort that will not be refused. They set off through the dark streets. Vali became aware that he was accompanied by at least forty men. He was a prisoner, no mistaking it.

'You arrived by fishing boat, prince. It's a strange choice for a king's son. Has Forkbeard no drakkar to transport you?'

'My lord,' said Vali, 'we were shipwrecked on the Wide Islands. A storm came from nowhere, a creation no doubt of the sorcerous Haarik. Our gifts for your lord were lost, but so important was our mission that we continued as we could.'

Vali knew it was a risk to appear vulnerable. A real man would spit at a storm and land his ship safe, or at least that was what the skalds said. Despite this, Vali had heard of enough heroes who had gone to the bottom, though few in coastal waters.

Skardi was thoughtful. 'And the purpose of your mission?'

'Why peace, my lord, peace. Now Forkbeard and my father

sit with eighty drakkars ready to send a sword storm to Haarik. Once the fire of battle lights, it may not be easy to put out, nor to confine it to one land. I need your king's word that he will not interfere as we take our rightful revenge and raise a spear din in Haarik's halls.'

Vali had lost face over the shipwreck; now he tried to regain it with talk of war.

Skardi gave a curt nod, giving away nothing.

'Our drakkar,' he said, 'is waiting.'

29 The Drum

Drown, drown, just drown. Stop fighting, just drown. Adisla willed her self to sink but couldn't do it. She was too good a swimmer and her body insisted on trying to survive, even in that cold swell.

There was shouting from the ship; the sail peeled back and men were pointing at her and yelling through the rain. The man in the four-cornered hat was there and had a drum in his hand. He began to beat it and to sing.

Adisla wanted to swim away from the boat but her instinct for preservation was too strong and she simply trod water, pumping her legs while willing her body to go under. Her skirts had filled with water and were heavy now, constrictive and tiring.

'Freya, take me. Freya take me.'

She lost sight of the ship, then she lost sight of everything and knew she was sinking. Still she tried to breathe but choked. Then she was thrashing wildly, desperate to get up to the surface, desperate for air, her body moving to the demands of instinct not thought. But Adisla couldn't find the air. It was as if a giant hand was holding her down, irresistible, pushing her into darkness while her arms flailed for the light. Her lungs were bursting and she couldn't help but try to breathe in again.

And then it was calm and it was light and her mind wandered. She thought she was with Vali again, by the fjord on a hot sunny day, and they were laughing. The light weakened and dimmed and she realised she wasn't outside at all but in a cave whose floor was submerged in water. There was something in there, a presence that seemed to bubble from the darkness, a formless animosity all around her. But when she looked, it was only Vali and he was saying, 'Wait for me. I will find you. I am looking.'

But it wasn't Vali, it was the wolfman. She reached out to touch him, but then there was pain and there was light and screaming, and underneath it all a strange chant and the beat of a drum that she knew came from the odd man who had sat next to her on the ship. She didn't understand his words at all, nor did she like their sound – to her ears it was like a dog singing, rough and guttural, but inside her something stirred and she moved her arms, kicked off her skirts and struck out for the ship. The water seemed immense and strong, but the beat from the ship seemed to sustain her, and her movements became calm and purposeful even as she wept because she couldn't drown. A rope was in her hands and then arms were reaching down for her. She was hauled back onto the ship wearing only her pinafore and leggings.

There was a face above her – the man in the blue coat and four-pointed hat. He had a drum in his hands marked with strange symbols. The red on the band of his hat seemed terribly vivid to her. The man leaned towards her, pushed back her head and held his ear to her mouth. When he heard her breathe, he took the cloak Adisla had discarded when she had gone overboard and put it around her. Then he hugged her to him to make her warm, holding her and whispering to her in his strange language. The Danes shot her lascivious glances but the man's eyes kept them at bay. They were pale blue, the colour of cold sky, and the contrast with his dark hair was striking. Not a man in the crew doubted he was a sorcerer.

Adisla was coughing and shaking and frozen. There was an uncommon depth to the cold she felt. Whatever she had sensed in that cave had been real to her and meant her no good. But she had seen only Vali and Feileg, who she knew were her protectors.

The sorcerer crawled away down the ship and came back with a waterskin. She put it to her lips and drank.

The magician's face was only just visible in the dim light beneath the sail. He grinned at her and she started. His teeth were filed to points, like an animal's. He leaned towards her and said in halting Norse, 'Do not hurry to that place, lady. You will go there again quickly enough.'

30   Politics

The sun shone brightly on Vali during his time at Hemming's court but he knew things were going badly for him when the king didn't receive him immediately. It was a week before he was summoned to the main hall, a week in which he stayed in the longhouse he had been allocated in case he should bump into the monarch outside his halls. He knew that the meeting had to be on Hemming's terms – at the time and place of his choosing. So when the summons came it was welcome – a relief from boredom and the frustration of inaction, at least.

Vali went alone. It felt good to get out into the clean air after a week in the smoky house and he took the opportunity to look around.

Hemming's settlement was impressive, containing five big longhouses. There were ramparts – one with a gate – on every side of the settlement apart from that adjoining the winding sea inlet – or river as it now was. A smaller version of the sea wall being constructed at Haithabyr extended from the rampart into the water in a semicircle with a chain across the entrance from the river. Vali didn't know whether to marvel at the skill of its construction or despair at how difficult it would make escape. There were only a couple of lookouts on the sea wall but, thought Vali, how many does it take to raise an alarm? No ship could come or go unless the chain was lowered, and if Vali and his companions tried to escape overland, Hemming would simply alert the surrounding farms.

A jarl in a bright yellow tunic conducted him to the hall, a huge structure with bulging sides like a ship's. You could have fitted two of Forkbeard's halls inside it.

A door was opened and he went in. At the far end he could just see through the haze of the fire a tall thin man sitting on a large stone seat. As Vali was led forward he saw the king more clearly. He was richly dressed in bright blue silks, his eyes elaborately decorated with kohl and his lips smeared with the juice of berries.

Kneeling at his side was the drab figure of a Christian priest, his head shaved into a tonsure. He was scribbling on a tablet and Vali would normally have been intrigued to look at what he was doing. On Hemming's other side was a pretty woman in a long silk gown of pale yellow. She came forward to Vali with a drinking horn. It was a beautiful thing, polished and inlaid with silver.

The woman spoke in an exotically accented Norse. 'I am Inga, queen of the Danes, and I bid you welcome to our court. Drink, guest. Accept the mead of friendship from Hemming, king of the Danes, mightiest ruler of this Middle Earth.'

'My gratitude to the noble queen. I accept this drink in recognition of our friendship, now and in the future,' said Vali.

He took a sip.

'Formalities over?' said Hemming, who had been pre-occupied with a parchment. He handed it back to the kneeling priest and looked up at Vali. 'Good. You are welcome, Vali of the Horda, over and above the high words with which we honour you.'

The king spoke perfect Norse without a trace of an accent.

'Your majesty is good to see me so soon after my arrival,' said Vali.

'All other business ceased when we knew you were here,' said Hemming with a short smile. The king then sat in silence for a moment, staring at Vali.

Vali wondered if he was expected to say something, but he couldn't think what that might be so he just kept quiet.

'Why are you here? The truth.'

'To ask your permission for the Rygir to attack Haarik, or for you to order him to compensate us for our loss.' Vali did not like to lie but there was a saying, 'A lie to an enemy is no lie at all.' Hemming was a potential enemy so deceit was allowable, honourable even. An oath, however, well, that would be a different matter.

'That is not why you are here,' said Hemming. His manner was calm: there was no threat at all in his voice. Only the sudden restlessness of the priest gave Vali any indication that anything was wrong. The man glanced at the king and went pale. Vali remembered that, at least in word, these priests were opposed to killing, though confusingly they did eat human flesh. If someone lied in front of Forkbeard he could expect to be given to Odin before he had the chance to tell his next one. Was Hemming similar, if with quieter manners?

There was another long silence. This time Vali did feel the need to break it first.

'I am here on a fool's errand,' he said.

The king raised his eyebrows, indicating that Vali should go on. Vali tried to think fast. He needed to describe his mission in a way that Hemming would find acceptable.

'I was sick as a boy,' he said, 'and a healer in Rogaland tended me and cured me. I vowed to her then that any service I could do her, I would. Her daughter was taken in Haarik's raid and her mother begged me to find her and free her. It is an oath I made before Odin, lord. I had to act upon it. Forkbeard was not keen to help me find a lowly freewoman's daughter. Hence here I am, in the only transport I could muster. I am looking for a girl.'

'Go home then. An oath in front of idols and false gods means nothing,' said the priest. His accent was thick and strange.

Hemming held up his hand. 'To us, father, an oath in front of a goat or a duck is worth something. A man is only a man in as much as he can keep his oath.'

The priest remained motionless; Hemming puckered up his mouth in thought.

'Not the whole story, is it?'

'Lord?'

'Were you running towards this girl or away from Forkbeard?'

Vali smiled. 'Something of both, sir.'

'Lord of wisdom, help me now!' said Hemming to the rafters.

The priest smiled uncertainly.

Hemming shook his head and looked Vali up and down. 'So what am I to do with you?'

Vali said nothing.

'No, really, I want your advice. Come on. You started this mess, let's see you get us out of it. What shall I do with you?'

'Help me find the girl.'

Hemming laughed and waved the back of his hand at Vali as if to swat him away. 'She is Haarik's taken in war. And besides I don't think she's even his to give by now.'

'She's been sold on?'

The king didn't answer the question but sat back and gave Vali that appraising look again. 'What do you know of sorcery, prince?'

'Very little.'

'You are too modest. The lord Odin has his intelligencers and I have mine. Do you want me to tell you what my ravens whisper to me?'

The priest shifted again.

'Anything the king wishes to tell me, it will be my honour to hear.'

'You fight foes with neither spear nor sword. Mighty war bands fall before you, defeated by mobs of boys and old men. You consult gods in the mire. You miraculously escape the most secure captivity and consort with wildmen and shape-shifters. Seers and wizards from the four corners of the earth look into their ponds or take to their hanging trees, and the visions they see are of the son of the wolf eating up the world. A boy escaped from some hags of the north of your country tells, as he dies, a story about a great enchantment being laid, again for the son of the wolf. Is that not how you are known, prince, as the son of the wolf?'

'These stories are exaggerated. I am a sore disappointment to my father, I can assure you of that.'

'I hear that as well,' said Hemming. 'If I believed half the seer babble I'd hang you now and take the consequences.' He paused and seemed thoughtful, then looked straight at Vali. 'Understand my problem. Your father is stricken.'

Vali tried to stop the alarm registering on his face. He failed.

'Yes, I know. Your mother rules in his place. That makes you very important, for the moment. If one of your cousins or uncles seizes the throne, however, it makes you less important in one way, more in another. Your value as some sort of bargaining counter drops, but I think the new king would pay well to have you returned to him, breathing or not. On the other hand, were I to give you a few ships to conquer your homeland then a good many of your kinsman would rally to you and, with luck, I would have another king paying me tribute from overseas, the proper oaths having been extracted. That said, I'm always interested in short-term gain. Forkbeard is keen on seeing you again. You could still be valuable there.'

Vali opened his mouth to speak but Hemming held up a hand to silence him.

'What am I to do? I've enough problems to contend with without this.' He shook his head. 'I'm looking for a reason to let you go but I really can't find one.'

'I eat a lot and am expensive to keep,' said Vali. He tried to keep his manner light. If he had no bargaining power with the king at all, at least he could try to make him like him.

Hemming smiled. The priest stood and whispered into his ear. The king listened impassively while the queen asked Vali how he liked the mead.

The priest sank back to the floor.

'You are important,' said Hemming. 'I can see that without

employing seers and wizards. That's common sense. Son and heir of that prodigious killer, your father, the Horda will want you on the throne if you've got even a sliver of that old steel in you. My priest advises me to kill you.' He gestured to the man in the sackcloth, who actually coloured with embarrassment. 'His religion finds practitioners of Seid threatening. Coincidentally, word from the west makes me even more inclined to kill you. Haarik wants you as a gift for the northern sorcerers. That's why he came for you.'

'He came to plunder,' said Vali.

'Hardly. He must have known Forkbeard would have hidden his gold very carefully, particularly while he was away. Why go storming in risking war with the Rygir when there are West Men who can't muster a drakkar between them not a week's sail away?'

'I—'

'Why three ships? He has near sixty, you know. Well, fifty-nine after you relieved him of one. What can you do with three? Hit and run, no more. If he thinks Forkbeard is stupid enough to leave his treasure so near the shore then he's not the Haarik I know. It was people he was after, if not you then those close to you. That's why he went for the girl.'

'How could he know about her?'

'How do I know about you?' Hemming shrugged. 'Haarik doesn't have a large network of spies but he has his methods, I'm sure.'

'No Rygir man would dishonour his lord by spying.'

'Yes, he would,' said Hemming. 'Or he'll talk in drink at markets or to traders. Some with ambitions of their own will go further.'

'Name the traitor, and if I see him again he will die.'

Hemming shook his head.

'Well, I'd hardly be likely to do that, would I? The facts are these. Haarik wanted you. That's the word I hear. You. Which is why you become important again. I mean, I might allow you to accept his hospitality, for a consideration. On the other hand, if I do that we all know that King Authun has his ravens too, and your mother Yrsa even more. If I hand you over to Haarik, I anger your father. While I have no doubt my men could crush the Horda in war, I also have no doubt your father would make us pay a high price for the victory. He may be sick, or that may be a bluff. Whatever, I think there's a chance he would make a remarkable recovery and demonstrate his uncanny knack of finding the opposing king on the battlefield.' He glanced at his bodyguard. 'And it would be a shame to meet such a formidable, some say unbeatable, warrior and destroy the myth.'

'Kings are for glory, not long life,' said Vali, repeating the well-known saying.

'Your father seems to have combined both to alarming effect. It would take a brave man – though needless to say I long for such a chance to prove myself in combat against such as he – a brave man indeed, to bet on ending either.'

'I tell you this: Authun would let me die a thousand deaths before he gave you or Haarik so much as a coin in ransom. I am not so important. He can name an heir.'

Hemming tapped his knee.

'I disagree. You are important. Line of Odin and all that. What do you do in the far north-east?'

The question surprised Vali, as it was meant to.

'Nothing. I have been on one raid in the west but nothing further.'

'To the land of the Whale People? Vagoy, the wolf island, or around there in Ultima Thule?'

Vali recognised the old name for the islands at the end of the known world. He shrugged.

'What do you know of the wolf island?' said Hemming.

'Nothing.'

'Haarik's son was captured near there a year or so ago. I've wondered if that's anything to do with all this.'

'In what way?'

Hemming shrugged in his turn. 'Haarik loves his son,

though why I cannot tell. The boy's an idiot. I don't know. There's always been a rumour about the Whale People keeping a vast treasure up there – maybe he went looking for that. He's the rarest sort of fool if he has.'

'Why?'

'Because the northerners are as poor as prophets. There is no treasure. I've sent men up there myself to check, but it's a flat cold rock, nothing more. Whatever he was up there for, he's got lost, and Haarik wants him back. But then Haarik attacks the Rygir instead of going after him. It makes no sense.'

Vali was nervous. He drained the mead and the queen came forward with more.

Hemming went on: 'He could have you, but quite frankly Haarik went against my advice in raiding the Rygir, so I'm certainly not rewarding him with what he wants. What to do, what to do?'

'I intend to find the girl I'm looking for and live as a farmer,' said Vali. 'I want nothing to do with kingship.'

Hemming snorted. 'Well, you'll find that in this life what you intend rarely has any bearing on what you finish up doing, particularly as a king. If I let you go, you'll become king or die. Whoever became king in your place wouldn't want Authun's son hiding like a wolf in the byre. You'd be dead, and your family with you, within a year. Intend. Intend! I didn't intend you to come here. If you'd passed through Haithabyr without proclaiming who you were I would never have detained you.'

'We feared attack by the townsfolk.'

'Haithabyr is the world's biggest port,' said Hemming. 'People are used to strangers. You could have come and gone as you pleased. It isn't some farmstead where you have to sound your horn as soon as you're in earshot or risk doing the dead lord's dance.'

Vali felt stupid and angry. Why hadn't Forkbeard allowed him one of these holy men – sitting on his shoulder, recording his orders so they couldn't be forgotten, lost or argued about, and teaching him to speak like Hemming? Surely it was worth kneeling to their god for that, whatever you believed in your heart.

'If you release me, you have my oath of friendship.'

'Well, I had already considered that. I'd be something of a fool to let you leave without it, wouldn't I?' said Hemming. He smiled again at Vali. 'If you and your friends could contrive to die in an accident then many of the problems this causes me would be solved, you know.'

Again, Hemming's face lacked menace, though Vali could see the danger was greater than his manner suggested. He was businesslike and thoughtful. Forkbeard would have been screaming in Vali's face or sucking up to him.

'If your majesty releases me then I shall endeavour to do my best to fulfil his wishes,' he said. 'I intend now to go to Haarik and ask him for the girl.'

Hemming laughed. 'Make sure you ask him when you've got your spear halfway through him or you've very little chance of a pleasant answer. Anyway, Haarik didn't go home, so you won't find him there.'

'Where did he go?'

For the first time Hemming seemed on the edge of anger.

'Should I tell you that so you can hunt him down and kill him, he who swells my coffers with chests of silver and gold? If you intend to use me as your raven, prince, the least you could do is throw me a little corn.'

'I have none to give.'

Hemming turned his face away. 'No,' he said. 'You don't, do you? Go back to your quarters. I'll decide whether to kill you, sell you or keep you by the end of tomorrow.'

He extended his hand and the priest passed him up a piece of parchment. Queen Inga took the drinking horn from Vali's hands and a bodyguard led him from the hall.

31 A Plan

On his way back from Hemming's hall Vali came across Bragi and Feileg looking out at the small harbour, the wolfman seeming almost slight next to the bulk of Bragi.

'Hemming's men must have a thirst on them. Do you think we'll get any of that?' said Bragi as Vali came to his side.

On Skardi's order the chain on the harbour wall was being lowered to allow a small squat boat containing five huge barrels of wine to enter. Bragi explained that the whole settlement had been talking about the delivery. A boy had arrived with a message from the town while Vali was seeing Hemming. Veles Libor sends his best wishes to the king, his finest wine a small token of thanks for all the king does for the people of Haithabyr, said the messenger.

'It's an apology,' said Vali.

'Right enough,' said Bragi.

Both men knew the real reason for Veles Libor's generosity was that word had reached Hemming the merchant hadn't informed him of his contact with a foreign prince. It wasn't exactly a hanging offence but neither could it be overlooked. As soon as Veles could get his hands on quality wine he had sent it to the king to improve Hemming's deliberations on what should happen to him.

'I'll be surprised if he doesn't have to pay a lot more than that,' said Bragi. 'Authun would have had his head for such a crime if he'd been in the wrong mood.'

'He'd be a fool then,' said Gyrth, the Norse-speaking retainer who had been looking after them during their stay. 'Veles is the best-connected merchant in the world. The tribute he pays the king buys many a byrnie and blade. And look! It's

Styrman the skald. Where did they get him from! Styrman! Hey, Styrman!'

A man disembarking waved his arm in the air. He was tall and thin, though with a drinker's face, and he carried a lyre under his arm, not wrapped up at all. There, thought Vali, was someone who valued his reputation as a skald more than the health of the instrument that earned him a living. Every skald he had ever met had been showy like that. They almost had to be, in order to succeed in their profession.

'Veles sent his best boat east for me,' shouted the skald, 'and demanded that I accompany his wine here.'

'A story! A story!

'Tonight,' said the skald, 'when the mead is drunk and we are drunker!'

The wine was heaved off the boat onto the foreshore and some men began rolling the barrels up towards the king's hall while, from throughout the settlement, people came to see Styrman. Vali had seen skalds before and met a few popular ones, but this man seemed to have everyone's attention. From the shouted requests of the crowd, he could see why.

'Tell us of Ofeig the Hobbler and Ivar Horse Cock!'

A young man cried out, 'We will beat you in flyting. No insult contest can you win, you who was raised so womanly!' He was laughing but good-natured.

'I am afraid of flyting with you, young fellow. Your balls have to drop sometime and, should they do so during the duel of jibes, the noise might put me off what I have to say. Clang!'

The crowd seemed to find this hilarious, much funnier than Vali thought it was. Still the skald was well liked, it seemed, and if he was an expert in flyting it would be interesting to hear him. People would come from miles around to test their wits against such a man. It was said that a good skald could best a hundred opponents in an evening's drinking, each one dispatched with a different insult, usually in rhyme.

Vali looked out at the chain and then at the river beyond.

The longing he felt inside didn't even come to him as words, just as a sort of hunger, an ache in his stomach.

He had to find a way to get out. But even if he did escape from the settlement, Hemming would have no problem hunting him down. He would be stopped or killed by fearful farmers if he ran by land. By water the route was easier but still perilous – the best he could manage alone was a faering and even that would be difficult. It was some distance to the sea and the wind was uncertain. A drakkar would be on him before he reached the open ocean.

He walked back to the gloom of the house and sat down. There was no one there for a change, not even women. Everyone had gone outside to see the skald. He picked at some boiled meat in a bowl. And then he came to his answer.

The skald's performance that evening would give him his chance. But escape was not enough; he needed to do something to stop himself being pursued. If the Danes thought he was dead, then they wouldn't come after him. The wolfman was his double. He tapped a bone against the bowl and tried to think of a way around the path that had opened before him. He couldn't. Vali would have to kill Feileg, dress him in his own clothes and then make off. It wouldn't guarantee him escape – Hemming would certainly want to make a show of finding his guest's killers – but the hunt would not be nearly so enthusiastic as if he was looking for Vali himself.

He worked out the details. He would need to get a Danish cloak to wrap himself in. The guards would be drunk or distracted by the skald and Vali thought he could just walk out. The wolfman could steal a cloak. When he returned to give it to Vali, he would kill him. Vali said the words in his mind, to fix himself in his purpose: 'I will kill him.' It was the best way, he knew. And yet that vision kept returning – the cave, the wolfman's body bent into the shape of that strange rune, his own body, and that of Adisla, similarly contorted. He felt anxious. What would happen if he failed? The wolfman would kill him and Adisla would be alone.

Bragi had told him that his father Authun was famous for cold thinking – for seeing what needed to be done and doing it without regard to emotion or affection. Was it not rumoured that he had taken nine warriors with him to the mountain witches, knowing they would die? He had needed them so he had taken them. The wolfman was not Vali's kinsman either, but an outlaw who had killed many men.

Vali had not been disarmed – that would have been a dishonour too far and an admission that the Danes feared him. He only had to remove his sword when he entered Hemming's hall. He remembered the beach, the wolfman thrashing after him in the water, and thought that he should have let him drown. He couldn't account for what had made him risk his own life saving him. Perhaps it was fate, saving the wolfman for the greater purpose of aiding his escape, Vali thought.

As the idea fixed itself in his mind, he found himself seeking justifications for what he was about to do. Feileg was dangerous. He had exposed them by his actions in the town. He drew attention to them wherever they went. On top of all that, he had some attraction for Adisla that unnerved Vali. Could he trust Feileg if they did find her? No. He'd seen the looks the wolfman gave him and could sense what Feileg felt towards him. Feileg wanted Vali dead but he needed him to find Adisla. As soon as that was done, Vali knew Feileg would attack him.

'I am a wolf,' the wolfman liked to say. So he needed to be treated like one.

Still, Vali didn't relish what he had to do. It was, he told himself, simply his best chance. Would he include Bragi in the escape? Yes, of course. Whatever the wisdom of trying to make it alone, he couldn't kill a kinsman or abandon one to die. He had set sail to find Adisla but he would have done the same for Bragi. He may have found the old man a bore, but he was a bore he was related to, and that solid fact removed all debate.

Vali drifted off to sleep, allowing the familiar aromas of the

278

longhouse to take him back to his childhood at Disa's hearth. He remembered Adisla and the warmth of her against him in the long winter evenings as they'd sat listening to the old stories of how the dwarfs made treasure for the gods, or of the never-ending battle fought by the war dead in the afterlife. There were other, better stories too – tales of farm life, of how Disa had tricked her husband into wiping his arse with a nettle in return for a beating he'd given her, of the funny things they'd said as children, of how the Rygir had suffered, fought and fled before marriage and trade had brought peace – or so they thought – to their lands. To find Adisla again, to have her sit by him as they listened to stories in the night, he would kill a thousand wolfmen, skin them and hang out their hides for the ravens to peck at.

All he needed to do was wait for darkness.

32   The Wine Road

The flyting was in full session and the skald was doing well. A huge jarl had shouted that Styrman was skinny, mean and too lazy to find his own food – at least Vali thought that was what he said. He could speak good Danish, his time with Barth the thrall had seen to that, but in the tumult of the hall he had difficulty picking some of the words out. He heard the skald's reply as something like, 'Food scarce. Lord Fastarr, none can eat but he. Esteemed lord keep cloak on as you pass the pigs, lest you be a birthing sow.'

The crowd roared, banging cups and knives on the table. Vali, though, could not find the contest funny. He glanced at Bragi. He had told the old man not to get drunk, but clearly Bragi had interpreted that as, 'Don't get very drunk indeed.' He was guffawing into his beard and shouting, 'He's got you there, Fastarr! You asked for that one!'

'How can you tell what they say?' Vali asked Bragi.

'I can't get much of it, but you know it's quality stuff from the skald – you only have to look at the fellow,' said Bragi. He was enjoying, more than enjoying, wordplay in a language he hardly understood. Vali shook his head and returned to thinking about the business of the night.

The wolfman, Vali knew, was outside, sitting, as he always did in the evenings, down by the ramparts, staring into nothing. Feileg couldn't stand the noise of the hall and in company retreated into long silences, hovering between animosity and something like fear. It was fear, Vali knew, of the unfamiliar. Vali looked around at the Danish nobles, the huge hall, the rich attire of the jarls, at their strange manners; he heard their weird ways of speaking. He was happier with ordinary people. Was he any different to Feileg? Yes, he was, because he would live to see the dawn tomorrow and Feileg would not.

Vali thought of the ships out on the water, symbols of the freedom he wanted. Even a rowing boat or Veles' little delivery vessel would do.

He was ready. Everything had unfolded just as he had thought. The visit of the skald was such a big occasion that the longhouses lay empty. Only a single guard sat on the perimeter wall of the harbour by the chain and another at the gate. It was going to be easier than he had imagined.

Vali slipped out of the hall. It was late and the Danes had drunk their way through four of Veles' big barrels, or at least they had been emptied. Vali knew very well that on such occasions people filled up whatever they could, and quite a lot of the wine would be transported in bottle and pan back to the longhouses to be consumed at a later date. The barrels had been upended and the ends prised off, people filling containers by dipping them in, tied to cords if necessary, to get the last out. The push to be first to the wine had been an unedifying spectacle.

He whistled to the wolfman, who turned and came towards him. Vali could sense his hatred, which was as strong as it had ever been. He was glad – it would make his task easier.

'We go tonight and need cloaks,' he said. 'Take three from a longhouse.' He had noted that everyone was in their best clothes for the visit of the skald. Their workaday stuff would be there for the taking.

'I need no cloak in this weather.'

'You do, for disguise. Go and get them.'

Soundlessly the wolfman moved away, more like something liquid than solid, flowing from shadow to shadow. Vali steeled himself while Feileg was gone. His sword was leaning against the outside of the king's hall, along with Bragi's. It would take too long to draw though. Vali had a short knife and thought he would do for Feileg with that as the wolfman put on his cloak. Then he would drag him to an animal pen, change their clothes, walk out of the settlement and steal a boat as soon as he could. His nervousness made him restless, and he went back inside the hall.

The skald was causing general hilarity with his flyting, and people were queuing up to try to best him, though no one had managed it so far. They were standing on the benches, clapping and yelling, toasting and cursing him, and everyone was seriously drunk.

Bragi, who was – incredibly – wearing his byrnie, was prof-fering a drinking horn to a slave girl who was trying to fill it from a jug. He was making her task much more difficult by pulling at her dress as she did so to get a look at her breasts.

'Outside,' said Vali. 'Now.'

Even though he was mildly drunk, the old warrior caught the seriousness in Vali's voice and followed him into the cool of the night. Vali took him to the shadows.

'When Feileg comes back,' he said, 'I am going to kill him. It must be done quickly and it must be done without sound. The best place is in the shadow of the stable over there. It's dark enough and any noise will not be heard from the hall. It is necessary and I'll explain why once it is done.'

Bragi shrugged. 'The outlaw was lucky to live so long any-way. Strike true. You'll be a dead man if you don't. I'll be ready, whatever.'

'Yes.'

They heard the skald shouting inside the hall.

> *Five tuns of wine sends the merchant Veles,*
> *Only five little tubs to fill our bellies*
> *Let us tell this stingy merchant, 'Be cursed!'*
> *Ten fat barrels we'll need to slake our thirst!*

There was a tumult of applause and cheers inside the hall.

Feileg was back with three old cloaks in the light Danish style.

'Over here away from the hall, and I'll tell you the plan,' said Vali.

They stepped towards the stable. Vali was very conscious of the knife in his belt. He would make Feileg do up the clasp on his cloak himself. The wolfman was unused to such things, and while his hands were occupied, Vali would stab him to the heart. Vali willed his fingers away from the knife, careful not to give his intentions away. That rune, that writhing, sinuous, shifting rune, was in his head again, but he dismissed it. They reached the lee of the building and Vali passed into the shadow. He was eager for Feileg to follow, eager for it to be over. But Feileg had stopped dead. He let out a low growl.

'What?' said Vali.

'There is danger here,' said Feileg. His teeth came back from his lips and he sniffed at the shadows.

'There's no danger. Come here,' said Vali. He felt his heart pumping and his head light with nervousness.

'I will not go there.'

Vali swallowed. Now, he thought. Now!

'Walk on, you girl,' said Bragi.

'Shhhhhh!' said a voice from the darkness.

Now Vali did draw his knife.

A pale face loomed out of the shadow. It was a child – the slave boy the wolfman had released back in Haithabyr.

'Please follow,' he said.

'Keep out of this, child,' said Vali. Had he guessed what was on Vali's mind and was seeking to protect the man who had freed him?

'Scram,' said Bragi. He had automatically picked up his sword when he left the hall and now he wafted it, still in its scabbard, at the boy to swat him away.

'Veles will make you free.'

'How?'

'You will go by the wine road. Follow me.'

Vali thought for a moment and then abandoned his plan. If Veles had sent this boy then perhaps there was a better way out. The boy led them to the side of the king's hall. There were the barrels, open at the top.

'In,' said the boy.

Feileg shook his head. 'No.'

Bragi's hand went to his sword. 'We can just as quick kill you here,' he said.

The wolfman's eyes were blank.

'Fine,' said Vali. 'Don't get in, and stay here to face Hemming's wrath.'

'I am coming with you,' said the wolfman, 'but not in there.'

'There's no other way,' said Vali.

There was a blast of laughter from the hall. Someone had opened the doors.

'I won't be captured again,' said Feileg.

The boy spoke: 'You freed me. I owe you a debt. This is not captivity but freedom. Please, get in,' he said.

There were footsteps now, drunken horseplay, voices repeating things the skald had said and wild laughter.

The wolfman looked at the boy. He nodded and, in what seemed like a single movement, was inside a barrel. Vali got into another, but Bragi couldn't lift himself in. From Veles' boat, four men in tatty work clothes appeared. They tipped a barrel onto its side, and Bragi crawled in. Vali squeezed down as far as he could. He had just enough space to bend his knees, so his head came below the lip of the barrel.

'Stay inside,' said a voice, and then his barrel was tipped onto its side and rolled towards the sea. The end was open and Vali feared he would be seen, but the night was dark and everyone was drunk. The turning was nauseating though, and it was all he could do to stop himself from falling out.

At the water's edge he felt his barrel lifted into the air and loaded onto a boat. Then a cloth was put over the top end of the barrel and it went dark. He kept still for a while, hearing the scrapings and crashes of the other barrels being loaded next to his. How were they going to get through the chain? Hemming would never allow it to be opened at night.

There was the sound of approaching shouts and many feet

on the shore. The shouts became a chant: 'More wine! More wine! More wine!'

'Get back to your stingy master and come back here with a gift fit for a king!' It was the skald, shouting from the shoreline.

'The chain opens for no one!' It was the voice of one of the men on the boat. 'Wait till tomorrow. You can make do with ale until then.'

'More wine! More wine! More wine!'

The skald spoke again: 'Don't try to get out of it, you serpents. They'll open the chain soon enough if you tell them you're off on an important mission from the king himself!'

'More wine! More wine! More wine!'

'Hey, Feggi, lower the chain!' shouted a voice.

'Chain down! Chain down! Chain down!'

'Gladly, if the king says so!' The voice of the chain guard was very close.

'Hemming, Hemming, grant us wine! Hemming, Hemming, grant us wine!'

Vali felt himself shaking and cursed himself for his fear.

'Lower the chain. Never let it be said that I don't listen to the will of my people!' It was Hemming's voice. The king had been drinking by the sound of him. Vali almost laughed. From what he had seen of Hemming, he was a serious man who wouldn't care to get too drunk. Sometimes, though, he would have to show his people he was one of them.

Vali heard the oars lift and the boat moved forward. There was the stiff clank of the lowering chain and the boat slid out into the main channel, the crowd cheering it on.

Vali regretted not killing the wolfman – it would have increased his chances of escape many times if Hemming had thought him dead. All he could hope was that Veles had come up with a better plan than he had managed himself.

The journey was a long and uncomfortable one. He tried to concentrate on the rhythm of the oars, to take his mind off the cramp in his legs. Then the boat stopped and the boy whispered to Vali to keep quiet. Other men got on and the boat began to move again. Vali guessed there had been a change of oarsmen.

He was in agony now but didn't dare move to ease his legs. He tried to sleep but it was impossible. Eventually, when numbness had dulled the pain, he smelled the sea and saw light through the cloth draped over his barrel. The boat was still. He had to get out, he thought, or he wouldn't ever be able to move again. As he shifted, he felt a hand push him back down.

'Not long now,' whispered a voice.

'Veles?'

'Your servant always, my lord.'

Despite his agony Vali gave thanks to Loki that Veles was on his side. The Obotrite was the cleverest man he had ever met.

His barrel was lifted again and Vali felt he was going to be sick. Then he was put down – on another ship, as far as he could tell. He heard the barrels being lashed down and realised he must now be on an ocean-going vessel preparing for the rigours of a sea voyage. Again, Veles' voice was close by.

'As soon as we are far from the shore you can come out. I apologise for your cramped accommodation, but be assured I had the barrels made specially for this purpose. They are commodious compared to normal vats. You will be free to stand soon.'

'Thank you, Veles. You've taken great risks for me.'

'Thanks are welcome, especially when princes speak with gold,' said Veles.

'What will you do if Hemming finds out it was you?'

'I am the king's most valuable servant, so I doubt he'll suspect me,' said Veles. 'Rest assured the blame will all be yours. Now be quiet. We are still inshore and there are men close by.'

Vali heard the creak of a rope and the sound of the sail

taking the wind, but no one spoke. For an age he waited. He could no longer feel his legs at all, apart from his knees, which had been rubbed to rawness against the sides of the barrel. He heard a tap.

'Out,' said a voice, and the cloth was pulled away.

Vali couldn't move at all at first but eventually managed to push himself to his feet, bending to massage the blood back into his legs. Then he climbed out of his barrel, blinded by the sun.

'Veles,' said Vali, 'even if I never walk properly again, I am forever in your debt. I—'

He felt a thump in his guts, so hard he puked. He fell to his side, his hands grasping for support, his head banging against one of the stays of the ship's hull. His sight began to adjust to the sunlight and he heard a familiar voice.

'The merchant sold you.'

He blinked and rubbed at his eyes, coughed and looked up. The warrior's identity seemed to assemble in Vali's mind from a collection of parts – the long deep scar running from the forehead to the lip, the massive body, bigger than any man he had ever seen, the tattoos covering every inch of his flesh in scenes of battle and destruction, the pelt of the white bear draped over him.

'Remember me, prince?' said Bodvar Bjarki. 'You said you wouldn't forget.'

33 An Explanation

The journey north felt like a dream to Adisla. The midnight sun turned the sea to boiling blood as it dipped towards the horizon and when it rose again it cast crystal shards into a sky of fragile blue. Sea mists came and went, the coastal mountains looming and then fading away, massive but fleeting. The temperature dropped as they moved up the coast – not to freezing, though ice was visible on the mountaintops, but to a grey numbing cold.

There was no true darkness, no rest from the leering of the Danes. Only the strange foreigner with his filed teeth and his drum seemed to stand between her and them. She had no oar to row, no sail to work and, huddling terrified at the prow of the ship, she was frozen. The man with the drum tried to help, but his attempts to hold her were unpleasant. He was ugly, frightening and stank of fish, though there was no lust in what he did. He just put his arms around her and squeezed.

She shrugged him off.

'It is normal,' he said. 'Be cold then.'

He brought her food – fish from the ship's pot, boiled reindeer, hunted and cooked when they stopped to camp. He was a dead shot with his little bow – a curious squashed-looking thing. The reindeer he brought back to the boat had just one arrow in it, embedded behind its ear. There had been no stressful wounded chase for the creature and the meat was tender and lovely.

It was the foreigner who slept next to her in an improvised tent on the beaches, keeping her from sleep as he watched her with those strange blue eyes, but keeping her from harm too with the broad knife he kept at his belt.

Soon the midnight sun turned from the side of the ships to behind them. They moved among islands that seemed no more than mountains rising from the water, past immense bays and wide silver beaches where sea eagles wheeled against brilliant skies. Great pine forests stretched up huge slopes, and where the mountains parted there were glimpses of vast green plains.

The ends of the earth were supposed to be this way, and as the fogs swept over the boat she wondered if this was the road to Nifhelm, the misty hell she had learned about at her mother's knee. The lands of men were called Middle Earth for good reason. There were other areas, realms of gods and giants beyond their own, and mortals had no place there. Was that where the longship was going?

Haarik came and sat next to her. He hadn't spoken to her for the whole voyage but now he was bored. The ship was under sail in an easy wind, most of the crew were sleeping and he had nothing to do. He held her face by her chin and turned it towards his. Then he glanced towards his men. None was paying them any attention. He let her go.

'I miss my wife,' he said. Normally Adisla would have found his thick accent and mangled words funny. At Eikund they'd been visited by an entertainer who did a very good impression of Danes, and Haarik reminded her of him with his sing-song Norse. Now she just found him grotesque.

'You should bring your bodyguard. You won't take me without a fight and you are old and frail.'

The king laughed.

'To talk to,' he said. 'I need to talk. The company of warriors is a glorious thing but men need softer speech too, don't they? Well, I do. Do you know why you're here?'

'I took it that you meant to sell me.'

'You're already sold, in a manner of speaking,' he said, 'or rather exchanged, though it seems to me an uneven bargain.'

Adisla looked at him. Haarik wasn't a coarse or unpleasant man; in fact, there was something quite fatherly about him – not her father but the father she wished she'd had. She hated him, though. He – or his men – had killed her brother, stolen her from her homeland and sentenced her mother to death. Still, she wanted to discover her fate so decided to be as civil as she could, which meant she said nothing.

'You're to be swapped for my son,' he said, 'although I wonder why I'm bothering. Perhaps I should have appointed you my heir. Are you any good as a sea captain? Can you wield a sword?'

'Not among my talents,' said Adisla.

'You can't be any worse than him. He was sent on a raid to the Islands at the World's Edge. He ended up here. That really does take a special sort of stupidity. I say go west; he finishes up just about as far east as it's possible to go.'

'He was captured?'

'Yes, and by people who couldn't catch a cold. The Whale People have got him – can you believe that? Nothing more than a sharpened reindeer antler between the lot of them and they've taken him hostage. He was shipwrecked on his way up the coast north. Went too far up, got caught in the wrong current. One of two survivors apparently, one of whom – biggest berserker I've ever seen – shows up at my court with my boy's sword and this whale wizard. I ask this berserker, Bodvar Bjarki, what a disciple of Odin of the white bear is doing getting captured by a bunch of icicle farmers and he murmurs something about sorcery. Says they heard a rumour of sorcerers' gold and went chasing it, which in itself beggars belief.'

'You look for him yourself?' said Adisla. 'Have you no champions to do it for you?'

Haarik laughed. 'I'm an old-fashioned king, not one of this new breed more at home with the inky priests of new gods than a sword. My problem, my solution. And besides I'm afraid of what the boy might say to anybody who rescues him. He could disgrace himself further.'

'Is he so big a fool?'

'Why would he be here if he wasn't? Sorcerer's gold! If I had a piece of silver for every rumour of sorcerer's gold I've heard then I wouldn't need any sorcerer's gold. These people haven't got combs for their hair, let alone gold. Even if it does exist, couldn't he hear the warning in the name? Sorcerer's gold. That's not little children's gold or farmer's gold, it's *sorcerer's* gold. I wouldn't be surprised if they had just untied a wind knot and blown him onto the rocks for his cheek. Anyway, this berserk tells me they've dragged my boy halfway across the world and the blubber bashers want something in return. '

'What?'

'You. If it weren't for the shame, I'd let him freeze his nuts off for ten winters up here.'

'How do they even know me?'

Haarik nodded towards the reclining Whale Man, who was watching them with half an eye. 'Ask him. If he'll tell you, he certainly won't tell me. The deal is: I take him to Rogaland; he identifies you; I take you up here; I get my idiot son back. Everyone happy.'

He looked at her face. 'Well, almost everyone.'

The Whale Man had closed his eyes and began to snore.

Haarik eyed him with contempt. 'They're idiots, his people. They pay tribute to three kingdoms that they move through after reindeer so no wonder they're poorer than dirt. Do they do anything about it? Do they go raiding or fight to keep what they've got? No. I tell you this: any Finn or Swede who came knocking on my door asking for tribute'd be going home with more than a whalebone comb for his pains.'

'And yet one Whale Man walks into your court, and you risk your men in war with the Rygir, leave your court in the hands of vassals and sail to the ends of the earth just because he asks you to.'

'My son is my son,' said Haarik, 'for better or worse.'

Adisla looked out of the ship. The landscape was flatter

here – a rusty shore of rocks above the grey sea; above that a strip of green.

Haarik continued: 'Anyway, when we get my boy back we'll give our blades a nice wetting, piss it up for a couple of days if they've got anything worth drinking and then head back. You seem like a nice girl. I'll take you as a bed slave. I'll try to avoid letting the crew have you if it's possible.'

'Very kind,' said Adisla.

'And practical. Giving you to them makes as much trouble as it stops – they'd be fighting like dogs over a bone.'

Haarik wasn't being unpleasant. He thought he was genuinely doing her favour by offering to claim her for his own. Adisla swallowed and looked out to sea. The courage to take her own life had failed her so she had to accept whatever was coming. She thought of the ruin of Eikund and couldn't help but taunt him.

'Let's hope the Whale People are not as fierce as the Rygir,' she said. 'You have only sixty men. With eighty you couldn't take our farms.'

Haarik's face darkened.

'There was the hand of sorcery in that,' he said, 'as we were told there would be. That's why we took you instead of the prince.'

'The same sorcery the berserk muttered about?'

Haarik smiled. 'Very like it.' She could see he liked her wit, took it for good humour. She found it difficult to believe that he couldn't see the hate that was in her heart.

They were approaching an island, a long black hill rising out of the flat sea. The sun seemed to reach out to it in a tongue of fire across the water, marking a path to lead them in.

Haarik went on: 'There is something protecting Prince Vali.' He nodded at the Whale Man. 'He wanted the prince but seemed to know we wouldn't get him. You were second best.'

A noise was coming across the water, a rhythm different to the creaking of the ship or, had anyone been rowing, the beat of oars. It was faint but insistent, and Adisla recognised it as the rhythm the Whale Man had used to pull her from the sea. It was pulsing towards them across the flat water now like the heartbeat of some gigantic beast.

'How can I be important to him? I'm a farmer's daughter.'

The Whale Man looked up, his pale eyes focusing on her, his little white teeth gleaming in a row as he smiled and jabbed a finger at her.

'Wolf trap,' he said.

34   From the Fog

Vali was thinking even as he fell against the boards. They had one free wolfman and four less deadly but still unencumbered hands. It was an unenviable position to be in against Bodvar Bjarki and his crew, but if they allowed themselves to be tied up or otherwise immobilised, they were done for.

Bragi stood cursing beside his upended barrel. He was moving like an old man waking after a long sleep. The wolfman was nowhere to be seen. Veles was wearing a smile that looked as if it had been cut into his face with a knife, shrugging as if asking for understanding. Vali felt angry and betrayed. He had looked up to the man, wished he was his father. Not Authun, Haarik nor even Forkbeard would have stooped to such a deceit.

'Tie them!' said Bodvar. A man came forward with a rope.

Time seemed to slow. One of Bodvar Bjarki's men peered into the wolfman's barrel as Vali heard Bragi come to the same conclusion he had, in the warrior's more straightforward manner.

'Bollocks to that!' Bragi took a stiff step forward and cut off the head of the rope man. Bragi had his sword, thought Vali. Unbelievably, he had got his sword into his barrel.

There was a noise halfway between a vomit and a scream from Vali's left and a guttural, crunching sound. The man looking for Feileg had found him.

Bodvar Bjarki didn't have his weapon out, but almost before the head of his crewman had hit the bottom of the boat he stepped forward and delivered a blow with his fist. Bragi flopped to the boards as though he'd had all the bones knocked out of him. Then Vali saw the giant coming for him. He tried to dodge but Bodvar Bjarki didn't just have the size and strength of a bear, he had the speed of one. He picked Vali up by an arm and a leg and smashed him down.

Vali fell badly, smacking his shoulder, but he quickly regained his feet. Bjarki was bearing down on him again.

The prince saw the realities of the situation in an instant. He was on his way to an enemy – Forkbeard or Haarik, it didn't matter. He was valuable goods. Bjarki lunged for him but he rolled away and ran for the stern of the ship. He put his foot on the rail and turned to face the berserk.

'Call off your men or I will—'

He didn't get a chance to finish the sentence. Bjarki leaped at him. Vali had no choice: he jumped over the side. He heard the berserk curse as he missed Vali by a fingernail.

The cold rushed at Vali, crushing the breath from him. He gulped saltwater and was gripped by terror. His time in the mire had seeped into him and he now had a terrible dread of drowning. He had to fight to calm himself, to allow himself to swim as he could instead of panicking in the water. It wasn't easy. His limbs were cramped from the barrel, but a flood of fear washed much of the stiffness away and he began to swim.

The swell meant that sometimes the boat was the height of two men above him, sometimes two below. It was coming about, side on to him. As the water lifted him, he concentrated to clear his mind and he saw it was a snekke, not as sleek or as quick as a drakkar but it could have twenty pairs of oars and maybe even carry a relief crew. They couldn't fight that many but he did have one bargaining counter. He was wondering if he would even get to use it when he heard a voice shout from the ship.

'Get back on the boat, goat brains!' It was Bjarki, throwing him a rope. It hit the water next to him, but he didn't take it even though he desperately wanted to.

He screamed as loud as he could, 'Not until I have your oath you will not try to tie us or kill us.'

'You're in no position to ask for oaths!'

'Yes, I am,' shouted Vali. 'If I drown, where is your ransom?'

'Drown then!' Bjarki went to turn away but Veles appeared beside him. For a few moments Vali lost sight of them, then the berserk was calling to him again: 'You have my oath, as you requested!'

'And you'll kill any man who does try to tie me or my friends while we are on your ship.'

Vali couldn't be sure he saw Veles shrug, but he thought he did.

'You've learned something of bargaining, prince!' shouted the merchant.

'Your oath. No hand raised against me or my friends.'

'That too!' shouted Bjarki.

The cold shot painful spasms into Vali's limbs and he had to concentrate very hard to make his frozen hands take the rope. Then he was being pulled in and up over the side. Bragi sat where he had fallen, blinking and holding his jaw. Feileg was in a snarling stand-off with three spearmen.

Bjarki came forward and said in a low, almost confidential voice, 'You've got your bargain, prince. You wouldn't have died anyway, none of you. The old boy's part of the deal and I intend to save your wolfman for where people can see me kill him.'

'Where are we going?' said Vali.

'Back to Forkbeard,' said the berserk. 'You are the price of my freedom – that and a good whack of compensation.'

'It was dishonourable to swear to that,' said Bragi.

'I'm meant for death in battle,' said Bjarki, 'not at the end of a rope.'

'The king is entitled to compensation for any ransom he has to pay,' said Veles. 'And it will be a good one, because this is a prisoner of Hemming, king of the Danes.'

'We escaped,' said Vali.

'Do you really think so,' said Veles, 'or was that for the benefit of spies? This way Hemming gets to sell you to Forkbeard;

everyone else thinks you went there under your own steam. A neat solution, wouldn't you agree?'

'I will kill you, Veles,' said Vali, 'be assured of that.'

The merchant shrugged. 'I think you are suffering from shock at your own stupidity. Don't blame me, blame yourself. I am a merchant and a fixer. I buy and sell things according to their worth. You gave yourself to me when you came to Haithabyr unprotected.'

'You were my friend,' said Vali.

The merchant snorted. 'I had enough of the friendship of your peoples when you burned my home in Reric,' he said.

Bjarki butted in. 'Do I have to kill him, or are you going to tell him to behave himself?' he said, nodding towards Bragi, who was getting to his feet. 'He's part of the prize so it'd be a shame to lose him.'

Vali gestured for Bragi to be calm.

'You have a sudden concern for profit,' said Vali. 'Has this merchant infected your thinking?'

The berserk spat. 'I have none,' he said. 'As long as I can eat and stay dry then riches don't concern me. "Cattle die, kindred die, but I know one thing that never dies, the glory of the great deed." Does not the Lord Odin tell us this? My prize is renown and the fulfilment of oaths, which is why, when we come to dry land, I shall kill your wolfman. He is a mighty warrior and the man who kills him will be praised down the centuries.'

'I am not interested in the wolfman.'

'So what are you interested in? That girl? Forget her. Haarik has given her to the Whale People for his son.'

'What do you mean?'

Bjarki looked at him and laughed. 'I mean she is Domen's bride by now.'

'Speak plainly.'

'The Whale Men will have used her for their magic. But why should I tell you any more? My oath concerns keeping you from harm while you are on this boat; it has nothing to do with your peace of mind.'

'If you can find her you'll be well rewarded,' said Vali, already knowing the berserk's answer.

'Where's the fame in that?' said Bjarki and turned away.

Vali felt a strange exhilaration. This was the first real information he'd had on Adisla. He felt closer to her just hearing it. He looked around the ship. He saw some faces he recognised, but the rest were unknown to him. There were a couple of berserks, stripped to the waist in the hot day, their tattoos so thick that they seemed almost like fur. There were some warriors who looked like men of the Groa river, ten days from Hordaland on foot. They wore the distinctive plaited beards of those people. So Forkbeard was using mercenaries. Was he preparing for war? Or was he just keeping his own men at home to defend his lands while using hired warriors to settle his scores?

The River Men were not happy, Vali could see. Bragi and Feileg had killed their friends and only fear of Bodvar Bjarki kept them from revenge. As it was, they glowered at the pair, muttering threats under their breath but keeping their distance. Bragi was unperturbed and met their gaze with a soft smile that told them he was ready any time they wanted to try their luck.

Vali went to the back of the ship and sat with him.

'Well?'

'I don't know. Seems we're safe for the short term.'

'I meant, how are you?' said Vali. 'That was quite a smack he gave you.'

'I lost a couple of teeth,' said Bragi, 'but I've had worse.' He raised his voice. 'But then again I'm used to fighting big men, not these skinny berserks.'

Vali thought he actually saw Bodvar Bjarki laugh as he tied off a rope.

Vali went back to the matter in hand. 'What do you think we can do?'

Bragi shrugged. 'We can't sail the ship with two of us. If they're not going to kill us, I'd say we have to stick with them. The moment we're in sight of land, we attack.'

'I have no weapon.'

'Tyr, god of battles will, provide.'

'He may provide an early death,' said Vali

'I have lived a long time,' said Bragi. 'I am not greedy for years, only fame.'

There were around sixty men on the ship, two of them with axes ready and another three with spears guarding them, watching with expressions somewhere between anger and fear. Feileg simply sat at the back of the boat looking at his feet. Vali remembered that the wolfman hadn't liked travelling under sail but didn't see how he could feel seasick in such a large, stable ship.

He looked out. No land. He realised that they must have left Haithabyr on the opposite course to the one they'd arrived on. They'd been taken to the town and transferred to another boat which had then doubled back. That was why their journey to the open sea had been so long. Bragi said the inlet from Hemming's court connected to the river Edjeren and out to the Northern Sea by a man-made channel. That was the route they had taken. They were, Vali guessed, navigating now by the sun and the stars, which gave them a good chance of getting lost. That was his best bet. If the ship lost its way and had to set down on a strange coast he might be able to escape. He sat back against a spar.

'Sleep if you like. I'll watch these bastards,' said Bragi.

So Vali slept, or rather hovered uncomfortably between waking and sleeping.

The sea fell to a dead calm and the boat went on under oar for a while. In his semi-conscious condition the rhythm of the rowing seemed like something animal, a heartbeat. His mind seemed to enter the beat, to be taken over by it, and then the cadence seemed to change subtly. It was no longer so slow and easy, but faster and more frenzied. He began to dream – or so he thought – and he saw Adisla and Feileg and that strange rune. It seemed to pulse and move, to vibrate and thump, and he realised it wasn't the oars at all that were making the noise, but the rune. And it was not floating and incorporeal, as he had thought it to be, but was real, painted onto a surface. He breathed in and smelled hide and wood – a fire. The rune was shaking. It was painted on a drum. Someone was beating a drum with that horrid symbol on it. He looked through the rune and he saw Adisla – but where was she? She was at the centre of a circle of wild animals: wolves, bears, stags, even a huge eagle. But then his mind cleared and he saw them for what they were – men in animal masks. They were beating drums, drums peppered with that rune, which seemed to lift from the skins as they beat them, to go floating up through the night. He knew where they were going – towards him. They seemed to sweep over him, enveloping him in a swarm. He had the sense that the men were showing him that they had her. They were calling him, even laying a trail for him to follow. There was another thing there though, something old and hungry, something that prowled at the edge of his mind, watching. Its presence seemed like a blind shaft, a drop away into nothing, and the cold he felt from it was the same cold he had felt when Disa had worked her magic on him.

The drumbeat filled up his mind.

When he turned he saw the man he had seen at the shield wall, tall and pale with a shock of red hair.

'Help me find her,' said Vali.

'You will find her,' he said, 'and you will be lost. Welcome the sorcerer's gift. Your anger is now a gate for him and he can hear it opening. Let these little ones in.'

He had picked up a fistful of those spiky runes and sprinkled them over Vali's head.

'What does the drummer want from me?'

'For you to know yourself.'

'Who am I?'

The man held Vali in his arms and kissed him on the forehead.

'Would you know?'

'I would know.'

'Then know.'

He was drowning again, the filthy water obscuring his sight, filling his lungs and choking his consciousness. The drums were thumping in his head and, above them, he heard Jodis telling them to put him under. He saw himself in that chamber where the rune had been, knowing that it expressed himself, Adisla and Feileg, knowing they were inseparable. He realised what he had missed before – he hadn't seen where he was watching from. He felt a pain in his mouth like a pin, felt tight bonds about him, smelled blood and fire and felt an anger of injustice boiling within him.

He tried to speak his name, but all that came out was a howl of agony, a roar of injustice. He was the wolf.

'Get up. This is our chance. In the name of Thor's bulging nut sack, get up. What's wrong with you? What's wrong with you?' It was Bragi's voice, shouting, urgent. Vali could also hear screams – men hurling obscenities and threats.

He stood. Something bizarre was happening. The merchant Veles came flapping past him, waving his arms almost as if he was swimming through the air. Then, with an unexpected turn of athleticism, he pulled himself up by one of the ropes that was securing the big barrels and leapt inside, quick as a rabbit into a hole.

Vali looked around. A huge full moon turned the sea to crumpled metal, and no more than bowshot away was a broad bank of thick fog almost glowing in the moonlight. There came the sound of rain – or something like it – and everyone scrambled for cover, cowering beneath shields or ducking under the longship's rail.

He looked off to the side. Two drakkars, the real deal with carved dragons' heads, were upon them, showering their ship with thick black volleys of arrows. Where had they come from?

'Haarik! Haarik!' came the chant.

They were raiders from Aggersborg. If Haarik was on board then Vali wanted his blood.

There was a shore in sight under the bright moon. They had blundered too close to Haarik's land and were paying the price. Still, Vali would welcome being captured by Haarik – in a way. It would put him closer to Adisla. Logic though wasn't uppermost in his mind. Something else was gnawing away at him. What had the man in the feather cloak said to him? He couldn't think. His head was still resonating to the sound of those drums. Then all reason seemed to desert him. These attackers were the kin of the men who had stolen Adisla, killed little Manni, uprooted him from his home and the people he called family. Vali coughed. It was the same cough he'd had in the mire. His throat felt dry and tight, his head light, his ears seemed full of a throbbing beat. He couldn't order his thoughts, couldn't find direction.

'Danes, Danes, Haarik's men, thieves and murderers to be torn and wasted. Kill them. Kill them all. None alive, none alive. My oath is murder to them. I tear and bite, bite and tear.'

What was happening to him? Now he was shaking and coughing. Now he was freezing cold, just as he had been when Bragi had dragged him from the water of the drowning pool.

'Pirates! Prince, it's now or never. We should bargain with them. This is our freedom!' It was Bragi, but Vali couldn't concentrate on what he was saying. His head was spinning. It was as if the reality he had experienced in his dream, the reality of the dark waters, had replaced that of the attack.

Some archers in Vali's boat were returning fire although most of Bjarki's men were still struggling to free their weapons from sea barrels. Vali seemed to move through a soup of stress and anger, as if the men leaked these things from them in their sweat.

A drakkar came swiping past, its oars withdrawn, to broad-side their own, snapping off oars and sending men tumbling to the bottom of the boat. Only three men were left standing – himself, Feileg and Bodvar Bjarki, who was grinning and laughing behind his huge shield, a fine sword in his hand.

Grappling hooks came into the ship. The war jabber was in his ears, the stink of fear all around him. He felt as if the rune was hooked through his throat, pulling him up towards a terrible destiny. His blood pumped in his head like something was trying to burst from inside him. And then it did – a word that seemed more than a word, more like a vortex, a sucking piece of the night into which he would abandon himself.

'Fenrisulfr.'

It felt right, as if for the first time he was saying his name.

'They tied me as they tied my father,' he heard himself say.

'What are you talking about? We need to get to that ship.' It was Bragi.

'I will lap their vital ichors.'

'Prince, you're raving. At least lie down. You're going to be hit.'

'Fenrisulfr.'

Vali stepped towards the bouquet of the fight. It all seemed so delicious to him: the heavy sweats of fear and rage, and the blood, above all the blood, where the sweet arrow did its work, where the lovely sword cut and the pretty axe hewed.

'The fetters have burst,' he said.

And then the blood mire took his mind.

35   A Wolf's Treat

Vali woke. He was in fog. It was day and the mast cast long shadows into the air like the rays of the sun coming behind a cloud, but streaking the fog with darkness not light. The rays floated before him, a black web on grey, almost as if the creaks of the ship that broke the damp silence had been given visible expression.

He looked down at his clothes, or what was left of them. They were torn and dark with blood. There was a taste in his mouth – blood too. He felt torpid and slow-witted, as you might after a heavy meal in the afternoon sun.

'Bragi?' No answer. He had his hand on something soft. He looked to see what it was and screamed. It was a man, his ribcage torn away, his limbs broken, staring up from beneath him. Vali jumped to his feet. There was someone beside him. He started and was about to leap back, but there was no need. It was just his own shadow, a fog spectre cast by the sun, eerily solid. He looked about him. The boat was full of corpses ripped and mutilated in the most horrible way. Dead eyes stared at him; limbs reached for him; entrails snaked at his feet; the smell of death filled up his nostrils.

He staggered around, trying to get away from the dead men, but they were everywhere, from stern to prow. He ran in a crazy dance, lifting his knees high as if attempting to float above the corpses. He felt a hand clutch at his shoulder and he turned to see the wolfman looking back at him. Feileg was gaunt and pale, and a long deep cut ran from the top of his arm across his chest. Vali took a step back, tripped over a body and fell onto it. Repulsed, he tried to stand. The wolfman grasped him and pulled him to his feet.

'How long?' said Vali.

'A week,' said the wolfman.

'I've been unconscious a week?'

'Not unconscious,' said the wolfman.

'Then what?'

The wolfman looked at the bodies.

'You?' said Vali.

'Not me.'

'Why didn't you throw them overboard?'

Feileg stared into Vali's eyes.

'I was afraid of you,' said the wolfman.

The explanation did not make sense to Vali. The wolfman was easily his better in a fight and could do what he liked.

'Why were you afraid of me?'

'You are a wolf,' said the wolfman. 'I had to hide from you among these dead.'

Vali could not grasp what Feileg was saying. His head felt light and the day, even under the fog, too bright. He looked at the bodies. They were Danes, around twenty of them, and none had any signs of arrow strikes or sword cuts. Rather, their wounds were ragged and torn. One man had half his face ripped away, and it looked more as if he had been attacked by a wild animal than killed in battle.

Vali couldn't bear the corpses staring at him in that unnatural light any longer. He spent a few moments steeling himself and then began to tip them overboard into the sea, removing any swords and purses before he did so. The work was long and it was hard. Vali felt exhausted and had to take frequent breaks as his distaste for what he was doing became too much. Feileg's wound pained him and he was little help. The fog began to clear and birds to descend – mainly gulls but crows too. The sight of the crows gave Vali hope. They weren't far from land. Still, he made some effort to shoo them away. Had the birds mutilated the corpses before flying off as the boat slid into the fog?

Feileg helped him lift a stout Dane up to the shield rail. The man was much heavier than he looked and it was a terrible heave to get him there. They propped him for a moment to recover their breath, the corpse leaning over the side like someone seasick rather than dead. And then Vali realised what had happened.

'You did this to them, didn't you?' he said. 'You did this evil thing.'

The wolfman looked at him without expression. 'Prince,' he said, 'you must not talk to me like that, for you ate a wolf's treat.'

'Have you taken to talking in riddles, Feileg? Our human company has had a corrupting effect on you. Say what you mean plainly.'

The wolfman said nothing.

The Dane had clearly been decomposing for some time. As they lifted his legs over the side, his stomach split, enveloping Vali in a cloud of corpse gas. He retched. The man slid into the water and Vali shuddered, wiping away the vomit. There was a strange metallic taste in his mouth, not unpleasant at all, he thought. He looked at his hand and then down to his boots where he had been sick. More blood. Instinctively he felt his sides, his arms and legs. He hadn't been wounded but still he was retching blood. The wolfman continued to watch him without expression.

When the last body was gone, Vali sat down, opened a sea chest and took out a skin of wine, drinking deeply. It tasted odd, unpleasant even. He concluded it was off. Why would a man take bad wine on a trip? He tried another. That was off too, as was a skin of beer. It tasted repulsive, undrinkable.

Finally, he found a skin with water in it and drank from that. It tasted much better, though he was now aware of other scents, suggestions of things he couldn't name but that made him think of the death throes of the animal which had been used to make the skin. He perceived something else as he drank – more than a taste, a sense of who had used the skin before. It had been drunk from just before the battle commenced – there was the sweat of anxiety on it.

And then he realised that beneath the salt of the sea, the smell of the wet boards and the ropes, he could smell a thousand other notes. Grass, loam, reindeer, trees, drying sand and seaweed, even a smell so familiar and powerful it almost made him laugh. Wet dog. In his mind Vali saw Disa driving Hopp away from the fire, saying they'd be having roast dog for dinner if he sat any closer. He breathed in and knew they were near land.

Vali looked out but could see nothing. He could tell by the scent of pine needles that the nearest land lay to his east, away from where the sun was throwing its fog shadows. The ship was caught in a current and was far too big for him to sail, but he took the rudder and tried to steer it that way.

The wolfman just kept looking at him.

Vali's thoughts had been disordered by the corpses and his long unconsciousness. As they began to come back to normality, he realised he had forgotten to ask a very important question. 'Do you know what happened to Bragi?' he said.

'Yes,' said the wolfman.

'What?'

'You killed him.'

36 The Blood Mire

Vali did not, as Feileg did, remember the attack. Nor did he remember the huge moon reducing the world to silver and black, lines and a circle.

The drakkars had come upon them quietly from the fog bank. Feileg thought the ambush must have been directed by a sorcerer who was working for the pirates How else would Bodvar Bjarki's ship have been spotted at night, and through such fog?

He didn't know that magic was involved, though with a bigger ambition than plunder. In the caves of the Troll Wall, the witch was working to speed him to his destiny and on the flat rock of his island the northern sorcerer sat entranced for a week beating his drum and chanting his chants to bring Vali to him. So the Danish warlord had found himself unable to sleep tht night. The inside of his longhouse seemed unbearably stuffy and he had gone outside for some air. Looking out over the sea, he had seen a movement. It was a squall of starlings, wheeling against the big moon, turning and vanishing. It was then that he'd seen the Drakkar, out towards the horizon, skirting an incoming fog. It was potentially dangerous to set sail in such weather but the temptation was too great. His men had not needed rousing. A mob of them were at his door before he had picked up his spear. They too had found no comfort in their beds that night and had seen the enemy vessel. Two ships were crewed and launched before the fog had moved a boat length.

The attackers had lost sight of their prey in the fog but had been guided by the slow beat of Bjarki's oars through the murk. Both Danish ships had matched that rhythm to hide the sound of their own approach. From within the white world of the fog the voices of the men on the target boat, Vali's conversation with Bragi even, would have sounded loud and close by.

Leading up to the attack, Bjarki, noted the wolfman, had been nervous. The fog was approaching and the berserk headed out to sea to keep clear of any sandbanks or rocks.

Feileg remembered Bjarki suddenly freezing and telling the rowers to be still and silent. They'd heard it then, the straining of the pirate oarsmen as they rowed, the exhalation of effort mingling with the sound of the oars in the water like the wet breath of a dying giant.

'Weapons!' Bodvar had shouted. 'Weapons!' And the men had scrambled to their barrels and chests. War horns had announced the attack, followed in a heartbeat by arrows. The bowmen were not accurate shooting from one moving ship at another but they had caused panic, the warriors stumbling and cursing as they fought to be first to their spears. In the attack the distinction between captive and captor melted away and Vali, Bragi and Feileg were free to act.

Bragi had been screaming at Feileg, really bellowing, 'Get yourself a shield. If you want to live, get yourself a shield.' He had also been trying to rouse Vali, who seemed to be in a trance.

Feileg could not yet see the attackers, though a couple of arrows skidding on the boards next to him told him they could see him. He ducked down as some of the other men were doing. Bragi was shouting at Vali, begging him to wake up.

A gust of air enveloped them in fog and for an instant Feileg thought they were hidden. But then there was a thump on the ship, so hard it almost felt as though he himself had been struck, a rattle and a crunching as their oars were sheared away, and screams of exultation as the Danes leaped aboard.

The prince stood, seemingly in the grip of madness, muttering to himself and staggering as if drunk.

Three Danes jumped down but one was impaled by Bragi's

sword before his feet even touched the boards, and he collapsed into the other two. There was an insane scramble on the bottom of the boat as Bragi left his sword in the Dane's body and found his knife for the close work. The Danes were armed with axes, but with Bragi on top of them in a pile had no way to swing them. He gutted the first in an instant. The second tried to get up, but Feileg drove a powerful kick into his head and leaped on him, tearing with his nails and teeth. Bragi was on his feet. He sheathed his knife and regained his sword. Then he leaped into the press of the fight slashing, striking with his pommel, kicking, biting and punching.

Bodvar Bjarki was an impressive sight, blocking with his shield, hacking with his sword, driving in with his knees and head. He was fighting three men at once and it was they who were giving ground. 'Odin! Odin! Odin!' he was screaming. He was so big that Feileg was reminded of when he'd played with his father as a child, leaping on him, being thrown away and leaping on again.

Other Danes appeared next to Feileg and for a time he lost all sense of anything but his own preservation. Faces came at him, weapons blurred, he dodged, struck and bit, broke limbs, tore eyes from their sockets and stamped on his fallen enemies. There was another massive crunch, the air filled with splinters and he fought to retain his balance. A second ship had sheared their oars away on the other side.

The fighting happened in waves. Men would engage, fight, prevail or die, then part to stand shouting insults at each other and looking for openings before clashing again. Bragi was howling, 'We are nobles of the Horda and much gold will you win for our safe return,' but it was useless. The Danes were set on killing them.

One came at Bragi, two then three. The shield he had taken up had been reduced to smithereens and he was fighting with just the iron boss, punching out with it and hacking with his sword. Someone struck him to the face, cutting away part of his chin, but the jarl just shoved his beard into his mouth to secure his dangling flesh. Four were on him, five. Two Danes confronted Feileg, and he couldn't reach Bragi.

Everything changed when someone struck at the prince. Feileg saw an axe swing towards Vali's head, but then the axe was flying through the air and the man who had been holding it was clutching his throat and screaming. Feileg saw Vali plunge into the Danes, and the rhythm of the battle changed. The ebb and flow became a flood tide, an unstoppable immense surge that pushed the Danes back, smashed them down and tore them to nothing. Vali's speed was breathtaking and his strength even more so. He reached Bragi, who was almost dead on his feet. The first Dane had his neck broken as Vali took his head in both hands and twisted; the next was simply battered into the sea. Bragi struck the third with his sword to the shoulder and Vali leaped on him, the two going down together. The last two no longer liked the odds and retreated onto their ship.

Bragi scanned for enemies, straightened his bent sword under his foot against a timber and slid his knife into his belt. That done, he put his hand up to the flap of skin at his chin and called out to Vali behind him, 'Well, you remembered something I taught you, though you did a good enough job of hiding it for long enough. I ...'

Feileg watched as Bragi looked at the prince. Vali was kneeling beside of one of the fallen men, chewing into the flesh of his face and trying to rip the meat from the bone with his teeth.

'Prince, I ...' Bragi put his hand on Vali's shoulder.

Vali gave a boiling growl.

'Prince,' said Bragi, 'you are bewitched. Prince, friend, please '

He never finished his sentence. Vali stood and in the same movement threw Bragi onto his back. Then he was on him, biting at him, tearing his skin, punching and kicking. Feileg saw the old man's head loll as Vali poured in blow after blow, but Bragi was a formidable fighter and responded with blows of his own. The two men rose, locked together, crashed back over the rail of the ship, fell into the enemy vessel and rolled apart. Danes surrounded them. Four, five, six men tore into the pair, attacks coming in from all sides. Vali lost his footing. Axes and spears were raised but Bragi got free of his opponent and charged headlong at Vali's attackers driving three of them to the boards. Bragi lost his sword and much of his hand to an axe but Vali broke the axeman's neck with a blow to the head.

Bragi went down, locked to an opponent. They broke, shoving each other away as they stood, but the Dane had snatched the old warrior's knife from his belt. Bragi reacted immediately, driving his head forward into the man's face, sending his opponent crashing over the rail of the ship into the sea.

Vali seemed to catch the idea. He tossed two men over the rail into the water and turned to face the rest. The Danes fell back, a half-circle of them around Bragi and Vali, too scared to come on but with nowhere to retreat to.

Bragi was unarmed, all his weapons gone in the fight and his right hand a bloody ruin, as was his face. He smiled at the prince. 'All my life I've dreamed of doing this with you. You're a great scrapper, as long as you concentrate on the enemy. But you want to watch those berserker mushrooms.'

Vali swayed uncertainly in front of him.

Bragi put a hand on his shoulder.

'I'm proud of you, lord. You're a mighty man, and it does my heart good to see you fight like that. I'd have lost my hand before if I'd known it would have that effect on you.'

And Vali took him, leaping on him like a wild animal and tearing out his throat with his teeth. Bragi instinctively reached for his sword with his bloody hand and for his knife with his good one, but they were gone. He staggered back, his blood engulfing him and engulfing the prince. Vali shoved him to the deck, where the old man lay writhing, his hands tearing at his belt for the weapons that were no longer there.

The Danes around them seemed to decide as one they wouldn't take on Vali and scrambled onto Bodvar Bjarki's crippled ship. The pirates on the other ship took this for a renewed attack and came pouring over in numbers themselves. Feileg fought hard and lost track of time, then he saw Vali leap back onto the centre boat with a terrible snarl.

Some of the Danes seemed transfixed, stopping as if turned to stone. Feileg had heard his father tell stories of this – the battle fetter – where Odin descends and strikes the enemy motionless. Others, though, were not affected and came forward to meet Vali. The fighting was terrible. Men lost their footing and were stabbed or trampled on the blood-slick boards; friend struck friend in the confusion but Vali seemed untouchable. Opponents fell back from him as if blasted by a gale, pushing back to their own ships. Some made it. Those who didn't were crushed, torn or broken by Vali's merciless attacks with teeth and hands.

Feileg took a blow across the shoulders and staggered, but then his opponent was down, felled by Bjarki. He was not berserk – he hadn't had the time to chant his chants and consume his brew of mushrooms – and when he spoke Feileg recognised what he said for sense.

'We have to take one of their boats. Leave him here. He is berserk like I've never seen and will harm us as much as the Danes.' Bjarki was no fool and realised that a common enemy could make for strange friends. He pointed to the ship where Bragi lay.

Feileg nodded and jumped across. He went to Bragi. The wound at his neck was terrible and his eyes were dim. He was reaching around, searching for something. The wolfman instinctively knew what to do – he had spent his earliest years with berserks, after all. He picked up a fallen spear and pressed it into the warrior's good hand. Bragi's fingers curled around it and he drew Feileg to him. His voice was hardly audible and Feileg had to crane down to hear it.

'I taught him many things,' he said, 'but I never taught him that.'

Bragi began to laugh and then stopped. Feileg touched the old man's face. He had died as the men of his people would have wanted to, thought Feileg, with a weapon in his hand and a joke on his lips.

Only a few of the Danes remained on the boat and the fight had gone out of them. Seeing the berserk and the remains of his crew climbing across towards them, they rushed back the other way to join what was left of their comrades on the far boat. Only Vali remained between the two groups on the middle ship. The Danes knew they were facing a monster rather than a man and had already started cutting the ropes they had lashed to Bjarki's ship at the start of the encounter.

On the oarless ship, red with blood, surrounded by bodies, Vali was suddenly still, looking about him as if slightly puzzled. A pair of eyes appeared above the rim of one of the barrels. Someone was still in there, Feileg realised.

'Now or never Veles Libor,' shouted Bjarki.

The merchant stood in the barrel looking at Vali. He trembled as he stared at the prince. Even from twenty paces away Feileg could see him shaking.

Veles looked towards Feileg's ship, his movements very slow as if he feared he might draw attention to himself. Then, with a very surprising turn of speed, he levered himself out of the barrel, ran to the rail of the boat and rolled over to join the wolfman and the berserk, flattening himself to the bottom of the boat as if he was still in the middle of an arrow storm. Bjarki gave a snort of contempt but Feileg was minded to throw the merchant into the water. Luckily for Veles, the wolfman had other things to think about.

'Can we take the prince with us?' Feileg asked Bjarki.

Busy cutting ropes, the big man shook his head. 'He'll still be berserk. We'll follow the current and try to keep him in sight.'

'And if we lose him?'

Bjarki shrugged. 'We'll pick him up easy enough if we let ourselves drift. If I stay tied to him I'll have a mutiny on my hands. He's bewitched and the men won't stand for it.'

The fog came over them again, the taunts of Bjarki's crew following the Danes as they disappeared into it. Vali was only a shadow on the corpse boat, though one last rope still connected it to Feileg's ship.

The rope was cut and the boats began to move apart. Feileg looked at the body of Bragi. Then he turned to Bjarki. He pointed to the old warrior's corpse. 'Tell tales of him,' he said, and then jumped to join his brother as the fog bank swallowed them.

37   The Hunters

It had been three days since Vali had woken and he felt very strange indeed. He was uncommonly energetic, hardly slept, felt stronger and had no urge to eat at all.

The scents of the night were enthralling to him and he would sit under the stars breathing in the many odours of the boat while Feileg chewed dried fish from the Danes' provisions. The days seemed alive with sensation: the sun on the water was a field of diamonds, the sky a limitless and entrancing blue and the wind, when it came, brought a bounty of scents in a thousand varieties he had never noticed before – beach tar and wet stone, bird droppings, stranded fish – each one containing its own notes, its fascinating signature. When the skies bloated with cloud he could smell the rain coming in and sense which way the wind would turn. None of this seemed strange to him, or rather he was aware of his heightened perceptions as something new but they didn't feel wrong or unusual. He felt more comfortable with his new senses than he had with his old ones.

He thought of Bragi – sometimes he could think of nothing else. Had he killed him, as Feileg had said? The wolfman had called him 'battle blind' but would not explain further. Vali felt so distant from his old self that it almost seemed possible ... No, the wolfman had got it wrong. Feileg had mistaken what he had seen. The mess of battle had confused him.

Then, in a rising sea, his eyes confirmed what his nose had told him – land, a strip of rusty red cliffs against the iron black of the ocean. He took the rudder, saved from the side-swipe of the pirate ship by the curve of the hull, and tried to turn landward. It was frustrating work. The current was pulling across the shore and the ship responded sluggishly when it responded at all. Feileg was no use, slumped in his usual position, sat with his head between his legs, staring at his feet. But they were getting closer.

The coast was unpromising, with few beaches and fierce cliffs making a landing very tricky at best. He steered, allowed the current to take them, steered again, let go again. Then they were racing under dirty brown cliffs a boat's length away. The sea was getting higher, the wind whipping up about them. Vali didn't think he would have much of a chance if the boat struck the rocks. He looked at Feileg. The wolfman would have none.

The boat was pushed into the cliff by a wave, crashed into the rock face, and bounced off, spinning round. Vali let go of the rudder. Nothing to do now but hope. They were speeding backwards, the cliffs racing past so near Vali could have touched them. The boat wouldn't survive another such impact, he knew. Again they turned, and again, and then another crunch and the boat was still. The ship had come to rest on a sandbank. It was no more than a couple of boat's lengths to a narrow beach.

Feileg stood up. 'I will swim,' he said.

'I know you can't even if you try,' said Vali. He picked up a spear, a bow and a sword from the bottom of the boat. He was feeling very peculiar: one instant his head was thick, as if he was drunk, the next it had a sharpness he had never known. 'Get some provisions. If we're lucky you'll be able to wade to shore.'

The wolfman did as he was bid, and Vali stepped uncertainly into the water. It only came up to his thighs. He began to wade with the wolfman watching him. He made it easily – the sea was chest deep at most. Feileg followed. Vali was surprised to see how hesitant he was. Could someone so fierce in battle really be afraid of wet feet?

They were on a small beach beneath a long broken cliff of that reddish rock. Vali said nothing, just made his way towards it. The cliffs were tall but uneven and climbable and they found their way to the top quite easily, Feileg pausing to take some birds' eggs. The view was immense. They had reached a spot overlooking a green land of birch forests falling towards long fjords and a wide grassy plain stretching to distant mountains that rose like black dragons on the horizon.

Vali breathed in. He smelled smoke on the wind and something else. Cooking meat. He held his hand to his forehead and squinted into the distance. There, beyond the barrier of a fjord, over a short hill in the grassland, a plume of grey reached up, curving in the wind. It was a fire.

'What is this land?' said Feileg.

'I don't know,' said Vali, 'but I intend to ask.'

The two made their way around the fjord and over to the grassy plain. The fire was three day's walk away but still Vali did not feel hungry. He thought of the blood he had vomited. It was possible something was wrong with him, though he didn't feel at all ill. In fact, he felt uncommonly well, like that point after a drink of beer when you first feel its effects – your tongue seems looser, your wit quicker, your body more able, and yet a dullness stalks you, as if your reason and discernment are fading away. Reindeer herds were moving in the distance, he could tell, and thunder coming in on the wind.

Feileg gathered herbs to dress his wound but it was clear to Vali the wolfman was not well. He was sweating heavily and visibly hot with a sweetness to his breath that Vali could smell ten paces from him. The prince was irritated to have to stop to let him rest, irritated beyond reasonableness, he recognised, but he wanted to press on. In fact, he was angry with Feileg, and that anger seemed caught up in how he had been feeling since he had woken on the boat. Why couldn't he leave him? He just couldn't. He felt utterly bound to Feileg, like the rain was bound to the land.

He had tried to kill him at Hemming's court and told himself the intervention of the boy had saved Feileg's life. But in reality his own will had failed. As his senses changed and his thoughts distorted, Vali realised why he had not been able to stab him. The wolfman felt like kin. The thought was heavy inside him, but he couldn't acknowledge its weight any more than he could deny it.

A storm swept over them hard and cold but Vali did not pause. The fire was invisible now but he still could scent its wet embers through the downpour. There was another smell too – the sour smack of the wolfman's wound. Vali tried to ignore what it was doing to him but a bubbling growl seemed to fill his mind and he struggled against acknowledging it for what it was. A call for blood. Blood. The taste and the scent of it had not left him since the ship and he could not shake its savour.

They found the remains of a camp as the sun was beginning to dip behind a large black peak, spreading a span of rays across the sky. There was no one around, but the earth was flattened and there were the cold ashes of a fire and the smell of animal skins on the grass where people had slept.

'They went inland,' said Feileg.

Vali nodded. He knew. 'Then follow,' he said. He spat. For a day he had been salivating heavily.

The prince seemed possessed to the wolfman. Feileg looked at him with fear in his eyes and he did as he said.

The storm had gone and the sun was rising by the time they came upon the reindeer hunters. A new fire had led them there, seductive in its smell of cooking meat.

A single family was gathered around two squat conical tents of birch poles and reindeer skins. The tents were open at the top where the sticks met, and in one of them was the small fire that had drawn Vali and Feileg in. Of more immediate concern, however, were the two men who challenged them a bowshot from the camp. A bowshot was an appropriate measure of distance because both of the hunters had strange short bows in their hands. Arrows were stuck in the ground in front of them, not nocked, but available for easy access.

Vali felt his blood rising in his veins, ready for the fight, and tried to tell himself there was no need. Yet his focus had shifted, it seemed. His first response was to think of murder. He felt a hand at his side and his sword was drawn without him touching it. Feileg tossed the sword towards the bowmen and sat down on the ground. Vali exchanged a glance with him. The wolfman was wounded but Vali had only ever seen him respond to newcomers with seething anger before. Now he acted as Vali himself would have wanted to act, had he been in more control of his mind. Vali remembered the raid on the monastery. Hadn't he made a gesture like that once? He tried to recall that thought, to drop an anchor to hold him still in the tide of animosity that was engulfing him.

The hunters, who wore dark blue coats trimmed with red and gold bands, gave a friendly wave and walked towards the brothers. They were an interesting people, thought Vali, with dark hair and blue eyes like his own. They all exchanged smiles, and the hunters said something in a strange language and sat down in front of them. Vali didn't understand a word.

The wolfman was opening his pack with weak fingers. He offered the hunters wine in a skin, which they drank from gratefully. It was the same skin Vali had tried. He had thought it was bad but the hunters seemed to like it well enough. One of them gestured towards Feileg's wound and then to the camp. Vali stood to follow them but realised that Feileg could not get up. He had spent the last of his energy on the overnight trek. The prince had never seen the wolfman weak before. He knew what had happened – his wound had turned. There wasn't long for him now.

Vali forced himself to think, to be the boy who had grown up around Forkbeard's farms, the young man who had loved Adisla and had vowed to die for her. That dirty mire water was in him though, and he struggled to frame his thoughts. It came to him that he should help Feileg to his feet. He crouched, put the wolfman's arm around his shoulders and got him up. The human gesture seemed to restore Vali and his head cleared some more. These were Whale People or their kin from the

320

interior of the country who lived from reindeer. Hemming had said that Haarik intended to exchange Adisla for his son. Perhaps they would know where or who this Domen was that Bodvar Bjarki had spoken of.

At the camp the men made signs for the brothers to sit inside one of the tents. A woman was in there, holding a young child. She looked at them with wary eyes but pointed to some furs for Feileg to lie on. Vali lowered the wolfman to the ground and then went outside. The interior of the tent was unbearably stuffy. He needed to be under the sun.

Feileg lay breathing heavily on the deerskins. The pace Vali had demanded had nearly killed him. The wolfman was convinced that some sort of sorcery had taken the prince but he was still determined to follow him. Something had moved in Feileg when he had spoken to Adisla and he was set on following his impulse to find her until the end. He breathed in the aromas of the tent: cooking and curds of goats' milk, reindeer hide and the birch fire. Feileg found it all immensely comforting and recalled evenings sitting in the dark with his brothers and sisters and listening to stories of adventure and glory. He had had no idea he was different then, marked for a special destiny among the wolves. Feileg had not wanted to be inside for years, but now he was content. It was Vali who sat in the open, head bowed and looking at his feet.

A man came in. He was smaller than the others and wearing a hat of four corners, like a parcel of cloth folded back on top. He nodded and smiled a greeting, sat down and put a hand on the wolf pelt Feileg wore. The wolfman felt no threat and allowed him to pull it aside. The man examined the wound. He shook his head and ran his fingers lightly across it. Then he turned and said something to the woman. She brought Feileg some stew in a bowl and he ate it gratefully.

'Ruohtta,' said the man to Feileg. He pointed at him and made a gesture of lying down on his side and turning up his eyes. Feileg realised he was telling him he was going to die.

Feileg had never feared death. When he was with his family

he had been told it was glorious; when he was with Kveld Ulf he had seen it as simply a happening – a transformation, a different kind of day among other days. He thought he would be happy to die in the little tent with its domestic smells, among the kindness of these strangers, although the peace of that place, the company of the children and the women, the smiles of the man in the four-pointed hat, made him want to live. He wanted this for himself, he thought. The words 'I am a wolf' came to him again, but what wolf ever thought that? He was separate from his forest brothers, for all that he had been raised to be like them. The man in the hat got up and left.

Outside, stew was brought to Vali. He ate a little and drank some of the fermented milk drink he was offered. He could hardly stomach it and accepted only out of politeness. He smiled at the woman who had brought him the stew but the gesture was for him, not her. These rituals of etiquette and manners seemed vitally important to him now. He needed a link to the everyday, the human, he thought, to keep him from – what? He didn't know, but he was afraid of the feeling within him, halfway between nausea and elation. It was something that seemed ready to evict him from his own head. The prince knew he was losing something valuable to him.

Everything felt different. He had thought before that the sensation was a bit like being drunk, and that impression was stronger now. There was a feeling of freedom, like when the wine first takes effect. There was the knowledge that he was entering a different sort of consciousness. There was even some fear, but this was accompanied by an odd delight, an inner snigger that said, 'Go on. Give in to it. Step away from yourself and change.' He did not know where he was going, nor what had happened to him, but instinctively he knew he had to fight it. Mad thoughts jostled in his head: I am becoming not myself, but how can that be? Myself is what I am, therefore I am leaving myself to become myself. Myself is more than one thing. I am uncontinuous and broken, I am ... He struggled to find a word to sum up how he felt. And then it came to him: hungry. Yes, he was hungry, but not for anything that the pot could provide.

He looked inside the tent and realised that Feileg would not be coming with him. He wanted to leave right now, to find Adisla. The love he bore her seemed to take on even more importance. It was like a light seen through rain by a lost traveller, something to guide him to safety. He saw her face as he'd seen it for the last time when she'd kissed him goodbye – fearful, anxious but full of love for him.

Vali waved to the man in the four-pointed hat. He willed his unwieldy brain to concentrate on what he needed to do, using Adisla as the focus for his thoughts.

The man came and stood next to him. Without a shared language, they struggled to communicate.

'Haarik's son?' said Vali. He scratched in the dirt a picture of a ship then mimed it being wrecked by smashing his fist into his hand. He drew a crown and mimed snatching it.

'Domen,' he said. 'Where is Domen?'

The man smiled at him and made a calming gesture with his hands. Then he turned, ruffled the hair of one of the children, kissed the woman who had brought the stew and set off across the plain towards the distant mountains. Vali felt helpless. He sat outside the tent with the reindeer family watching him, saying nothing.

He began to lose concentration, to just exist beneath the changing light, the moving clouds. Vali didn't know how long he had been sitting there when he felt a hand on his shoulder.

'No tribute.' The man spoke Norse, however badly.

The man was back, and with someone else just like himself in a dark wool tunic and four-pointed hat. Beside them was a roped reindeer. The nervousness of the beast seemed to flood over Vali; he could taste its fear.

Instead of a bow the newcomer had a broad shallow drum in his hands. Vali started. It was just like the one he'd seen in his dream on the boat, where he'd glimpsed Adisla surrounded by those odd masked figures. This one though wasn't decorated with that crooked little rune that had tumbled from the skins of the drums in the vision, but with scenes of hunting and fishing.

'No tribute.' The man said it again.

'No tribute,' said Vali. 'I'm looking for a person, not furs or gold.'

The man smiled, and Vali saw that he had two extra teeth in his upper jaw. He knew this was how the Whale People chose their holy men – by physical peculiarities like withered limbs or odd-coloured eyes. Veles Libor had told him as much. The thought of the merchant's name filled Vali with nausea.

'Domen?'

The holy man looked at him blankly.

'Domen. Drums.' Vali pointed at the drum. 'Domen.'

'Vagoy?' said the holy man.

'Domen.'

The holy man shook his head and gestured inside the tent, pointing at Feileg. He scratched a sort of rough circle and a wavy line in the dirt. Vali didn't understand. The man took up a rock. He scratched out a little hollow in the earth, put the rock in it and poured some water from a container around the rock.

'Vagoy,' he said, pointing at the rock. Then he howled, splashed at the water and mimed beating the drum.

Vali suddenly saw it – he was showing him an island, an island full of wolves where the drum was beaten.

'Domen?' said Vali, pointing at the rock.

'Ahhh! Dooerrrrrmaaan,' said the man, and Vali realised he had got the pronunciation wrong.

'Yes, Domen.'

The man nodded.

'Jabbmeaaakka,' he said. Then he pointed at the tent, shook the flap that covered its entrance, said slowly, 'Hel. Goddess. Fight,' and snarled with a grabbing gesture.

Vali pointed about him: which way?

The holy man gestured east, waving his arm several times to indicate that it was a long way.

Vali didn't wait. He got to his feet immediately and strode off in that direction but the man called after him in his incomprehensible language. The prince turned and the man pointed at him, then at himself, then east again.

'You will take me?' said Vali. He echoed the man's gestures.

The holy man gave a slow nod and disappeared inside the tent.

38   What Is Within

The sun set, which it had not since they had left the south. Autumn was coming and, soon behind it, winter. Feileg could almost taste the ice on the air.

He had a freezing fever and his body shook with cold. They brought him out under the deep stars and laid him next to a fire. He smelled the chill on the grass but the flames were fragrant and kept him warm. A little girl stroked his hair and her mother brought him blankets. A small platform made from the stump of an uprooted tree was set down at his side. A stone was placed on it, along with a stick carved into the likeness of a man. Cheese and meat were laid out. Spruce twigs were put there too. The reindeer was tethered close by. The reindeer man came to Feileg. He touched his wound. Pain shot through Feileg and there was blood on the man's hands. The man stood and walked to the reindeer, smeared the blood across its face and back.

Something was cooking on a pot, though Feileg knew it was not food. It had a bitter aroma to it that he didn't like at all.

Vali was there too, sitting looking out to the east, talking to nobody and with no one trying to talk to him.

One of the hunters took a cup from the pot and put it to Feileg's lips. He swallowed and, as he did, he recognised the taste – it was very similar to the brew that Kveld Ulf had fed him during their rituals, the drink that unlocked the doorway to his wolf nature.

The reindeer man drank himself and passed the cup around. He went to Vali and offered it to him but Vali was blank and distant. The reindeer man was insistent and pushed the cup to the prince's lips. Vali suddenly seemed to awake from his trance, took it and drained it.

Then the drumming began and the reindeer man intoned a harsh but beautiful chant. A hunter accompanied him on a small bone flute and Feileg lost himself in the music. The drumming went on and on, as the chanting rose and fell like the sea, or like the voices of his wolf brothers in the hills.

The skies were wide and beautiful and Feileg saw bright streaks flashing across them. He saw the people around him, caring for him, and he thought them very like his own family. He saw the face of his mother looking down at him, telling him she was sorry to have sent him away and he could come home now.

The reindeer man was there, but he wasn't the reindeer man; he was a reindeer and his antlers were made of stars. There was another presence too. The stars seemed to have taken shape and fallen to earth in the form of a man who rode a horse of stars and carried a bow of stars which held an arrow that was a comet.

'Ruohtta ... Ruohtta ... Ruohtta ...'

The other hunter had the reindeer to the ground, though it brayed in protest. Then it screamed. There was the sound of sawing. Something was put into Feileg's hands – a pair of antlers. He held the antlers out how the reindeer man showed him. The chanting went on and on. He saw the man of stars raise his bow but it was not pointing at him. He knew the figure for what it was – a god of death – and it had come for him, but the hunters had tricked it. The comet arrow flashed towards the reindeer. There was a final hideous bray from the animal and then it was quiet.

Feileg trembled. The women and children came to lie close to him, warming the chill of the fever away, but the chant went on. The man of stars had not gone; he was fitting another arrow to his bow, though none of the hunters seemed to notice.

Vali listened hard to the drumming. It was in him and around him and did not beat alone. From behind the mountains where the fat moon dipped another rhythm answered it. The taste of the holy man's brew filled him up and he thought he might vomit but then he felt the drums commanding his own heartbeat.

Someone was speaking to him from a long way away. The sound of the drums seemed to have a physical form, like a rope winding over the mountains to twine around him and pull him in, and he heard a voice from far away in that odd foreign language rasping out its chant.

'Jabbmeaaakka ... Jabbmeaaakka ... Jabbmeaaakka ...'

Vali knew that the name was chanted in hate, not invocation. Something wanted Jabbmeaaakka dead and he was caught up in that wish.

The brew was percolating through his mind, stripping away his reluctance to yield to the hunger that was calling to him. He looked at his hands. They were beautiful, and he spent a long time studying them. It had never occurred to him before just how long his fingers were, how pointed, more like talons than anything human. His teeth felt uncomfortable, too big for his mouth; he couldn't stop licking them. There was that taste. There it was, iron and salt and a depthless beauty that held all the pull of roasting meat to a hungry man. The blood, the deep and alluring scent of blood, was in him.

'I am strong.' He said it out loud. The drum was faster now, the voices harsher.

'Jabbmeaaakka ... Jabbmeaaakka ... Jabbmeaaakka ...'

And then the rhythm seemed to take a mad tumble, fast as a rock fall. She was there, he knew, the thing they had been calling to.

He saw a child with a woman's face, gaunt and lined. She was covered in gold, and precious gems stuck to her skin as if she were some shining snake. She was watching as the drumbeat curled around him to draw him on.

The beat was telling him something. He had to go on a long journey. She was there – Adisla, the one he had come to find.

His final thought, when it came, did not arrive from outside. It was not a stream of symbols seeping into his mind with the rhythm of the drums, though that is what the rhythm seemed to intend. Neither did it come from the grotesque girl-woman who looked on from the firelight. The magic around him was just a spark to a fire, igniting something far bigger than itself. The thought came from himself, from within. He spoke, to give it form.

'I must fortify myself,' said Vali.

He stood. He felt very long and sinuous, more like something made of shadow than flesh. Things were moving around him. Vali reached out to catch them, to break them, to feed on them. He felt a blow and brushed it away. He heard screams but was lost to the taste of the meat. He fed deeply, feeling the stress of his prey seep into him with a gorgeous tingle.

'I am fortified,' he said. There were some broken things on the ground, things that had been useful to him, things that had been going to help him, direct him and show him the way. He didn't need them any more; he knew where he was going. He was going towards the drumming.

39   The Nature of Magic

Adisla had now been on the island for months and to her surprise had been treated very well. It wouldn't have been her first choice of a home – a long flat rock rising out of a turbulent and cold sea – but her fear that she was to be some stinking Whale Man's bed slave had not been realised.

The people were kind: they brought her meat and bitter bread, berries and salted cheese, even gave her a rough beer to drink. She was also allowed to sleep alone – in a low conical tent which was open at the top to allow the smoke of a fire to escape. Although the tent was tiny, the little old woman detailed to care for her was skilled at building the fire and Adisla found it less smoky than a longhouse.

Her arrival had been terrifying. The whole rock had seemed to swarm with men – thirty or forty of them, all in animal masks, but not like the pelt that Feileg wore. These were skilfully constructed from supple twigs, shaped into the likeness of a bear or wolf, a bird, reindeer or seal, and covered in fur or feathers to terrible, frightening effect. The men drummed and sang and peered at her closely, but they didn't touch or harm her.

Haarik had been given instructions on where he might find his son and been told that a scout was watching from the mainland, ready to ride a reindeer hard to the young man's slaughter if he tried anything. The Whale Men had dealt with Norsemen before and were careful to extract oaths that they would not be harmed once Haarik's son was released. For all his talk of violence, the king looked pleased to leave. He had a warrior's distaste for magic and wanted to collect his son and then put as much distance between himself and the island as possible.

Most of the Whale Men soon left the rock — including the sorcerer who had travelled with her — but Adisla remained with the old woman to care for her and in the silent company of a man called Noaidi. He was small, even for a Whale Man, dark-haired with very blue eyes, and he habitually wore a wolf mask as he moved about the rock. At nights he usually went down towards the sea on the open ocean side and sat at the mouth of a huge cave, playing his drum and singing in a way that seemed to echo the sounds of the wind. Noaidi said nothing to her for days. And then, when she had been there about a week, she realised she had not actually tried to speak to him.

One night when he didn't go off to chant Adisla saw him remove his wolf mask and go to his tent. She went across and knelt at the entrance. He was lying on some furs and the little fire had been fed until the inside of the tent was as hot as a smithy. In the firelight, without his mask, he was a shocking sight. He must have been around twenty-five but was terribly drawn, his cheeks hollow and his eyes red. He hardly seemed to notice her at first and she saw he was trembling.

'Why am I here?'

Noaidi looked at her. 'I am sorry,' he said. He clearly had to think hard to remember the words and spoke Norse in a thick accent that reminded Adisla more of a cat than a man.

'You speak our language.'

'I know your people. Too well.' He smiled a brief smile and she could see that he was very ill indeed.

'Then why am I here?'

The man thought for a moment. He coughed and took a swallow of water from a cup. Then he gestured her into the tiny tent. She crawled in and sat down, very near to the blazing fire. It was uncomfortable but she wanted to question her captor. The sorcerer seemed if anything rather cold. He smiled again though, and seemed pleased to be able to talk to someone, although he was breathless and his words were halting and slow.

'I will not lie to you. In our visions we saw a spirit that we foresaw would do us great harm – Jabbmeaaakka, the death goddess, lady of dark places and the dark places of the mind. The prophecy was clear: she would destroy us. So we looked for magic to protect ourselves. First we struck at her. It did not work. A year ago the spirit met one of our men in the underworld. The underworld in here.' He tapped his head. 'She killed him. Like that.' He snatched with his hand at the air, as if crushing a fly. 'But we saw that the spirit was making powerful magic, magic that she began years ago, before she even knew she was beginning it. Now we seek to turn that magic against her. So we looked for you.'

'Why me?'

'We saw, in here –' again he tapped his head '– that the way to turn this magic was through you. Her weapon will be our weapon. We need powerful magic to do this. There is another spirit, a wolf god. We can set him against her if we can bring him here. He will come – looking for you.'

He was shaking quite badly now.

'And what happens when this spirit arrives?'

'Through you,' he said, 'he grows teeth.'

'Do spirits have teeth?'

The man swallowed some more water.

'Spirits and gods take many forms. They are here –' he tapped the ground '– and they are everywhere. You are just here.'

'And you?'

'Everywhere. Sometimes.'

'How?'

The man tapped the ground again.

'This is solid when this –' he tapped his head '– is solid. When this –' his head '– becomes as water then this –' the ground '– can flow away. When it does, I fight the goddess. Our minds tangle and we battle each other.'

'How?'

'Through resolve and persistence. I steal her magic. We are winning.'

'It doesn't seem to do you much good,' said Adisla. 'You look fit to die.'

'The things I win from her . . .' He seemed to be having more difficulty framing his words. 'I would not take them unless it was necessary.'

'Does she harm you in this struggle?'

'Not so very much. She seems weak or distracted. I cannot tell. To do what we need to do, to make the thing that will kill her, we have to steal her power from her. The damage is not in the taking of it but in the having. There are things of great power – runes, symbols older than the gods. I rip them up by their roots and take them from the death goddess and plant them in my mind. Sustaining them, it seems, is what costs.'

'And these runes will help you call your wolf?'

'I think so. I cannot tell. Sometimes I can sense him, sometimes not. Sometimes he is a man, sometimes a wolf. I see his face and I know he will come. I am sure of that.'

'How are you sure?'

'Many ways.'

'Be careful the wolf doesn't use his teeth on you,' said Adisla.

Noaidi nodded. 'I have gone to him in dreams and called him. When he arrives I will bind him. He will use his teeth where he is meant to – when he grows them.'

Adisla continued to question Noaidi. She discovered that Noaidi was not his name but rather a title given to sorcerers in that region. His real name was Lieaibolmmai, which Adisla found very difficult to say. He had become a magician because as a child he had shown the gift of prophecy.

'All my life,' he said, 'I have seen this day coming. All my life I knew that Jabbmeaaakka would strike at me.'

The fire in the tent burned on and the two of them fell into silence.

Adisla thought Lieaibolmmai seemed a gentle man and couldn't believe he was planning anything bad for her. After a long time she asked the question that was concerning her most. 'Am I a sacrifice?'

'I don't know.'

She looked into his eyes and saw nothing to reassure her.

'Am I to suffer?'

'No,' he said but looked down and would not meet her gaze. 'Magic is like speaking. You know what you want to say, but when you speak, not the exact words you are going to use. His mind, he who is coming, must open, it must be shocked into opening. Then the spirit will come to earth fully. Perhaps his mind can open without you, perhaps not.'

'Which spirit?'

'The wolf, the wolf who will protect us.'

Then he would say no more.

After a month, under a sky of slate, men came over from the mainland in boats. They took Adisla to Lieaibolmmai's cave in the hollow light of the late day. It was a huge wound in the side of the rock, three times as high as a man and more than three times as wide. It was strewn with rubble and dipped down into blackness. The sorcerers lined up at its mouth, peering into the dark through their animal masks.

'Down,' said Lieaibolmmai to Adisla. He was not friendly now but serious. He was wearing his wolf mask so his face was invisible, but she could see that under his red robes he had become terribly thin. His voice was quiet, like a fever sufferer's, and she saw sweat at his neck despite the cold of the day.

'For what?'

'This is where the spirits are,' he said. 'Here they can come through. Here the wolf comes to earth.'

'I will not go.'

Lieaibolmmai swayed slightly, as if her refusal was causing him pain.

'Until he comes you are safer here.'

'I will not go.'

He took off his mask and looked at her. 'Please,' he said

with gentle eyes. 'It is easier if you agree.' One of the other Noaidis came to his side and supported him. Lieaibolmmai was trembling, standing as stiff as a tree in his battle to stay on his feet. A man who was willing to put himself through such an ordeal was unlikely to tolerate much more resistance.

Adisla thought of what she had done to her mother, of the grief that had dogged her every day since the raid and her apparently remote chance of ever returning to a normal life. Then she went down with the Noaidis. Remarkably, Lieaibolmmai came with her.

At a point where the passage narrowed and dropped so much that she had to bend her head to continue, it fell away into a shaft. There was a flat boulder leaning against the wall, a great slab. Underneath it were some wooden wedges. Adisla looked at it and shivered. They were going to seal her in.

Lieaibolmmai caught her look. 'Only a precaution,' he said. 'If he is human, as we expect him to be, there will be no need for it.'

Adisla wondered what he meant but decided she would rather not know the answer and said nothing more.

A Noaidi showed her how to wrap a rope around herself in order to climb down. There was no light as she descended, just darkness and the smell of wet rocks. She went down about the height of five men and found herself on an uneven floor. Lieaibolmmai was lowered, limp as a hanged man. He untied himself and sat panting for a while. Then he gently pushed her forward through the dark.

She felt her way, a hand on the ceiling, another on the wall, her feet testing for further drops. It seemed that they went a long way forward. Then she felt the passage open out and Lieaibolmmai told her to stop. He struck a flint, set some tinder burning and lit a whale oil lamp. A wolf's head loomed at her from the dark, its teeth bared and its eyes angry. She screamed but quickly realised it was only a carving, though very disquieting. The sickly light showed the cave around her smeared with runes, a tiny stream of water filtering into a pool at the back. He pushed the flint and tinder into her hands, set down a pack beside her and took off his thick reindeer coat.

'For your comfort,' he said.

'What happens here?' said Adisla.

'Magic is like speaking,' said Lieaibolmmai. 'Let us see what we are required to say.'

'What am I waiting for?'

'You will see in good time.'

'How much time? How long must I spend in here?'

'Not long, I think. It is hard to tell. We are working the magic as best we can. He is not easy to find sometimes. Today. Many days. I don't know.'

Noises drifted down from above: drumming and chanting.

Lieaibolmmai gave Adisla a sad smile. Then he turned and was swallowed by the dark. Adisla heard the sound of the Noaidis heaving him up and then the slither of the other rope as it was pulled in. She was alone in the blackness and the damp.

40 Wolf Hunt

Feileg woke. Around him were the voices of ravens. His fever had gone and his wound was healing. He sat up and looked around. For a heartbeat he didn't understand what he was seeing. Where there had been a family, a fire and welcoming smiles, now there was only ruin.

Of course, he had been among corpses before, and corpses he had made too, but never anything like this blood swamp. The bodies had been devastated: men were unrecognisable from women, children from animals. How long had he lain there? He looked at the bodies. They were beginning to rot.

The scene did not repulse Feileg or make him retch as it might have someone who had not spent half his life as a wolf, but it did make him shake. Since he had been looking for the girl, humanity had come back to him; suffering had started to mean something. He felt the years that had been denied to these children, the tendernesses and the joys. He thought again of his own mother, the break from his family that had felt like an amputation.

Feileg pondered what to do. He had no idea what these people's customs were or how they preferred their dead to be treated. The birds were there and he knew that the wolves would come down when the darkness held for long enough to conceal them. It seemed a good way to him, so he just set their stone back on the stump that served for an altar, put the drum beside it and left.

It was not difficult to track Vali. The ground was wet, though not sodden, and the prince's footprints were clearly visible at points, blood on the grass at others.

Feileg thought of what he had seen on the boat, the tempest made flesh that the prince had become, thought of the sight of him among the dead bodies, feeding. The wolfman, for all the killing he had wrought with hands and teeth, had never eaten human flesh. He never had the need in the winter, when animals were weak and easy prey, nor the opportunity in the summer, when most travellers went by sea. And besides, Kveld Ulf had not taught him to eat men. The shape-shifter knew the diseases that could emerge from cannibalism and the madness that it brings.

Feileg was sure that Vali had attacked the reindeer hunters. Whatever enchantment the prince was under had consumed him. And yet Feileg felt he had no choice but to follow. Vali was looking for Adisla, which meant that Feileg was bound to him. When Feileg freed the girl and she married him, he would ask her to release him from his vow and he would kill Vali.

Feileg followed Vali's trail east for days, relying on scent, tracks and hunter's intuition. In a pass through some black mountains, he came across a cave. Vali had stayed there for days, he could tell. The prince had not been his normal fastidious self, and on the ground at the mouth of the cave was human shit. Feileg saw that it was sticky and cloying and it smelled of blood. It confirmed what he already feared.

He didn't want to sleep there, so he followed Vali's trail across the pass.

As he continued east, it became colder and the skies more grey than blue. The vegetation turned to scrub, a stunted tundra of dwarf trees and shrubs that seemed to cringe from the wind. Shelter became difficult to find. Feileg ate what he had taken from the ship – he hadn't been able to bring himself to take the family's food, even though he had known he would need it. He drank from streams and hid in caves and holes when it rained. Weeks passed and he began to find indications that Vali was not moving as quickly. He was stopping regularly, sometimes in caves, sometimes in the open, but there was a different smell to the mess he was leaving now.

Beneath the human scent was something else. Feileg knew it better than any smell in the world. It was wolf.

After days more travel the mountains ended and Feileg was at the edge of a broad plain going down to low hills by the sea. After some scouting, he found a place where the grass was flattened. He followed the trail and saw a mob of ravens ahead of him. They scattered to the sky as he approached, rising like the spirit of the corpse they had been eating. The dead man had been a hunter. His squat bow was nearby. Feileg took it along with the arrows. He hadn't shot a bow since he was a child, nor used any other weapon, but now he would accept any help he could get. The ravens were watching from a distance. 'You'll eat when I'm done here and not before,' Feileg said. He knelt to the corpse. The skull was sheared in two. No bird had done that.

Half a day's walk yielded another find. He could see something had rested beneath the lee of a rock and, from the flatness of the grass, that it had been there for some time. Leading away were prints but they were not Vali's. This was something bigger, still on two legs but with a huge stride. Feileg sniffed at the footprints and the same signature came back: wolf. As he went on, there were other tracks too – reindeer and broad sled marks on the wet grass obscuring all signs of the prince. The clouds hung black over the land. Great petals of snow began to fall, settling cold upon his skin.

With Vali's trail gone, Feileg simply followed what looked like a path towards the sea. How long had he been on the prince's trail? The moon had been full twice and when it could be seen was now a silver sliver in the night sky. But it wouldn't be visible that night. The weather was closing in but there was no prospect of shelter nearby. Over the two months his strength had returned and Feileg kept up a good pace. Then he spotted the island. It was a long flat loaf of rock, like a reflection of the clouds, a white tear into the dark fabric of the sea.

He had no coat, only the wolf pelt, a pair of ragged trousers the Danes at Hemming's court had given him out of pity, a shirt and a cloak he had taken from the ship. He had something else he could use to protect himself from the cold but hesitated to do so. He had kept them around his neck since he had taken them from a body on the Danish ship but hadn't yet had the courage to put them on. It felt like a betrayal of Kveld Ulf to even carry them. But he saw the sense now. Most of his life he had simply tied pieces of reindeer fur around his feet in the cold. Now he pulled on the pair of boots. They were a little too big but good enough. He wondered if he should stuff grass inside them to insulate them, as the farmers did.

In his mind he heard Bragi's voice: 'Are you going soft on me, son?' Feileg smiled to himself, the memory keeping him warmer than any of his clothes.

He could smell something on the breeze – reindeer. He stopped and listened. He heard the clicking of their hooves, that distinctive sound reindeer make even on soft grass, and he could tell they were standing. On again, on through the whitening world, running now to keep the cold at bay, hoping to kill a reindeer and crawl inside its carcass for the night for warmth. In the dying light he saw movement and realised that the reindeer were not alone. There were figures of men about them, and the beasts were tied to small flat wooden sleds.

Feileg slowed to a walk. Across on the island he could just about see figures making their way to the top. Some sort of assembly was taking place. He came to a small cliff over a short beach of silver shingle. The sea below him looked angry. From across the water howling and drumming filled his ears. He started to feel very odd, almost as though his limbs weren't his to command. He walked on to where the reindeer were and saw something like his own reflection. A man beside a sled was wearing a wolf pelt, almost like his own, but white. Another wore a coat of black feathers and had his hair shorn and spiked to resemble a bird. They ignored him, finished tying the legs of their animals and made their way down to

340

the beach. He followed them across to the sea, where they began to push a tiny boat out into the heaving water.

Feileg was acting on impulse now, the howling and the drumming filling his mind. He had to find shelter. The men could find him shelter. Throwing away the hunter's bow and arrows, he ran forward, helped push the boat out into the water and got in with the two men. They didn't say a word; just helped him aboard for the short but terrifying trip to the island.

The boat grounded on a tiny beach beneath a cliff and they all climbed. The jabber was intense now, and his companions pulled out their own drums to join in as they ascended. At the top Feileg found himself on a plateau. Fifty men in animal masks faced him, all drumming, shrieking, barking and roaring. The sight paralysed him.

Then, as if on a command, a sudden silence. The men parted and a small man in a wolf mask came forward. He was frail and clearly in pain. He approached Feileg, gazed into his face, then turned to his brothers and said something in a strange language.

The drumming took on renewed life and hands grasped Feileg. Charms and icons were shoved into his face, water thrown on him, and then he was being carried across the island. He fought and tore and knocked men to the ground, but the press of numbers was too great, and he was shoved and manhandled, kicked and clubbed across the island. Ropes were produced and thrown over him; when he shook them off others replaced them. The drumming seemed to be draining him of strength, and finally, inevitably, he was bound. By this time there was no need. The drums had entered his head, robbing his limbs of movement.

They dragged him to a cave, a gaping mouth that seemed to transform the hillside into the jaws of some ugly monster. He was mobbed into the hole by the dancing firelight of lamps and long shadows reached out like spider legs as if to inspect him as he descended the slope into darkness. Then, where the floor fell away, the man in the wolf mask came forward, holding a torch in one hand and a bright iron knife in the other.

'Lord,' he said in Norse. He bowed his head and turned Feileg to face the dark. In one movement, he slashed the bonds on his arms and pushed him hard in the back.

Feileg tried to turn to strike him but couldn't seem to make his body respond. He dropped into the dark. It was a heavy fall and he was stunned for a couple of breaths. When he recovered his senses, he could hear someone panting, trying to control themselves but taking in great gulps of air in panic.

'What are you?'

'Lady?' said Feileg.

There was another cry. He was sure it was Adisla. Even through her sobs he was certain it was her voice.

'Is it you? I swore to protect you, remember? Adisla, is it you?'

'It is me,' said the voice.

'Lady,' he said, and she came to him, hugging him and saying his name.

Above them the drumming stopped.

Lieaibolmmai turned to his brothers. His voice was weak but he was resolute. 'We have unbound him now and the spirit will find him. In hunger the wolf will out, and he will do what he needs to do to welcome the god. '

Now the animal cries and howling struck up again, but in a higher key.

Adisla held Feileg to her in the darkness. 'Are you going to kill me?'

'I am going to die for you,' said Feileg, unpicking the bonds around his ankles.

Above, Lieaibolmmai sat down and took out his drum. It was two months into the final stage of his wolf-summoning chant and the sorcerer was sweating heavily. His magic had been growing stronger by the day since he had battled Jabbmeaaakka, goddess of the underworld, but still he had not been sure the wolf would come. It had taken years to frame the magic correctly to call him, years of toil. Then he had torn something from the goddess, a bright gleaming rune that seemed supple and to grow like a tree. He had thought on the rune in his chanting and had felt the wolf move towards him. Then, just two weeks ago, something had changed, and he had lost the creature, or so he thought. But now he had arrived, and he was just as he had seen him that first day in the mire. His face was exactly as he had seen it in his vision. The sorcerer could begin the transformation now.

It would be the work of another month, maybe more, to get to where they needed to be, but Leiaibolmmai was willing to wait. He had sent instructions to his whole nation, called every man of knowledge from wherever he hunted whales or stalked the reindeer, and now he was to reap his reward. He knew that many of the Noaidis were weak and would not last the course of the magic, that some had untold miles to cross to be there, but he was content. Some would fall away but others would take their places. He and those who began would be able to rest and rejoin the ritual as they saw fit.

He felt physically drained but ready. The battle with the goddess had strengthened him magically. He had ripped her knowledge from her, seen her accomplices die and forced her to hand over their secrets, the screaming runes that he had torn from the grasp of the dead sisters. But the battle had unbalanced him too. The runes buzzed within him, denying him sleep, filling him with odd energies and unwelcome sensations. Lieaibolmmai was a gentle man but not strong enough for those terrible symbols. He felt constantly sick, unsettled and not a little mad.

He thought of a rune like a spear, long and pointed. He concentrated on that — it would give him purpose. It did, though an unaccustomed anger rose up in him too. The runes were unmanageable and vastly dangerous, some raging like torrents of images and sounds that threatened to sweep away his sanity, others with a calm presence disguising deep undertows into madness.

*

The chanting went on and the nights lengthened. Magnificent smears of colour appeared in the sky, the foxfire that meant the celestial fox spirit had been called to their gathering. Lieaibolmmai knew the omens could not have been better. The fox was the most magical of creatures and had blessed their ceremony by beating his tail until sparks flew across the heavens in shades of glowing green.

He concentrated on the image he had seen of the dark goddess's lair in his mind, that terrible cliff. He needed to implant that into the mind of the wolf, so that it knew where to go when it emerged transformed from the cave.

For two weeks the chanting never ceased. Feileg and Adisla lost all sense of time in the darkness. There was only the food in the pack and just the tiny stream of water to drink. Adisla, less used than Feileg to physical hardship, began to fade.

Feileg, though his body remained strong, was losing his grip on reality under the relentless chanting. He sweated and coughed as the image of the Troll Wall came into his mind. It was not strange to him as it was to the sorcerers. He had hunted in that area many times, walked the land at the foot of the mountain and looked up at it in awe.

'Act, and then you will leave this trap. Set out for your destiny,' he heard a voice say in his head. 'Kill and be free.'

He felt compelled to do something, to step closer to something, but he couldn't see what it was, and the feeling made him miserable and uncomfortable. He was like a slave who finds his master screaming instructions at him in an incomprehensible language, wanting to act but not knowing what to do. Adisla felt him trembling. She was weak and terribly hungry.

Outside, up on the surface, in the hollow light of an Arctic dawn, Lieaibolmmai felt beyond tiredness, unnaturally awake. He had broken from the ritual to eat a little, to rest his voice and to try to sleep for the first time in days. He almost didn't hear the chanting now. The runes were all around him, as if they had lives of their own – hanging in space, fizzing, snapping, hissing, sometimes even sounding with rich musical notes. They had helped him though. He had achieved that higher level where he could feel the animal heart of the wolf in the pit and talk to him, direct him, show him where to go. He had contacted the wolf many times in long and difficult rituals, spoken to him over vast distances and heard him answer as a beast. The man in the pit seemed just a man. And yet it was him, he knew: the runes had shown him his face. He took it for another confusion of the magic, another product of his self-induced insanity.

A howl split the grey air. Lieaibolmmai shivered, not recognising what was strange about it but feeling disquiet anyway. The other Noaidis on the rock glanced at each other. They too thought it had sounded odd. The perspective was wrong, if sound can have a perspective. It sounded far away, hollow, but it was loud too, as if near. No one thought of the simplest explanation: the creature was much bigger than any wolf they had ever heard before.

In the cave Feileg sat up, feeling a cold dread. He knew better than anyone that the cry of the wolf was unnatural.

Lieaibolmmai had a terrible ache in his head but still he smiled. The wolves of the plain were greeting the wolf god's arrival, he was sure. The howl from the mainland was repeated. It was very loud, thought the sorcerer, very loud indeed. Unease rippled through the Noaidis but excitement too. The howling was just a side effect of the magic. Their defender was coming, they were sure.

Down on the beach a youth was getting out of a boat, calling to them. From his accent Lieaibolmmai recognised him as an eastern Noaidi, typically late for the ceremony. He was glad to have that thought, pleased to be linked to a world of mundanity away from the dreadful presence of those runes.

'The wolf! The wolf is coming! The wolf is here!' the young man was shouting.

Lieaibolmmai huddled into the fire. Did the boy really sense the wolf, or was he just trying to make up for in enthusiasm what he lacked in timeliness?

'Pick up your drum and join in, brother,' a man next to Lieaibolmmai called down, his voice hoarse from chanting.

'A black wolf with eyes of foxfire! He is there, out on the plain! He is there!'

'He is within,' said Lieaibolmmai.

A gust of air chilled his shoulder. He turned to look at the Noaidi next to him, surprised to see that, though momentarily the man was still standing, he didn't have a head.

41 Werewolf

Vali was lost, really lost. The drums no longer called to him.
He could still hear them in his mind but he felt no desire to follow them any more. The beat was more urgent. He understood
its demands. It wanted him to step forward inside himself, to
become what he could. He found it easy to ignore. He had
killed some things and that had helped him grow, he recalled.
And when he had grown, the drums had lost their power. He
was stepping forward all right, but under the impulse of his
own magic, urgent and compelling as a tidal surge.

As his body rippled with vigour, his mind contracted. He
had difficulty following any chain of reasoning. Images of his
life were there and gone again like mountains under fleeting
cloud. A yearning, an adolescent itch for action, was upon
him, though he couldn't think what he wanted to do. He
didn't sleep for days, and it seemed to him that he didn't quite
fit in his skin. His heart would beat fast for no reason and he
feared he would die, then a smirking calm would descend and
he would start to feel unaccountably pleased with himself.

He looked at his body and it seemed to him a very fine
thing. His hands were strong and large, his muscles huge
and pronounced, and his teeth felt like shining knives in his
head.

He was aware that he had forgotten a great deal. He couldn't
remember how he had come to the cave. For a moment or
two he would recall why it was important that he found out
how he had come to lie naked underground far away from
anything he recognised, but then it would slip from his mind
and all curiosity about his condition would disappear. He had
no difficulty, though, recalling the deep savour of the meat
that moves and then is still, the prey that had surrendered

its power to him, and it seemed that, as he digested the flesh of his victims, the memories, or rather the sentiments and attitudes of those he had consumed, were digested too.

Vali spent a while playing with rocks on the floor of the cave, knocking one into another as if he was a child; he sat with endless patience, watching the snow fall as a woman waiting for a hunter to return might; he pictured the man he had surprised in the valley, saw the shaking hands trying to nock an arrow to the bowstring. The memory of the archer's fear was delicious, recalled like the scent of baking bread.

When Vali slept his dreams were full of Adisla but they were full of the wolf too. It was bound, agonisingly bound, the fetters digging into its flesh and that awful sword holding open its mouth. Vali had one of those strange feelings that only make sense in dreams and blink away with the morning light. He was dreaming about the wolf, he knew, but it seemed to him that the wolf was dreaming about him too, or rather was simply dreaming him. He felt he didn't exist outside of the god's mind and the boundaries between himself and the wolf were insubstantial things, as nothing to their shared communion of pain. He felt its constriction as his own, a crushed, tied, pinioned sensation that would suddenly relent and snap into release and contentment. When he awoke, his limbs were longer and his teeth bigger.

He didn't know how long he lay in that cave – weeks or months – but it was cold when clarity finally came to him, in that moment between hunger and satiety. It was as if, his appetites in balance, his mind was free to think.

He went outside and looked around. Snow was falling, the sky was heavy and the light was flat. It was dusk. The air was full of scents. Over the hills behind him a bear was moving – late to its hibernation, he could tell – and down on the plain people were gathering. In the far distance was the sea, purple and blue, and in the sea an island. Men were going to it, he could smell them moving across the plain. Their odours of sweat and grime were powerful and alluring. Reindeer were with them, one or more geldings, their piss and shit unpungent.

Voices came through the still air. He listened. There were three distant heartbeats, one animal, two human. Now he could see them: a man and a youth driving a reindeer pulling a sled, to which was attached a pack of provisions and a shallow drum.

He saw them look up at the cave, but they didn't spot him. They were clearly thinking of resting there for the night as the snow became heavier. They were debating something, one pointing on down the trail, the other up into the cave. Vali could see that the two were hurrying to something and wondering if they could make it by nightfall in the worsening weather. The man held out his hand and let the snow fall on it. Then he shook his head and the travellers began to make their way up the slope.

Vali shrank away inside the cave, right to the back. Saliva rose to his mouth and his limbs felt looser. The men were at the mouth of the cave now. A stone came whistling in, then another. They were checking for wild animals. He heard them speak to each other. When he peered out from his hiding place in the shadows, he saw them examining something on the floor. The man rubbed it in his fingers and looked at the youth. Then he shrugged and stood. Vali saw he had a spear. The man stared hard into the cave, picked up another stone and threw it past Vali.

There was a roar. Vali felt his heart racing, his muscles clenching, his head dizzy. The youth leaped back with a shout but the man was laughing. He had pretended to be a bear. The joke seemed to calm them both and they set about building a fire and bringing the reindeer up. The creature wouldn't come inside, and eventually the youth gave up and left it tied at the cave mouth.

The smell of the fire comforted Vali and penetrated into his mind far more deeply than any aroma he had ever known. The smoke seemed unlike any other smoke he had ever smelled, and he could tell the tree that had been used for the fire had been a strong one, fed from an underground stream, not felled for its wood, just a few branches taken.

Vali thought of Adisla. Her presence in his mind was now all that kept him from giving in to the beast inside him. If he could find her, he might feel better. Something had happened to him, he could tell, a sort of illness. Vali did not want a cure, though, didn't want to go back to what he had been; he just wanted to feel right, not to have this terrible sensation of dislocation and restraint bearing down on him. It was love like a hunger, sharp and selfish.

The men cooked, but their own odours were far more appealing to Vali. The sweat, the saliva, the secretions of the glands of their hair and skin, all seemed sizzling little calls to murder. Then a sudden wave of repugnance took him and his thoughts nauseated him.

The travellers were tired and the fire was warm. They both fell asleep where they sat, still in their furs. Silently Vali came forward. He was surprised to see how small they were. Light on snow removes all perspective and it had been impossible to tell their size from a distance. These men were dwarfs, people who had seemingly walked out of a story. The man, standing up, would hardly have come up to Vali's waist; the boy was even smaller. The reindeer began to fret. It was tiny too, full grown with wide antlers – and old – but much smaller than he had ever seen a mature stag before. And the cave mouth had shrunk. When Vali had come in, it was too high to touch. Now he almost had to stoop to stand up in it. Some strange shrinking magic was happening, he was sure.

Vali sat down by their fire and warmed himself. Thoughts brawled in his mind. He thought of Disa, of the fire at her home, of winter evenings with Adisla by his side; he thought of blood, the smack and savour of the kill, he thought of Bragi taking his arm on the longship, telling him everything was going to be all right; he thought of the ruin of his rage, the bloody dead.

He watched the sleeping men and had the urge to kill them. Something was stopping him though: it was as if the ghost of himself was haunting what he had become, drawing him back from the inevitable. The fire was warm and fragrant, and he lay down. He slept and dreamed he was himself, a man who loved a woman and thought that was enough.

There was a shout. It was light. One of the tiny men was yelling and the other had a spear. Their movements seemed very slow and cumbersome to Vali. The man threw the spear. Vali just stepped around it.

The smell of their dread swept over him, urging him on to attack, but he fought the impulse. The dream of the person he had been was in his mind – he could still be that man. He tried to speak, to tell them they had no need to be afraid, but when he did he was shocked. A low rumble filled the cave, like thunder in the hills. He was growling, he realised.

The youth was on his hands and knees, trying to scramble past Vali. The man had picked up a stone and was hurling it at him.

'Kill a hundred of them for me.' The words were harsh but an echo of what Adisla had meant came back to him: 'Return. Be with me again.' The memory suffocated his anger and he was paralysed. The boy had got past him and was screaming to the man to do the same. He did, diving under Vali to where the reindeer was going wild.

The men released the panicking animal and just ran for it, almost falling down the slope in their haste. Vali went to the cave mouth, sat breathing heavily and watched them flapping over the plain towards the shore. The snow had stopped but it was still difficult to see any distance.

Vali felt shaken. He had had the overwhelming urge to kill them, but he had fought it – fought whatever disease or enchantment was on his mind – and he had won. There was a way back to Adisla.

The men ran for a while and then stopped. They looked

back at him and saw that he hadn't pursued them. They stood talking and, presently, Vali could see they were having an argument, sense their stress on the breeze. Then one walked off towards the sea and that distant island while the other called and caught the reindeer. He took something like a broad dish from a pack on its back, let the animal go and began to walk back towards Vali.

Vali felt nothing as he watched him come, no more than he did when he looked at the sky or the sea. The man approached slowly. He was beating a drum. The rhythm was different to the one Vali had heard that had led him to this place, the one that had vanished as he came to the cave. It was slower and more deliberate, and backed with a forceful chant. Vali smelled fear but also excitement. The man came closer, stopping eventually at the foot of the scree slope that led up to the cave mouth. Here he stood fixing Vali with a stare, banging the drum and making gestures towards him.

It all meant nothing to Vali, who was lost in himself, holding the door to the slaughterhouse of his thoughts hard shut. He knew what he wanted to do – eat this fool in front of him and then chase down his companion and do the same to him. But he wouldn't. Why not? He had forgotten the reason; he just knew it was important to restrain himself. Vali could hear the drummer's heartbeat, sense the blood flowing through the cavities of his body, almost taste his presence on the air.

The man's breath was hot with excitement, his skin basted with fear. He brought the drumming to a climax, hammering out a frenzy of blows on the skin, gave a heavy last strike and threw his drumstick onto the ground in front of Vali, his eyes wide with challenge and expectation. Then his expression changed. His spell had not worked. Vali, now more wolf than wolfman, tore out his heart.

42 Success for the Sorcerer

Panic swept the rock. The resting Noaidis tried to help those still lost to the power of the drums and chanting. Some woke easily, others not at all and had to be left to death as their brothers sought what little protection the bare island provided.

Lieaibolmmai found himself flat on his face concealed in the dark of the cave entrance, digging in his furs for his little knife. There was a squelching noise like a man walking through a swamp, and he saw the monster put its back paws through the chest of the Noaidi in the bird mask.

The gigantic creature was hideous. Its black wolf's head with eyes of shining emerald sat on a body that was a twisted stand-off between man and wolf, though three times the size of the biggest man Lieaibolmmai had ever seen. The creature loped on all fours, its back limbs and front left those of a wolf, while its front right, which it used to tear and smash the Noaidis, to pull them into its crushing jaws, was the arm of a freakishly big human.

The sorcerers had been taken completely by surprise. Some were slashing at the creature with their knives, some were throwing rocks, a few were shooting arrows from squat bows, but most were scrambling for the boats that would take them off the island.

Lieaibolmmai cleared his mind. Hadn't he bound the wolf? He had gone to it in its dreams, called it with his drums, commanded it into the cave and done all the magic as the runes had revealed. He had also heard the girl with the wolf and it was certain they were known and important to each other. And hadn't the wolf appeared in exactly the form he had seen in his visions? So what was this thing?

He felt himself pissing where he lay. He had to control himself, to think clearly.

Then he understood that he had been deceived. Somehow the goddess had tricked him. He had snared a wolf but not the one he was looking for. And yet he had touched its mind, run with it in the wide dark of the mountains, breathed its joy in the kill. He could not understand it.

Lieaibolmmai was an honest man. He had no delight in the dark magics he had been shown and looked for power only to defend himself rather than for its own sake. He knew what he had to do – to give the girl he had uprooted and the wolfman he had enchanted and damned a chance. He went further into the cave and threw down the ropes.

'The wolf is here,' he said into the darkness. 'Stay until it has finished killing. I will do my best to control it. I will—'

He never finished his sentence. A primordial sense told him that something was behind him, something worse than a neck-break fall. He stepped forward into the darkness.

At the bottom of the shaft Feileg and Adisla heard Lieaibolmmai crash to the ground beside them and then his scream. He had torn his arm from its socket and couldn't stifle his agony.

Then something else dropped softly down the shaft, some sort of creature.

In the blackness there were retching and coughing noises. The creature hacked, growled and snapped again and again. She heard it snuffle forward, its snout testing the darkness. Adisla was close to collapse. She could concentrate on nothing, think of nothing but the awful scraping sounds coming from the creature's throat, within which she seemed to hear some words.

'My love,' it said. 'I have found you.'

43 A Sacrifice

Vali. That name still described what faced Adisla in the black of the pit.

How much change must you go through before you are no longer you? How many planks can you replace on a ship before you have to say that you have a new boat?

Vali's jaws dripped with the blood of the sorcerers, his mind was full of the scent of their panic, and yet, now that he had found Adisla, a glimpse of who he was came to him, indistinctly, hardly discernible, as a distant shore might appear through haze. This was the girl he had loved since the instant he met her. He fought down his other perceptions – the delicious aroma of anxiety that clung to her, the succulence of her flesh, even her threat. She was not him, and every living thing that was not him now seemed hostile and dangerous.

'No,' said Adisla. 'No.' She could see nothing in the darkness, nothing at all, but that made the creature more terrible – its rasping voice, the heat of its breath.

'I have found you, as I vowed,' said Vali. 'Come from this place.'

Adisla shied back, reaching for Feileg's hand.

'What are you?' she said.

'Your love. Vali.'

The Noaidi was trying to bite back his pain but his suffering escaped him in suppressed groans. Vali felt the attraction of the holy man's agony, calling him to feed. His skin felt alive, his muscles drawing power from his questing hunger.

'Keep away from me,' said Adisla. Her body convulsed as she clung to Feileg in the dark. Vali could see them clearly and felt his lips draw back from his teeth, his legs prepare to spring. He willed himself to be still.

Feileg spoke. 'It is him. I saw the beginning of this change. It is the prince.'

Adisla was shaking her head.

'Let me take you from here,' said the wolf.

Adisla drew in her breath and backed further away. 'I will not go.'

'Better that than the damp and dark,' said Feileg. 'Go. If it is your turn to die then you will die.'

'I do not fear death, only him.'

'He is as the Norns wish him to be. Now go.'

Still she did not go. Feileg pushed her forward. Then fear killed all her thoughts, and she did not resist as Vali gathered her up. Her weight was nothing to him and he lifted her to the top of the shaft and then pulled himself up using his human arm. Three Noaidis stood at the mouth of the cave. The sun had risen behind them, turning the rocks inside to burning gold and revealing Vali and his burden to the sorcerers. They let fly with their bows. Vali turned his back to them to shield Adisla. The arrows hit him hard but didn't even break his skin. Vali put the girl down, turned again and made a stuttering, snarling run towards them. They fell back and scattered. Vali returned to Adisla.

She tried to summon her strength, not for herself but for him.

'Do you remember what you were?'

'I remember the betony you gave me when I first went out to fight. I remember you at the river, the sun on the water and you racing your brothers from bank to bank. I remember how you kissed me when we last saw each other. I remember you, Adisla, so I remember me.'

Adisla looked at him. Somewhere in his expression, in the inclination of his head, she could see her Vali. It *was* him, so how could she be afraid?

'Do you know what you have become?' said Adisla.

The creature bowed its head. It stammered, 'I am a b-better thing.'

'No, Vali, you are not. You must come back to me,' said Adisla. 'We must break this curse.' Feileg was beside her. He had climbed one of the ropes Lieaibolmmai had thrown down the shaft.

The wolf spoke: 'It feels like a blessing. I am so strong and the world is so beautiful.'

'We have had only one blessing in life, and one curse,' said Adisla. 'Each other. You have found me and I will find you. There are sorcerers who will help you, and we will take them the gifts they ask to save you.'

To Vali, Adisla's body sparkled with scents, sang with her fear. And there was another sensation too, something even more persuasive. They would be together for ever if he ate her. They would be the same person. What closer love than that is possible? *No!* Her connection to him was stronger than hunger. Her love burst over him like cool water on hot iron and made a blade of his will.

'What would you have me do, Adisla?'

'Wait here, on this island.'

'I cannot command myself.'

'Then let us command you. Vali, this is a trap and a refuge. Go within and let us keep you here. We will bring your salvation, I promise.'

'I will starve.'

'Your hunger is worse fulfilled. It will be a noble agony and, I promise, my love, it will end.'

The great beast craned its head in something like thought.

Vali saw the flight of the arrow and knew it was going to miss him, so he ignored it. He hadn't thought where else it might go. It struck Adisla in the leg, spinning her to the ground in a hard fall.

The bowman died for her, killed not for his arrow but so that Vali's hunger could feast on flesh that was not Adisla's. She was trying to stand, her stricken movements firing all his wolf senses, impelling him to take her.

He leaped towards her and stood above her, the man he had

been struggling to spare her, the wolf he had almost become simmering in resentment at that restraint. No. Yes. No. Yes. Yes.

The wolfman shoved at Vali's side, punching and slapping at him, trying to shake his attention from the stricken girl. Slowly the wolf turned its head to him, the black bulk of its body almost featureless against the light of the cave mouth.

Feileg was shouting at Vali, trying to get through to him. 'After her there is no way back! After her this, always.' Blood filled up Vali's senses. He seemed almost to teeter above Adisla, rocking and keening as he struggled to fight the pull of her distress.

There was a scream from below. Lieaibolmmai had tried to climb from the shaft but the ruin of his arm made it impossible and he had fallen. The wolf lunged at Adisla. She felt his breath on her face, his teeth brush her neck. But Vali, still there inside the wolf, pulled his animal body back, slammed Feileg to one side and threw himself into the shaft after the sorcerer. He tumbled down, crashing to the floor.

'I am lost,' said Vali, not in the wolf's growl but in the voice of his mind, 'and I will never be found again.'

Lieaibolmmai scrambled back through the darkness, back away from the thing he had summoned. He knew he had lost to the goddess and his duty was clear. 'Seal us in!' he shouted. 'Seal us in!'

At the top of the shaft Feileg was heaving at the flat boulder. He couldn't budge it. Adisla stood, stumbled, stood again and added her weight. A Noaidi ran in to join them. They rolled the stone down the wall until it was level with the shaft.

Adisla fell to her hands and knees at the edge of the pit. She looked down to see a pair of green eyes reflecting the light of the rising sun. The rumbling voice echoed up the shaft.

'Forget me,' it said, and Feileg dropped the boulder over the hole.

44 For Love

No drumming, no chanting. The remaining Noaidis were numb, slumped on the bare rock as if still entranced. Already the birds were descending, ravens and crows dropping from the sky, their cracked cries sounding something like delight.

Noaidis helped Feileg pile more stones over the boulder to ensure that the beast could not escape. Adisla watched helpless, her leg now agony after the initial shock had subsided. When a Noaidi approached her, Feileg snarled at the man, but he had a small bag and made a sign for the wolfman to be calm. Feileg allowed him to draw the arrow and dress the wound. Adisla was beyond screaming as the arrow was withdrawn and sat vacantly on the rock. The Noaidi pushed water to her lips, gave her reindeer meat and flatbread while Feileg returned to pile on more stones.

Feileg could hear the screams from the shaft. He wondered how long the creature's resolve to stay in the pit would last. It had food in the shape of the sorcerer. Would that feed its growth? Would it become strong enough to get out? Never mind. They would be long gone by then.

When they could get no more stones on the pile, Feileg rejoined Adisla and put his arms around her. She returned his embrace but not as warmly as he wanted. She was grateful to him and pleased they were both alive, but she did not love him. He had heard what she had said to Vali and knew she was prepared to die for her prince. Despite herself, tears came into Adisla's eyes. Feileg stroked her hair. He had vowed to kill Vali because the prince had captured him and taken him from a wolf's life. But for that moment in the cave, knowing what it was to love someone and to feel that love in his arms, Feileg should have regarded him as his saviour.

'We will free him.'

'How?'

'I told you I have many treasures in the hills, and I spoke the truth. I will present them to the witches, put myself at their mercy and ask them to save your prince.'

'And then?'

'I am a wolf,' he said, 'and have had enough of tomorrow and yesterday. I will die or I will not. I will go to the hills or I will not. I will exist or I will not.'

She thought of Vali looking up at her from the pit. She had seen something of the man in those strange green eyes. She loved and admired him more than ever when she thought of his courage. He had allowed them to seal him in. He, unlike her, had the bravery to die. But then she looked at Feileg, so like him in appearance, so different in personality. In some ways it was as if the gods had answered her prayers, given her a low-born man in Vali's image – someone she could marry, perhaps could love.

'I will follow you,' said Adisla.

'There is no need. The witches are not always merciful.'

'More merciful than the fates?' said Adisla. She looked at him and squeezed his hand.

'There will be great danger,' he said.

'Feileg, I'll follow you because you came here for me and you saved me. I see that you are the first among men. I'll follow you because I want my Vali back, but I'll follow you for baser reasons too. I have no home to go to. My mother is dead in the most awful way and I can never look on that place again without that memory. If I cannot be with him, I'll be with you. And if I cannot be with you then my life is over.'

Feileg now knew that he would have what he so desperately wanted if only the prince died in that hole. All he had to do was fetch bigger and bigger rocks, perhaps even persuade the Noaidis to bring some over by boat, and make sure that thing was sealed in until it starved.

Adisla had tears on her face as her eyes turned to the great heap of stones over the shaft.

'Come on,' said Feileg. 'We will go to the witches.'

45 Buried Treasure

Veles Libor was not in a good mood. His promise to King Hemming that he would find a way to rid him of the prince and make him a little money at the same time had come to nothing. The deception of the escape – played for the benefit of the mob – had been a good one but he hadn't foreseen the pirate attack. Hemming would fall into a fury if Veles returned without Forkbeard's gold and would assume he had pocketed it himself. That, thought Veles, would be a problem to dwarf the unenviable difficulties he was already facing.

He couldn't believe how quickly they had lost Vali in the fog. They'd scarcely cut him adrift when he disappeared and there had been no sign at all of him since.

'I'd just cut loose from this king if I were you,' said Bodvar Bjarki. 'You could disappear east and he'd never hear of you again.'

'Neither would anyone else. A merchant without a prince to protect him is nothing,' said Veles, 'and besides, his name is worth ten on every hundred to me.'

The berserk was ungovernable, he thought. The crew would have been mutinous if they had not been so depleted and weakened by the attack, and the ship was low on provisions. His actions during the battle had made him an object of contempt to the men and he had to endure being called 'barrel man', 'keg creeper', 'tun tickler' and whatever other less than inventive nicknames they could come up with.

Despite this, Veles now assumed informal command of the vessel, in that he determined its next move. This was not because he had any authority with Bjarki or the hired crew but because he was the only one who seemed to have any idea what they might do.

They stopped at the little market at Kaupangen, where he managed to sell some of the taken battle gear for a reasonable price and to hire five passably hardy-looking Danes to replace some of the men lost in the battle. He made sure the Danes knew who paid their wages and picked them for their brawn and stupidity. He wanted stupid – it was an essential requirement for the expedition he had in mind. He had lies to tell and didn't want clever men finding them out. The crew was down to twenty-six – five for him, at least in theory, and nineteen for the berserk. The odds were very far from ideal but they were better than they had been.

Luckily for Veles, the berserk wanted Vali as much as he did. Bjarki had vowed to take the prince to Forkbeard and that was an un-negotiable promise, so for the moment he found Veles useful. Bjarki was a brute but not a fool, and he knew the merchant's brains would be useful in the hunt. After that, well, who knew who had been killed in the pirate attack?

Veles looked at the berserk. He was no mind reader but could guess what Bjarki was thinking. The merchant needed to make himself indispensable to him.

When Veles settled to thinking about a problem then, if there was an answer, he usually found it. At Haithabyr he had heard whispers that Haarik was using Vali's farm girl to ransom his son. He had not told Vali this because he had very quickly seen that the prince wasn't in a position to pay for the information, nor to offer any other sort of benefit. However, now he saw a happy meeting of needs between himself and Bodvar Bjarki. The girl had gone north. Haarik had gone north. The prevailing current would take Vali north if he wasn't shipwrecked on the way. Veles would take his ship up the North Land coast, find Whale People and ask for information about the girl, Haarik and the prince. Find either of the first two and he would find the third, he thought.

There was another reason to go north. He had heard of an island where the Whale People made sacrifices to their stupid gods. There was a rumour of gold there. Bjarki was convinced it was defended by sorcery but Veles thought otherwise.

In truth, Veles had very little respect for magic or for any god. He had seen his children playing by the fire with the Whale People's holy objects, hung embroideries of the Christ god on his walls for decoration, heard people all over the world singing the praises of Wuoton, Odin, Raedie, Svarog, Spenta Mainyu, Jesus and other gods. All seemed the same to him – pictures and carvings beautiful but empty.

He put more faith in himself, the swords of Hemming and the power of coin than he did in the supernatural. The sorcerer who had made his child's mask hadn't been protected by his magic from whoever took it from him; Jesus had been taken to the cross with no angelic defenders, no bolts of fire from the sky smiting his enemies. Veles had actually laughed when the missionary told him the story of the crucifixion. What had the mighty god done to avenge his son? Torn the curtain on the temple. Cross Hemming and you'd suffer more than a ripped wall hanging for your pains.

So, the prince was in the north and Haarik was in the north and even this girl who seemed so important was there. He suspected magical beliefs figured in her disappearance and a look around the Whale People's holy sites might uncover her. The prince wouldn't be far behind. Veles thought he'd give it a go. It was better than returning empty-handed to Hemming, and maybe there really was gold up there, though he doubted it.

The journey was excruciatingly slow, hampered by argument and indecision. The whole trip should have taken them a couple of weeks, even against the current. Instead it consumed months. The berserk wanted to go after Vali but didn't seem to realise that they first had to find out where he had been. There was no point randomly hurtling around the coast, as Bjarki seemed to want to do. They needed to ask if there had been a shipwreck, if strangers had passed by, if anyone had taken captives.

The Whale People were simple and friendly folk. They started out hostile and threatening, waving spears and screaming but if you gave them a coin or two they thought you a very fine fellow indeed and no threat – otherwise, why would you have given them the coins? So they wanted to please. Yes, there had been a shipwreck. Yes, strangers had gone past. Yes, there were captives. In their little dwellings on the headlands behind beaches, in their tents and by their fires Veles listened to them tell their stories of great storms, men with burning eyes and princesses of southern kingdoms tied to reindeer sleds and taken north to marry water spirits. The most recent of the stories, he guessed, was around fifty years old.

He had been freezing on and off the boat for two months when they came to where there was no further land to the north and the coast turned east.

'What now?' said the berserk. It was cold, very cold.

'We go on,' said Veles.

'To what end?' said the berserk. 'The prince is wrecked on the coast. We should turn round and look for him.'

'Tell me, Bjarki,' said Veles. 'Is this near where you were wrecked with Haarik's son?'

'Half a day's sail south,' he said. 'We never did get to the sorcerer's gold.'

'No. Perhaps we should just take a peek down the coast and see what we can see.'

Bjarki shook his head. 'They enchanted me. I became weak.'

'You'll suffer fewer enchantments if you don't drink their wine.'

'It wasn't wine.'

'I dread to think what it was,' said Veles. He knew very well – fermented milk, a drink he always found deeply unpleasant and one he'd had enough of in his travels.

'It was enchantment,' said Bodvar, 'not the wine. Drums. They made me weak.'

Veles raised his eyebrows.

'Well, I've been weak all my life, so I have no strength for these sorcerers to rob. Come on, just a peek. I think I can only guarantee a rock in the sea, but who knows? You might get enough to pay Forkbeard his compensation. You did vow to pay him, didn't you? You should do something to show your mettle. You do have something of a history of failure.'

Veles was treading a fine line between goading the berserk to action and enraging him.

The berserk looked at him. 'I saved you,' he said.

'And now I will save you. The prince, if he is alive, will be on the holy island. If not, then their holy men will have heard of him. And these are peaceful people – they lie down at the first threat. If there is no treasure then there will at least be fine furs to be taken.'

'They are sorcerers.'

There was no point in appealing to reason any more. The best way was to agree that the Whale People were powerful sorcerers – in which case they were doing rather badly – and that their spells needed to be taken seriously.

'I have thought of that,' said Veles. 'I have brought this mask with me. They use it in their ceremonies and it deflects their power away from you.'

'Then the mask is mine,' said Bodvar Bjarki.

'As you wish,' said Veles. 'But if we are enchanted, I shall rely on you to come to my rescue.'

Bjarki nodded and took the wolf mask from Veles. He put it to his face. It was tiny against his massive skull and the ties at its back hardly reached around his head.

'This will protect me?'

'All of you, the crew included.'

'Good. If you are lying, Libor, then I'll cut off your head.'

Veles thought that if he was lying and the sorcery was real Bjarki might not be in a position to cut off anyone's head. If the sorcery wasn't real, well, he was sure the mask offered good protection against people clicking their fingers and banging their drums at you. The berserk didn't really think things through, thought the merchant.

The boat travelled east down the north coast into the falling cold. The sea didn't freeze but they began to see smears of white on the landscape. The little ballast fire did something to keep him warm but Veles couldn't quite stop shivering. It was a sort of crafty chill that you could banish momentarily by the fire or by adding another fur but that always seemed to work a freezing finger in – a cold of the bones, dropping from iron skies.

Two weeks past the turn east they came to what he thought he was looking for, but when they stopped, the local Whale People told him that the island he was seeking – Domen, also known as Vagoy, the wolf island, the blood-red rock – was further east still. He gave them a little money and said he would prefer that island to be beneath his feet as he spoke but only a couple then said that it was. The Whale People weren't liars, he knew, just very eager to please.

'Is there treasure there?' asked Bjarki, but Veles did not translate this. Instead, he said, 'Do your people hold it very holy?'

'It is the place where our ancestors are. It is the mouth of the other worlds.'

'And offerings are left there?'

'More riches than you can imagine.'

'That's quite a lot,' said Veles in his own tongue.

'What did he say?' said Bjarki.

'I don't think we're going to be disappointed,' said Veles.

They went on, and a week later, under a sickle moon, spotted the island. The dusk was flat and cold and the island rose from the sea in a featureless hump with a thin snow covering.

'This?' Bjarki was at his side.

'Fits, doesn't it? The blood-red rock?'

'Looks more black to me,' said Bjarki.

'Use your imagination. No, on second thoughts don't bother,' said Veles. 'Just find a landing spot, will you?'

'Will the prince be here?'

'I think we've established that I don't know,' said Veles. 'Something may be here that may lead us to him. If not, there may be something else for us. And if not that, then the next time I hear of treasure in Ultima Thule I'll be able to tell whoever it is they're talking rubbish. Or perhaps I won't. Perhaps I'll send them up here to freeze their backside to the boards as I've done.'

The ship reached a small beach, grounding easily in the calm sea. Veles noted that anyone on the island wouldn't get off without help. There were a number of little boats across the narrow strait drawn up on a mainland beach but none on the island itself.

Veles disembarked, as did the berserk and his men. Bjarki had his sword drawn. Veles glanced at it. In his experience a sword was more of a liability than a help in some situations. What was the berserk going to do if two hundred baying Whale Men appeared to defend their holy island from invaders? Wasn't it better not to appear threatening? Particularly and especially if you actually were offering a threat.

They made their way up a rusty slope of loose stones. Veles thought the Whale People had chosen a very unpromising location for their gateway to the gods. He had been in many such places and some of them were very pleasant – gardens in the sunshine, vineyards even.

Veles shivered. He wanted to get out of this place – but not until he had found what he had come for.

'Aha!' said the berserk. 'Maybe you are right, Veles.' He was holding up a fine reindeer coat. 'This'll fetch a decent bit when we've given it a scrub.'

Veles looked at the coat. It was well made and relatively new. It would fetch a reasonable price, he thought, though he was more inclined to put it on against the cold. He stroked the fur and something came off on his hand. Blood.

'That, as my mother used to say,' said Veles, 'is the mule of stains, and very difficult to get out. It's dried on too. It won't fetch much.'

They went on and found other things. There were drums and shoes, clothes and packs. Everywhere there was blood. Then they came upon their first body. And another. And another. All were awfully mutilated.

'It's a corpse hoard,' said Bjarki, 'a trove of slaughter.'

Veles might have argued with his choice of words but not with the sentiment. The top of the island was a field of the dead.

'Lord Odin has had some fun here,' said Bjarki. He had the wolf mask over his face. He looked slightly ridiculous, as it only stretched to just below his mouth.

'Indeed, indeed,' said Veles. He looked around and was glad he had given the mask to the berserk. Whatever had done the killing seemed to favour men who masqueraded as animals. There were about thirty corpses, or what the birds had left of them. A wolf's nose jutted out here, a gigantic beak there. The ears of a huge Arctic hare lay at his feet. Veles could read what had happened. The coats and drums had been dropped by people who had not wanted to risk anything hampering their escape.

He kicked over a mask with his foot. There was a head inside it.

'Looks like somebody beat us to it,' said Bjarki, 'though they've left enough furs. Doubtless their ship was too laden with gold.'

He was more used to this sort of sight than Veles and he picked his way through the corpses while the merchant caught his breath and composed himself. Veles looked about him. He wanted to be certain that whoever or whatever had caused this mess had gone from the island. The bodies had not been there for very long and the ravens still had some rich pickings. One pecked at a corpse next to him, watching Veles as the corpse itself seemed to watch him through the eyes of a stag mask. He didn't like this at all and shooed the bird away.

His confidence in the non-existence of supernatural powers was always stronger by a fire, drinking with his fellows, than it was in such wild places.

The crew spread over the island, looking to loot the unlootable. There was the odd fur, the odd knife, but these people had been very poor. Their drums might be worth a bit, Veles thought. He could always sell them back to them, or offer them as curiosities to the courts of the south.

'Here's your treasure!' It was Bjarki's voice, shouting from somewhere down the slope towards the open sea.

Veles couldn't see where he was calling from. He walked down. This slaughter must have been some sort of mass human sacrifice, he thought.

'Some Blöt, eh?' said Bjarki as if reading his mind. 'Old King Hrutr did nine slaves at midsummer one year, but this beats that head or rump however you look at it.' He pointed into a cave. 'Down there,' he said. 'Look.'

Veles squinted into the darkness. He could see nothing. Anxiety gripped him. He wondered if Bjarki was luring him into the dark of the cave to kill him. No. The berserk would have had no qualms at all about splitting his skull in broad daylight, in front of a market-day crowd if the mood took him. If Bjarki had wanted him dead, he would be so already.

'Do you have any way of seeing better?'

Bodvar Bjarki picked up a dead brand from the fingers of a corpse with as little disquiet as if the man had still been alive and simply passed it to him. Veles struck a flint, kindled the sparks on some wood shavings he had in his pouch and applied them. The torch flamed and the men went down.

Shadows danced around them as they descended. The light of the torch seemed merely an absence of dark, not a thing of itself. In it they saw runes painted on the walls.

'Can you read them?' said Bodvar Bjarki.

'Treasure,' said Veles, 'and good fortune.' He had never bothered too much with runes, preferring the Latin alphabet. He could read them but with difficulty. He wished they did say that, but it seemed to be the normal bilge about spirits and gods.

'How did you see in here?' said Veles. It seemed very dark to him.

'It's obvious it's a tomb,' said Bjarki.

'So you haven't actually been in here?'

'I have no intention of letting you out of my sight, merchant. I don't trust you. You'd strike a bargain with the men, maroon me here, sell the boat and cheat them out of the profit if I gave you as much as half a chance.'

'The idea never occurred to me,' said Veles. It hadn't actually, but it was good to know Bjarki feared a mutiny, and kind of him to suggest a way it might be done.

The passageway stopped at a large mound of stones. There was no sign of collapse on the tunnel roof, so Veles took them to have been placed there. On one large block a rune had been carved, a jagged sideways swipe with a line through it.

'What does that mean?'

'I've never seen it before,' said Veles.

Some other men were behind him now, peering through the wavering light.

'It's a holy sign of their people,' said one.

'Very likely,' said Veles, 'and whoever did this slaughter has taken care to secrete something here.'

'What?'

Veles shrugged and smiled. 'We won't find out until we open it, will we? I suggest you get to work.'

Bjarki grunted. Then he began on the pile of stones.

46   From the Dark

Saitada sat in a shaft of light that cut through from a finger-width opening in the side of the upper cave. She watched her image looking back from the blade of the sword.

She was much older. How much? She didn't know. The un-burned side of her face was not pretty any more: her skin was tight on her bones, pale from lack of light, dirty and cut.

Saitada had been a long time in the dark. The witch caves were endless and deep. She had not known at first that her boys had been taken and had remained underground, trawl-ing the blackness with her fingertips, reaching for a hand, the brush of some hair, listening for the cries of her children in the dark, living off the water of streams and food she could beg from the witches' servants.

For years, Saitada hadn't known why her children had been taken. But crawling through blind chimneys, emerging from dripping sumps of rock where her mouth had stolen the inch of air between the water and the tunnel ceiling, taking candles from the boy servants and watching the light struggle against the deep dark, she listened and she learned. The witches, who from their lowest caves could hear a hare's breath on the mountainside, to whom the rock and the ice of the Troll Wall were just a veil through which they saw from sea to sea, did not notice her, and she did not know to think that odd.

The older witches of course did not speak, and the boys knew only that they needed to fear and to serve them. Neither yielded any information about what had happened to Saitada's children. The girls, however, initiates new to the dark, shiv-ered and trembled and clung to what they had been. Saitada came to them, sat with them, hugged them and calmed them, though she never thought to say anything. The girls needed to talk, to confess their fears as they would have to their mothers. They told her, among other things, of the threat that was coming, of the deaths and the terror of death. They told her too about two boys who would become one wolf to kill the murderous god. One boy's body would host the spirit of the wolf, the other would be his food, giving his brother the strength he needed. The witch queen had taken the boys and only one would live. Saitada never found it strange that she could understand the girls' language. She only knew that her babies had gone.

They were always in her mind, their memory like a tumour that ate everything else she had seen, everything she had been. After years alone she was not a person, just a love and a hate encased in flesh – cherishing the thought of her children, loathing the witch queen who had taken them – watching death begin to creep through the caves.

The girls had all died when Saitada's grief was at its height. She had gone to the deep dark, where she had thought she would die, when five of them were dead, and emerged to find none alive. The boys were all dead too. From one she had taken tinder and lit a candle. She had no idea why she had come back – her own motivations were now a mystery to her – but in a week her purpose became clear. She had come back to watch the witch queen kill her sisters.

Some went in their sleep; some were strangled and some burned. The majority would have died from neglect, with no boys to tend them, but Saitada brought them food from the sacrifices. It wasn't kindness. She saw the distress the murders caused the witch queen and didn't want starvation or thirst to spare her a single one. Saitada saw how the deaths drove the queen on to madness and she sought to guide her hand, leaving rope or tinder, stakes or, once, a long pin that she found in some cloth left as a sacrifice. The queen quickly put Saitada's gifts to use.

Saitada watched for the arrival of the god the girls had talked about but saw nothing. Rock, pool and stream remained the same in the yellow light of a candle stub; the torpid air and dripping damp didn't change when the flame was spent.

When the witches were all dead, she tried to kill the witch queen herself. She could not go through with it. Twice she pulled the queen from the Pools of the Dead by a rope at her neck; once she took a little knife, pressed it to her breast but then drew back. Were the runes protecting the witch queen? Even Saitada could sense them now, chiming and splashing and fizzing in the blackness as the witch endured her daily sufferings by water and cold. Frustration began to overwhelm Saitada and she spent a long time trying to think how she could strike her enemy down. But every time she moved against her she faltered.

She found his sword in the lowest caves – it thumped against her knee as she stumbled on the uneven floor. She knew what it was the instant she held it – the slim curve in the jewelled scabbard, the keenness of the blade when it was drawn.

He could kill the witch. He could kill anyone. Saitada knew only one thing about him – his name. Authun. It was enough. She took the sword and went up towards the light.

47 Descent

Feileg could not sail so they were forced to travel by land. The landscape now looked entirely different to when he had come north, a wide field of white leading to distant mountains. But he knew well where they should go – a wolf can always find its home – and he headed south under the swirling skies with Adisla behind him. With her wound she could not walk far, but Feileg sat her on one of the reindeer sleighs and led the animal. The Noaidi who had owned it had not appeared to claim it. The wolfman loaded the sled with good reindeer coats, a tent, furs, snow shoes and boots, and took some flints and plenty of tinder. He also took a spear. He didn't need it to fight but wanted a sign to warn anyone they encountered to look elsewhere if robbery was on their mind.

The Noaidis who had survived were in no mood to argue. By the time Feileg finished piling the stones all but one sorcerer had gone. The man had marked a stone with a rune, put it on the heap and left.

To Feileg the rune was vaguely familiar. He wished he had asked what it meant but he had no language in common with the holy man. Was it a seal to magically hold the beast in place? Or was it something else, a warning maybe?

He thought on it as they headed south for the Troll Wall, as he made up the tent and the fire within it and brought Adisla the things he had caught and killed for her. The wolf is the king of winter, and Feileg was almost happy, bringing in his kills and allowing Adisla to cook them rather than eat the meat raw as had been his habit. It was the life he had glimpsed as he had kissed her by the post where she had cut him free.

Adisla, however, was withdrawn. Her tears had been replaced by silence. Vali's condition, she was sure, was her fault.

There was no logic to her thinking, but she couldn't shake her conviction that her liaison with someone so far above her social standing, what she had done to her mother, even her capitulation in agreeing to marry Drengi, were all to blame for what had happened to him. She had grown up with a powerful belief in magic, been raised to learn healing and even some divination. Things were linked, she felt. Her mother had said people stand at the edge of an ocean of events that touches unseen islands and shores. She had allowed something bad to grow between her and Vali. Now something far more terrible had grown within him.

But as they rested by their fires and Feileg described the amazing events of his childhood, the hopelessness she felt about her relationship with Vali bore the seed of hope for a future with Feileg. Slowly, she found she could talk to him. She spoke about her youth with Vali and then just about herself and her life with her brothers and, most of all, her mother. The wolfman listened without comment, and when she told him what she had done to Disa, he just sat for a while before saying, 'I wish I had known such love.'

'To kill her?'

'To save her,' he said. 'She was fated to die and she knew it. Better quickly, at her daughter's hand, than after the torments of the Danes. She chose the instrument of her death — you, who she loved. You are no more to blame than if she had used the knife herself.'

'I wish I could believe it.'

'Do you think your mother would have wanted this grief for you?'

'No.'

'What would she have wanted?'

Adisla looked up into the shining whorls of the night sky. 'For me to get on with my life, to meet a good man and bear fine sons,' she said.

Feileg smiled. 'Then make that your aim,' he said.

Feileg, she could see, was not a wolf. The shaman had not

taken his humanity with his chants and brews. Feileg was a man, plain and simple, someone who had been raised to savagery but who had reclaimed himself from it. He would make a good husband, she was sure, and she would have been proud to be his wife, had the fates put them together before.

The days were short as they travelled through the mountain passes, but when the moon was bright, Feileg pressed on.

'Do you know where you're going?' she asked him.

'The south,' he said. 'The mountains there are like a fold from this sea to the Troll Wall. We will follow the coast as best we can and then use them to steer us to where we want to go.'

Adisla was left breathless by the beauty of the northern winter, of the bleak hills and the blinding plains, though she found the country barren and threatening compared to the softer features of her coastal home. The journey was rough and bumpy, though the sled was warm beneath the furs and she even managed to doze.

They had been travelling for weeks and the snow was thick when the land in the distance seemed to buckle into ridges of black. As they got nearer they saw them, the Troll Peaks, rising up in crests like the gigantic waves of a solid sea. They appeared daunting, though the way to them was easy – the ground frozen solid, rivers turned into roads. Occasionally they came upon a family hut. There were signs of life – or rather lives that had been. No one came to greet them; no dog barked; no child called out. Clothes left in the sun to dry had bleached and rotted before they froze.

Adisla looked at Feileg and shrugged as if to say, 'What happened here?'

He shrugged back. 'These hills leak nightmares,' he said, 'they always have. Perhaps it all got too much.'

As they moved through the country at the back of the Troll Wall it seemed the leak had become a flood. Everything was abandoned, everything in ruins; not a house was inhabited.

They followed the hills inland, skirting them before

climbing up through a narrow valley. In the heavy light of evening wolves howled invisibly from the ridges.

Adisla, who could walk well by now, looked at Feileg in alarm, but the wolfman was calm.

'They are my brothers,' he said, 'and they are welcoming me home.'

He returned their call and Adisla saw them. What she had taken for rocks were animals, now moving down the slope. Feileg smiled and cut the fretting reindeer free of the sled.

'The animal has served us well,' said Adisla.

'They would have him, tied to the sled or free,' said Feileg. 'This way he dies free. It is what he was meant to do.'

There was no way out for the reindeer – wolves ahead and behind. It turned one way and then the other, a pattering run forward, a pattering run back. And then it stopped. In a moment the pack was on it.

'It didn't even try to run,' said Adisla.

'It knew there was no point. Why die exhausted? It's bad enough to die without being made to work for it.'

'What are *we* doing?' said Adisla.

'Working for it,' said Feileg.

'You sound like Bragi.'

'Thank you.' He hadn't told her the old man was dead. She had enough to contend with.

The wolves fed, and when they had finished Feileg shouldered the tent and they walked on up the pass. The pack followed behind. The mountain in front of them had seemed big from a distance. Close up it was immense, bigger than anything Adisla had ever imagined, an enormous barren sweep of grey and white rising out of the valley floor and disappearing into cloud at the top.

'If I saw the world tree,' said Adisla, holding Feileg's hand and looking up at it, 'this is how I think it would look.'

'We are going into it,' said Feileg.

'How?'

'We need to find a wolf trap,' said Feileg.

Adisla thought of Vali, transformed and starving in that horrible cave. She let go of Feileg's hand and said no more.

Feileg led the way up the mountain and Adisla's wound began to pain her. Feileg saw her limping.

'I can go on my own. It might be better like that.'

'I'll stay with you,' said Adisla. 'I am linked to you now. I'll die in this wilderness without you.'

Feileg longed to hold her, to tell her how he felt about her, but he saw the resolution with which she drove herself on, her dedication to the prince, and he concentrated on picking a safe route for the climb.

The lower reaches were easy enough, snowy but not deadly cold as long as you kept moving or had fire. There was even a track winding across the mountain. Adisla had always imagined mountains as unrelenting climbs but this one had frequent breaks in the slope. They scrambled up scree or through fields of boulders, then along ridges where they seemed to go sideways rather than up. As they ascended, the path cut across slopes so steep that Adisla had to dig the butt end of the spear into the snow field to prevent herself sliding off the mountain. The light was bleak and drained of colour. Feileg stopped where the path gave out on a broad area of barren scree, a shoulder in a ridge that went up into ice. In the snowless lee of a big rock there were several pots on the ground, along with two or three bottles.

Feileg picked up a pot and sniffed it. 'Butter,' he said, 'but licked clean by my brothers.' He took up a bottle and removed the wooden bung.

'Mead,' he said. 'This is as far as normal men can go without being certain of madness. It's where offerings are left, but no one has collected them. Look!'

He pointed to the side of the track behind them. Adisla saw a dark area.

'That was a wolf pit, to protect the offerings,' said Feileg 'Men fear the witches, wolves do not. I snapped its spikes.'

'How do they ever get anything before the wolves?'

'They have servants, and they take it quickly,' said Feileg.

Silently, a wolf had come to his shoulder. It nosed the ground before glancing at Feileg and going on. The animal had almost looked as if it was asking for instructions.

They went on, up, up and then down to a valley, up again and down into another valley. Here the land was barren and rocky. A river plunged almost as a waterfall off one side of the hill, tumbling into a wide pool before leading away down the mountain. The wolf with Feileg streaked across towards the pool. Just in front of it he stopped and picked something up in his mouth. Adisla and Feileg followed. The wolf had a human hand, a child's, in its mouth.

Feileg breathed in. 'It is near here,' he said, 'very near.'

They searched for two days but found nothing. There was little dry wood for the fire, food was running low and Feileg didn't have time to catch anything – he was scouring the mountain, directing the wolves back and forth like a shepherd with his dogs. Adisla sat in the tent and tried to keep warm, resting her aching leg.

Feileg returned to the pool.

'Nothing,' he said. 'The wolves can tell children go all over this mountain, but the tracks go over and over each other. They drink here and then go up there. Then they come back. Or so it seems.'

Adisla looked at the water. It was very clear and strangely not frozen. They were a good height above the valley floor, and even down there the river was solid and any pools were frozen a hard blue. This was still liquid.

'There is no ice here,' said Adisla.

Feileg looked at the water. That hadn't occurred to him. He dipped his hand in. It wasn't warm, but it was nowhere near as cold as it should have been. It was clear too, very clear.

'Enchantment?' he said.

'Perhaps. Is this an entrance, do you think?' she said.

'Maybe one of them. There are supposed to be many, but neither I nor the wolves can find them.'

'Will you go in?'

'Yes.' First he built a fire inside the Noaidi tent. Then he spent a few moments puffing and blowing beside the water, rubbing his hands and stamping his feet. Adisla wondered what he was doing and thought he looked far from confident. He went in up to his waist.

'It is not cold,' he said, 'not at all.'

He went in deeper, made of few back and forth movements, tried to dive but immediately came back to the surface choking and coughing. Then he tried again, but with the same result.

'Are you all right?' said Adisla.

'Yes.' He was shaking. He steeled himself and put his face into the water. Then he did dive and didn't appear for a couple of heartbeats. He came back up in a flurry of flapping arms and kicking legs, beating at the water with his hands and gulping down mouthfuls. Gasping, he managed to find his feet and stagger to the fire, where she cradled his shivering body in her arms as the Noaidi had done for her when she had gone over the side of the ship.

He regained his breath. 'There is something down there, a lip on the bottom. It is possible to go underneath. I will try again.'

'Wait a moment, you need to rest,' she said.

She had never seen him look like this. For the first time since she had known him, the wolfman had fear in his eyes.

'What is it?' she said.

'There must be other ways in.'

'Is this a way in?'

'There is a rope and it is secured to something. I think it's a guide. But there will be other ways in. The boys can't take everything in this way. It would all be soaked.'

'This is the way in we have; why search for another?'

Feileg looked at the ground. 'I don't like the water,' he said.

'Oh Feileg,' said Adisla. She squeezed him to her. He looked into her eyes and on impulse she rested her lips on his in a light kiss. Feileg didn't know what to say, still less what to do.

Adisla slipped from his arms, took three big gulps of breath and dived into the pool.

48   The Pool of Tears

At first Saitada had gone north by mistake, through deserted farmsteads, past houses where now only rats sheltered from the cold. She had picked up some things of use to her there – two mouldy blankets which provided some warmth, enough rags to cover her face, bind her feet and wrap the sword, and a cup in which to melt snow for water.

It had been three days before she had seen smoke from a hut, and when she had spoken the name Authun and gestured to ask if he was there, the people had laughed and pointed to the south past the Troll Wall. They thought she was a simpleton but still poured their advice into her ears. It was not safe to travel to the south. The land around those mountains was cursed. Nightmares of death and torture had come down from the slopes and now no one could stand to live there. The witches, it was said, were dying and their magic had poisoned the land. Saitada listened and said nothing more. She could understand them, though she didn't know how.

That night the son of the house decided to have a look at what the old beggar had in her bundle, but as he went to prise it from Saitada's fingers he caught a glimpse of that burn on the side of her face and went back to his bed. In the morning, ashamed by his actions the night before, he gave her a warm cloak, some old boots and a rough tunic that the dog had been using for a bed. Saitada bowed to thank them for their hospitality and turned for the long journey south.

Authun's people had not forgotten him, and at the farms and among the flocks they told her where she needed to go. The snow was lighter in the south, though the wind was cruel Still, the people kept to the tradition of welcome for travellers that existed throughout that land, took her in by night and pointed her on her way the next morning. She found him two days' walk into the Iron Woods.

A hunter took her half the way in out of pity for her face and showed her the direction she needed to take – to keep among the birches and come down if the woods turned to only firs, to keep the slope to her left, the Pole Star to her right and to trust to luck for the rest. After so long in the dark the night made her dizzy and her head felt open to the sky. And what a sky. It was shot with fire, swirls of green and red that seemed to her as if the gods had lit their beacons to rejoice in what she was doing. She didn't stop to stare. Her purpose and her need for warmth drove her on.

It was the following evening and the moon was full when she met him. He was sitting on a rock looking into a pool. Much of it was frozen, but where the pool was fed by a small waterfall the water was still free. His long silver hair shone in the moonlight like water itself, or like a prophecy of how the waterfall would look when the cold finally took it. He did not look at her but remained focused on the pool. Without turning his head, he said, 'Do not look to me for battle, stranger; there are enough widows screaming in my dreams.'

Saitada did not reply. The king had no fire and no cloak and was so still that the plumes of steam that came from his freezing breath made her think of a mountain wreathed in mist. Eventually he looked up.

No spearman or berserk could have made him stand, but Saitada did.

'Lady, I have thought of you,' he said.

She bowed her head.

The king went on. 'That thought drew me here.' He pointed to the pool. 'He is in here, the man you saw me send to the ocean floor, and the other kinsmen I threw away. It seems to me that this is a magic pool, fed not by the hills but by the tears of the widows and orphans I have made.'

He turned to look at the waterfall and then back to her. No enemy could have put him in such a state of agitation.

'I am sorry,' he said. 'I am sorry for what I did to you. Your face haunts my dreams. I took your children and left you to monsters. And for what? To influence fate when we know all fates are set at birth. The child will not bring everlasting fame to the Horda, or if he will, in no way that I can see. And if he does, what of it?'

Still Saitada said nothing. She did not hate the king. He had done no more than move her from one place to another, she thought, as she had been moved from the smith to the farmer to the priests. It was her fate in life to be a slave. He had not, as the witch had done, parted her from her children.

Authun did not see it that way and felt the shame build further in him. Already that shame had taken him from his kingdom, from his family and his battles to sit in the freezing woods, listening to the voice of the waters for year upon year and going to war on the person he had been. And yet, when robbers came, when bears struck at him or the winter bit, he could not let himself go, could not die, and fought always for life. He hunted when he would rather have starved, drank when he would have died of thirst. Saitada had been wrong. Authun couldn't kill anyone at all. He couldn't kill himself. He couldn't step over the threshold he had pushed so many others across. The dishonour of that hovered above him like a mighty fist that could smash him at any instant.

'What would you have me do, lady?'

Saitada pointed to the north.

'You want me to go with you? For what? You gave me pity and despair. What other gifts do you have for me?'

Saitada stared into his eyes and said the first word she had ever spoken in his language other than his name, the word she had heard whispered through the witch caves on the trembling lips of the boys, on the hushed breath of the girls.

'Death,' she said. She walked forward and put the bundle she was carrying into his arms. He opened it and in the pale light of the woodland night saw the scabbard of the Moonsword.

He drew the sword and watched the cold spark of the moon run the length of the blade.

'Then I will follow you,' he said.

Saitada turned and began to walk out of the forest.

49 Manifestation

The witch's energies had been directed towards Lieaibolmmai – towards giving him enough power to bring calamity on himself. She had provided the noose. He had put his head inside it and jumped. When he died under the teeth of the wolf, her mind became free.

She had been in the wolf's mouth, the lowest cave, lying naked upon the teeth of stone to demand the gods recognise her suffering with revelation. She wanted to open that door that led even further into the earth, to the bound god, his serpents and his bowl. But she couldn't find him. The passage-ways he had inhabited were still there but there was no sign of Loki, nor even a resonance of his presence. In her pain, frustration and madness she did not even notice that the sword she had enchanted was gone.

Lieaibolmmai's passing had come to her like a lightening in the atmosphere, the feeling of a house with its doors left open to spring after a long heavy winter.

She struggled up from the jagged rocks and stood in her blood and her filth. Although the queen knew her way through the tunnels by touch, she had prepared a little lamp for the end of her ordeal, knowing that she would want the comfort of light after travelling to such dark places. She lit it and felt a tingle of relief course through her. At her feet was the little piece of leather with the Wolfsangel rune carved on it. She touched it and felt the resonance of the symbol inside her. It had returned to her. Yes, Odin was dead, taken by the only thing that could take him – the Fenris Wolf come to earth. She had given the hanged god his runes, let him come to his knowledge of himself, and he had cast the spell that had killed him.

She stumbled up a passage to where a spring spilled from the ground. She cupped her hand to drink, and as she lifted the water, some passed through her fingers. It fell, she thought, too quickly. She picked up a pebble and rolled it in her hand. It dropped from her fingers and bounced on the rocky floor. Too far? It seemed so to her. Only Odin could frighten the rocks and the streams, only Odin could make the air depart and the seas pull away. He was still alive. Despite her best efforts, he was still alive.

The witch queen – though she was now queen only of herself, her subjects all lying slaughtered – sank down in the dark, trembling. The air was moving in the passageways. She knew what it was – the breath of the god. He was coming for her and she was alone: no sisters to augment her power, no army of witches to send against him to weaken him. Had she been tricked? Had some deeper magic than hers turned her hands to murder?

The witch felt her mind twist. The god crowded in on her, inhabited everything around her, seeped through the passageways and caves to surround and suffocate her. Odin had come for her – Odin, lord of the hanged, Odin the berserk, Odin the frenzied, dangler, screamer, spear inviter, old one eye, Odin the mad, Odin the poet, Odin the rain, Odin the rock, Odin the dark and Odin the light. He waited at every turn of the tunnel, hid in every pool, but flickered away as she snatched a hand into the blackness to catch him, splashed footsteps through the dark as she chased to confront him.

And if Odin was there, where was the wolf? She had thought the northern sorcerer would bring Fenrisulfr to flesh on earth and destroy himself. But if the drum magician was not Odin, then the wolf could not have manifested. She was sure the wolf would only be fully present when the god came into his knowledge of himself. Sanity came to her now only in glimpses. She had killed, she had suffered, she had striven towards magical insight. Now worms seemed to gnaw through the labyrinth of her thoughts. Structures and links were missing from her mind, ways blocked, burned and broken. So other paths had been found, bored through the lattice of ordinary assumptions, building precarious bridges between areas of her mind that had only ever communicated indirectly. Others would have called it madness, but to the queen it was a blessing which she had won through her years of murder and pain.

A realisation sparked inside her. She was the first of magicians, a sorcerer without parallel. She had hidden her intentions even from herself, afraid that knowing her own plans would compromise her with the god. If he knew she was acting against him he would strike. But, deceived, she was safe. While her energies were directed at a false target, the god would think he had time – he might dally, hesitate. And in so doing he had given her the chance to bring the wolf to the cusp of existence in the best possible way – by getting someone else to do it for her. Her visions told her she had even hidden from herself the true nature of the spell and which boy would be used to house the spirit of the god come to earth. Odin had not been able to force this secret from her because she had not known it herself. So the god had not seen the peril he was in until her protector was ready.

She recalled the knot at the throat of the first dead girl – the dead lord's necklace with its three tight twists, and she knew it had been a message – one thing hidden inside another, inside yet another. It was magic of the deepest depth, magic that works independently of the sorcerer – of her and through her, yes, but it could not really be said to be her doing. This was not spell casting; it was a force she had welcomed in as a child, something that now cast her.

The witch's thoughts floated free of reason and into the realm of magical thinking, beyond logic and sanity but with the strongest possible connection to reality – the connection of death.

She clasped the rune to her, the one she had etched on the piece of leather. She held it to her lips, touched it with her tongue and breathed in its aroma. The smell was something beyond animal skin. It tasted of tears, funeral pyres and of the staleness of waiting. Loss.

The wolf was coming but needed something to take the final step, a suffering to propel it into flesh and chase the human out. There was something living in the upper caves, the warmth of the air on the witch's skin told her. It wasn't a rat and it wasn't a bird. She looked at the rune on the leather, its meanings spilling into her mind — storm, werewolf, wolf trap. The girl, she knew, had come and now the queen sensed her importance. She was the trap to draw the brothers in. The pieces of the magical puzzle were falling into place. The girl was there, the brother would come, only the wolf was missing. The rune seemed to pulse in her hand. Three in one, a knot of misery, denial and slaughter. Odin was very near. It was time to summon her protector, the dead god's enemy. It would not be easy. The wolf had grown, she could sense, and was close to his full power. A creature that could stand in front of the master of magic and snap off his head would not respond to a witch's call. Something more was required to compel his attendance. The witch, whose mind was so linked to the caves that she could feel every movement within them, knew the girl had entered the hoard cave. She would go to her. She touched her tongue to the rune again. This time it tasted of blood.

50 Alone

What if there is no air? What if this leads nowhere?

Adisla tugged at the rope with increasing desperation, able to see nothing at all. The passage from the bottom of the pool was long, dark and entirely underwater, and she had gone too far down to turn back. She pulled and pulled, hand over hand, hand over hand, fighting down panic. The ceiling of the tunnel was smooth rock but she kept hitting her head, which forced her to bend her neck down so her shoulders took the impact instead.

She struggled against the urge to breathe in or give up, to hammer at the ceiling and waste energy. Then, abruptly, the passage rose. Air hit her face and she swallowed it down. She opened her eyes to blackness. She could see nothing at all but crawled out onto the rough and potholed floor of a cave. She pulled herself up to sitting and felt something between her fingers, cold like autumn grass.

'Hello.'

The dead air of the cave seemed to cling to her skin. Dead air. That was the smell – something was rotting. Adisla composed herself and reached for the pouch at her side for the flint, steel and tinder Feileg had taken from the Noaidi. The tinder was useless – she could feel it was soaked – but the flint and steel would work. She took them out, struck them together and the corpses were upon her, rotten faces looming from the dark. In the awful instant of the flint's flash she saw three dead boys. It was not grass she had touched but hair. Adisla offered a prayer to Freya. She was almost glad of the dark now and shrank back against a wall.

She waited for Feileg to come, holding her knees into herself for the small comfort she could take from hugging something.

But Feileg didn't appear. She had thought her example would encourage him. Had she been wrong? She forced herself to listen to her breathing to make sure time was really passing, that the eternity she felt was in reality no more than a few heartbeats. Feileg still did not come.

She tried to think what to do. Return to the surface, she decided. Adisla felt for the rope and prepared herself for the haul back. It would be easier, she told herself – she knew how long the tunnel was. She took the rope in her hands and tested it. Yes, it was secured at the other end. She could pull herself through. Then she thought of Vali, enchanted and forsaken in that pit. If Feileg was incapable of coming through the tunnel, there was no guarantee another entrance to the witch caves could be found.

A terrible thought struck her. What if Feileg had drowned in the tunnel? Would she find his body blocking her way? Trembling and terrified, she forced herself to think. This was the Troll Wall and the witches had been the death of countless heroes. Who was to say that Feileg would be any different? For Vali's sake, she had to go on without him.

Adisla steeled herself and searched the boys' bodies, hoping to find a lamp. She found only the amulets at their necks. She took one. It had done the child no good, but who was to say it wouldn't help her? Crawling past the boys, she cut her knees on the floor. Never mind, she was going to have to get used to that. When she was sure the corpses were behind her, she struck the flint again. In the brief flash she saw the passage going on and down, and went ahead before striking once more to check her way. She didn't expect to see anything much, but thought she might at least get some warnings of drops, low ceilings or falls. Nevertheless, she proceeded cautiously, feeling her way forward. It was painful progress and it was slow.

She hoped she would find Feileg again. He had told her that he had a great treasure in the hills. Feileg was naive and didn't have the guile to lie about something like that. If he said he had treasure, he had treasure. It would be something she could use to bargain with the witches to get them to use their magic to bring Vali back to human form. She could offer her word she would deliver it. But what was the word of a woman? Perhaps Feileg would have been useful: they would more readily accept the oath of a warrior.

She tried to smother her deeper thoughts. For as long as she could remember she had loved only Vali. Now she was terrified of him, and Feileg, with his honesty and kindness, offered her the chance of a simple life away from the affairs of kings and sorcerers. Adisla's love for Vali had devoured her, Feileg, her mother, everything it touched. But for that love, the Danes would never have come for her and her mother would still be alive, little Manni too. She couldn't abandon the prince, though, no matter what.

Questions of the heart were for the sunshine and the open air. In the tunnels of the Troll Wall she had more pressing concerns. Adisla had never known such dark. It seemed like a beast smothering her, her flint a little thorn that she jabbed into its belly, forcing a momentary retreat, before its dead weight came down on her again.

How would she call a witch? What would she say? Adisla didn't know. First, she thought, she needed light. There was plenty of detritus on the tunnel floors. Surely she would come across a lamp eventually? It was impossible to believe that the dead children she had found had spent their whole lives in the dark.

She crawled on and on, her fingers numb from striking the flint. At the end of one cramped fissure the ceiling and the floor came together into a narrow slash in the rock. She crawled forward and pushed her head and arms into it. Then she struck her flint and nearly dropped it in awe.

She did not notice the cavern, the spears of white that dropped from the ceiling, nor the folds in the rock where dead witches seemed to peer out at you. She saw only the blazing gold piled high to the ceiling, splendid as a bonfire. She struck again and again, and among the swords, the byrnies, the goblets and the plate, the jewels and the coins taken in tribute from nightmare-tormented kings for twenty generations, she saw something far more precious – a fish-oil lamp.

It was quite a drop to the floor from where her tunnel came in and she knew there would be no turning back once she had gone down. Adisla withdrew her head, wriggled round and lowered herself down feet first then dropped into blackness. Agony shot through her leg as she landed and she let out a cry that echoed back at her. She had twisted her ankle – the same leg that the arrow had struck. Even as she held it she could feel it begin to swell. No matter. She needed light. She struck the flint and crawled to where the lamp was. Her fingers curled around it and she shook it. It was nearly full. Again she hit the flint. Five, maybe six, tries and she located what she was looking for – something that would burn, a tattered cloak in some rich material she had never felt before. She found the edge of the cloak, teased off some threads and struck the flint. Adisla had made a fire this way thousands of times at home but now it seemed impossibly difficult. Her fingers were bleeding from catching them on the edge of the steel by the time an ember took. But then she had the lamp alight and looked around at the glory of the witch queen's hoard.

Her fear did not subside as the dark shrank back but it changed in nature. Before, the tunnels had seemed full of unseen eyes, invisible and hungry mouths. Now, in the silence of the huge cavern, she was afraid that she might be alone. Adisla realised that she might well die in these caves, witches or no witches. In some ways, to be alone was the worst monster of all. The gold was incredible but, she realised, useless. She couldn't drink it, she couldn't eat it, and it almost mocked her.

The pain in her ankle was growing. Was it sprained or was it broken?

There was a distant noise, a stirring like a breath but much louder. She told herself it was the wind, but the air was still. She wanted to extinguish the light and hide but knew that she had chosen to face whatever was in those tunnels. There it was again. What was it? Adisla's throat was dry and she had to struggle with herself not to snuff out the lamp.

Cold prickled her skin and she began to shake. The lamp was guttering, or was that her imagination? Panic gripped her. Adisla scrambled up but had forgotten her ankle. She screamed and fell to her knees, nearly dropping the lamp. The flame guttered and nearly died. She forced her hands to pick it up and held it high to look around.

A terrible child stood over her, haggard, filthy, with the face of a woman and the eyes of the drowned.

And then Adisla was calm. She realised that she had not seen the lady properly in the dark. This was no cave-dwelling hag, this was a queen. The lady extended her hand and her kind smile told Adisla to forget about all pain, the anguish she felt for Vali, her desire to find Feileg, even the agony of her ankle. It would all be all right, thought Adisla. She knew that this lady had suffered torments beyond imagining and could take all those that Adisla felt and wash them away. The lady was dressed in a fine robe embroidered with gold; a beautiful necklace burned at her throat and a crown of sapphires shone like ice in the sun upon her head. Even the dark seemed to peel away around this lovely woman.

'I need you to help my Vali,' said Adisla. The lady smiled and Adisla understood that she knew that and was already working to free him. From the lady's demeanour, Adisla felt certain that even now Vali was on his way to meet her and that soon everything would be settled. This lady had great powers and could break any enchantment that Vali had suffered.

Yes, everything was going to be all right. The lady had looked into her mind and sent her a vision to bring her peace. Adisla saw herself on a farmstead in the sun, children about her who ran giggling from old Bragi as he staggered around pretending to be a bear. There was someone else next to her,

Feileg or Vali, she couldn't be sure which. She felt secure, though, loving and loved among the people she valued most in all the world. The lady had shown her that future and she was grateful to her.

Adisla took the witch's hand and Gullveig led her to the lower caves.

51 Reward

In the north, though the wind was a knife and the sky black with snow, Veles Libor was not cold, he was sweating. Underground, the wind didn't cut him and the snow didn't touch him. In the swaying torchlight he pulled away the rocks. He would toil alongside the Norsemen because he knew them well enough to realise that should he not do the work some might think he was not worth a share of the reward.

He knew that the hardest part would come if they found any treasure. Bodvar Bjarki owed him nothing; the crew owed him nothing and they were not men of his king. So he had to rely on two things – his sharp wits and his companions' dim ones. Accordingly, he talked constantly of the robbing ways of southern merchants and how one fine warrior had been tricked into giving half a dragon's hoard for a worthless belt that a merchant had claimed was that of the god Thor, capable of giving its owner a giant's strength. In truth, he hadn't really thought there would be any treasure and had run out of ideas as to how he would pay Hemming the ransom for the prince. However, anything was worth a go, and the crooked treasure mark and the great pile of stones looked very promising indeed. So he needed to make his companions see his worth.

'To get the best price for plunder, you need an experienced merchant on your side,' he said. 'When I think of all the proud warriors who have sold great treasures never knowing what they had, it makes my heart weep. I tell you this, if I had that dragon's loot to sell, I would have got twice what it was worth. But then again I know where to find the buyers.'

Some of the men were naive farm boys with little experience of anything and they lapped up what Veles was saying.

Bjarki, however, was a different matter. The berserk had to realise that if Veles got back to Haithabyr with their plunder Bjarki would never see so much as a bushel of oats in reward. However, Veles thought he could convince him that bargaining skills might be useful in a neutral port where Bjarki didn't have to fear the merchant's connections. Also, Bodvar Bjarki owed compensation. If he took anything but coin back to Forkbeard, the king would place his own value on it, which might leave the berserk with still more to pay. The merchant thought he'd use all these arguments when the time was right.

The piled stones were finally clawed away and they stood looking at a great flat slab. It had on it the same rune as the first rock they had removed, a jagged line with another through it.

'What does that mean?' said Bjarki.

'It is a curse,' said Veles. 'The treasure in here will need very careful handling if the men who take it are not to be struck down. In Byzantium this sign was used to slay the emperor himself.'

'Where is Byzantium?' said one of the farm boys.

'He means Miklagard,' said Bjarki.

'Where is Miklagard?' said the farm boy.

'West of here and down a little,' said Veles. 'Big town, lots of sorcerers used to allaying curses. This did for them.'

Bjarki snorted. 'I have my own way with curses,' he said and tapped his sword. 'I've never met a sorcerer who can put his head back on when you've cut it off.'

'Then you have never met the wizard Ptolemy. He is a friend of mine and it is something of a party trick,' said Veles.

The farm boys inclined their heads, impressed.

'I would like to test that trick,' said Bjarki. 'Perhaps I'll take you back in two pieces and see if he can stick you back together again.'

Veles went quiet. He knew enough about human nature to see that Bjarki was quite capable of carrying out his threats.

He didn't bother pointing out that, by the berserk's own account, he had been trapped by a sorcerer. Perhaps the death of the men who had enchanted him had made him bolder, or had the ridiculous wolf mask given him courage?

'Shall we get this done?' said one of the men. 'I don't like this place. It grows crow food and I have no desire to let it make a meal of me.'

Bjarki nodded and went to the slab. He was a massive man but his arms were not long enough to span the stone. He tried to get his fingers behind it but it had jammed against the sloping end of the passage. Then he crouched and tugged at the rock at its front. He couldn't get the purchase to move it.

'Allow me,' said Veles. He took up one of the wooden wedges lying on the floor and hammered it with a stone into the crack between the slab and the passage wall. Then he sent a crewman down to the beach for water. The man came back and Veles poured the water onto the wood.

'Do you hope to wash it away?' said one of the farm boys.

'Yes,' said Veles. After a few moments the wood began to swell and the gap between the wall and the slab widened. Bodvar Bjarki nodded, impressed, as Veles drove in more wedges.

'I am a magician in my own right, as you can see,' said the merchant with a smile.

Eventually, the gap was big enough and Bjarki stepped forward. He forced his hand in and pulled. Nothing happened. He spat and he swore, working himself up into a rage, mumbling under his breath, 'Odin, war merry, lord of death. Odin, destroyer, wrecker, mighty slayer. Odin means frenzy. Odin means war. Odin, Odin, the mad, the half blind. Odin! Odin! Ahhhhhhh!'

The slab lifted. Bjarki heaved it into the vertical, where it teetered for a heartbeat and seemed that it would fall back into place, but then it tipped towards him. Bjarki leaped back and the stone followed him with a crash. There was a rush of stinking air from the hole in the cave floor, and even Veles, a man of iron stomach, found himself retching. Two crewmen had to turn aside to vomit. Even Bjarki recoiled, though he stepped forward again pretty quickly.

'It's a tomb,' he said, 'and a fresh one – you can smell the rot. Come on, lads, it's a good sign. No one's been here before us. Here's my freedom from my oath to Forkbeard.'

He kneeled and secured a rope to a projection in the rock over the hole that seemed designed for the purpose.

'This is good,' he said. 'They've helped us out here, boys.' He grinned. 'Last one down's a pauper.' Then he lowered himself into the blackness.

What was in that pit? Vali. No, not Vali. Something had Vali's thoughts but they no longer defined its personality. They were loose and unconnected, shooting stars, here and then gone. His memories and experiences were pulp, running into each other, friendship and love no more important than the feel of the rock under his feet, the cold of the cave.

At first he had accepted being in the pit because of his love for Adisla. He knew how near he had been to killing her, and though the sound of the slab sealing him in had filled him with despair, he had also welcomed it. While he was trapped he could cause no more harm. When he'd seen the stricken Noaidi, his animal self had taken over and he had accepted his fate for quite different reasons. He had food, the pit was sheltered – why would he not want to be there? Then the food had run out and he had beaten the walls with rage, leaped at the rock sealing him in, tried to dig his way out and eventually, as any beast would, accepted his fate and sat down.

By then he could hardly remember who he was. His humanity seemed like a shoal of silver fish, turning and moving in the water, suddenly possessing shape and form and then scattered to chaos by massive jaws.

Veles was not far behind Bodvar Bjarki. He cut his hands coming down the rope and cursed as he hit the rubble of the floor.

Someone threw down a burning torch. Veles picked it up and peered around. He touched the wall – something sticky was on his fingers. He licked at them and then wiped his tongue with his sleeve. It was blood.

In front of him Bjarki was edging forward, sword drawn.

'There are emeralds here,' whispered the berserk. 'Look. They're huge.'

'Very likely cheap agate,' said Veles, 'I will need to value them properly.'

But they weren't emeralds or agate. They were eyes.

52 King and Queen

The darkness was not the same as the last time, thought Authun. On the way into the caves from the back of the mountain the woman had taken flint, steel and tinder and a big bundle of candle stubs from a hole under a rock. She lit the candles, one off another, as they descended. But when one blew out the darkness did not seem to cling too close or to seethe with animosity and harm.

The woman had prepared him before they went down – in her way. She had taken the wolf's head pebble that hung by a thong at her neck and tied it around his neck.

'For luck?' he said.

'Death,' she said.

He let her tie it. He felt no different, and as far as he could see it was only a piece of stone.

The king found it hard to credit that this entrance to the witches' caves was so easy to find. It was virtually signposted – a narrow crawl running into the side of the mountain, identified by sacrifices left at its mouth. The tunnel had the shape of a long-handled spoon, spreading into a tall chamber at its end. Access to the actual caves was through the roof of the tunnel, reached by stacking a pile of flat rocks and hooking down a rope with a stick. Anyone could have got in. The split in the cave roof was far from obvious but Authun wouldn't have trusted the entrance to stay hidden if the caves had been his refuge. It would only take a hunch from a curious warrior and the enemy would be in. Why had he gone up the Troll Wall when this was available just on the other side?

Authun wondered if he was heading into a trap. He reminded himself that no one coming to those caves would see anything the witches didn't want him to see. So, were they

402

allowing him in? He had looked at the uncollected sacrifices at the entrance – bottles and pots, anything that couldn't be taken by animals. Were the witches even there?

Still, he wasn't scared. Certain of death and welcoming it, there was no room for terror in his life. So the bodies of the boys, the rat-eaten corpses of the girls, the puffy flesh of the drowned women in the ponds and the rotting, blackened faces of those who hung by ropes from spars of rock only caused him the discomfort of remembering how many people he had sent to similar fates.

The constriction of the tunnels, however, was another matter. Authun was not afraid of death but he had no desire to suffocate, his own arms sealing his mouth and nose in a tight gullet of rock. Some of the passages were scarcely wider than his head and he had to squirm and wriggle his way through. He began to see why this entrance was not so well guarded as the others on the Troll Wall side of the caves. An enemy coming in this way would be hugely vulnerable. A warrior can't fight with his arms pinned above his head. So the route was easy in some ways but at the same time very tricky, even without the witches sending their nightmares stalking through the passageways.

As he descended he became more and more sure the witches were dead. How could he have held on to his sanity so long in those tunnels if they hadn't been? What had killed them? They rested by the light of a candle by an underground pool. The pool caught the reflection of the ceiling in the candlelight, turning it into a shimmering golden disc. He looked at Saitada. Had this woman become a witch? Was she now their servant and was he there to kill whatever had caused so many deaths in the tunnels? He put the thoughts aside. They were no good to him. He would just concentrate on what he would do. Act, as always, do and kill until he himself was killed. He wanted no more murders, but when the fight presented itself he would not shirk from it. He knew no other way.

After what he thought must have been a day in the caves

he became aware of a soft glow answering the light of their candle from down the tunnel. He looked at the woman and put his hand to his sword. She shook her head, which he took for an assurance of safety.

Drawing quietly closer he realised that the light was a reflection of their own candle from a mass of gold. Weapons, armour, rings and jewels were piled to the ceiling like a miser's dream. It was said the witches had collected tribute and plunder for a thousand years. It seemed too short a time to collect such a hoard.

'How many have died to reach here?' he said, as much to himself as to the woman, and then almost laughed. For most of his life he would have rejoiced in this, taken all he could and returned in glory. Not now. He hardly understood the purpose of riches any more. Jewels were called the tears of Freya, after the goddess who was said to weep them. He had thought it just a story for winter. But now he saw that tears and precious things have their fates tightly bound.

He touched a byrnie and a shield. Both were dull with age but very finely made and in good repair. The woman shook her head. She meant, he thought, that he would not need them for the battle he was to face. Something though – intuition or just the desire to die as he had lived, in war gear – came over him. In all his lonely meditations and nightmares of regret, some simple warrior's habits had proved unshakeable. In an uncertain situation he would take whatever advantage he could. He put on the byrnie, found a gilded iron helmet to fit him and took up a splendid shield that bore the sign not of the wolf but of the raven. Odin's sign.

Saitada set her candle on the floor, sat on the most comfortable stone she could find and watched him dress. She said that word again under her breath: 'Death.'

There was movement in the mouth of a tunnel. Authun's sword was out, liquid in the candlelight. There was another movement in a tunnel to his left. Then she was in front of him, not three paces away. It was a girl, a wasted and haggard child, dressed in a long and bloody white shift. In her hand was a broken spear shaft, the end burned in a fire until it was a wicked tapering shard, a blackened needle.

Authun had only ever seen her face twice before and then only in glimpses. But he recognised her – she was thinner and madder and starved and white but he recognised her. The necklace at her throat burned with all the colours of war. She was the witch queen.

'Lady?' said Authun.

'Death,' said Saitada, pointing to the child.

The candle went out. There was a noise from somewhere deep in the caves. It spoke to Authun's body rather than his mind, pulling the skin into bumps on his arms and neck, drying his mouth and making his heart pump. It was fear given sound – the howl of a wolf.

The witch spoke. Her voice was hardly audible, cracked and weak. 'Odin?'

Saitada struck a flint, and Authun saw in the flash that the queen was gone. Saitada struck again but could not make the tinder catch.

'Odin?'

Saitada struck a third time and the witch was on him, driving the spear towards his head, but Authun caught it in one hand. The witch had no strength in her child's arms. Authun reversed the thrust and smashed the butt of the spear into her eye. She shrieked and it was dark again.

Authun couldn't understand why she had thought to attack him this way. She could boil a sleeping man's brains five days' travel away, why fight him like this? Then he thought of the amulet at his neck. Protection against magic was, after all, what they were for.

'Get me light, girl! Strike that flint!'

Then something hit him like an avalanche.

53   The Battle in the Hoard Cave

Feileg had cursed himself for his inability to dive into the tunnel. It wasn't a matter of bravery; he simply couldn't do it, like he couldn't fly. His limbs wouldn't obey his commands: his attempts to push himself down into the pool only met with choking frustration.

Adisla had gone and his mind was in a terrible confusion. All he wanted had been his in the fleeting moment of her kiss. He wished that she could have just walked with him off that mountain and gone to his home in the hills instead of plunging into the pool. She had gone to meet the witches, to rescue the prince. He had no other course of action. He loved her, so he had to help her.

He waited for her to come back. It got dark. When it became light, he tried again. Useless. His body would not do as he told it.

He searched the mountain for an entrance in increasing desperation. In a bowl of rock above a dizzying drop there was a cave that looked promising – long and narrow with sacrifices at the mouth – but when he went inside there was the smell of humans but no sign of an entrance. Besides, the ceiling looked dangerously split. He thought it might fall at any instant, so he went back outside. He ran all over the mountain, looking for anything that resembled a way in. There was no alternative, he decided, he would have to try the Wall. He knew the entrances there were easier to spot but also that they were almost impossible to get to.

He climbed to the top of the great cliff, up to a knife-edge ridge on which strange tall outcrops of rocks like the fingers of a monstrous hand stretching for the sky loomed above him. These were the trolls that gave the Wall its name – rumoured to have been turned to stone looking at the beauty of the sunrise. He looked out over the land. He was so high up that it would take him, he thought, twenty heartbeats to hit the ground if he fell. Clouds drifted by beneath him. The route he had followed to reach this point was threatening enough; the overhang below him was almost unimaginable. But he had to try. He lowered himself, kicking his legs into the vast space below him, his feet feeling for a shelf, a hold. But, as in the pool, his body took over and he pulled himself up. He sat in the freezing wind on the edge of the Wall, hating himself for his cowardice. Then he saw something down on the plain.

There were two travellers far below. He would have ignored them, but then he heard something he had never heard before. It was a howl of pain, a thin blade of sound that seemed to quiver, not in the air but in his head. He knew who it was – Adisla, calling to him to help her. He saw a vision of that jagged rune on the sorcerer's stone and felt a pull like a rip tide impelling him on. Feileg, to whom the language of the wolves was as plain as speaking, knew what the howl had said: 'I am in agony.'

He *had* to get to her. Perhaps the travellers below would know an entrance to the caves. It was an idea born of desperation rather than good sense.

He watched them move around the Wall, and when he was sure of their route along a ravine he set off to meet them. Then doubts crept in. How long had he haunted these lands as a wolf, smashing and tearing and taking what he wanted? His experiences since the prince had captured him had made him forget who he was. These people would see him as a wild animal and very likely flee. He decided to follow them at a distance and watch for a time before approaching. Still, he would have to be quick. He descended the mountain in swift silent leaps.

He followed them from the top of the ravine around to the back of the mountain. At first he thought they were beggars. The woman was dressed in rags and the man no better. Only

407

the curved sword that the man carried in his hands said that they were people of a different station altogether. Feileg, who had no real appreciation of gold or jewellery, was still dazzled by the magnificence of the scabbard, catching the winter sun in white flashes.

He decided to wait until night, take the man's sword while he was sleeping, then he could bargain it back for information. But they did not stop to make camp, travelling on as the sun weakened to a smoky dusk. Eventually they came to the long cave that Feileg had already inspected. He followed them inside using all his hunter's stealth and watched as the woman piled flat slabs one on top of another. Then she reached up with a stick and fished something from the crack in the cave's ceiling. It was a knotted rope and she began to climb it.

Feileg felt like running forward, pulling her out of the way and climbing the rope into the dark, but had noticed the bearing of the white-haired man. He was old but he was strong. The wolfman was confident he could take him in a fight but saw no point. And the woman? Feileg knew the sisters never left the darkness so she wasn't a witch. However, she seemed to know the caves and might lead him where he needed to go.

So he watched. The man held a candle while she climbed, then she lit another at the top and he went up. The rope was then pulled up and the light faded. Feileg gave it as little time as he dared, grabbed the stick and leaped up onto the pile of rocks. He poked around above him with the stick until he snagged the rope and tugged it free. Then he pulled himself up into the dark. Something else was under his hand. It was a pole and he guessed it would be used to knock over the pile of rocks and cover the tracks of anyone entering the cave. He left it where it was.

After a steep climb he came to where the rope was fastened. Here, the fissure sloped into a level tunnel. There was no light at first, but a wolf is a creature of smell, not sight. The human musk and the fish stink of the candle led him on until, faintly, he saw a glow.

He followed the trail down through the tunnels and the cracks, trusting to the scents when he couldn't see a light. Feileg knew his chances of finding Adisla in that labyrinth were very small indeed but these two were his only hope. He didn't know where they were going but they were going *somewhere* and they had light. That had to be better than crawling purposely through the dark.

As he descended, Feileg began to feel there was something else in the darkness, something that didn't wish him well. He had no wolfstone to protect him, no gift from a god to keep him safe. The dark seemed like an animal itself, one that rubbed against him, licked his flesh, knew him even. Something, Feileg sensed, was crawling over his mind, sniffing at his thoughts, marking them with its own scent. The witch, he could tell, knew he was there.

On instinct, he tried to lose himself, to cut away that human part, to just be a wolf hunting in the dark, as Kveld Ulf had taught him to be. He felt the pressure in his head lift and move away. She had gone, but he knew that to get what Adisla wanted — to bring back the prince — he would have to confront the witch face to face. Even at a distance, her presence had seemed like a spider creeping over his brain.

Feileg was sweating now. The candlelight had stopped moving forwards. As he drew nearer it became stronger, its glow more golden. He edged his way to a corner and looked round.

The old man with the sword was standing in front of what seemed to be a hill of gold. The treasure was piled from the floor to the ceiling of the cavern, and the chamber was not low. The man had put on a byrnie and a helmet and was holding a shield that seemed more for show than war. Feileg looked at the way the man stood in his war gear, the confidence that seemed to shine from him. He knew this would be no easy opponent, no merchant's bodyguard to be smashed and dashed.

In front of the old warrior was a child, a haggard girl in a dirty bloody shift, carrying a broken spear shaft.

Then the light had gone. In the flash of a flint being struck Feileg saw the man and his companion, but the girl had vanished. Another flash. And another, and the girl was there, stabbing at the warrior with her spear shaft. Feileg saw her fall and then it was dark again.

And Feileg knew. The ragged little girl was the witch and the only hope for the prince Adisla loved. If the warrior was attacking her, that made him his enemy. It was flat dark but Feileg could hear the man breathing, smell his sweat, hear the movement of the rings on the byrnie.

Quiet as a wolf over snow, he sped towards him and struck.

Anyone Feileg had ever faced had been put down by his first attack, and Authun was no different. The king went sprawling to the floor with Feileg on top of him, but even as he hit Authun, Feileg knew he was in a fight. There was no fatal breath of shock for the king, no moment where he needed to work out what had happened to him and adjust. In an instant he had locked out the arm Feileg had put to his throat, driven into the elbow joint with the heel of his hand and forced the wolfman off him, twisting to stand as he did so. All that without sight.

If Feileg had been a less flexible man, Authun would have had him at his mercy, using his arm to pinion him through the shoulder to the floor. Instead, Feileg rolled away and broke Authun's grip, but now the momentum of the fight had changed. Authun was standing, Feileg was on the floor, barrel-rolling away from him.

Feileg felt the king's shin in his side as Authun kept pace with him. The warrior was keeping contact with him so as not to lose him in the dark. Feileg flipped back and heard the sword cut the air.

Feileg was now on his feet. The king's byrnie jingled like a reindeer sled as he moved and told Feileg exactly where he was. The wolfman sprang again. The king could not see him but heard him exhale as he leaped. Authun crouched behind his shield to offer a smaller target and the wolfman went over his head, falling badly on the uneven floor.

There was a mournful sound from far away, like the mountain wind, though they were too far underground to be able to hear that.

All the air had been driven out of Feileg's lungs by his fall, and Authun moved towards him, drawn by the sound of his panting.

The noise again. It couldn't be wind, not here. And it sounded more animal. Authun struck into the darkness but his sword sparked on the floor. There was another flash. Saitada was trying desperately to light a candle. In the instant of light he saw the wolfman about to spring.

Feileg hit him again, but Authun blocked with his shield and bounced him aside. Authun could sense his man was tiring. He wished he had a shorter weapon than the Moonsword with him. If he let the wolfman close with him, he could finish him at close range with a knife.

The flint hit steel once more and Authun caught a glimpse of his opponent. It was enough. The Moonsword sliced out and caught the advancing Feileg across the thigh. The wolfman screamed as he crashed into Authun. The king battered him down with his shield. Feileg was howling, but a deeper sound stopped Authun dead — a rumbling snarl like a rock slide. It was a very large animal, probably a bear, and it was close. The noise distracted the king and the wolfman rolled away.

Feileg couldn't stand — that much was clear to Authun, who could hear him dragging himself away in the dark. With another enemy so close, Authun couldn't risk grubbing about to finish him off, but he knew men in battle could get up from terrible wounds and Feileg's groans gave him away. However, the wounded wolfman was useful to the king. If there was a bear in the cave it would be drawn to the coughing and groaning man on the floor. Then Authun would know where both his opponents were.

Finally, Saitada had the candle lit.

The wolfman was trying to get up while behind him floated two points of green light. When Authun's eyes adjusted, he felt himself shiver.

It was a wolf, but bigger than any wolf he had ever seen. It was bigger than any man, half again bigger than any white bear. How had it got into the caves? The tunnels were surely too narrow. The creature snapped its jaws and looked at him, coughing and hacking.

'Fa ... fath ...' If Authun had not known better he would have said the beast was trying to speak.

He made himself loosen his grip on the Moonsword, shook the tension from his limbs, breathed out and walked towards the wolf. To his right Authun noticed the wolfman crawling away. Let him go, he thought. He would be dead from loss of blood before long, and even if he survived wouldn't be back to attack him any time soon. The fury that allows a man to forget mortal wounds is a short-lived thing, Authun knew.

Five paces from the creature he stopped. He was struck that its front right limb was more like a human arm than the foreleg of a wolf but most of all he noticed its teeth – each as big as a boat nail.

The king smiled. This was a rare death, he thought, one worthy of the tales of the skalds, but there was only the scarred woman there to witness it. He almost wished he hadn't mortally wounded his previous opponent. His old friend Varrin would have loved to have died fighting such a monster, he thought. The face of the drowned man came into his mind again. He had killed him, and for what? What had been made by his ambition, what future secured, what treasures won?

The beast hacked and coughed again. Was it trying to speak? It didn't matter. Authun had wanted death and here was his perfect enemy – the opponent who could not be pitied, the monster, the useful fiend who could be struck without compunction.

Authun raised the Moonsword. It was as if the animal caught his intent the instant it arose in the king. It snarled forward in a blur, knocking him to the floor. The byrnie saved his back on the rough stone but the wind was knocked from him.

Authun could not let that concern him.

Feileg bit down his agony and watched in the flickering candlelight as the king rolled away from the beast's jaws, wriggling underneath it to slash up with his sword. The wolf was cut, its blood splashing onto Authun's face.

The creature howled and leaped away from Authun but did not take long to recover. It charged again, but this time swiped at the king's sword arm with its man-like arm. Authun had been ready to duck the charge but the attack on his weapon surprised him. He'd expect that from a man but not an animal. There was a clatter as the Moonsword went flashing across the cave. For the first time in his life Authun had been disarmed in battle.

Now the fight really started, the wolf driving into the king with tooth and claw, the king turning and ducking, dodging and jumping and – when that failed – catching the attacks on his shield.

Even through his pain Feileg had to admire the old warrior. Though empty-handed and fighting such an enemy, he didn't lose his head. All the time, as he slipped past the creature's attacks or rolled and twisted away, he was working his way towards where his sword lay. Feileg had to wonder why the warrior's companion didn't help him. The woman just sat in the candle glow, calm as if she was listening to a story by the fire.

The king was getting close to his sword. He was unharmed, though the animal had torn holes in his byrnie and ripped his shield to splinters. Feileg summoned his strength and crawled forward. The battle was almost on top of him, the old warrior crouching to feel for his sword. Feileg put his hand on the Moonsword, picked it up and dragged himself away into the shadows.

Authun did not pause; he simply readjusted his retreat, giving ground with each one of the wolf's attacks, back towards the hoard of gold and the weapons that lay within it.

Feileg pulled himself to his feet and limped towards the nearest tunnel. Pushing himself along the wall of the passage he made his way into the darkness, the sounds of the fight fading in his ears. He felt his way down and down. The tunnel seemed endless but he couldn't afford to rest. He drove himself on, away from the old warrior, away from the teeth of the wolf, and after some time had the sense that he was in a larger cave.

Then he heard something, a whimper. It was some distance away, and for a moment he dared to think it was Adisla. He ran his hand across the wall of the cave and limped on, clutching his wounded thigh with one hand, the Moonsword pressed under his other arm. The wall opened into another corridor. It was small, mercifully small, not much wider than a man. The beast would not be able to get down there. From below he heard the voice again.

'Help me.' His stomach leaped. It *was* Adisla.

He pushed himself on, the going terribly hard on the uneven floor.

'Help me!' The voice was louder now. Yes, no mistake, it was her.

Around a curve in the tunnel he could see a light.

54 Tracking

The creature was hungry. The need to eat saturated his mind as the first light appeared like the nimbus of the sun from behind a rain cloud at the edge of the great slab that sealed him in. But he had not lost his animal caution and watched from the darkness to see what it was that had freed him. Wolves do not rush in until they know the odds, and the creature, who only had a weak notion of his invulnerability, wanted to see his opponents before striking.

But then they had come down into the pit and other beast feelings had taken over. If an animal stays somewhere long enough, it regards that place as its den. The creature felt threatened.

He heard words he didn't really understand: 'Let me go first. This treasure may be delicate and I should assess how best to move it.'

'We are taking everything from this tomb, merchant. Do not make me leave your body in payment.'

There was no idea of revenge in the wolf's brain as he snapped off Bodvar Bjarki's head, only hunger.

There was only hunger too as he watched Veles trying in vain to climb the rope out of the pit. He closed on him, ripped open his back with a single bite, gulped down a gob of meat, pawed him to the floor and tore away the flesh from his belly, sucking on his sweet entrails as the merchant screamed.

Vali might have been pleased to see Veles suffer for what he had done to him, or might have thought that it was too strong a punishment for the crime he had committed, but he was scarcely there inside the wolf to have feelings either way. He was not one thing any more; he was a crowd, a mob, each of its members screaming for attention. The sorcerer, the Whale

People, the family of reindeer hunters, the pirate Danes were all in him, or rather he *was* them, his consciousness a wild jumble of digested thoughts and personalities. His mind was like a marketplace, each bidder yabbering to stake his claim. Above them all though was the keening voice of the wolf, providing direction, impelling his body to action.

Panic flooded down from above. Men were scrambling to replace the great slab of rock that had sealed him in, but no one could shift it. They gave up and ran.

The wolf was out of the pit in a bound. There were things in his way, things that yelled and beat at him, so he swept them aside, cracked them in his jaws, allowed their juices and ichors to calm the hunger of his long incarceration.

When they were all dead, he lay down, heavy with what he had eaten, his brain torpid, his body growing as it put its meal to work under the frozen moon and the green fire skies of the winter's unyielding dark.

He was not Vali. His body was like a twisted musical instrument and the prince was a tune it could play, but it did not then, nor for a while, not until he heard her cry the agonised howl that called him to life inside the beast.

In the lowest cave of the Troll Wall it appeared to Adisla that she lay on a wonderful bed of straw covered with luxurious furs. She was back in her house. Her mother was there and Barth the Dane, Manni and all her brothers. The calm that had come down upon her with the lady's presence seemed like the snugness of her bed on a winter's morning.

Adisla knew the witch queen wanted her to call Vali. Adisla spoke his name. The witch looked into her eyes and stroked her hair. She wanted Adisla to repeat the name, she could tell, and she did so gladly after all the lady's kindnesses.

The witch queen looked down at Adisla and nodded to herself. She had been trying to work through the girl, to channel Adisla's tender thoughts in order to send them to the wolf and summon him. That, it appeared, was not going to work.

Gullveig allowed the barbed rune to surface in her mind. It made her shiver. Its presence felt almost toxic, as if she held it too long it would burn her, destroy her even. Then she sent it to the mind of the girl before her.

Adisla screamed as her illusion fell away. She was not in her bed at all; there was no house, no loving family around her. She was pinioned on a narrow wedge of sharp stones at the end of a tapering cave. The stones cut her and the weird light of oil lamps cast shadows that seemed like long cruel fingers, reaching out to tear her flesh. She was in agony.

As the rune spilled from the witch's mind, Adisla saw what was intended. She saw visions of death – hers and Vali's, Feileg's and Bragi's, in that life and in others, stretching away into time. And she saw what the witch herself didn't see. She saw Gullveig's true name, and that knowledge was more terrible than the bonds that tied her down, more terrible than the sharp rocks that cut her, more terrible even than Vali, transformed and murderous. Adisla knew that the lady wanted her to call Vali, and now she knew why.

'I will not,' she said.

Someone came into view. It wasn't the lady, but a pale and terrible child with an aged face. The witch queen opened her mind and it was as if all the ghosts and dreads that Adisla carried with her rose up to engulf her and drag her down. She saw her mother dying, Manni dead at the door, Vali slavering and grunting in that pit. Desperate to stop these nightmares swamping her, Adisla needed something to cling to, to blot out the vile images. The rune, shimmering and twisting in front of her, was her salvation, she thought, though she didn't know where that idea came from. She stared into it, focused on it and knew in an instant that she had made a terrible mistake. A blinding white light burst onto her eyes as the rune seemed to sear into her like a branding iron burning into her mind.

A howl burst from her lips and from her soul. More than a sound, it was a magical emanation. Vali, sleeping as a wolf on the rock, heard it as the witch intended and understood what it meant. It shook him from the fug of digestion. He stood upright on his back legs and looked to the south-west.

Feileg, watching Authun and Saitada from the top of the Troll Wall, sensed it too at the precise moment he decided to follow the travellers around the mountain.

The witch was pleased. Her magic couldn't call the wolf any more, he was too powerful, but the magic the wolf had weaved himself out of his connection to this girl was enough. He would come, she thought, to do her bidding.

On the island Adisla and all she had meant to him came to the front of Vali's thoughts. She was in danger, he knew, and he needed to go to her. The sea channel between the island and the land was nothing to him, the wide plains and the mountain passes were nothing, nor fjords or swamps, valleys or cliffs. He took them all in devouring bounds, eating the distance between him and the girl, racing to the source of her cry at a pace no human, no horse, not even a bird could hope to match.

The resonance of her agony was his guide, a stream he could follow to its source. The frozen night of the far north melted into a pale dawn; farmsteads and sleigh trains flashed by; he flickered through forests, scattered herds of reindeer on wide plains, dropped from mountain peaks like a falling star and flew on towards his target as a warp in the light.

The caves slowed him. He forced his body down through the tunnels, only the power of his will strong enough to push him through. He didn't think where he was going; Adisla's scream called him on. In the shove and squeeze of his descent Vali came to himself, although it no longer seemed unusual to him that he had the form of a massive wolf, nor that the caves glittered with a million scents. His memories came back to him but they only increased his pain. The woman he loved was suffering terribly and the only meaning of his life was to find her and take her agony away.

Then he was standing before his father, Authun, in a cave full of gold. The king was terrible in his war gear. Vali tried to tell him that Adisla was in danger. He knew that his father would not understand his concern for a farm girl but he wanted to implore him to put that aside and help him. Then Authun had struck at him, and it was as if Vali was an unwilling passenger in his own body, his protests useless as the wolf drove forward to attack.

Again the voices crowded in on him, again the dreadful howl of the wolf echoed through his head, a sound that he knew was as much part of him as his love for Adisla. He was losing his way, surrendering to the fury of the animal he had become. Authun was down, his shield shattered, his weapon gone and the wolf was on top of him, Vali fading away like a drowsy rider on a hot day surrendering direction to his horse.

'Help me.' It was her voice.

Authun was hitting him with something. He felt nothing.

'Help me.'

Vali was reaching out, trying to make the wolf's body answer her call.

'Help me!'

The wolf paused its attack and stood panting over the old warrior. Authun didn't stay still. He rolled from under the wolf and made for the hoard pile, pulled out a jewelled sword and spun to strike at the animal's back, plunging the weapon down with two hands.

The sword dug into the wolf's spine and snapped, Vali felt nothing. He sent Authun sprawling to the floor with a back-handed blow from his forelimb.

'Help me!' Finally Vali had control over his movements. He broke from the combat and made his way down the passage following Adisla's call.

55 Fenrisulfr

Feileg was sick with the pain now and had to pause. After four breaths he limped on again. There was the smell of fish oil. Someone had a lamp down there. Yes, he could see the glow. He pressed on towards the light, the tunnel narrowing to a crack. He breathed in and slid sideways through.

The cave was no bigger than the inside of a longhouse, the ceiling falling to the floor at one end and forming a wedge of jagged rocks like an animal's jaws. Adisla was there, lying bound on the sharp stones, soaked in blood. Feileg's heart leaped as he saw her.

The witch, her face a mask of blood from a ruined eye, was standing staring vacantly into space, a broken spear shaft in her hand. She had a piece of rope around her neck, tied with an elaborate knot at the front. Feileg recognised it as a hangman's noose, Odin's symbol. The wolfman was terrified of the magical child, appalled by what had happened to Adisla, but he forced himself to speak.

'Lady,' said Feileg, speaking to the witch but limping as fast as he could to Adisla, 'we are on an errand of great importance. A friend is bewitched and has taken the shape of a wolf. He is here, in the tunnels. We need you to use your arts to cure him. I have gold and can pay.'

Adisla was shaking and Feileg could see she had lost a lot of blood. She was tied down by leather cords secured to rusty pins in the rock. Feileg used the Moonsword to cut them. Then he held her to him and kissed her on the forehead. She was weak, scarcely able to move but she was saying something. Feileg bent his ear to her mouth.

'I have seen her mind,' she said, 'I have seen her mind. Run. Feileg, run.'

Feileg shook his head.

'I couldn't run if I wanted to, and I do not want to,' he said. 'I will stay here with you. It'll be all right. She will do what we ask, won't you, lady?'

Still the witch said nothing. There was a thump from the top of the tunnel.

'She put me to those rocks, Feileg. I have been cruelly treated.'

'Then she will make amends or she will die. She will cure him.'

'No, you don't understand.'

'She is all we have. We must make her do as we ask.'

'No Feileg, no.' Adisla was shaking and sobbing.

The wolf, Adisla sensed, was an expression of some huge and terrible magic. Gullveig imagined herself as manipulating this force, but Adisla, allowed into the web of the witch queen's mind, had seen with saner eyes. Something that was part of Gullveig but – at the same time – external to her and much more powerful was bending her to its own will. The thing, whatever it was, felt cold and hungry. It looked for death in the jaws of the wolf, and that death was linked to Adisla's own and to those of Feileg and Vali, again and again in an endless cycle of rebirth and slaughter, all that carnage expressed by the pulsing of that rune.

'He will kill her again and again, for ever and ever, and us too. I have been in her mind; I have seen this thing happen. You must kill her before he does. He will act out the prophecy and we will be doomed.'

'I will not allow him to kill her,' said Feileg.

'How can you stop him?'

'This sword cuts him,' said Feileg. 'I will drive him off. No wolf wants to bleed.'

He tried to sound confident, but he put more faith in the witch's powers than he did in his own sword skills.

There was another thump, closer now, and a terrible howl. The witch turned her head in its direction. The tunnel was too narrow, Feileg was sure, for the wolf to get through. That would allow the witch to work safe from its jaws.

Feileg looked down at Adisla. 'You will have your prince back,' he said.

'No,' she said. 'No. I have seen. I have seen. Kill her, Feileg, kill her before it is too late. We can fight a monster; you cannot fight a god.'

'She is our salvation.'

'She is our death, eternally and again and again, you and me, Bragi and more, torture and horror without end. Always she looks for death in the jaws of the wolf. Kill her. Kill her before he does.'

'Adisla, my love,' he said, 'the wolf is here. He has come. He could keep us in here for ever. I am no swordsman, and already a mighty warrior, a man brought up to arms from his earliest years, has proved no match for him. The witch must help him. Can you speak to him again? Can you calm him and allow her to work her magic on him?'

'He is death, always death. He was a breath from killing me in the north. Do not bring him here, Feileg, do not bring him.'

'He is here,' said Feileg.

Adisla gave way to terror and just shook in his arms.

The noise was still closer, a deep and angry growling but coupled with something else. Feileg, who had eaten countless times with his wolf brothers, recognised it. It was the sound of tearing flesh, of joints coming apart, of bones being pulverised. And then there was a third sound, an occasional pitiful whine, like a wolf caught in a hunter's trap. The monster was wounded.

'She will save us or she will die.'

'If she dies by his teeth then we are lost. It is what she wants. Strike at her, Feileg, strike at her.' Adisla was pulling at his shoulders. She was raving, thought Feileg, driven mad by what she had endured.

The witch was still staring ahead, the spear shaft raised.

Feileg wondered if she meant to strike Adisla with it but couldn't summon the will. Another thump, much closer, and with it that grizzling note of agony. Feileg stumbled as best he could back to the tunnel.

There was a wave of breath, hot and fetid, which hit him like a fist, driving him back into the cave. The snapping jaws of the beast were no more than three paces from him. It was forcing its way through, so desperate it was smashing its own body in the attempt.

This was Feileg's chance to kill the beast. It was momentarily stuck, its back legs scrabbling at the ground, its shoulders crunching and cracking in the narrow gap, its head twisting and straining forward. He raised the Moonsword but could not strike. His mind went back to the escape from the beach, to the water. Vali had saved his life. It was more than that though. The prince had been his double, the person he could have been but for a twist of the Norns' thread, and now he felt bound to him.

He fell back. 'Use your magic, witch,' he said, gesturing to the tunnel. 'Use your magic or I will kill you both.'

Still the witch said nothing, did nothing. He raised the Moonsword above his head as if to hit her but even then she didn't move, just stood holding that spear as if about to strike at an unseen enemy.

Feileg turned to Adisla. 'When the wolf gets into the chamber, I will occupy it. You circle around and get out into the tunnel. It will be stuck in here for a time. If you can speak to him then do. After that she will cure him or she will die.'

'Kill her, kill her.'

There was no more time. The wolf had made it and smacked onto the floor like a fish onto a slab. It seemed boneless, almost: only its back legs were moving and one of them seemed dislocated at a terrible angle.

'Go!' said Feileg. 'Go!' He pulled Adisla to her feet.

She swayed and would have fallen, but Feileg, from somewhere, found the strength to support her, taking her arm over his shoulder and plunging towards the tunnel. They made it only a few paces before collapsing.

The wolf was writhing like a hooked eel on the floor of the cave, the witch still immobile with that spear in her hands.

'Death and agony, always and for eternity,' said Adisla.

Feileg shook his head. 'This, for eternity,' he said and hugged her to him. 'The love you sent to me when we parted at the pool, the love we share now. Go, Adisla, and go with that love.'

He looked at the wolf. Its body was reforming. There was a sound like someone cracking a joint of mutton and the shoulders became recognisable again. It stretched out its forelegs and they too snapped back into shape.

'You'll die.'

'I am not afraid to die. I am more afraid to live if I cannot save you. Go. Go! You once risked your life by setting me free, now I do the same for you. Go!'

The wolf breathed in and there was a tearing noise as its lungs pushed its ribs back into position.

Adisla squeezed his hand and kissed it.

'Leave here,' she said.

' I will come back to you. I vow it.' He shoved her into the tunnel.

'Feileg!' Adisla's arms stretched after him, but he had gone back and she had no strength to move.

The wolf had got to its feet, complete and whole. In the small cave Feileg realised just how big the animal was, its green eyes the size of shield bosses and its teeth a hand span each. It towered over Feileg and the skinny body of the witch. It looked at Adisla in the mouth of the tunnel, at the torture rocks and at the witch. Then it fixed the witch queen with a hard stare and drew back its teeth. She was unmoved, just staring ahead with that spear raised.

Feileg saw what he needed to do. He had hated Vali, resented him for tying him and for being loved by Adisla. But hadn't it all been for the best? Without Vali he would have never known what it was like to be loved, to feel a kiss returned or see an affectionate look in a woman's eye. His destiny had been tied to that of the prince, and though it would have been simpler to cut him where he stood, fighting was not the way forward. He'd had enough of that.

Feileg put down the Moonsword at the monster's feet.

'Prince,' he said, 'come back to yourself.'

The wolf hacked and coughed and words began to form. 'I am here ... I am here ... I am known to you ... I am ...'

It seemed to be having difficulty framing its thoughts.

Feileg spoke. 'This lady, this child, she is your cure. Bow down before her and do as she bids. Her magic is famous in all known lands. Let her help you, Vali. For the love you have known. For Adisla, relent.'

The wolf lowered its head and bowed down before the witch queen.

For the first time Feileg saw the terrible child move. Her head turned towards him and her gaze met his. Feileg felt those spider claws scuttle across his brain again as a rush of thoughts and sensations. He saw what a fool he had been. The wolf was all that was standing between him and what he wanted. With Vali gone, Adisla was his, her past cut away, her future free. He thought of his disgust at seeing the prince gnawing at those bodies on the ship, Vali's slaying of the brave Bragi, his murder of the hunters. Why should he be cured? He had forfeited that right with his murders.

Feileg took up the Moonsword and struck.

Adisla screamed as the bright arc of the sword flashed through the air to sink into the animal's flank, but the blow was inexpert and poor. The wolf rounded on Feileg, driving its teeth into him, ripping away the flesh from his side and smashing him to the floor. The animal threw back its head, opened its jaws and swallowed the meat down. Adisla was too weak to move.

The witch smiled. The next stage was now plain. It was more than a spell though; it was an expression of something eternal, powerful and undeniable – like a rune, she thought. Yes, a rune. She stroked the piece of leather with the thumb of one hand while the other still held the spear shaft.

The wolf snarled, muscles bubbling on its body as its brother's blood dripped from its lips. It was transforming, not so much physically this time, but magically, the witch could sense. That was the key, as the rune Loki had given her had shown – the two brothers becoming one. It was all in place, all ready for the final stage.

The witch reversed the spear shaft, wedged the butt on the floor and leaped forward, impaling herself so that the point came out of her back.

To Adisla, reality seemed to fall apart.

56 The Dead

The witch was a little girl again, lost in her first memories. What were her first memories? The dark and the cold, the faces of the women smeared with their ghost paint, the weak light of torches and the damp smell of the caves.

> *They say with spells in tunnels dark*
> *As a witch with charms did you work*
> *And in witch's guise among men did you go*
> *Unmanly your soul must seem.*

The voice, the witch queen knew the voice. If was him. Who? Him. The mocker. She giggled. Yes, the mocker who was not so clever as he reckoned. Loki, the liar, who thought he could stand apart from the affairs of the gods and laugh. Not so. She had hooked him in and made him play his part too. Did he think those fetters just held his body and that his mind was free to wander the worlds as a man? No. He was snared and trapped and pinned and tethered, shackled and bound in every movement of his thoughts. She had done for him, that red-haired fellow, that night caller, that smirker and snickerer and enemy of death.

Had the women of the Troll Wall known who she was? They had made her their queen when she was six. She had all the runes, all of them, as no mortal ever had before. Had they known?

The truth had been obscured from the witch, but as the spear sent its energy of pain throughout her body, she saw what it was. She had killed them, every one, the girls, the boys and her sisters; she had slipped into their minds at night to whisper suicide; she had strangled, drowned and burned them in their trances and she hadn't done it to weaken herself, as an extreme measure to preserve the magical gains of the sisterhood, but because she was a fearful and jealous god who despised them for their power. She had hidden her intent from herself, afraid that her earthly form might rebel and try to avoid its fate. She touched the triple hanging knot at her neck. One thing hidden inside another inside another. She had thought she had hidden the wolf from himself to hide him from the god. In fact, she had hidden him from herself. Now the deception unravelled and she knew who the wolf had come for. It had come for her.

The spear seemed perfect, and the position she lay in on the floor perfect too, an illustration of the rune that had guided her. She had made a Wolfsangel of her own body.

She was everywhere, controlling; she sensed every mind on earth and could influence and touch them. In the moment of her greatest pain was her greatest magic.

She said her own name: 'Odin.' Her voice was cracked from years of disuse but the force of the god's will pushed the sound through the reluctant throat.

The body of the witch was bleeding, blood spreading in a wide pool. The wolf put down his head to lap at it. Adisla could not take her eyes off what was happening in the cavern.

The witch stood. She pulled the spear from her belly and looked at the wolf, who looked back at her.

'I have called you here to do this,' she said.

The wolf drew back its lips, exposing its teeth.

'It was this way, and it will be this way for ever,' said the witch, 'though it will never be easy for you, Fenrisulfr.'

To Adisla, it seemed that the caves no longer existed. She was at the centre of a huge blackened plain, where the shadows of ravens seemed to sweep over her, where smoke tinged the air and the cries of a dying battle could be heard.

The witch too was different. She was dressed not in that bloodstained shift but in man's armour. She was carrying a shield and in her hand was a cruel spear.

428

'I am Odin,' said the witch, 'all hater, all seer, lord of the hanged, lord of the slain, lord of madness, wisest in magic and battle bold.'

The wolf began to keen.

'Come, Fenrisulfr,' she said. 'You are the slaughter beast, my enemy and my accomplice.'

The wolf sprang as the witch forwarded her spear and stabbed. Then the wolf had her by the throat, shaking her body like a dog with a doll until her feet came off the floor. Adisla saw strange bright shapes scatter from the witch, some fizzing to the ground, some melting like snowflakes on warm land and others hitting her. A sense of flow and current seemed to go through her, then a frozen feeling as cold as the north wind, then something that stamped and steamed and breathed was in her mind. Finally, a smell like fresh grass came to her and a sense of warmth like a spring day. These were runes, she knew, each with its separate power. They told her so. They spoke.

The witch had dropped her spear and was beating uselessly against the wolf's muzzle. The animal did not relax its grip but tightened its jaws ever harder about her. Adisla saw rain showers, sunshine, a great tree that seemed to stretch up to the heavens, horses, a hearth. All the witch's magic shook from her in the animal's jaws.

Then the scene faded; the walls of the cavern returned. The wolf stood over the witch, guzzling her flesh.

Adisla felt the power of the runes and was restored and strong, all mysteries peeling away. Now, she knew, the magic was complete. The witch was Odin. The god had achieved what it wanted – death, its own and the queen's, which were the same thing. The knowledge-seeking god had deepened his knowledge of death by experiencing it. The runes it had shed as its earthly self died seemed to burn within Adisla, offering insight and unhappiness.

The wolf fed, consuming the witch's flesh in snaps and gulps. Then it shivered and coughed, shook, and finally lay down.

Adisla took up the Moonsword.

The wolf looked at her and spoke. 'Do not. I cannot command myself if you do.'

Adisla raised the weapon above her head. It felt unbalanced and unwieldy. Feileg had hit the creature with all his strength, and though he had cut it, he had not killed it. She would not stand a chance.

'I am ready for death,' she said.

'Not death,' said the creature. Its voice was low and rough, the human words forced through the wolf throat and mouth.

'Is it you, Vali?'

'Her death has freed my mind from the bloody swamp. It is me.'

'You are the worst of marvels,' she said.

'I am afflicted, but this was an ending. There are sorcerers. We can find them. There is a way back for me.'

'At what cost? How many have you killed, my love?'

'I do not want to kill any more.'

'A wolf kills, Vali.'

'No, Adisla, no.'

'I have seen the truth. Feileg was your brother and you killed him.'

The great animal bowed its head. 'The wolf killed him.'

'You are an enemy of the gods. I have seen. This is your purpose.'

'I will be myself again, Adisla.'

Adisla shook her head, tears cutting bright lines through the dirt on her face. 'But I will never be me. We have loved outside our station; we have offended the gods. I want to go from you, Vali. I want to die.'

'If you die, my love is so strong that it will call you back from the halls of the dead.'

'I will live again, Vali. When the god died, a sharp magic entered me and I am certain that it means rebirth. But I will live again without you. You are hated by the dead god.'

'I am part of his plan, as I saw on the field of the slain.

He needs me to fulfil his destiny. I am his enemy and his helper.'

'I want no part of that Vali.'

There was a noise from behind her, though she didn't turn to see its cause.

The wolf bent his head towards Adisla. 'I love you,' he said.

'Then forget me.' She lifted the Moonsword and stepped forward to strike him.

Vali felt himself shiver. He knew he could not help but respond to a threat, but he fought with all his will not to attack her. He understood who he was now – a god killer, reborn in a thousand lifetimes to hunt down Odin in all his incarnations. What room was there for love in that? What place even for himself against the vast magical forces that laid claim to him? He wanted her but he would kill her if she moved against him. As with so much in his life, he had no choice – the wolf would answer violence with violence returned a thousand times.

The sword was bright in her hand and the sound of anger was in his throat. He tried to frame the words. 'It isn't finished. We will live again, and I will never rest until I have found you and felt you love me as you once did.' But the words didn't come, just the blood-hungry snarl of the wolf.

Adisla closed her eyes and struck, but the blow didn't land. Authun was behind her and took the sword from her hand as it came down, stepping in front of her and pushing her back with the same movement.

Vali crouched. He looked at Adisla and knew that his dreams had been crushed by the jaws of the wolf. They had parted and all reason to live had gone from him. He was trapped for ever in an immortal body with no more company than his undying misery, linked more to the death lust of a demented god than to the woman he loved so much.

He saw the cruel sword in the hands of his father, felt the cut, still bleeding, in his side, no matter that all his other wounds had healed. The Norns, he thought, had paused their weaving for him, and it was up to him if he wanted them to start again.

He wanted it all to melt away, to be as it had been. To him Adisla was still the girl by the fjord, lying with him in the grass under the brilliant sun. But that was just a dream now, and he had travelled too far for it ever to be reality again.

He turned his eyes to the warrior. Authun returned his gaze.

At last, Vali forced out a word: 'Death?'

'Death,' said Authun.

The Moonsword flickered in the lamplight; the wolf's eyes and teeth flashed from the dark.

When it was done, the sword lay on the floor and the wolf was still.

Adisla came forward to look at the corpses, her body shivering and her mind numb. The strange woman with the ruined face was bending over Feileg, stroking his hair. Adisla went to her and looked at him. His blue eyes were open, looking up into nothing. There was a cruel wound in his side where the wolf had torn into his belly. He wasn't yet cold, but there was no breath in him and she knew for certain he was dead.

She took him in her arms and kissed him. In her mind she felt the shimmering presence of the rune that had seemed to burst with the scents of spring, to patter and babble like the sound of rain by a stream. Rebirth. She tried to send it to him, to make him whole again, but that art took years to learn and its cost was madness.

The woman with the ruined face was looking down at her, and Adisla understood what she said with her eyes: 'There is a way.'

The woman took up the lamp and left the cave. Adisla lifted Feileg in her arms. The runes seemed to shine inside her as she did so, and he did not feel heavy, nor was the entrance to the cave difficult to pass through. She followed the light up through the silent tunnels to where she could feel fresh air on her face. At the end of a broad cave, where a bright shard of light split the dark, the woman stopped and put her hand on Adisla's arm. Then she kissed Feileg on the forehead and touched Adisla's cheek.

Adisla walked on. She smelled wind, rain and the cold coming off the sea.

The shard of light grew. She walked on. At the mouth of the cave she looked out from a ledge near the top of the sheer Troll Wall, the ground far beneath her feet. A vast distance of land and sea lay before her, glorious in green and blue.

She kissed Feileg and held him to her.

'For hope,' she said and stepped into the light.

Saitada had followed to the ledge. From somewhere a wolf was howling. She understood what its voice was saying: 'I am here. Where are you?'

She stood listening for a while. Then she turned back to the caves.

57   Travellers' Tales

The hunters were three days into the forest looking for the wolves. There was a new pack in the area, they were sure. Sheep had been killed and even an old horse. They had taken their bows and their bait and headed into the trees, looking for signs of the animals. They had found nothing and were beginning to think they had wasted their time.

Then, as the long dusk of summer settled over the trees and the moon hung full in the sky, a traveller had come to their clearing, asking to share their fire. He was a strange-looking man, tall and pale with a shock of hair that was an almost unnatural red. Still, he had a skin of mead with him, and they let him eat with them in return for a few cups.

The stranger was good company and funny too, but as the brief night approached conversation turned to religion.

'I see you are men of the new faith,' said the traveller, gesturing to the cross one of the hunters wore at his neck.

'We are Christ's,' said a hunter. 'You are a man of the old ways, I can see.'

'I like to get as many gods as I can for my money,' said the stranger. 'It seems to me that all the Lords of Asgard give a better bargain for your sacrifices than the one god of the east.'

The men laughed.

'There are places in this land where you'd lose your tongue for saying that,' said one.

'Yes, the meek and merciful god can get in quite a bate when he's crossed, can't he?'

'It's no sin to defend the word of Christ,' said another man.

'Even if that word tells you that such a defence is sin?'

said the traveller. 'Are you recent converts or born into the faith?'

'This time five years ago I crawled on my belly before idols, then the way of grace was shown to me,' said the first hunter.

'Why did you change?' said the stranger.

'I was a slave and the church paid for my freedom,' he said. 'Christian men should not be the slaves of pagans. So says the holy father.'

'And you?'

'The same,' said the second hunter.

'It wasn't so for me,' said the third, who was quieter than the other two, and cleverer.

'What was it?'

'I felt the old gods were savage,' he said, 'and this new one offered a gentler way. He so loved the world that he sent his only son to die for our sins. It seemed a beautiful story, how the god took flesh as a man.'

'You never saw that with Thor, did you?' said the first hunter.

'I don't know about Thor,' said the stranger, 'but it is well known that the old gods often took flesh as men.'

'How so?'

'Have you not heard the stories? Of how the gods can split off a hair and grow it as a man, how their incarnations forget their godly origin and live as ordinary people. More of a challenge to be a god and not know it, I think, than to walk secure in your divinity as Jesus did.'

'Tell us one of these stories,' said the first hunter. 'I am in the mood for a tale and far enough away from the priests to not mind hearing one.'

So the stranger told them a story of how the old mad god Odin had a dream one day that he was a witch in the earthly realm. But the dreams of the gods are not like the dreams of men: they take flesh. The witch became powerful in magic and the god became jealous of his earthly self. So he sprinkled

435

prophetic visions on her, like seeds onto the field. Then the great god Loki had a dream too, of a beautiful slave girl who took a hot iron to her face to spite her owner. And Loki fell in love with his dream and came to earth to sire two children with her. One was the Fenris Wolf, who will eat the gods on the final day. The other was just a man. He gave them as gifts to a king and to the witch. A gift from Loki is no gift at all, though, and the wolf ate his brother and the witch before the king killed it with his dying blow, just as the wolf will kill Odin on the final day before it too is killed. In this way it is said that Loki and his children are both Odin's enemies and his helpers – they smooth the way to his destiny, though that destiny is death.

'It pleases the gods,' said the stranger, 'to see the stories of their fate acted out in the earthly realm. The wolf and Odin have fought down the centuries and will fight down those to come. It's easy to see where, if you know how to look.'

'So Judas was Jesus' helper, was he, by your reckoning?'

'Judas helped Jesus die for the sins of man, it is said,' said the traveller. 'Well, if that was against the will of God it wouldn't have happened, would it?'

'It was the will of the devil, working through Judas' hands,' said the first hunter.

'The will of the devil that all sins be washed away?' said the stranger. 'Then he is a strange devil indeed.'

The men laughed some more.

'We are luckier than you, sir,' said one. 'We only have to listen to what the priests tell us, not think about it.'

'If God sends us these wolves, then that's enough for us,' said the first hunter.

'You should ask Loki,' said the stranger. 'He is the one who sends wolves.'

'We don't pray to idols, sir,' said the second.

'No,' said the traveller. 'Then perhaps you should pray to your own god that Loki doesn't send you a wolf anyway, if the fate of the king and the witch are anything to go by.'

'That sort of wolf we can do without,' said the first.

The men sat by the fire and drank and talked until late. The stranger, who knew the woods well, told them of a cave a day west, following the north bank of the river.

'It is a famous wolf den,' he said, 'and though hunters take the animals again and again they always seem to return.'

'We will watch for it, sir.'

The next day the man was gone when the hunters awoke. They had no better plan than to follow his advice. It was nightfall again when they came to the caves, which were set in a small cliff a hundred paces from the river and five men's hcights above it.

The hunters looked around and were pleased to see wolf droppings along with some small evidence of kills. They camped nearby, sure that the wolves were out hunting and knowing that they would not return with men in the area. Nevertheless, the next day they tried the caves. It was a clear blue day and the moon was still visible, bright in the morning sky.

They made the short climb to the mouth of the biggest cave. The first hunter took a stone from the ground and threw it in while the other two stood ready with their bows. There was a noise from inside but neither loosed an arrow into the darkness. It wasn't impossible that a traveller was sleeping in there, and as good Christians none of the men wanted a murder on his hands. The hunter threw another stone. There was a scuffling sound and the hunter caught a glimpse of something. It was paler than any wolf. A pig maybe?

'Master wolf, come out, come out wherever you are.'

Nothing stirred. The hunter moved closer and his eyes began to adjust to the dark. He gasped when he saw what was inside the cave. It wasn't a pig or a wolf, but a boy, about six years old with a shock of dark hair. He was in a terrible state, thin and filthy with eyes that seemed too big for his head.

'It's a boy!' the hunter called over his shouldcr.

He took an apple from his bag. The boy shrank back into the cave.

'It's for you – go on.'

The boy didn't move.

'I'll have it then. See.'

The hunter bit into the fruit but the boy just retreated further.

The hunters were limited men but not insensitive. They could see that winning the boy's trust would be no quick job. As Christians, they thought they had a duty to help him – the parable of the good Samaritan had been impressed on them not two Sundays before – and they decided to wait until he learned to accept them. They would, they agreed, treat the boy as they would a nervous animal. So they stayed near but not too near, hunted for birds and small game, cooked them and left the food with water at the cave mouth. None of them could understand how he had lived. Pagans were known to abandon sickly children in the forest but this boy had proved anything but delicate.

Gradually the boy became less wary, and the hunters were able to get closer. The moon was a slim crescent by the time he finally took the hand that was offered him. They decided the best thing to do was to get him back to their village and hand him over to the priest.

It took four days to get out of the forest. The boy was dreadfully restless at night, throwing off the blanket the hunters had given him and scratching and howling in his sleep. The clever hunter felt very sorry for the child and put out his hand to stroke his hair. The child suddenly seized it. He was dreaming, the hunter could see, but his eyes were wide open, staring up at the sickle moon.

'Adisla,' he said, 'I will find you.'

Acknowledgements

Thanks to my wife Claire for all her support during the writing of this book and her correct prediction of its eventual shape. Also to Emily Turner for, as usual, her informed and intelligent comments on the text. Likewise to Anno for the monumental task of reading the huge first draft. Thanks to my dad for, among other things, the early introduction to science fiction and fantasy.